THE HARSHER THE TRUTH, THE SWEETER THE LIES

THE COMPLETE TRUTH AND LIES DUET

SYBIL KNIGHT

THE HARSHER THE TRUTH

SOCIALS:

Email: authorsybilknight@gmail.com

Newsletter: www.sendfox.com/dahliaandsybil

Facebook Group: www.facebook.com/groups/dahliaandsybilslittedevils

Instagram: www.instragram.com/author.sybil.knight

Facebook Page: www.facebook.com/authorsybilknight

TikTok: www.tiktok.com/@queensofchaosbooks

Amazon: https://www.amazon.com/stores/Sybil-Knight/author/B09QW5R3MB

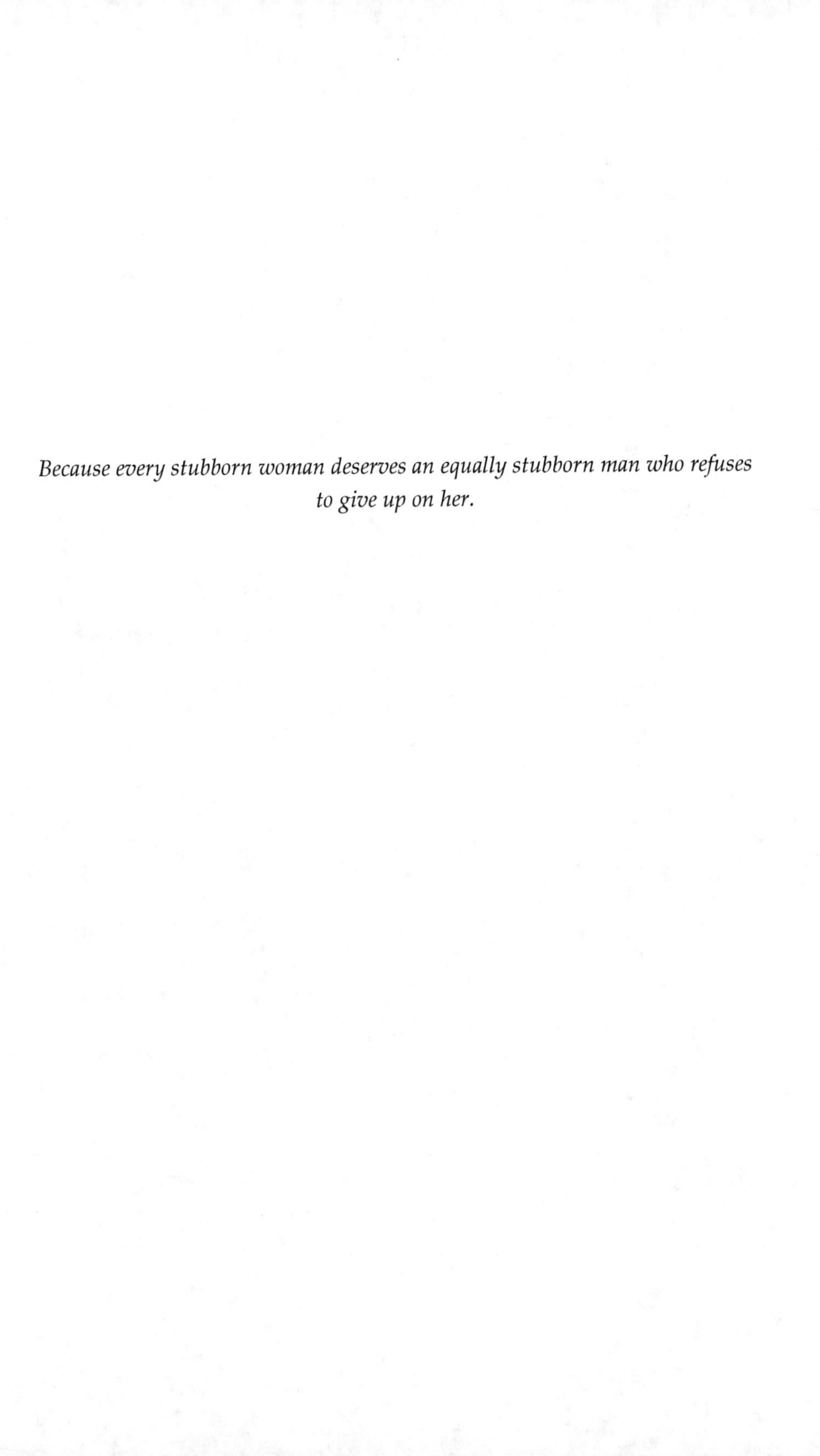

*Because every stubborn woman deserves an equally stubborn man who refuses
to give up on her.*

AUTHOR NOTES:

Before proceeding and/or placing judgment on the author or the actions of the characters in this narrative, please keep in mind that each individual responds differently to trauma. How someone copes doesn't make them any more or any less deserving of empathy. The author asks that you refrain from judging the characters or their actions based on how you would, how you think you would, or how you think they should respond in any given scenario. People are not cookie-cutter and nothing was done thoughtlessly or without proper research and consideration.

TRIGGER WARNINGS:

This book is recommended for a mature audience.

The enclosed content includes triggering situations such as (but not limited to) the following: on-page sexual assault/rape of a main character (not involving the romantic interest), profanity, detailed violence/gore, infertility, mental diseases and disorders, loss of a parent, amputation, motor vehicle accident, alcohol misuse/abuse, off-page accidental death of a pet, threats of violence and murder, kidnapping, physical disabilities, stalking, sexualization of female characters, gender inequality, obsession/possessiveness between romantic leads, criminal actions such as bribery and extortion, and crossing professional boundaries.

BLURB:

TESSA

Shut up and look pretty, sweetheart.

The instructions were simple.
1. Do as you're told.
2. Don't ask questions.
3. And always smile.

Men find it more attractive when you smile.

Unfortunately, the job description forgot the part about not punching your partner square in the jaw. *Guess they should have been more specific?*

Not that life lessons really mattered to a dead guy. Or the other halfwits looking to clean up his mess. If only the truth had been as easy to bury…

But the past, yeah, it had a way of creeping up on you. Especially when you forgot the most important rule:
4. Don't mix business and pleasure. *Again.*

STERLING

If it comes down to the story or you, I will choose the story. Every damn time.

She couldn't have been more clear. But that organ in his chest? The one that quickened when a certain smart-mouthed, pain-in-the-ass tabloid writer entered the room. It had a bad habit of hoping what it heard was wrong. And not giving a damn if it wasn't.

After all, she had said it herself: It takes two people to end things. One to leave. And the other to let them.

Yep, much like everything else in their relationship, he wasn't about to make it easy for her. No matter how harsh the truth…

Or sweet the lie.

PROLOGUE
THE FIRST DANCE

THE GUEST

THE CRISP, *off-white envelope with embossed lettering was tucked inside his jacket pocket, the weight of the contents far heavier than the cardstock itself.*

It wasn't wedding crashing. Not when you received an invitation from your ex, regardless of her motives. His eyes scanned his surroundings, faces both familiar and unfamiliar in equal waves while he sat the stranger amongst them.

This was it, right?

The thought popped into his head as he cataloged the banality of it all. This was what every woman wanted, what every decent man should give her.

The flowers, the white dress, the three-tiered cake, the partygoers whispering their compliments and criticisms in the foreground like judgmental gods in the presence of mortals.

Yes, this was where the story ended, where the chapter concluded, and the characters lived happily ever after. Or whatever it was they said at the culmination of every fairy tale, as the pages whittled down and the book closed.

There was no last-minute plot twist. No "ah-hah" moment. No sudden turn of events that could unexpectedly alter the finality of these words. Because, as if circumstance begot reason, he understood there was no undoing what had been done. What had veered the story. His story. And her story too. So off course.

He wasn't blind to the truth. He knew what their vows signified. Those promises uttered in a breathy whisper as he watched her make them without a hint of duress. Without regret. But mostly, he knew now what he should have known back then. At the beginning. It was inevitable. Because this supposed storybook ending was just that. An ending. With none of the revelry.

Cross the T.

Loop the E.

The End...

———

But then again, that was the irony of his presence. Here. Today. That the conclusion of one narrative was merely the start of another.

He should be thankful that they could both finally move forward, and he was thankful. For her, anyway. She deserved this life, the normalcy of it, the kind of life he would have never been able to give her. Or anyone else.

Because he wasn't normal. And nothing about his life was either.

CHAPTER 1
THE CONTENDER

THIS WAS NO HAPPILY EVER AFTER, Tessa scoffed to herself before glancing up at the thirteen-foot vaulted ceilings. *Nope, there was absolutely no chance in hell this marriage would last.*

She dropped her glare and eyed the remaining fanfare with disdain. The crystalline chandeliers and polished silverware evoking the same repugnance most would reserve for rodents and cockroaches looking to scurry under the closest kitchen appliance. She could feel her lips curl, her nose twitch in a manifestation of outward disgust.

And immediately relaxed her posture.

She knew better. She should remain apathetic and attempt to assimilate with the societal *beau monde.* The entitled blue bloods who'd narrowed down their ancestry to the Founding Fathers themselves—or at least claimed to. It wasn't that she hated the elite as much as she despised their existence in its entirety. The idea that people held a monetary value that could be bought and paid for as easily as a transaction at a grocery store checkout. The belief that self-worth was determined by factors outside one's control such as: age, race, gender, birth order…

The conformity—the sheer injustice of it all—churned the acid in her stomach until it ate away at her own morality. But now wasn't the time for inner reflection. She had a job to do and failing to school her features would only serve as a hindrance.

Then again, perhaps her obvious aversion would provide all the more camouflage, she mused. After all, how better to conform with the crème de la crème than to appear unfazed, underwhelmed even, by such a blatant display of overindulgence?

She hadn't *exactly* been invited to this affair; however, *trespassing* still felt like too harsh a term. There were no posted signs specifically "prohibiting" her entrance to the reception of the soon-to-be Mister and Missus. At least, none that she had seen thus far. Her intrusion was further morally justified by the sheer superficiality of the hired security team—who upon first glance of her aristocratic features (credited by her mother's French lineage) enthusiastically escorted her to the reception hall, all the while playing little mind to her partner in tow.

COREY

Corey could only shake his head at the theatrics that had just transpired in front of him. Tessa was a shark in open waters, a predator having spotted, smelled, sensed her first drop of blood before it dissolved and became one with the seawater. She walked like she belonged; she talked like she belonged… The only changing variable was the setting. The journalistic where and when. Even her partner wasn't entirely sure she *did not* belong.

There may actually be a story there.

He chuckled at the thought. But that theory would have to be explored at a later date. Today, they would focus on the frivolity of the privileged and pedigreed: who was secretly married, who was a bastard love child, who did Miss Scarlet kill in the conservatory with the candlestick?

Their normal repertoire.

His eyes nearly doubled in size as he watched Tessa wordlessly flip the posted notice clearly forbidding the entrance of press "of any kind" beyond the threshold, as she fluttered her lashes at the overly distracted security officer. As if implying an "out of sight, out of mind" rationale for their uninvited attendance at the evening's festivities.

That's not how things work, he groaned at her internally.

Or is it? Her red Cheshire smirk seemed to rebuke in response as she casually grinned at him, a single eyebrow raised in challenge, with that knowing glance over her shoulder. Again, he couldn't help but shake his head. Only Tessa…

She was the star of the show and he was her what exactly? Some sort of hired help. That's how it must have seemed anyway, as he struggled to keep pace with her long, cat-like strides.

So much for "escorting" her anywhere, he continued to ruminate.

Though he was certain no one would have believed that fact to begin with. He would have been better off posing as her driver, rather than her husband for the evening. Not that Corey wasn't a sight in his own element. He was tall, broad, muscular. His short blonde hair and striking green eyes would easily catch the attention of a cougar or two; but where he was an accessory for the affluent, Tessa reeked of wealth and status… old money even.

If only they knew the girl behind that painted-up mask, the rich fucks would likely choke on their champagne and caviar.

The "Tessa" he had the pleasure of experiencing was the girl next door. The girl who could and *would* drink a six-pack with the rest of them, after a long day of editorials and deadlines. Her hair was often thrown up in a bun as she would glide across the conference room in jeans and a t-shirt. That presence, the way the woman carried herself, was the one element that was unchanging. It perpetuated confidence, guile, a certain magnetism even—that could first infatuate and then consume a man—whether she was clothed in rags or couture.

Not him, Corey was sure to clarify to no one in particular. But to an unsuspecting pawn, Tessa's allure could be intoxicating. Noxious. And here they were, in a room inundated with unclaimed chess pieces all looking to maneuver towards their opponent's queen, and all steps away from falling into that queen's gambit.

TESSA

And now we wait…

Tessa tapped her freshly manicured index finger against her perfect pale jawline. Most journalistic investigators would take notes, covertly placing microphones in brooches and hairpins. But that would be a novice move among the *bien nantis.* Instead, she would watch. Patience, not only a virtue, but Tessa's ever-present confidant.

She should hold more stock in words, given her chosen profession. Yet experience had shown her *on more than one occasion* that it was the unspoken articulation that carried the most weight. Especially among the current crowd. Sleek silver lies would often spew from the tongue while rotten truths were held close to the heart, choked down and stifled.

So it was her job, as well as the journalist's secret indulgence, to read between the lines—between those lies—and to find the bigger picture. Quite literally sometimes. After all, a picture was worth a thousand words. Or, as in Tessa and Corey's case, thousands of dollars.

The honesties were unmasked by the small nuances. A glance here. A glare there. She just needed the slightest opportunity. Something little. Subtle. A scowl. A seemingly inconspicuous smirk. A light, surreptitious brush of an arm. Something she could sink her teeth into. It was the small, uncontrollable moments she sought. She waited for.

The moments when no one was watching and the truth would peer out, just long enough for her to grasp and grab hold. It didn't take much, only the thinnest thread of latent candor. She felt like a predator —a lioness stalking her prey—and the thrill stimulated every nerve in her body, awakening her most visceral impulses. When presented with a choice between fight or flight, she effortlessly selected fight every time. But this fight was not accomplished with the use of physical force. Not today. This was just as refined an interaction as the ones she pursued.

Bingo!

Tessa's internal radar sparked on high alert, almost in unison with her inconspicuous camera flash. She had him. Good looking? Yes. But good looks were a dime a dozen–and much like a mistress–they lost their appeal over time. No, it was his presence that drew her in. He had a story. She could feel it in her bones. Her core reverberated with intrigue and her mouth was peppered by the metallic apparition of blood. Or perhaps the thrill really had caused her to bite her lip a little too hard. At this point, she was too hyper-focused on her mark to care for the difference.

That familiar, calculated grin again painted her lips as she beamed down at her screen. Yes, it was archaic to use her phone—she knew as much—especially with the professional equipment she had at her disposal. However, the sophistication of the image was not the priority; it was its overall authenticity that was essential. And this job taught her that authenticity was always in question with a camera crew, overhead lights, and a microphone in view.

She laughed at the image.

But who would question a partygoer tightly clutching her cellular device in a venue that catered to and promoted self-centeredness and superficiality? Especially a woman as elegantly tailored as she was?

Not a damn one of them; that's who.

The image was exactly what she wanted, Tessa discerned as she studied the captured likeness. His expression was candid, soft. Pained? Maybe. As he stared—*or perhaps gazed was a better word, definitely not gawked*—at the newly appointed Missus. It lasted only a moment. But she was an expert in moments, and thus, had eagerly captured his.

This was all she needed. Just this image. This lead. And the rest of the story would write itself. At home. With the help of Inspector Google and a pint of cookies and cream ice cream, her greatest friend and biggest foe.

She would dissect this man. Piece by piece. A surgeon skilled at incising duplicity. Yes, there was definitely something there. She could taste the intrigue and it was sweet. Bittersweet.

She sucked in her cheeks, chewing on the flesh there, and nearly giggled aloud. Her hand shot up to quickly stifle the sudden outburst of emotion, before she accidentally compromised her position.

"I beg your pardon, Miss." The authoritative tone both startled and roused the journalist from her speculative trance. "But I believe you have something of mine." With that ambiguous introduction, the man behind the tone—the same man who'd obsessed her ruminations mere moments ago—effortlessly plucked Tessa's cell phone from her grip and attempted to unlock the screen.

"It has a passcode, you know?" she chided, gesturing towards her stolen device before folding her arms over her chest. "However, if you wanted my number, all you needed to do was ask."

Yes, she would diffuse this situation with a little harmless flirting.

Her posturing further emphasized her elongated neckline and the dangling jewelry cascading into the deep-V of her fiery-red gown.

"I'm aware there is a passcode. Or, rather, that there likely is one," the man-in-question smiled at her. *Well, almost smiled?* "Though that's hardly relevant when the screen is unlocked." *Now* he smiled, as he continued to hold the phone just out of her reach.

Tessa's demeanor flared from sirenic to incensed; however, to most men, hot with eroticism and hot with belligerence held very little distinction. And yet, he hadn't even flinched at her blatant display of provocation.

Time to up the ante, her inner voice instructed.

Tessa refused to let the smirk fall from her lips, even while she clenched her teeth behind them. Again, with dexterity very similar to a feline prowl, the journalist stalked closer to her newly labeled adversary. Her movements were abrupt, unexpected, and daunting enough to ruin even his carefully poised composure.

"You didn't answer the question about my phone number, *mon chéri,*" she purred, her body suddenly slinked across his lap and her breath now warming his freshly shaved jawline. The tailored guest didn't move, almost as if he didn't dare.

"You didn't ask a question," he rebuked, the inflection in his voice ever steadied. Not an ounce of hesitation. "You made a statement. However, *I* do have a question..."

Tessa had no intention of removing herself from his lap. She glanced up at him, her fingers now curling the ends of his tie. The seconds ticked by—for dramatic effect of course—the scene almost intimate if it weren't so *public.* "You, *mon nounours,*" she emphasized, flawlessly switching from her mother's native accent to her father's colloquial one, "may ask me anything." Still not a hint of levity from this man.

A story indeed, she considered.

COREY

Corey was sure to catch Tessa's unsolicited maneuver with his camera phone. "The insurance shot" she had enthusiastically christened this tactic—though she appeared to be the only one amused by her wit at the time.

He quickly glanced down at the photo. Tessa was sprawled across the stranger's lap, crinkling the man's once-pressed suit and loosening his neatly tucked dress shirt. While the sight was both compromising and salacious, a more naïve viewer would find it almost tender.

And that's exactly what she planned, wasn't it?

The realization finally dawned on him. Blackmail. How had he not seen that one coming? Was that what it had always been about? And he was only just now realizing it?

Corey stood in the background, watching the playful banter between the two. The man seemed to hold his own—he would give him that. Most men and women alike fell under Tessa's spell long before she even unleashed her charm to its full extent. But there she was, having already relinquished her cache of French endearments and her mark appeared unfazed.

Maybe he has something against the French? her partner quipped to himself. *Well, Tessa did always enjoy a challenge.*

Corey continued to observe the pair for several minutes before determining that perhaps it was finally time for him to intercede. He protectively shoved his phone back into the pocket of his dress pants and quietly, reluctantly, trudged over to his ever-beguiling cohort.

Time to get this show on the road, he huffed, as he had no intention of earning himself a pair of silver bracelets to match all the silver spoons in attendance. Corey was far too pretty for prison. At least *he* thought so.

STERLING

Before he could respond to the woman's overtly flirtatious double entendre, Sterling's attention was drawn to the sizable figure trekking in their direction. The man seemed intent on disrupting this ongoing charade—the sexualized female currently clinging to his lapel in an effort to distract him from his sensibilities.

Boyfriend? Husband? Maybe. No, he concluded.

Her knight in shining armor was far too composed at this predicament for there to be anything romantic between them, and Sterling had noted the lack of a ring. For no reason other than his livelihood was dependent on his ability to discern the finer details. His prowess was built on his keen sense of observation, and his instincts told him this man was more than likely a brother to her. Except there was little semblance there, even if only one parent had been shared.

So a fraternal bond, he continued to deduce. *Years old though. Almost as if he were used to her antics, both bothered and bemused by her. Closer than a mere colleague or acquaintance. A symbiotic relationship. Interesting, considering they were of opposing genders and both clearly aesthetically pleasing.*

"Does a cat have your tongue, *mon beau?*" The woman continued with her pretty French words.

If someone had stolen his tongue, he was certain she would be behind it, he thought to himself. He rolled his eyes in response.

"Then what is it that you wanted to ask me? In exchange for my property, that is, of course," she prompted.

There it is.

He smirked. Her pronunciation was definitely sprinkled with irritability now. Barely noticeable. But it was there, manifesting in a small undertone and slight emphasis when she spoke the word "property." This was her game, and yet she was clearly tired of it. Much like a cat done playing with an injured bird.

How befitting.

"I merely wanted to enquire if you do this often?" he spat.

"And what is it that you think I'm doing?" She sought to provoke him, a challenge resonating in unison with her tonality and purposefully defiant facial features.

"Attacking and mocking a helpless crippled man," he growled, his upper lip curling in disgust—whether it was at himself or the woman in front of him had yet to be determined.

CHAPTER 2
THE FIRST ROUND

STERLING

SHE'D LAUGHED AT HIM. Actually laughed in his face. It was a boisterous, lighthearted sound. And probably the first sincere reaction he'd seen from the woman.

Great, she was mocking him.

He shouldn't be surprised. And yet, for a moment, he closed his eyes in silent resignation. But that small break in character was all the emotion he would surrender. She would get no more from him, he vowed.

"First of all, I would *never* attack or mock a *helpless crippled man...*" she retorted, simultaneously composing herself while breaking his train of thought.

"Then what do you call this...?" He gestured towards their current struggle.

"Well, this... *this* is rude. Had you let me finish my explanation, instead of cutting me off mid-sentence," she chided.

He raised a curious brow, conceding to her antics with an open palm. "By all means..."

"As I was saying, *mon ami*, first of all, I would never do as you have so thoughtlessly accused. The very idea further implies that you should get to know me better." She paused and teased at his collar before continuing. "And secondly you, sir, are by no means helpless or crippled. Far from it in my expert opinion," she whispered close to his ear, her voice audible only to him, her breath warm while the slight movement remained intoxicatingly personal.

This conversation was ridiculous. "Is this a joke? If not crippled, what would you call it?" He stared out into the crowd, partially addressing the young woman and partially taunting himself.

She hummed for a second, as if carefully choosing her words. "Crippled is a man without tact. A man without wit. A man who fails to observe the world around him and learn it's not always as it appears. A man who is incapacitated by his chosen ignorance. You are not that man. You are as hindered a man as I am a woman." She allowed a bout of silence to fall between them, her thoughts seemingly distant and far from this moment, then added, "Yes, outwardly we are both regarded by our physicalities. Dismissed even. Because of our most prominent distinctions, by those with little depth of character. However, the same puppets who pass judgment, in turn, play into our strings. We use that ignorance as ammunition. Myself—in how I superficially live up to the expectations of a vapid, wanton plaything—to be used and thoughtlessly dismissed on a whim..."

She silently averted her gaze as she brushed her hair behind her ear and continued to trail her fingers down her cheek, passed her chin and neck, before lightly grazing her cleavage.

"And you—in how you equate the functionality of your legs with the functionality of not only your mind but also your manhood. We both know that's not true, *chérie*," She skimmed her fingers against his waist this time. "However, we use the insecurities of lesser men and sometimes even our own innermost selves, to produce the desired outcome. Hence, you threw out the word *crippled* as one would use profanity. For shock value. With the expectation that I would yield out of guilt or discomfort. Or both. *No?*"

The distraction was just long enough for Sterling to catch the camera flash in his peripheral.

"*Son of a*—I shouldn't be surprised. Is anything about you real? Not part of some greater scheme?" He cursed and nearly dropped the woman to the ballroom floor, shoving her captured cellular device back into her grasp. "Just take it and go! Use whatever photos of me you'd like but you *will not* make a spectacle of my cousin or *her* wedding day."

TESSA

This was a command, not a threat. And not intimidation. His cadence remained unshakable and didn't discern even a hint of the anguish that his eyes betrayed.

Interesting...

You would think that she would be taken aback at this point—quick to flee under the accusations and scrutiny of a wretched man in a wheelchair. But, instead, the journalist was nearly giddy.

He was annoyed with her. Not entranced. Not unnerved. And perhaps not even attracted. *Why?*

Tessa leaned in, a new thrill driving her tactics, something slightly more valuable than monetary gain. "Real? Now, that depends on your definition of the word, *mon nounours*. It's true that most of what I do serves an underlying purpose," she hummed. "But *this* time, it's my words that do not."

"Whatever it is you seek to accomplish with this game you're playing, I suggest you cut your losses, sell your tabloid photos, and move on." At this point, he seemed beyond any hope of reconciliation, dismissing her presence with a cavalier wave of his hand.

"Tabloids?" She snarled, repulsed by the insinuation. "Is that what you think I do?" She smoothed out the creases in her designer gown, more offended than if her mark had tried to shove a twenty down her top.

Tessa wasn't sure why she was suddenly so distressed by his implications. This is what she was accustomed to. These chauvinistic assumptions built her career, after all. And these displays of public sexism had always made her that much more dangerous; yet she felt insecure and exposed. This time. In this moment. And what was most harrowing was the unestablished causality of these emotions over a man whose name she didn't even know.

What was it about his appraisal of her that somehow mattered? She had long since outgrown her need for outside validation. Or so the journalist thought...

"Blackmail then?" the man prompted, breaking her daze. "From old money or new?"

She wasn't entirely sure why he kept the exchange going. Then again, she wasn't entirely sure why she did either. "Neither, you?"

"Both," he responded flatly.

"Ah, so family money and *nouveau riche.*" She mulled over the concept. "Self-sustained. How *bizarre...*"

"The accent, real or fake?"

Tessa smiled wide this time. Wide and earnest. "Both, *mon petit nounours.*" She sat down beside him, transitioning from vixen to perfect gentlewoman in an instant, while purposefully accentuating her enunciation. She rested her elbow on the table, her hand against her temple, and tapped lightly. "My mother is from *La Rochelle* and my father is a Midwesterner. I grew up with the language but I can exaggerate it at will," she confessed.

COREY

He feared his partner had gone too far this time, having forcibly accosted the affluent man in the wheelchair, especially at such a high-end affair.

Corey held his breath as he waited for the onslaught of security that was sure to ensue. And yet, surprisingly, Tessa's transgression was well-orchestrated enough to somehow remain unseen.

When finally within earshot, he paused. Unsure how things had evolved from a verbal altercation to a game of twenty questions, Corey was paralyzed by confusion.

That was *his* Tessa now…

Well, not his.

He dismissed the awkwardness of that thought. Because she wasn't his in that way. But the real Tessa. That smile was absolutely real, its authenticity proven by how the levity reached her eyes, her grin slightly crooked and her nostrils flared in amusement. He wasn't entirely certain how to proceed, or if he should interject at this point. She seemed to be enjoying herself. He took another deep breath before advancing.

"Tessa, my darling." He approached hesitantly, the strain in his voice apparent as he attempted to subdue his natural speech pattern. "You seem to have wandered off."

STERLING

Darling?

Sterling's eyebrow raised in response to *Tessa's* bewilderment, as though the girl had forgotten her fallen veneer and was stumbling to regain it. She didn't seem like the type of woman to stumble often. Therefore, this slight misstep, this break in character... it intrigued him.

Much more than it should, he openly admitted to himself.

She appeared startled but amused by the onlooker's feigned sentiment, the forced haughty accent doing little to camouflage the man's humble upbringing. Sterling could not help but note how foreign the term seemed to taste on the newcomer's lips. Almost... *sour*. He'd deciphered their relationship correctly, he decided.

However, why did that realization invoke such a rapid heartbeat? It seemed to palpate in his ears and, alarmingly, it sounded from within his own chest.

"You're absolutely right, *mon chou*." The woman's intonation was different this time, far less flowery and yet seemingly more... endearing. Authentic. "How inconsiderate of me! I'd become preoccupied—you know how shiny objects tend to catch my eye. Speaking of, this is Mister...?" She turned, her gaze shifting from her companion to the stranger amongst them.

"Sterling." He nodded in acknowledgment.

"First name or last?" the man prodded with poorly guised amusement.

"Both." Sterling huffed, no longer emitting interest in continuing to converse.

"Ah, like Madonna? Or Cher?" the overgrown outsider jibed. "All right then, Mr. *Sterling*. I suppose my wife and I should go offer our congratulations to the newlyweds."

"Right. Though, forgive me for my frankness, but why in the hell would you do that? It's not as if either of you were invited." And those were his parting words, as Sterling nearly backed over the guy's feet and proceeded to distance himself from the troublesome interaction. And that troublesome woman.

COREY

"Well, what was that all about?" Corey turned from the fleeting partygoer to face Tessa.

The smile continued to adorn her mouth. "I think he likes me."

"I think he *hates* you," Corey countered.

She chuckled, grabbed the crux of his arm, and guided him towards the doorway. "*C'est la vie.* That's life," she murmured wistfully. "What can we do?"

"*Que sera, sera,*" her partner hummed in response, butchering the pronunciation with his Irish-American twang peppered by an odd mix of something southern, while haphazardly attempting refinement.

Tessa shook her head as they continued down the sidewalk, the pretentious ballroom filled with its pretentious patrons shrinking in the distance. "That's not French, you know."

"But it sounded good, aye?"

"Not even a little bit." She snorted, and her counterpart grinned.

Corey loved this girl. Wholeheartedly.

Girl, not woman, he distinguished.

Because in these rare intervals of time, she was that girl again. Carefree, unburdened by the drudgeries of the adult world, and vulnerable. He regarded her with both fondness and intimacy in their purest forms. Not something tarnished by romantic interest, but rather adoration and respect for this person unconditionally and regardless of her gender.

Her femininity—while eliciting his more protective nature, he would admit—was of no other circumstance. And were it to ever come into consideration, he knew these sporadic moments of reprieve would be lost to him forever. Losing that part of her, this glimpse of her, was not something he was willing to risk for a more physical one.

Not ever. And he knew she felt the same.

TESSA

There were no questions about her intentions when it came to Corey. Tessa never once played games with him. In fact, she despised it whenever he saw her act this way; however, the journalist had no choice when it came to her career. It didn't matter how much she downplayed her exterior, she'd always been met with misogynism. And a slew of men who assumed having a cock somehow increased their number of brain cells. It didn't.

Over time, Tessa had learned to use the ridicule she faced advantageously, instead of seeing it as a hindrance.

They wanted a Barbie doll? They got one. But just long enough for her to get what she wanted as well. A story. *The story.* The one that paid and paid generously. While it wasn't the kind of investigative journalism she'd envisioned—mostly deep dives into the repugnant and unscrupulous inner workings of the affluent—she had made a name for herself. *Finally.*

Well, kind of...

In order to gain professional recognition, as well as protect her anonymity while undercover, she only ever published her initials. Although she never specifically gender-identified under the pseudonym, readers often assumed she was male. The blatant societal sexism, ironically enough, had accelerated her journalistic esteem whereas once it had been inhibited.

The truth was, she hadn't been lying to Sterling.

Though she couldn't blame him for doubting her motives. There were days when she herself couldn't differentiate the lies she told from those she didn't. Almost as though a piece of her tangible self died each time she played a part.

The journalist hoped that wasn't true. That she hadn't begun to assimilate with her numerous alter egos. She hoped she was merely succumbing to a brief instance of stagnation... Boredom.

But after the unexpected exhilaration that seemed to consume her after her only authentic exchange with the brooding wedding guest, his terse dismissal left her feeling... dejected.

———

Having returned to her small apartment—small because she had no need for anything more gratuitous and not due to limited financial stability—Tessa continued to fixate on the strange interaction with that strange man.

Strange and magnetic, she continued to muse.

To say there was "something about him" was too simplistic; there was much more than just something. But what? She chewed on the end of her spoon before robotically shoving it back into the empty ice cream carton. She had been so lost in thought, she hadn't even realized she had eaten the entire thing.

Ugh, she huffed.

She needed to focus. She needed to write or she might find herself obsessing over this man all night. Her fascination needed a more productive outlet. She grabbed her cell phone from the entryway table where she had tossed it and plugged the device into her laptop.

Okay, let's take a closer look.

Tessa paused, glaring at the error message on her computer screen. Then proceeded to dislodge her phone from the USB cord before reattaching it. She narrowed her eyes at the returning accessory failure, hissing inwardly while holding her breath, and flicked open the cell phone backing.

That son of a bitch!

She growled outwardly this time, discharging a slew of French profanities aimed at both Sterling and herself. He'd stolen her SD card. And not just stolen it. He'd choreographed the entire exchange—she was sure of it.

She paced. It was what she did to help her think. Dissect.

The conclusion was simple. Her mark had played her. He was the *toreador* baiting his opponent with flowery affectation. Waiting until the very last moment—both impassive and shrewd—before unveiling his deceit with a methodical flick of his wrist. Too callous to even revel in the resulting onslaught. And she...

Tessa seethed with sudden realization. She found herself to be no better than the frenzied beast, antagonized, predatory, and *sure as hell* she was seeing red.

You've messed with the bull, mon ami...

CHAPTER 3
THE HORNS

TESSA

IN TRUTH, she didn't need the pictures. It was only on the rare occasion that she would even publish them. Instead, her methodology centered on studying the small nuances she'd frozen on film. She would focus on those images with the same scrutiny as a forensic scientist trying to connect the dots amongst the unsavory aftermath of a crime scene. She searched for context clues, needles in the haystack.

It was an unorthodox form of investigative journalism, she knew. However, it was how her cognitive inner workings thrived. She needed that puzzle. She needed to solve for the hypothetical X in order to appease her inquisitive nature. It was how the journalist had functioned for as long as she could remember. Find the problem first, then determine how you got there. Unearth all the defining factors. This was how Tessa effectively married analytics with creativity. Her composition was poetic, precise, and unconventional; it was her journalistic signature.

However, the fact that she didn't necessarily need the photos did little to alleviate the rage bubbling beneath the surface.

Okay, it was more than bubbling.

The proverbial pot had already bubbled, boiled, and erupted in an ebullition of shock, contempt, and humility. Before finally settling on defiance. She could not act on impulse, she decided. He would expect a hotheaded counterattack.

Tessa returned to her compulsory pacing from her workstation to her apartment window and back again.

Especially if he assumed she worked for the tabloids. She rolled her eyes. No, anger would be predictable. As would further melodramatics. The next interaction must be completely outside his expectations. Outside his need for control and his appreciation for polite society. It had to encroach on his every level of comfort.

She smiled—that long, curled, Machiavellian smile. There was only one strategy that would shake a man who seemed to turn his back on the world, who anticipated her next move long before she'd skimmed her piece across the chessboard.

But first she had to find him.

————

Having effectively transitioned through the seven stages of loss—because that's what it had been to the woman who was accustomed to setting the trap rather than being ensnared herself—and after several more days, Tessa was finally settling into her phase of acceptance. However, that did not mean she *accepted* defeat.

No, instead, it was far more accurate to say she had voluntarily recognized the challenge. And perhaps was a little enticed by it. She told herself she wanted to face Sterling to prove her intellectual superiority. To best that man at his own game. *Her own game as well.* But if she was completely honest with herself, completely transparent, she would admit it was partially an excuse to see him again.

She had plenty of men who would willingly fawn over her, who had promised her the world. And more. But Tessa never wanted the world. She never sought the monetary, tangential affirmations that were easily laid out as offerings in exchange for her romantic favor. She hated to be called "pretty" or "beautiful" or any of the other ornamental blandishments—it made her feel hollow and eerily alone.

She didn't want to be revered or held up on a pedestal as one would exhibit the fanciful curiosities they'd acquired over time. She wanted a more abstract proposition. A more physiological—rather than physical—antagonist. A man who would not concede to her every beck and call just to win her affections. Who would be willing to draw out her vulnerabilities rather than demand them. Though the concept seemed foolish, Tessa was unable to dismiss her optimism entirely.

But she'd wasted enough time in this state of introspection. She was much more prone to action. After all, she was still in possession of the insurance shot—the photo Corey had taken of her and the elusive Mr. Sterling—as well as a certain element of surprise when it came to planning the next interlude. It was a decent starting point. For both her yet-to-be-addressed article and yet-to-be-established reintroduction.

She was certain Sterling and Corey alike had concluded that the second photo was planned in an effort to secure leverage and coerce a reluctant mark—hence the clever terminology. However, that wasn't entirely true. The journalist wasn't looking to ensure the man's compliance, as much as she was looking to safeguard her physical well-being. The photo served as a discreet accounting of her last known associates. A documented: who, what, when, and where. Should the journalist need a backup plan.

The thought sent a considerable chill down her spine; she knew that the fear was justified and yet it was no easier to embrace. It was a frailty she didn't dare mention aloud and she was especially not willing to impart it today.

Maybe you're not the only one who's broken.

She confessed as much to the open air in her bedroom, and to a man who didn't know her and couldn't hear her, as she packed a crumpled notebook into her leather messenger bag before tossing the familiar weight over her shoulder and exiting. Her hair was twisted haphazardly into a bun at the top of her head while a favorite click pen hugged the edge of her right ear. This lackluster rendition was a far contrast to the vixen from the days prior. But certainly not any less formidable.

———

The phrase the "man is an enigma" had never felt more appropriate before now. Because this particular man didn't seem to exist. Tessa huffed. After hours of researching, she was no closer to narrowing down the identity of the figure self-purported as "Sterling." He may as well have introduced himself as "John Doe."

She'd probably have better luck if he had. At least in that instance, she would have a first and last name to go by. Tessa rolled her eyes.

She had sorted through articles about silverware, birds, coins, business names. Anything and everything filtered through her search engine—with such little information to narrow down her scope—and *that* was assuming he favored the traditional spelling.

Her mark had mentioned that the bride was his cousin. Well, to be completely factual, he'd said "his cousin" and "her wedding day" in the same sentence, which led to the assumption.

Tessa began mindlessly chewing her pen cap, as she was known to do while deep in thought. Admittedly, many pens had been decommissioned this way.

However, Googling the family tree had landed her with another dead end. She continued to ruminate. The journalist had already discovered that the bride didn't have any cousins—first or second, to be more specific. Which could only mean one of two things: the bastard had full-blown lied about their relationship, *or* he had given Tessa just enough for the information to be both truthful and inconsequential. And the man did not appear to be a liar...

The change of scenery—having left her apartment and now seated in her office—had helped refresh Tessa's perspective. She needed to solve this Rubik's cube; there was no question about it.

COREY

"The website's up…" Corey chimed in, leaning his shoulder against the doorframe.

He'd been watching her for several minutes before breaking her concentration. To say he had never seen her so obsessed would be a veritable lie. This was Tessa's MO. Her obsession was both her brilliance *and* debility. She would hyperfocus on the details most would overlook. She would find a story where he was certain none had existed before, as if the woman could almost will it into materialization. He knew this would likely be the case again; however, logic resounded in his ear.

Because there *was* something different in this instance. He couldn't determine exactly what it was. But there was *something*. Perhaps Tessa's intuition was rubbing off on him, or maybe it was just his lack of sleep finally catching up. Either way, she appeared slightly off… almost personally invested in this man and his identity.

Corey hoped this wasn't the case. As much as he cared for his partner, as much as he wanted her happiness, he didn't trust the rest of the fuckers out there. *Their marks*. Any of them. Men like that—the elite, the wealthy, the privileged bastards born at the top of the food chain— they were all used to having the world handed to them. They focused on materialism, favored the tangible over the unquantifiable. And

Corey feared what value someone like that would put on Tessa's heart if freely given. His dread grew exponentially when he noted the spark in her eyes that his tidbit of information had clearly evoked.

"Is it now?" She responded in an almost singsong voice.

"It is," he confirmed. "But why are you so interested in this guy in particular?" Corey propelled his weight from where he was angled at the entrance of her office and positioned himself beside her. Tessa was already perusing the official wedding announcement and press release posted by the bride's family.

"I'm not sure what you're implying, *mon chou*." Her retort was guarded, her tone resonating both warmth and warning. "He's the mark. There *is* a story there. Why else would he be so elusive? Besides, he thinks he's bested me. And you know I can't have that."

She glanced up at Corey briefly, then dropped her gaze to the computer screen and continued to scroll.

"There it is!" Her loud proclamation nearly knocked her counterpart from his seat. She ignored his plight and tapped on her monitor. "You see it, don't you? That's not a look of a man happy for a *cousin* on her wedding day. That's a look of a man lost. A man who *has* lost. And that's my story." She paused before returning to her rant in near-whispered contemplation. "What's the history there?"

Again, while Corey was not entirely sure what *Tessa* saw, or what theory she'd likely already concocted when she focused on the blurry man in the background, he would agree there was probably more depth to the image than he could currently perceive. It took a keen eye to narrow in on Sterling amongst the crowd. But once Corey did, beyond an expression of torment, he detected a quiet acceptance.

This was someone who not only acknowledged his fate but seemed to have a willing hand in it. And it was as if the sudden realization had slapped him back to reality.

"The bride wasn't his cousin," he blurted aloud. "She was *his*. An ex. An ex-girlfriend. Fiancée. Wife. Whatever. But she was *something* and I bet he pushed her away. Or let her go. The groom—that's the cousin. And the bastard's use of a pronoun for the girl… it was meant to dissuade more than just *our* interest. My guess is that it is a reminder to dissuade his own as well. A psychological prompt."

Corey began to mimic Tessa's enthusiasm, as he robotically paced back and forth across the office and mindlessly rubbed his index finger and thumb against his five-o'clock shadow.

"We should search through old engagement and wedding announcements. If we assume the information he provided is correct." He spun on his heel to face her now. "And he really is from old money, then there would be something about the pairing published. Even if it was kept under wraps. There's no such thing as full discretion in *that* world."

"Precisely my thoughts," Tessa purred with a smile that could not have been wider if it were painted in place. She gestured towards the empty coffee mugs conveniently stacked just out of reach, as her elbow made light playful contact with Corey's lower abdomen. "So… what are you waiting for?"

"*Really…?*" He rolled his eyes with a blustered breath before reluctantly obliging. Mugs in hand, Corey trudged towards the break room, grumbling to himself in feigned annoyance. "Always the bridesmaid and never the bride…"

CHAPTER 4
THE INTENDED

STERLING

SHE HAD BEEN RIGHT ABOUT one thing; he did observe the world rather than try to live in it. Sterling would never admit this concession to her but he could, at the very least, admit it to himself—however begrudgingly.

He tapped the SD card against the top of his desk while staring blankly at his computer screen. He wasn't entirely sure why he continued to hold on to the tiny piece of plastic, but for whatever reason, he couldn't throw it away either. Ideally, he would have preferred to delete the stolen images rather than confiscate all of her device storage; nonetheless, she hadn't given him much of an option at the time. He couldn't allow her to play her games during Madelyn's wedding; he *wouldn't* allow her. Had the setting been anywhere else, he may have prolonged the interaction, entertained her antics for a bit longer. Surely he would have figured her out by now, if only he'd been given the opportunity.

Continuing his "should have, would have, could have" train of thought, Sterling *could* not bring himself to destroy the damned card and yet his urge to view its contents felt too much like an invasion of privacy.

Not that she cared much for his, his subconscious countered.

His intentions weren't depraved. He didn't seek to gawk at any private moments hidden in her phone's history, nor did he wish to blackmail her—though he wouldn't deny that both thoughts had crossed his mind at one point or another. Instead, guilt surged and ebbed at his core. The images could be important. Irreplaceable...

And yet—to be completely transparent—morality was not Sterling's only drive. He'd also become somewhat obsessed with knowing more about the woman. Perhaps it was the mystery by its very nature that haunted him. And once solved, once her true self came to light, his mind would be free from any further thoughts of this woman. His piqued curiosity had to be far more alluring than her actual embodiment. Or so he told himself.

Indecision was not Sterling's usual state of being and the feeling unnerved him. He could ask his secretary to take a look...

He pondered the idea, before ultimately dismissing it in frustration. He wasn't a coward nor was he one to delegate *sensitive* undertakings.

How had this one woman completely disarmed him?

It had to be the normalcy of the interaction that rattled the usually controlled blue blood. She was clever and she knew it. And yet, she had spoken to him as she would have spoken to any other man in the room. Not because she saw him as weak. And not in the predacious sense.

The tapping of the plastic continued with his thoughts. *Tap, tap, tap.*

Sterling had become accustomed to the standard reactions: aversion and avoidance. But she wasn't cruel. And she wasn't intimidated. She hadn't glared at his chair, regarding its proximity as an affliction in itself. Nor had she maintained the expected social distance, afraid his disability was some sort of contagion that could be passed from person to person. Despite her capacity for deceit, this reaction—or rather lack thereof—hadn't been part of her con.

Eyes were telling, even the most composed, and hers had not flickered with disgust or pity. Or even the air of superiority. Not in the usual sense anyway. She *did* feel superior, but it had nothing to do with his physical shortcomings. He had assumed that, in her own opinion, her arrogance was well-earned among most. Even if her intellect was no match for his.

He chuckled. And momentarily glanced at the SD card, continuing the *tap, tap, tap.*

This was maddening. He slammed his fist against the solid-wood desk.

No, she was maddening…

It was his last thought before shoving the card into his laptop port. And before his conscience could convince him otherwise. He peered down at the computer screen and braced himself. His instinct was to cringe—much like a man sticking his hand in a cage—uncertain if he was about to be embraced or bit. It was foolish and yet, even with that acknowledgment and understanding, his posture remained stiffened and his brain screamed: *beware of dog.*

And beware, he should…

———

Having permanently deleted all the photos from Madelyn's reception, Sterling scrolled through image after image as if he were transfixed. He wasn't entirely sure what he expected to see, but *this…* this was not it.

This girl was normal and completely extraordinary in the same instance. There was no other way to appropriately describe her, he'd concluded. He had learned nothing and everything about her in these few moments. She was absolutely that woman he had met that night. Intoxicating. Infuriating. But in an abundantly different way. Or maybe exactly that way…

His thoughts were jumbled and incoherent, and he couldn't adequately decipher them, let alone express them. With each click of his mouse, he saw more and more of the real person behind the painted veneer she liked to present. He saw her real smile and how, when it was authentically drawn out, it rose slightly higher on the left side—no longer controlled and perfectly placed. He remembered that smile. She had given it to him that night, or perhaps he had stolen it without her realizing. Either way, it had been his for a brief period of time.

He wondered how many others could say the same.

He saw how her eyes could light up in both feigned annoyance and genuine enjoyment when her photo was taken candidly. She seemed to know she was classically beautiful and yet she didn't appear to know how truly captivating she was at the same time. She didn't like to be that woman she pretended to be. The disdain was evident, her orchestrated expression darkened and discouraged in comparison to these unfiltered ones.

That being said, she still loved the thrill of winning… of besting her opponent. Whether the casualty knew it or not was completely irrelevant to her satisfaction. Because *she* knew it.

The woman was complex, a creature both faultlessly optimistic and deeply jaded about mankind. Like a strategic game of cards, her face was an anatomical contradiction, emotion laced in duplicity.

And if nothing else, she was compelling; like a siren in the darkness, she beckoned him. While he was the ship all too willing to sink along the shores.

She had a tendency of wearing yellow most days in some fashion or another: yellow pens tucked behind her ear, yellow mugs grasped tightly in her hands, yellow sunglasses hiding her intense green eyes, a yellow belt cinching her hourglass figure.

He wondered if she realized this or if the choice was subconscious. Was she drawn to the color? Much like Sterling was drawn to dissecting her?

He studied the last image on the roll, having scarcely realized that his examination had already come to an end. Except it wasn't an *image;* it was a video.

She had been honest with him about her parents or who he could only assume were her parents by the undeniable resemblance between her and them. Tessa was a near facsimile of her mother, though with somewhat softer features. The man—whose thinning hair was peppered with age—mishandled the camera view in the stereotypical "parents and technology don't mix" way, while the woman issued muffled instructions in a thick French accent.

Once the screen was properly adjusted and the couple was collectively framed, the woman began to speak:

Tessa, notre petit chou, we are so proud of the woman you have become. And remember, no matter what happens, success is not measured by the worth others put on it but by the value you find in it. Nous t'aimons. We love you!

The message cut off with a flurry of hand movements, a close-up of the man's palm, and a view of what appeared to be a living room ceiling. The video was several years old, evident by the date and time stamp on the file, and Sterling surmised that it was likely rewatched countless times over.

He nearly laughed at the sad irony in it; the woman had spoken about intrinsic value. And he suspected that this tiny piece of plastic held immeasurable significance to its owner, a loss that was beyond compensation. He didn't understand one's attachment to their parental figures, not firsthand anyway; however, he did recognize the normalcy of it. And part of him wished his mother and father had been so openly supportive. He wondered if the couple on the card were still living and, more so, he wondered how he was going to find this paradox of a woman and return it.

Still lost in contemplation, accompanied only by the continued rhythmic tapping of his fingertips—the plastic square discarded to the side of his desk—Sterling ignored the knocks on his office door. He was too far entranced to hear anything outside his internal monologue.

He didn't know where to even begin to search for Tessa. He didn't have more than a first name and a handful of photos. The guest list would be useless; after all, she was never a guest to begin with. And he doubted anyone picked up on her antics. She neither belonged nor stood out amongst the crowd that day.

Well, to say she didn't stand out would be a lie. *She definitely stood out.* Just not in any way that would be helpful to him now…

The knocking persisted.

"Yes, what is it? Come in already," he finally growled at the unrelenting sound. "For fuck's sake, what could possibly be so urgent?"

"Well, sir, I knocked several times and you didn't bloody answer. You could have been dead for all I knew!" the voice rebuked in a satirically formal diction, colored by a hint of a British accent. The man loved to slip the occasional colloquialism in, as if to remind everyone of his time at Oxford. And with an overdramatized entrance, the figure —now recognized to be his business partner Charles—threw his hand to his heart and gasped.

"And if I were dead, how would knocking help in the slightest? Last time I checked, dead men don't answer doors…"

"Very true. *However*, I didn't want to interrupt the process either. If my memory serves me correctly, and it always does, I'm still listed in your will…" Charles paused for a moment as if daydreaming about his cohort's demise, then added, "And I really could use a new car—I'm thinking a baby-blue P72 would look pretty in my driveway…"

"Funny… because adding a sixth to your collection is a fiscally responsible decision, coming from the man I trust with my accounting." Sterling rolled his eyes. "Now, tell me why you're really here?"

"Ah, yes. Right. Back to business." Charles straightened his imaginary tie, flattened the imaginary wrinkles in his pants, and adjusted his imaginary glasses. "Miss Owens is here to see you, sir." His voice was, mockingly, an octave lower than it was when he'd first entered.

"Miss Owens?… I don't have anything on my calendar for this afternoon…" The desk was inundated with folders, all of which had been ignored for the entirety of the morning. And Sterling's calendar was buried somewhere underneath.

"She said the matter was pressing. Something about her property in the city?" Though they were the same age, Charles appeared much younger, especially as he stood there and rocked back and forth on his heels like an impatient child. He claimed that it was his humor that kept him youthful, while Sterling's scowls had aged the man beyond his years. But in truth, he believed it had more to do with a clean shave versus his counterpart's usual five-o'clock shadow. Though it wouldn't kill the guy to smile either.

"Fine, yes. Send her in." Without raising his glance and still searching his desk, Sterling waved his hand in reluctant concession.

"Oh, good. Because the girl followed me up here anyway!" the would-be inheritor confessed as he turned and reopened the office door.

"Girl?" Before Sterling could look up and finish his thought process, the hinges had already pivoted in the casing and *she* was standing at the threshold. Ripping the SD card from the port while simultaneously slamming his laptop closed, he paled.

"Lucien Conrad Sterling," she hummed. "It's a pleasure to see you again, *mon nounours.*"

CHAPTER 5
THE KNOCK-OUT

THE QUIET WAS DEAFENING as seconds ticked by like hours. While he had been preoccupied with finding her, she'd hunted him down instead. And somehow, he hadn't even fathomed the possibility of such a plot twist. He was anchored in place, as if any sudden movement might shatter the reality and the girl would disappear.

Like an apparition only he could see.

"Silly me." Charles broke the tension with an exaggerated palm to his forehead. "I forgot to mention Miss Owens never actually *scheduled* an appointment. She just showed up at the office today." He turned to face the girl. "Tessa Owens, it appears you're already acquainted with Lucien so I will forgo a more formal introduction."

The distraction was exactly what Sterling had needed to recover his composure. Even so, he couldn't help but regard her fondly. He leaned back in his chair, his hands steepled and an arrogant half-smirk across his lips.

The socialite he'd met was gone, and in her place was a girl every bit as impressive. Her hair was freed and fell naturally over her shoulders and down her back. Where once it was framed by a designer gown, her hourglass figure was now adorned in black jeans, brown leather boots, and a matching jacket.

There were those who mistakenly assumed that elegance and grace and sophistication were a birthright for the upper class, characteristics signed over with their title once their bank account listed enough zeros.

They were wrong.

Wealth had nothing to do with it. Rather, it was how someone's entire being could fill a room upon entry while emitting these attributes. No matter the attire. No matter the influence behind it. It was how the person carried themselves. Regardless of circumstance. And this girl just... had it. His gaze traveled along her neckline to her white blouse before landing on the thin yellow belt that circled her waist.

His smile grew, as if of its own accord.

"... Your belt. It's yellow." It was an odd statement, he knew. But he was compelled to say it all the same.

"How observant," she challenged, her arms crossed, and yet her inflection was playful.

"It suits you." Sterling shifted his weight forward, his elbows planted firmly on the desk and his eyes narrowed. "How did you find me?"

This time, it was her grin that widened as she pointed to the SD card he was trying to conceal in the palm of his left hand. "You have your tricks.." she responded, her outstretched finger then turning to tap lightly on her breastbone, "and I have mine."

A nod was his only reply, partially in agreement and partially at a loss for words. Charles was chuckling to himself as he leaned in the doorway, clearly amused by the spectacle.

"I'm sorry. Please forgive my lack of manners. Tessa, this is Charles." Sterling gestured to his cohort. "Charles Fox... partner to the firm, the executive of my familial estate, and legal representative. His duties include: being a constant pain in my ass, while reminding me of both the financial and judicial ramifications shooting him would cause."

"Ah, yes!" Mr. Fox issued his most authoritative delivery. "Jail... and lots of fines. Many, many fines." Removing himself from the entryway, Charles pivoted to exit. "And on that note, I will leave you two to discuss the… a… property…" Without waiting for a rebuttal, he secured the door behind him, his footsteps quickly echoing down the hall.

At the mention of the reason behind her sudden appearance, Tessa closed the distance between herself and the desk separating them. She sunk into the leather visitor's chair and mimicked Sterling's posture, elbows in place and paralleled to his. She reached for the tiny black square, then paused.

"So." Her green eyes locked on to his darker ones. "Did you enjoy the nudes?"

The memory card escaped from his grasp and bounced on the wood surface before settling between them. His mouth remained slightly ajar. "The what?" he scrambled. "There… There weren't any… a… nudes…"

A grin curled Tessa's lips as she propelled herself off the desk and into the back of the chair, her demeanor relaxed. She looked like the cat who ate the canary. "Don't sound so disappointed, *mon beau.*"

TESSA

She'd promised herself that she would behave accordingly. That, despite her instinct to outsmart and outmaneuver, she would approach this man without her usual smokescreen. And she had every intention of keeping that promise.

Until the moment she'd walked through that office door.

She sighed. Some impulses just couldn't be suppressed. She was enamored by the psychological warfare at play and the effort needed to get a rise out of the man in front of her. He was a... challenge. Unlike anything she'd seen in recent years, and the journalist had never been one to back down from a challenge.

All things considered, this very well could have been the real girl. She wasn't trying to seduce. She wasn't succumbing to his idea of her. Or, rather, who they both thought she should be. And there was no means to the end. The only actual gain was her own personal enjoyment as she watched him squirm.

And squirm he did.

Though she was proficient in the art of stoicism, contentment now sparkled in her eyes. Even amongst the dead air that most would find disconcerting. She sat across from Lucien, a first name she had just recently learned, the only words between them hanging and unspoken.

A smirk further heightening her cheekbones while discomfort reddened his.

She'd spent the last several days solely focused on deconstructing this man; a detail her colleague would be none too happy to hear. Especially considering the information she'd ascertained was irrelevant to their article.

However, their shared theory *had* been correct.

Five years prior to her most recent nuptials, the illustrious Madelyn Beaumont—now Madelyn Beaumont-DeLacy—had been engaged. And as Tessa had announced upon entry, the would-be groom's full name was Lucien Conrad Sterling, a title that sounded like money.

And it was.

His family was nearly as blue blood as they came, owning every bank in the city, with their ancestral crest practically printed on each denominative bill; subsequently, little else was mentioned about them. A small factoid the journalist found strange in itself.

Although there had been no publicized acknowledgment regarding the dissolution of the betrothal between the socialites, Tessa surmised that it likely had something to do with whatever led Lucien to his current state. While the engagement photos had shown a smiling man standing beside the Beaumont bride, presently, smiling seemed like a distant memory and that same statuesque figure was confined to a chair.

Using every resource at her disposal, Tessa was still unable to determine the root cause of this turn of events. The media outlets had been close-mouthed on the matter in the years following—a happenstance that didn't occur organically. She was certain deep pockets were necessary and that copious amounts of cash must have exchanged hands.

His next appearance in print transpired two years later with the uprising of his architectural restoration firm, a multibillion-dollar venture. By that time, however, Lucien had distanced himself from his familial name and entitlement. Very few individuals, outside those closest to him, realized his connection to the prominent financiers. He'd even gone as far as to drop his first name in its entirety; the man was singularly referred to as "Sterling" in every publication moving forward.

There couldn't have been more intrigue if the journalist had written his backstory herself.

————

The lingering silence allowed Tessa a more thorough appraisal of her male counterpart. Though she had initially deemed the man as handsome, it felt far too superficial a word upon closer inspection. His eyes were a deep, dark brown; they would lighten a shade when he was amused while turning a near black when agitated—an effect she'd experienced firsthand. And more than once. His jaw was tight and squared in reservation, softening just slightly when he observed something he found gratifying, as it had when he took note of her belt.

Unlike their first confrontation, he hadn't shaved this morning. But the stubble only further accentuated the angles of his mandible. Her visual examination concluded with a sweep of his broad shoulders and well-defined chest muscles before landing on the natural stretch and flex of his biceps, now fidgeting beneath her scrutiny.

It was evident that he'd not allowed himself to waste away in that chair, she thought. *Nope, not at all.*

What he feared he'd lost with the use of his legs, he seemed to try to make up for with his upper body. This was a man with an indomitable presence, no matter his self-reported inhibitions.

The silence was an interrogation measure used to break willpower. Most didn't like the unease a hushed room instilled and would unwittingly fill it like a sinner in a confessional. And so she sat: legs crossed, eyelashes fluttering, and lips planted. However, what she hadn't foreseen was that, being well aware of this stratagem, he did the same. It was a true-to-life chess match, each having successfully captured the opponent's pawn. But there were still many more pieces up for grabs on that board.

And Tessa would patiently await his blunder before… check and mate.

———

Neither certain how much time had elapsed, the two jolted in unison at the sound of the heavy wooden door slamming against the wall. Somehow, the tension seemed to be vacuumed out upon its impact. And in perfect synchronization, Tessa giggled, her hands rushing to her mouth to stifle the sound while Sterling attempted to turn his chuckle into a cough.

Stalemate.

"You two..." Charles barged in on the dead-locked impasse, pointing a disciplinary finger at each of his transgressors before resuming his reprimand. "How do you expect a guy to be able to eavesdrop on a conversation without... you know... conversating!" He sighed and motioned towards the hallway. "Do you know how long I've been standing out there with my fucking ear to the door? I'm pretty sure I'm going to need a chiropractor after all this..." He began rubbing the back of his neck in a blatant attempt to evoke sympathy.

Apparently, Charles Fox had been the only one broken in their twisted battle of wills.

"Good thing you're up-to-date on your insurance premiums," Sterling teased, but his eyes never left Tessa's silhouette... even as she turned to face their inquisitor.

"Sorry to disappoint, *Charlie dear.*" Though she didn't seem very sorry. He threw his arms up in exasperation and stormed out, mumbling to himself, while Sterling raised a curious eyebrow at the journalist's familiarized pet name. "I'll take that as an *apology accepted!*" she called to his back, as Charles disappeared around the corner for the second time that day.

Tessa shook her head and laughed, before rising to her feet and approaching the large set of windows behind the desk. The office building was old brick-and-mortar and the hazed panels were likely historically preserved, or very accurate replications. She pressed her hand to the glass, unable to discern if they were, in fact, the heavy leaded encasements she'd been expecting from the era.

"The panes are original, the weights were restored, and the frames are refabs."

Startled by the intimate presence of the voice at her back, Tessa spun on her heel. And consequently lost her footing. She reached out in an attempt to catch herself, but instead propelled full-force into the man now seated beneath her.

"How is it that you keep finding yourself in my lap?" His question came out in a gruff whisper.

She wasn't entirely sure herself. But, at the time, she didn't entirely care either. The hands that held her in place were just as solid as they had appeared at a distance, while the smell of his cologne was subtle yet stimulative.

Her arms had instinctively encircled his neck as she landed, her hands interlocking in a sort of damsel-in-distress death grip. The journalist's heartbeat was so loud and so rapid that she was both certain and mortified at the belief he could hear it too. Removing her head from the crux of his jawline, Tessa glanced upward, noting his labored breathing. It was comforting to see that she hadn't been the only one affected.

"I don't know..." Her mouth was hypnotically close to his as she confided, "But I must say, I rather like it..." Despite the gravitational pull, neither party edged closer.

"Is this all part of some game? Some con of yours?" She could feel the pounding in his chest quicken against hers, as he asked the question.

"No." Her voice was breathy, her pupils dilated.

"And how can I tell the difference?" She wasn't sure who had moved forward—but somehow—he was nearly talking into her lips. She could taste the significance behind his inquest. But she wanted to taste something more.

The kiss was soft. Tender. Yet impassioned all the same. His fingertips grazed along her cheek before resting at her chin as he tilted it upwards. He was controlled and gentle, a stark contrast to her frenzied thoughts. Much like how it started, Tessa didn't know who had pulled away first.

"If this were a game, I wouldn't have stopped you." She continued as if the conversation had never paused.

"Was it *you* who stopped *me*?" He brushed his thumb against her slightly puffed-out lower lip, his eyes locked on hers.

"I would have..." Her assertion came out weaker than she'd intended.

He smiled down at her and shook his head. "I'm not so sure."

The man's confidence was overwhelming, thereby thrusting her wayward senses firmly into place. She removed her arms from his shoulders and pulled herself back upright. To her feet. Having combed her nails through her hair before tucking the loose strands behind her ears, the journalist had regained her sobriety. The mesmerism had been broken and neatly filed away, to review and reassess at a later date.

"I guess you'll never know then, *mon ami.*" She adjusted her top and straightened her jacket as she headed towards the exit.

"Fine. If not a game, then what was it?" he probed. It wasn't a plea but an implication that hung in the air between them.

Tessa stopped mid-stride and rested her hand on the brass doorknob. Without turning to look at him, she responded, "Honestly, I have no idea..." Her face was out of his direct line of sight, but she smiled at her own abrupt self-awareness.

"When will I see you again?" His movements were quicker and far more soundless than she could have predicted. He had closed ranks, currently positioned but a few inches from where she'd fled.

Glancing over her shoulder, the journalist finally met his gaze with a proposition on the tip of her tongue. "I found you. Now it's your turn." Then she marched out of the office, stopping halfway down the hall for one final taunt. "At least you get to start with a first *and* last name."

And just like that, with a parting provocation and as cryptically as she'd appeared, Tessa was gone.

CHAPTER 6
THE TOUCH-MOVE

STERLING HAD no idea exactly what had—or perhaps hadn't—just happened. This morning he'd been perplexed. But now, he was completely disoriented.

For a moment, he'd felt like his old self. Deliberate. Decisive. Dominating even. But that moment was fleeting. And then, all of a sudden, he felt empty. Emptier than he could remember feeling since…

He shook his head. There wasn't time for any of that self-pity bullshit. He wouldn't become *that* guy. Over the years, he had seen his fair share of sympathy, especially on the faces of those closest to him. And for fuck's sake, he wasn't about to see it in the mirror too.

The scent of her perfume still clung to his shirt and remained the only concrete testament to her actual presence. Curiously, her SD card still lay where it had fallen; she hadn't even taken it with her as she'd bolted out the door. His teeth clenched at the memory of kissing her, the feel of her weight curled up and against his torso, and the faint pressure she had placed on his thighs. He couldn't explain it. But it hadn't been like that night when he first saw her.

This time, when he'd looked down, there had been a vulnerability in her eyes—a slight ripple in her polished exterior. And for a split-second, before her cognitive faculties could tell her otherwise, it was an insecurity she had wanted him to see too. But then again, almost as if it had been regenerated, her veil dropped right back into position.

Flawless… like it hadn't moved at all.

"So what'd you do to scare this one off?" True to his meddlesome nature, Charles—who'd likely been within earshot of the door anyway—interjected, hitchhiker thumb gesturing behind him.

Sterling shrugged, glaring down at his computer screen and pretending to read what he now just realized was actually a spam email.

"A shame. I liked her too. Seemed fiery. You know, like the kind of girl who could clean up nice and all… but at the same time, you're a little afraid she just might kick your ass, then ravage you in a back room?" Charles stopped when he reached the desk. He leaned forward onto the polished veneer, arms spread and palms flat. "So…? You going to call her? Tell me you at least got her phone number?"

Sterling had no intention of answering the barrage of questions being obnoxiously tossed his way. Instead, he glanced up once—his blank expression saying as much—before continuing to stare at his keyboard.

Charles sighed, and a hand gripped the edge of each one of the armrests, as he sunk back into the chair. The same chair where Tessa had just been. He crossed a leg, ankle-to-knee, as he carefully considered his next words. "In all seriousness, *did you see that girl*? When's the last time someone like *that*…" He paused, first pointing to the doorway, then tapping his index finger on the upholstered leather for emphasis. "…just walked in here? Or better yet, *just willingly walked into your office*?"

"Pretty girls walk in here all the time," Sterling rebuffed the implication.

"I didn't say *pretty girls*," Charles clarified, dragging a hand across his face. "I *said* a girl like *that*. A girl who can actually stand to be in your presence… No. I'm sorry. A girl who actually *likes* your presence—wait! Is that her memory card?" He reached out to grab it but Sterling quickly intercepted.

"How'd you know about this?" Eyes narrowed, Tessa's mark held the plastic square up and into view.

Charles grinned and reclined into his seat before replying, "Who's idea do you think it was to call her *Miss Owens*?..." Clearly thinking he was clever, he paused to sarcastically dust off his shoulders.

Sterling had never been one to pay attention to the specifics when it came to his clientele. Names. Addresses. Phone numbers. Niceties. That had always been Charles's department. They were all just faceless voices to the disgruntled architect. *Irrelevancies.* All he was interested in was how old the structure was and how much of it could be salvaged.

"Huh. She did all that research to find you. To get *that* back. And then she just *left it behind.* Interesting. Don't ya think?"

What was truly interesting was how in less than ten minutes, the woman was able to not only con her way into his office but also get his closest friend to act as a willing co-conspirator. However, it did explain the familiar pet name she had imparted earlier.

"It doesn't matter." Sterling returned to his brooding. "You saw her run out of here. She blew me off."

"Are you trying to convince me... or yourself? I heard what she said to you in the hallway. She found you. *Now it's your turn.* She dared you to do it. So go find her." He cracked his knuckles before leaning in. "Be honest. You've always preferred the chase anyway. When have you ever wanted anything that simply fell into your lap?"

Ironic choice of words, considering *this time*, it just so happened to be *exactly* what Sterling wanted.

TESSA

Fils de pute! Son of a bitch!

What the hell had she been thinking? Oh, right. She hadn't been thinking and therein lay the dilemma.

In trying to get into his head, he had gotten into hers. Her heart was fluttering as if it were seeking to untether itself and erupt from her chest cavity. This was absurd. She didn't know why she was so flustered.

He was just one man. And it had been just one kiss. He was a mark… like any other. And it was a story angle; howbeit one she'd gotten a little sidetracked on.

It happens to the best of us…

Except it hadn't been about the angle, not in the slightest. She sighed. Whatever that interaction *had been*, it had nothing to do with an article. And everything to do with her actually enjoying his company, as unfathomable as that may have seemed.

He'd been confident with her, in a completely different way than she had been accustomed to. Completely different from how he had been during their first exchange. Though his ego wasn't the issue—she had met plenty of confident men in her life. In fact, those were her favorite to take down. In the "the bigger they are, the harder they fall" kind of way. But this hadn't been that sort of confidence. This... this had been earned. Because she had freely given it to him. Because she had wanted to. And he'd wanted to take it.

Oh mon Dieu, c'était mauvais.

This was bad. She felt trapped, caged within the confines of her own emotional stockade. And for the first time, in a very long time, she had the instincts of flight. Though it was then that she quickly discovered she had a bigger problem—far greater than crossing the line of business and pleasure.

Her eyes widened with sudden comprehension, a hand muffling her gasp. "I forgot the card!" she exclaimed aloud, frozen midstep on the busied sidewalk. And worse still, part of her wasn't entirely sure if it had been accidental.

Swinging the door open with a little more force than she had intended, Tessa rushed into her apartment. She threw her suitcase onto her bed and piled it high with handfuls of clothing, taking little notice as to what exactly she was packing. She shoved her laptop into her leather messenger bag, sprinkled it with whatever pens were within reach, and tossed in her notebook. She took a quick survey of her bedroom; however, in her current state, she wasn't sure if she would have even noticed if she had missed anything. She turned off all the lights and lowered her thermostat setting, before grabbing her luggage and sprinting back out the door.

She took a deep breath and pulled her cell phone from her back pocket as she entered the elevator and began the descent to the lobby. Having replaced her device storage capabilities several days ago, she sent a flurry of text messages to Corey, explaining her intentions and reminding him where she hid her spare apartment key back at the office.

One of the perks of journalism was she could work anywhere and on an autonomous schedule. That was exactly what she needed at the moment—some fresh air and a chance to escape for a little while. And there was only one place she could go to do that and only one person she could do it with.

The only man Tessa had ever loved and the only man she could ever run to in such a disheveled state.

COREY

Looking down at his phone, Corey scrolled through his last few messages. He'd been waiting back at the office for Tessa to arrive and it was unlike her to be running late. Her typing seemed frenzied, incomplete, and somewhat incoherent. But he was able to understand the overall gist of what she was relaying, even if she had thrown a few French words in the mix absentmindedly.

Something was up, he thought to himself.

She wouldn't run off to see Jack, especially with an article due, unless something was really wrong. He wouldn't press her just yet. It wouldn't get him anywhere, except maybe on the floor with a few knuckles to the gut. But once she was settled in, he needed to check on her. He opened her desk drawer and removed her spare key from its usual hiding spot before adding it to his key ring.

In the meantime, he would keep an eye on her place. And possibly her refrigerator.

STERLING

He'd never realized how common of a surname "Owens" was until he began searching for one in particular. After reviewing the first few pages of possible addresses, a thought finally occurred to him. He was never going to find her this way; it was too wide a berth for him to narrow it down to a single girl. But he still had her photos...

He was more likely to find some sort of lead that way than anything he was currently doing.

Scanning the images for the second time—instead of focusing on the one girl he couldn't stop focusing on—he scrutinized every detail beyond her. By the midway point, he stumbled upon what he was looking for. Or at least he hoped so. He'd seen it in a cluster of photos taken inside what he deduced must have been her apartment.

Outside the windows that overlooked the city skyline, there was a distinguishable archway in the distance. It belonged to one of the oldest buildings in the area and had been historically returned to its original grandeur last summer. All the intricacies had been handled personally by Sterling's company and, as it so happens, by Sterling himself. He smirked. And he knew exactly which complex held such a view. Now, pinpointing which apartment number would be a hell of a lot easier than aimlessly perusing the white pages.

It had been far longer than he would like to admit since the last time he put so much effort into something that wasn't structural, arciform, or dormered. But Charles had been right. As difficult as it was for Sterling to accept, Tessa was certainly much more than another *pretty girl*. In fact, neither of the terms did her any justice. She was strikingly beautiful and infinitely more woman than girl.

At first, he'd assumed it was how she had been painted up at the wedding—embellished by pearls and satin and shrouded by the ambient lighting. Similar to how a dream was always more intoxicating than reality. Though he was man enough to admit that was also what he'd wanted to believe at the time. However, the way she presented herself in his office cemented any notion that her appeal had been simply ornamental. Like the most perfect disaster, her exterior wasn't her only artillery in play; she was sharp, obviously educated, and relentlessly tenacious. She had and was willing to meet him blow for blow. So, if she really had been just throwing down the gauntlet, he would meet the challenge.

And raise her one.

"Did you find her?" Charles prodded from his usual perch in the doorway before closing the distance between them.

"I believe so." Sterling nodded, shutting down his laptop and typing an address into his GPS. "Why?"

"Because I'm coming along for the show," Charles affirmed. "Have to make sure you don't do anything stupid this time."

Sterling rolled his eyes. "Fine. But I have to make a stop first."

TESSA

She pulled up to the familiar wrap-around porch and took a deep breath before turning the ignition off. When the idea had first come to mind, it felt like the right thing to do. But as she sat in the glow of the streetlights after the two-hour long drive, all she could think about was putting the car in reverse and peeling out of the driveway. She swung the car door open, letting it slam as it closed in order to alert the residents of her arrival. Her suitcase in one hand and her bag thrown over her shoulder, she approached the large wooden door.

Bracing herself, the journalist tapped lightly and waited. It only took a few seconds for it to fling open, for the warm gruff voice to address her. "Tess…" The man stared down at her inquisitively. "What are you doing all the way out here? Is everything all right?"

Tessa shook her head, trying to restrain the same tears she'd been holding back since she first set out to her destination. She dropped her luggage on the porch with a *thump* before enveloping him in the tightest hug she could muster while burying her face in his shirt.

"Can I stay the night?" she pleaded, her voice soft and vulnerable.

Without having to respond, he picked her bags up off the ground and escorted her inside, the door closing quietly before it was locked in place.

CHAPTER 7
THE SILVER FOX

COREY

MIDBITE OF TESSA'S secret stash of Fudge Ripple, Corey craned his neck towards the repetitive knock sounding from the hall. It must have been too much to ask for a grown man to enjoy a little ice cream post-shower like any other normal, functioning adult. Especially one squatting in a colleague's apartment while indulging in the quietude the privacy allotted him.

Refusing to let the unwelcomed guest ruin his guilty pleasure, and with carton in hand, he begrudgingly trudged over and flung the door open. Corey leaned against the frame, licking the spoon as the minuscule towel around his waist clung there. Just barely.

"Yep...?" the Irish boy with an oddly southern drawl questioned, glancing casually at the two confused men in front of him. "What my girl do this time?" After another mouthful and still chewing, he continued as he pointed the silverware in their direction. "Full disclosure, I cannot be held accountable for her shenanigans. Even have an agreement saying as much. Insisted on it after the first time. There's no controlling that one."

He recognized the one as Tessa's mark; if he hadn't, the chair would have been a dead giveaway—*unless pissing off guys who couldn't chase her down was her new thing.* The other guy's identity? He had no clue. Both men were silently gawking at his unabashed state of undress.

Sterling was the first to speak up, clearing his throat in discomfort. "A… right… well… I just stopped over to return her possessions. She had, um, left them behind when she came by the office yesterday." Sterling reached into his coat pocket, pulling out Tessa's missing memory card and a small white box that Corey didn't recognize as hers.

"She's actually not here right now—wait… did you say yesterday?" Corey again directed his accusative chocolate-coated spoon at the seated man. "Are you the reason she ran out of town so abruptly and headed over to Jack's?"

STERLING

For what felt like the millionth time since having met this girl, he found himself speechless. First, she'd fallen into his lap and kissed him; then she'd run away, taunting him to come find her; and now, his would-be chivalric gesture is met by this half-naked man at her door who proceeds to tell him about some other guy she'd taken off with. And somehow Sterling was at fault?

He wasn't sure how to answer any of it. Nor did he really want to.

The architect chided himself for being the least bit surprised, but even more, for feeling so utterly disheartened.

Ironically enough. He inspected Corey from top to bottom. *Had he been able to stand at the time, he'd tower over the Irish cowboy. Rather than have to glare up at him like he was.*

But did it really matter anyway? In the end, she had gotten one over on him and he'd allowed it. Subtly regaining his composure, Sterling shoved the items into Corey's outstretched hand.

"I'm sorry. But I cannot speak for her choice of actions," Sterling responded as tactfully as he could conjure up at the time, as he readjusted his lapels and buttoned his jacket. "If you could just return those to her, it would be greatly appreciated." He veered towards the elevators before Corey's audible observation stopped him in his tracks.

"I would, except *this* isn't hers." Corey exited Tessa's apartment and stalked down the hall, obviously carefree when it came to his God-given attributes. "Aren't you even gonna ask Jack's last name?"

"And why would I want to do that?" Sterling scoffed, pivoting to face the man. "What would be the point?" He reached over to reclaim the box.

"Because, it's *Owens*. Jack Owens." Corey nonchalantly returned the rectangular parcel along with the memory card. "Whatever you did, you sent her straight home and into the arms of Papa Bear. So I recommend you giving *that* to her, yourself, in person." He crossed his large biceps over his wide chest, then continued. "I'll even make you a deal. If you have a business card on you, once I'm dressed, I'll text you the address. In return, you agree not to mention this whole *eating her ice cream and wearing her nice towel* incident. That woman will stab a man over some Häagen-Dazs."

Mouth still slightly agape, Sterling's suspiciously tight-lipped counterpart pulled out his wallet and revealed a crisp metallic card. *Silver Fox Restorations.* Corey plucked it from Charles's grasp and, with a bemused salute of farewell, strutted back in the opposite direction. After several moments had passed, Sterling elbowed Charles in the side with a reproachful glare.

"What the hell? Are you suddenly mute?"

Smiling almost robotically, Charles signaled a 'mind-blown' gesticulation, followed by a theatrical clap. "That. Was. Amazing! Like watching a live-action soap opera," he uttered in astonishment. "There was love… loss… a rival suitor… then finally the twist ending!" He stared blankly. "I can't wait until the next episode. You think she has an evil twin?"

With an audible *thump*, Sterling aimed a closed fist at his partner's rib cage before again maneuvering towards the elevators.

TESSA

As defeating as it felt to tuck her tail between her legs and hide out back home, there had always been something so reassuring about actually being here. She sat in the kitchen with her father—a tall, imposing figure and absolutely the only man to earn a piece of her heart.

No one else could ever stand in comparison. She had been close once, and that once embedded the ideal she had known all along: *Jack Owens was the exception.* To him, she was never a disappointment or a failure. He never asked her to be any more or any less than herself; *that* had always been just exactly enough for him.

From the time she had been a little girl, he stressed the importance of her intelligence over her physical aesthetics. It had been the world around her that constantly insisted otherwise, that one man. And that one instance. While the repetitive reminders of her supposed inadequacies as a female only sought to further root her staggering insecurities—the realization that she had almost willingly handed over a small part of herself, to have it discarded before it had even left her grasp.

Looking back, it had been the embarrassment over her sheer gullibility that had broken her down; more so than any tangible wound she had suffered, it was the knowledge that she had played a complicit part in her own invalidation that shattered her self-worth. All those years her father had put into building her up and yet she was so effortlessly weakened. With that in mind, whenever she felt her sensibility buckling, she returned to this house and to this kitchen to find her solid ground.

Mulling over her theology, she knew how it sounded. Like one single broken heart was all it took to close her off from humankind. But it hadn't been that simplistic. It hadn't been just that incident. It had been every person... every mark from that day forward who reiterated her worst fears. Who saw her as nothing more than what she offered on the outside. Who never once tried to look deeper. She had given them the chance—each and every one of them—to morph from a hedonistic philanderer to someone worth a damn. And each had failed miserably. That is, until she'd met Sterling, and he'd shattered her fortitude in a completely different way altogether.

"All right, Bumblebee." Jack pulled up a stool and handed her the traditional cup of hot cocoa. "Tell me what's going on. It's been a while since we've had an impromptu visit. *Not that I'm complaining about having you home.*" His smile was more creased than she'd remembered it being, his hair more white than gray. Though even harrowed by age, the retired military man held firm his authoritative bearing.

"I don't know, *Papa.*" Tessa shook her head and stared down into her mug. "I just feel completely—*je ne sais quoi*—out of sorts, I guess. Like I'm at a crossroads and not completely certain that I am who I thought I was... Maybe it's all the undercover assignments. Maybe I'm losing myself in the midst."

Thumb gently lifting her chin, Jack forced her eyes to meet his. "Hold your head high and proud, kiddo. Because what do we do when we fall?" he prompted.

"We stand back up..." She grinned at the familiar phrasing, the last few tears trailing down her cheeks.

"And when we fall seven times?" he continued, wiping each tear away before tugging at her ear.

"We stand up eight." She laughed, her anxiety momentarily eased. "Though I'm not so sure that philosophy is appropriate in this instance, *Papa.*"

"Problems are often much worse in our minds than in reality, Bee. The fact that you're here questioning everything is proof in *itself* that you are exactly the person we raised. You don't blindly accept what is in front of you or what the easiest solution is. You don't follow the course; you've always set it. *Changed it.* You may not feel like yourself and it's because you are not the same self. Not as yesterday and not as tomorrow. Life experiences shape you. Change you. Or else you would remain stagnant and small-minded. And, Miss Owens, though you may accuse me of being biased—you have always excelled far beyond mediocrity."

This time her laughter was earnest and full-bellied, amused rather than tense. "Now how can I argue with that, *Papa*?" Still grinning, she paused. "If only I had your voice playing in my head all day. Instead of my own."

"Ah. But then what excuse would you have to come see your old man?" he jibed, sipping from his own mug.

She lifted hers in salute. "The hot chocolate! Of course!" He chuckled at her reply while gesturing *touché*. Tessa sighed, her expression suddenly solemn. "How is *Maman*?"

COREY

Whelp, there was no turning back now, Corey thought to himself after pressing send on his most recent text message.

If Tessa wasn't going to kill him for cleaning out her freezer, she sure as hell would be planning his demise when two men appeared on Jack's doorstep. Then again, depending on how things turned out, Jack might take on the job himself.

It was times like these that he wondered if he was some sort of masochist, begging for a swift kick to the groin. Truth be told, Corey had no fucking clue why he chased the guy down the hall and gave him the advice he did. He probably should have just let them both think he was Tessa's live-in boy toy; but there'd just been something about how crushed he'd looked. Not angry. Not dismissive.

Crushed.

There was more going on between the pair than either party would willingly admit. Corey could sense the mutual infatuation just under the surface, an interest blocked by two-pronged egotism. And had it been merely superficial, he would have been the first one to send Mr. Money-Bags packing. In fact, had the stranger uttered a single insult directed at the girl he loved like a sister, he would have been met with closed knuckles to his chin.

Yet, despite being faced with Corey's lackadaisical bare-bodied form at Tessa's door, Sterling had not only remained reserved; but the rich crit had also politely returned both her storage device and whatever trinket he had been hoping to sway her with. That had to mean something. No matter how much either one of them would argue otherwise, Corey had the gut feeling that this was the right thing to do.

At least, he hoped so...

STERLING

Sterling had been tapping his hand against his knee involuntarily for the last forty-five minutes, a habit triggered by nerves. And his clear tell, had he been playing cards rather than making questionable life choices. Right now, he wished it was money he had on the line…

He was being reckless and, more than likely, this was an even bigger mistake than having engaged the girl in the first place. And yet, somehow, this is where the architect had found himself. She was an expert at putting him in awkward situations. Or maybe he was just an expert in walking into them—like a moth to the light. A two-hour drive for what? To have a door slammed in his face? To have her laugh at him and ask what he was thinking?

What was he thinking? And when had he become so self-loathing? Except, he knew exactly when…

Prior to the *accident*—as everyone liked to refer to it—Lucien was impossibly cocksure. He could captivate an audience, force every eye in the room to follow him by sheer will alone. Women had always been nameless and faceless, only in a different way altogether; he'd never been moved by the vapid, wanton china dolls, who bit at his heels while hoping to marry into his family name. Or more so, his family money. They all came and went, rebuffed, when he refused to promise them anything more than a night or two. Now that he was older, he didn't know why he had entertained them at all in the first place; his only excuse being that he had been young and dumb at the time.

But not that dumb…

When the self-inflated twenty-something-year-old had first laid eyes on Madelyn, he'd been enchanted by her. Yes, enchanted was the only way to describe her hold on him. It was the first instance in which he was at the tail-end of a rejection.

Perhaps Charles had been right about him always choosing the road less traveled. He laughed to himself.

But it was true. She had no interest in Lucien. His intentions. Or his lineage. She had one of each on her own, after all.

And Madelyn Beaumont had neither the time nor the energy to "entertain his foolish preconceptions" as she had so eloquently dubbed them. This spurn—the evident cold-shouldering—thrilled the young man, emboldened him even. He had to *and would* win her over. He'd never lost before and he wasn't about to start then.

Over the next few months, and as he prepared to bear the weight of his family's legacy, Lucien had slowly torn down her walls. Until she became just as enamored with him as he was with her. While it may have seemed counterproductive to lament over something that could not be changed, he did so as a reminder. He'd been a different man back then. A man, though confident, who was willing to settle for what was expected of him. And from him. Instead of breaking free to make his own way, as he had done in his later years. Somehow, as insane as it might have sounded, he had been less of a man then than he was now. Chair be damned.

Not that he should compare the two, but Madelyn—other than initiating the chase—was a stark contrast to Tessa. Even with as little as he knew about the girl. Where his ex-fiancée had been soft, docile, and content in her sheltered world; Tessa was harsh, fierce, and driven to rebel—she was the phoenix that could not be caged. The flame that could be observed but never grasped.

He knew he probably looked like a madman, grinning to himself. But at this point, what did it matter? A crippled madman it was.

"Isn't it your *job* to talk me out of poor decision-making?" Sterling barked, noting Charles's whimsical stare. "I'm fairly certain this borders the line of stalker-like behavior. Don't you think?" He was speaking his inner fears aloud. Ultimately, it was true. He had only met the girl twice and here he was, tracking her down at her parents' house.

"That's the funny thing when it comes to the legal intricacies of courtship," Charles hummed, arms crossed as he glanced down at his seemingly manicured fingernails. "The difference between an overtly romantic gesture and flat-out criminal stalking is all in how it is viewed by the recipient."

"Well, that's comforting… Shouldn't you want to keep me *out* of jail?" Sterling refuted. "Instead of escorting me there?"

"Now that you mention it, I *have* been waiting for the chance to use the 'helpless man in a wheelchair' defense for some time." Before Charles could look up with his own patronizing grin, Sterling's cell phone launched forward from the back of the vehicle and landed square against the man's jaw. "Never mind! With such violent tendencies, maybe a little jail time would do you some good!"

TESSA

It was nearly dusk on the second day since Tessa attempted to find solitude at her family home, hidden far from the distractions of the city. She'd tucked herself into her favorite loveseat, hair piled high on the top of her head while loose strands randomly escaped and framed the natural coloring of her unpaletted face. The air was thick with the scent of chocolate-chip oatmeal cookies as her father sought to impede her already meandering work ethic.

She couldn't resist her impulses as the aroma enticed her from the nest of pillows she'd created and drew her into the kitchen. Just as Tessa was about to grab one of the still-cooling desserts, her bare feet inching over the cold tile floor, a pounding echoed from the front door. Jack turned, the noise having alerted him to his daughter's presence, and playfully whacked her outstretched hand with his spatula before directing her to see to the unexpected guest. She snapped her fingers and narrowed her eyes as she approached the sound.

The breeze caused her to blink a few more times than necessary as she hurled the screen door open, nearly making contact with one of the men positioned there. Locking the swing-bar in place, Tessa allowed her gaze to travel from the wooden boards along the porch, upwards, before her eyes met a recognizable glare.

"Oh, I'm sorry. I didn't see you there..." Mid-apology for the mistaken collision, she froze, her pupils widened in disbelief. *Son of a bitch...* "So it seems you found me."

CHAPTER 8
THE GUT-SHOT

TESSA

IT WOULD HAVE BEEN a lie to say she wasn't taken aback by the sight of him; an even bigger falsehood to say she wasn't pleased as well. But Tessa had never been the type to fold her cards after only the first draw; she was much more interested in the slow play. Arms crossed, she leaned into the doorframe—as headstrong and impertinent in a pair of joggers and a tank top, as she would have been in a ballgown. Her posture emphasized that she knew she was breathtaking, even in her disheveled state. And that she didn't care. She was no longer the shell-shocked creature she had been in the days prior. Unsure. Broken.

No, on the contrary, this was exactly the woman her father had raised her to be.

"You seem surprised." His gaze bore into hers, almost as unwavering. But where Tessa was impassive, he was impassioned. It was the effect the two seemed to be able to place on each other, the sensation that the earth had stopped spinning on its axis and everything else had stilled. Like a clock that had been halted mid-tick.

"Oh, I am," she admitted. "Not by your ability, though. More so by the follow-through." Unshod, her bare toes inched onto the weathered threshold. Sidestepping her admirer, she approached his cohort instead. "That is an awfully long drive, *mon lapin*." She reached up to reposition Charles's collar. "What brings you here?"

He gulped beneath her touch; the flesh along his neck reddening at her carefully exacted maneuver. Tessa could feel Sterling's glare, narrowed and direct, his cogs turning as he tried to interpret the inter-action. And that was precisely her logic; she had sought to assail the more fragile target first. She beamed up at her flustered guest, lashes fluttering and expression coy.

"I… we… We're returning your stuff… The stuff you forgot." The normally extroverted wisecracker combed his fingers through his hair, neither moving forward nor back. "We…we… We have some proper-ties in the area we are looking into."

With a final tug to his neckband, the journalist released him, her hands resuming their crossed platform. "Ah, really? Where?" She aimed the question at both men this time. "I'm sure my father could assist you. Except during his service, he's lived in town his entire life."

As if prompted, Jack Owens shadowed the entryway, dish towel in hand. "These your friends, Bumblebee?" He nodded towards the visitors.

Charles echoed the endearment under his breath while attempting to stifle a laugh. *"Bumblebee?"*

A single eyebrow raised, and sporting an expression as deadened as his tone, Jack warned. "Her mother urged me to soften the nick-name years back. Claimed it scared the other kids when I called my girl *killer* at the playground. But don't you be fooled, boy: the thing may be small, but yell *bee* in a crowded room and everyone goes running. It's not the size of the creature they fear, but the intensity of its sting." He turned his back in more of a command than an invitation and ordered, "Come on in. It's time for dinner."

Grabbing Charles by the hand, Tessa yanked the unwilling guest through the doorway while he twisted to face Sterling over her shoul-der. He pointed and mouthed the words *"evil twin"* before disap-pearing into the house.

STERLING

He should be jealous—the *average* man would have been. But as previously determined, Sterling preferred the unconventional. In fact, he was still trying to decide if he should consider her artificial display with Charlie *blatant antagonism* or an outright compliment. Observing her bravado, rather than being subjected to it, was an art form all its own. He watched as she instantly adapted to each new circumstance, a chameleon by its very definition. She didn't miss a beat; it was as though the entire scenario and all possible outcomes had already been scripted. And all she needed to do was recite her lines. Each movement had been natural yet precise, graceful but calculated. Like a dance edged in subtleties.

She had concentrated her efforts on Charles because of how easily the man would crack. Hell, her hapless victim had surrendered before she even had to lay a hand on him. This much, Sterling had already surmised. What he couldn't understand was why, in this instance, she had favored a swift submission over her usual strategy? Was it possible Tessa was acknowledging that she had been bested? Realizing that he had seen through each layer of carefully applied deception and been introduced to the girl beneath it all? Or perhaps, even more unlikely, had she willingly chosen to disengage her opposition? Was the gravitational pull between them deeper than even her serpentine devices dared to reach?

TESSA

Dinner had been quiet but oddly comfortable, considering the questionable happenstance; only in the Owens household was it customary for company to be threatened before being fed. Granted, her father had been one hundred percent accurate. Tessa did have one hell of a left hook.

She shrugged her shoulders in silent agreement.

Placing a silver dessert tray in the center of the table, Jack gripped the back of Charles's neck, causing the poor guy to nearly jolt from his seat. "Come now. I'll show ya' where you fellas will be spending the night." Again, the offer was formulated as an instruction.

Charles dropped the cookie he had raised, though his mouth remained ajar. "Oh, no. We couldn't impose. We, ah, we planned on staying at the hotel downtown," he stuttered.

Mr. Owens didn't respond; instead, the imposing figure continued towards the guest room. As if unsure what else to do, Charles stood—equally wordless—and followed the man while Sterling and Tessa erupted into a bout of combined laughter.

"He does make it almost too easy. *No*?" she posited.

Sterling nodded, the air again falling silent as he glared into his black coffee before taking a swig. "I've been meaning to ask... I couldn't help but notice the ramps. Since you obviously hadn't been expecting us all the way out here, I take it you didn't break them out just for me?"

She was startled when the warmth of his hand closed around hers, providing the reassurance she didn't know she needed until it was already there.

This. This was exactly what she had been hoping to avoid—what she was running from—the emptiness she felt at the thought of him letting go and her sudden impulse to hold on that much tighter.

"Already dismissing my ability to predict the future?" she jested, looking to ease her own apprehension rather than his, before adding with a sigh, "My mother. She just doesn't have the same strength anymore. When she refuses to eat, she can barely make it out of the car after a doctor's appointment. But when *Papa* bakes her favorites, he'll find her up that flight of stairs, reorganizing the linen closet as if she were ten years younger. He built her those ramps after the first bad day. He never wanted her to feel that helpless again." Then Tessa bounced from her chair, as if the thought had unexpectedly struck her. "You two should meet!"

STERLING

Tessa had shot up from her chair as though she were animated by a self-imposed electrical current before, and assuming he'd follow her, she bounded through the kitchen and down the hall. She, of course, had assumed correctly.

Like father, like daughter, he mused to himself.

The corridor was wider than Sterling would have expected from the structural era. Although an expansion could have been made in later renovations, the architect took note of how the double-pocket doors and Victorian-bronze knobs spoke to the original construction. The high ceilings, intricate archways, and hand-carved woodwork had been well-preserved over the years, but it was the aerial view that had piqued his interest. If only he were able to take a closer look at the plastered ceilings...

From his current angle, he couldn't tell if they had been restored or just impeccably maintained. Time, settlement, and moisture were not sympathetic to the opulent design; however, the obvious yellowing leaned towards its authenticity.

Sterling's preoccupation with architectural features derived from an early age and had initially centered around the historic financial repositories his family had inherited. While his parents conversed over which walls to blow out and which foundations to demolish, Sterling stockpiled antiquated vault doors, ornamental ironwork, and whatever carpentry he could salvage. He never understood how the same individuals hyper-focused on progeny could completely dismantle their ancestral monuments, preferring to replace them with whatever was newer, sleeker, and more modernized. His office building was the last concession he'd welcomed from them, and only because he knew if he had not, its future lay at the other end of a bulldozer.

The now obsolete credit union had originally served as the city's fledgling fire department before it was converted into a warehouse and then finally landed amongst his familial line of holdings. It had been his first conservation venture post-injury and consumed him for months on end—as he drafted and redrafted his blueprints, converting the archaic freight elevator into something usable so he could ultimately navigate the top floor. While his predecessors insisted their legacy was found at the other end of a bankroll, Sterling saw *his* etched in brick walls and masonry.

He had given up on the idea of ever having children, instead believing that his patronage could get passed down in every bit of stone and mortar he sought to maintain for future generations. Unlike an epitaph—cemented in sorrow and mourning, as forgotten as the dirt beneath it—these aging infrastructures could inspire enjoyment and admiration over lifetimes, as they did for him in the present moment. It was a far more beneficial use of his namesake.

At least he thought so. His forebears on the other hand? Not so much.

The hallway ended in what would have been traditionally used as a cigar parlor. Sterling waited at the entrance as the two women spoke quickly and fluently in French. Mrs. Owens was not what he had been expecting, despite having seen her briefly in the video message.

She was much thinner and slighter in frame, likely due to the malnutrition Tessa had recently mentioned. But all the same, she was a beautiful woman. With long auburn hair braided into a bun and not yet showing signs of gray. Her eyes were strikingly green and mirrored her daughter's. Though the edges were creased, she still appeared much younger than her age would suggest. At the moment, she was standing but her chair was only a few feet behind her.

Catching his stare with the corner of her eye, Tessa greeted him with a small, sad smile as she directed Mrs. Owens's gaze. "Lucien, this is my mother—*Emeline Leroux Owens*. And, *Maman*, this is the friend I was telling you about. He's in town... looking at some proper-ties." She purposely inflected her voice as she repeated Charles's less-than-clever cover story.

The woman's brows furrowed in confusion before she quickly placed a kiss on each one of Sterling's cheeks and continued to respond in her native tongue.

"No, *Maman*, only English," Tessa corrected; however, Emeline's speech remained the same—though perhaps slightly more frantic. "*Maman, nous devons parler en Englais.*" Tessa prompted again, shaking her head.

"I'm sorry, Bee." Jack entered the room, pushing past the doorway to cradle his wife close to his side. "She doesn't know how. Not anymore. I didn't want to ruin your visit with us or burden you... The doctors say the disease has attacked her language center. She's reverted completely to French over the last few months. I was hoping you wouldn't notice for a while yet, since that's your preference anyway. The specialist said she wouldn't even remember learning English..."

Sterling suddenly felt intrusive, though he couldn't bring himself to abandon Tessa in this moment either. He watched as her demeanor shifted between several emotions before settling on anger. She let out a flurry of French profanities, which Mrs. Owens had no problem under-standing and seemed to reprimand her for. Then turned to Jack.

"How could you not tell me!" She huffed, pacing a few steps forward and then pacing back. "You don't speak a word of French! I could have been here. I could have helped. Translated! What were you thinking, *Papa*? Be honest. No bullshit!"

"Words have never been a barrier for us, kiddo. After nearly thirty years together, I already know what your mother wants, what she needs. She doesn't have to tell me." As if she knew exactly what her husband was saying, Emeline smiled up at him, and Jack placed a kiss to her forehead. "Speaking of which, I have to get her ready for bed. Show your friend here to the study. I converted it to a spare room for those nights when your mother doesn't want to climb the stairs. You can visit more in the morning." He escorted his wife to the threshold, pausing to address Sterling. "By the way, my daughter's room is upstairs, across from mine. And I'm a *very* light sleeper—an old habit from the war."

"With all due respect, sir," Sterling replied, unsure if the man was actually serious or just busting his balls. "Unless there's an elevator, you won't be finding me up any staircase. You understand that's physically impossible, right?" He gestured towards his chair, but calmly tempered his annoyance.

Mr. Owens grinned; it was the first time his face had softened in direct view of his houseguest. "*Impossible?* Yeah, that's what they said when I only had three months to talk a pretty French heiress, who didn't know a word of English, into moving to the States with me." Exiting the parlor, Jack declared, "I did it in two. Boy, where there's a will, there's always a way."

———

He sat with her in silence for longer than either of them had realized. Ironically, like Jack had suggested, verbal communication wasn't necessary. There wasn't much Sterling could have said to take away her anguish, and he guessed there wasn't much she would have wanted to hear at the time anyway. But Tessa hadn't wanted him to leave and somehow he had understood her plea without her having to vocalize it. He allowed her to stare off into nothing, devoid of questioning or prodding, as he circled his thumb around the palm of her hand.

Unprompted, she was the first to break the lull. "I'm sorry…" Tears clung to her bottom lashes, teetering on the edge of despair as she battled to keep them from falling. "I'm sure this wasn't what you were expecting. *Telle est la vie, mon chèri,* huh?"

She stilled, as he wiped the grief from her eyes before forcing her to turn and look into his. "I've already learned that it's foolish to have expectations when it comes to you." He cupped her cheek with the rough, cracked skin of his open palm. "It would be like a blind man trying to describe the sky." His remark came out a little huskier than he'd intended; but then again, it usually did when he was in the same room as this girl.

"Hm. Maybe you *are* smarter than you look." She laughed as though finding comfort in the comparison.

"Did you seriously just insinuate that I'm dumb?" he gasped, seizing her wrist before she could react and causing her to topple into his arms. She shrieked in surprise and landed with a giggle.

"*C'est souvent vrai quand tu es jolie.* The pretty ones usually are." Tessa smirked at the same stereotype that had been the bane of her existence. She shifted from a position of submission to one of dominance. Straddling his lap, her knees pinning the outside of each one of his thighs, she forced *him* to look up at *her.* His hands reflexively shot to her waist to steady her movements as well as to keep her from fleeing.

"Ah. So you admit that I'm pretty?" he countered. "Though, as I'm sure you're aware, men prefer to be called handsome, rugged, dapper even..." His list of preferred adjectives was cut off by her mouth impatiently assaulting his.

Her lips were softer than he'd remembered, the taste somehow sweeter. Or maybe his memory just couldn't do them justice. All the same, she ignited every neuron in his body—even those long thought dead. He knew they were practically strangers and yet everything about this woman felt *right*. Felt seamless and extraordinary. Like the piece he had been missing for years.

Hell, the way she looked at him...

She loosened his collar, then turned her focus to the buttons of his suit jacket, yanking the material from his shoulders in an attempt to further liberate him from his constrictive clothing. In doing so, her memory card fell from the inner pocket as did the rectangular box he'd been concealing. Both landing with a muffled *thud* on the hardwood. The sound—although just barely audible—was distracting enough to catch her attention. She reached down and plucked the items from the floor, intent on discarding them on the end table at their side.

"Open it," he encouraged. Though, in truth, what had initially seemed like a good idea suddenly induced self-consciousness and apprehension.

Wordlessly, she did as she was instructed. *For once.* He could detect her quickened pulse when she exhaled the air she must've been holding back. And her head was tilted and her eyes were narrowed, as if she were asking a question without an utterance.

"It… it reminded me of you. Charles said it was weird. You can be honest if you don't like it. Flowers just felt too… cliché."

CHAPTER 9
THE HORNET'S NEST

TESSA

CLUTCHING the white box to her chest, the journalist was awestruck. That and somewhat perplexed.

It hadn't been the monetary value that rendered her speechless, though she was certain the price tag was more than she cared to know. No, she was accustomed to the practice of having thoughtless tokens tossed her way; too many admirers—both men and women alike—confused the size of their wallets with their desirability. Instead, it had been his considerable forethought that left Tessa feeling suddenly... *off-balance.*

Grazing her fingertips over each detail, she was thoroughly convinced that Sterling's choice had been exacting and deliberate. The adornment had been carefully nestled inside the crushed velvet navy-blue cushioning, old but delicately placed. The chain appeared to be platinum and pearl, each sequence slightly misshapen and patinaed over time, but the pendant shone as the true masterpiece.

Fossilized amber seemed to be artfully sculpted into an almost teardrop heart shape and then it had been mounted into the silver and rose-cut diamond setting. The pattern crisscrossed from the widest point before interlocking at the tip. Moreover, encased inside the yellow resin was an exquisitely preserved and petrified scorpion. Both fierce and beautiful.

"It reminded me of you."

She knew he was waiting for a response, likely one more animated than her state of reticence. *But how do you respond to that?* He was examining her, scanning for any indication of her displeasure. But he didn't goad her; he didn't force a reaction. He deferred his emotions to hers. However, she did notice that his grip on her had tightened—whether intentional or not—as though he feared she might run away again.

Cautiously lifting the necklace from its resting place, Tessa cradled it in her palm as she continued to trace out the intricacies. After only a few interactions and even fewer words exchanged, this man had found a way to personify her better than she could describe herself. She uttered the only dialogue she could muster at the time.

"C'est parfait. It's perfect."

———

Over the next hour, and despite the other available seating options, they remained as they were. Tessa had sprawled one leg across the curved armrest with the other dangling off the side, her back held tight to his chest. With each word he spoke, she was soothed by the vibration of his throat pressed to her shoulder while his chin rested comfortably at her collarbone.

She couldn't remember the last time she'd felt so at ease in her own skin. It was then that she'd been able to openly explain her mother's illness and how the dementia had crept in slowly at first—under the guise of forgetfulness and the natural aging process—before eating away at the invincible woman Tessa had known throughout her youth.

Emeline Leroux had traveled to the United States, as Jack had mentioned, barely knowing more than a word or two of English. In the year that followed—and in every respect all but self-taught—she became fluently bilingual. Though she had originated from a well-established family, Emeline had never again returned to her hometown, relinquishing both her name and wealth in agreeing to follow the handsome young soldier.

The Leroux bloodline was solely anecdotal for Tessa, her grandparents' existence stored in the mind of a woman whose memory diminished a little more each day. Believing they deserved the same regard they'd shown her father, Tessa knowingly accepted the fact that part of her family history would die alongside her mother's recollections.

She accepted it as much as she didn't care.

Recognizing that her initial sentiment may have appeared grim, Tessa sought to clarify the logic behind her familial indifference; while Sterling continued to listen without interruption or disparagement, absorbing any insight into her inner workings she would willingly impart. There had been moments she was convinced that his attentiveness was, in fact, a demonstration of boredom. She would turn, expecting to find his mind adrift but instead his eyes would meet hers with an encouraging nod. He would pull her back down against him, warming the nape of her neck with his measured breathing, and prompt her to proceed.

She rationalized that extended family—especially one that didn't want her to begin with—was inconsequential, growing up as she had and with parents such as hers. Emeline had been the catalyst for Tessa's education, advising her daughter on the importance of being well-rounded in conjunction with being well-versed. She stood by her belief that there were many facets of intelligence and academics were just part of a larger equation, and thus, motivated Tessa to expand her scope of knowledge outside of social formalities and comfort.

So, at her mother's prompting, the girl had studied literature, the arts, history, and photography in tandem with mechanics, engineering, business, and politics—acquiring such a vast variety of skill sets that Corey surmised his counterpart must be an international spy. He jokingly dubbed Tessa the *Female 007*, himself the cleverly appointed *Bond Boy*.

But most of all, Emeline had taught her daughter that wealth was always secondary to personal fulfillment; the woman could speak from experience.

Meanwhile, ever the proponent of his daughter's intestinal fortitude, Jack Owens had raised Tessa with the understanding that the only tangible hindrance to an accomplishment was self-depreciation. He repetitively vocalized his pride, insisting that true failure was achieved by never trying in the first place, while deeming each misstep she took no more than an exercise in perseverance. She had never been his *princess*.

No, Jack's daughter would never be labeled a damsel in distress, as he called it. She was his *killer*. The kind of girl born to cause a commotion. He trained her to box, build her own campfire, and change her own oil. Where many parents misguidedly focused on a burden-free life with their children, he focused on preparing Tessa for the obstacles she would face *without* him.

At no time, and under no circumstance, did the girl fear living up to his expectations. Just his legacy.

STERLING

He'd thwarted her attempts to move, no matter the number of times she'd tried to pull away. However, he didn't hold her there against her will. In fact, he had the inclination that she wanted to stay as much as he had needed her to. Her inability to relax against him for long periods of time seemed more of a compulsion—manifested by anxiety—rather than an autonomous decision. How seamlessly she melted back into his arms further solidified his theory. Every time and as if subconsciously, her restlessness stilled with the light pressure of his hands around the narrowing of her waist.

Sterling studied the girl as she spoke, while appeasing his usual affinity for observation. However, he wasn't looking to remain the outsider, nor was she a peculiarity he was hoping to dissect. Instead, he appreciated each word. Each recounting. Each autobiographical detail she voluntarily divulged. She'd guided the conversation, centered her small relinquishments around her immediate family and her upbringing. It was as though she sought to steer the architect away from anything too personal. And yet, ironically, that had been her fatal flaw.

Her parental relationships told him more about her than any self-portrayal ever could have, much like *his* would have told *her*. Even to the most absentminded spectator, it was evident that she maintained a staunch closeness to them. There had been a tenderness in her depiction of the couple. Her tempo would serendipitously quicken with enjoyment and her French would interject more fluidly. And yet before he could pause and remind her of the language barrier, she would habitually translate—a practice that, he assumed, had become second nature with her father.

Jack's pride had shown in his eyes at the mere mention of the girl. And not because of what she had done in life but because of who she had become. Courageous. Unrelenting. And resourceful. It didn't need to be said; it was intrinsically felt. Furthermore, the care her father had taken to preserve the grandeur of their old, well-loved home exemplified how the man defined value. There were some things that no amount of money could replace, a conviction that the Owens family seemed to collectively share.

While Sterling hadn't gained direct understanding from Emeline's words, the body language between mother and daughter spoke volumes. Tessa had grown into a girl as much a fighter as her mother seemed to epitomize. Even riddled with disease, the petite maternal figure projected dignity and strength. His heart—the cold, dead thing that it was—ached at the sight of the two and with the knowledge of what was to come for the woman he knew in narrative alone.

Yes. Her childhood had been a stark contrast to his, he thought to himself. Where her home emitted warmth and laughter even when faced with hardship, his had been formalized, cold, and distant. Just like the currency that bore his surname.

TESSA

"It's getting late, *mon nounours*." She sighed.

The fact that neither one of them had wanted to say it aloud didn't make it any less true. She begrudgingly removed herself from the warmth of his lap, stretching each leg to ease the cramps that had formed there. She felt the phantasmal loss the moment his hands left her hips, a chill where the heat had been. Crossing her arms, she stifled the urge to subdue her rising goose bumps.

"Come on. I'll show you to the study… and make sure you're tucked in properly." She winked, pointing and curling her index finger before turning on her heel.

Tessa led him to an enormous pair of antique pocket doors, delicately edging the weighted panels open to reveal the interior. This had always been one of her favorite rooms in the house. Breathing deep, she noted how it still smelled like the timeworn books it once held. She watched as the architect seemed as enamored with his makeshift sleeping quarters as she was.

While Tessa had learned that his architectural firm was restoration-based, what hadn't occurred to her was that he actually found enjoyment in it. It was a rare quality to observe in the affluent—usually the only thing they sought to retain was the blue tint to their blood. She couldn't help but smile at the immersive look on his face as he continued to examine the coffered ceiling.

"I'm shocked that we haven't heard hide nor hair from Charles," Tessa remarked as she slid the double doors in place before latching them closed. Turning, she stalked towards her captive prey—the newly gifted amber pendant bouncing in step against her low neckline, as if daring the man to stare.

"He texted that he's sleeping outside in our SUV." Sterling laughed. "He claimed your dad is crazy and threatened to *make sure he needs a chair of his own*… if he found him anywhere near your bedroom."

Tessa threw her head back in amusement. Little did either man know, Jack was not one to fight his daughter's battles for her. He had the foresight to understand she wouldn't be able to rely on his protection. Were she to find herself in a vulnerable scenario, the only strength his daughter should ever count on was her own.

STERLING

"*Papa* is all bark and no bite," Tessa professed, still smirking. "I'm pretty sure he gets his kicks from making you guys sweat. In truth, I think it's more of an invitation—if anything. Since we haven't been able to hit the bag in a while, he's probably hoping someone takes the bait, so he can make sure I can still land a solid punch."

Somehow Sterling didn't find her admission all that shocking—the apple certainly didn't fall far from the tree with this one.

She positioned herself as she had earlier: saddled on top and facing him, arms circling his neck. "But, now that Charlie's left us all to ourselves in here, there's something I've been meaning to ask… I know we've brushed over the topic," she said pointedly, running her fingertips along the sleek armrest of his chair. "But I think it's time we addressed the elephant in the room."

This was it.

The moment he'd been dreading. He closed his eyes and inhaled with the pang he already felt in his chest. He knew what she was going to ask. In actuality, he was surprised at how long she'd taken to bring up the subject. And yet, he couldn't squelch his underlying panic. *This* was why he avoided socializing in crowds, why Charles handled the firm's face-to-face daily operations.

The poking. The prodding. The constantly approaching him like he was a museum exhibit to be gawked at. Like his spectators had the right to know which parts of him worked and which didn't.

He'd been so immediately drawn to her because of how differently she'd treated him. Or rather, how equally. Then again, he knew the bubble she had initially created for him wouldn't last. Curiosity would always overtake even the best of them.

"Go ahead and ask." He groaned, his gaze penetrating hers as he ignored his growing impulse to look away.

CHAPTER 10
THE SLOW STUDY

STERLING

EVERY MUSCLE in his body tensed as he waited for her to formulate the question. The same question he'd answered, or refused to, or cursed at since the moment he'd discovered his entire world in shambles.

Even now, he could still see the look of horror, guilt, and pity on Madelyn's face upon hearing his prognosis. Though, in all fairness, it wasn't that hard to remember—considering that to this day, that look had remained imprinted there. He had yet to decide what had been worse, his fiancée's reaction or the devastation met by his parents. Not over concern for their son's future, of course, but rather for their sudden lack of a sole heir. In an instant, he'd shattered everyone's dreams, except his own, because he had never been permitted to have any in the first place.

Funny enough, this was the first time he realized that he'd never really had anything to lose to begin with. Not a single aspiration had belonged to Sterling alone…

From the time he'd been born, his life had been decided for him. His education. His profession. His impending marriage. It'd all been laid out in front of him like tomorrow's suit—one that he'd unquestioningly stepped into. That is, until he'd lost the use of his legs and, in turn, gained his backbone. It was true that his feelings for Madelyn had been earnest; however, he'd also never been given the opportunity to meet anyone outside his family's set income. Nor had he taken it. It was odd to think where he might be, right now, if everything hadn't veered so far off course.

He certainly wouldn't be in this room. Or with this girl. And that thought sent an unexpected twinge to his chest.

"Don't get me wrong, *ours en colère*." He was disoriented by the sound of her voice and incidentally freed from the trappings of his inner thoughts. Tapping on the left cylindrical spoke, she grinned as if bemused by his discomfort. "I know you come from money, but I have to ask… what is this? The Rolls-Royce of wheelchairs?"

Stunned, the architect blinked and tried to maintain his bearings. *Okay, that hadn't been the question he'd been expecting. And perhaps he wasn't smarter than he looked,* he thought and immediately regretted not heeding his credence from earlier.

"Only if a Rolls-Royce is made of graphene and manufactured in Sweden." His retort was natural and puckish as he choked back his laughter. "*That* was what you waited to ask me behind closed doors? Not about what happened…" He was a grown-ass man, and yet he could feel the heat creeping up his neck as he mindlessly tugged at his collar. "Or about what works? Instead, you want to know about the fancy chair?"

"Yep! Right now, in this moment, does it really matter what happened?" Her eyes glanced down suggestively before continuing to trail upwards to meet his gaze again. "And I'm already *well* aware of what works, Lucien. Lest you forget, I've spent more time in your lap than not."

He shifted in his seat under her visual anatomizing.

"As for bringing up the *fancy chair*, as you call it, I had to wait until we were out of earshot. I was raised to never comment on someone's financial status. *Maman* says it's rude." The look she gave him now was mischievous. And maybe something more…

———

She didn't flinch when he'd refused her offer to help climb onto the guest bed. He'd anticipated her leaving by that point—as embarrassed as he was—when he clumsily transitioned his weight onto the mattress. The same as he had done every night. Instead, she grinned and lifted her palms up in submission before plopping herself on the other end to watch. Though as to what she was so intent on observing, he hadn't the slightest. He wanted to be taken aback or annoyed by the way she treated him like a spectacle. But there was something about how her eyes regarded him that made Sterling think twice.

"And what exactly are you doing?" The accusation left him unwittingly and before he even realized he'd formulated the sentence. And yet, surprisingly, her stare didn't waver in the least bit.

"Trying to give you incentive to hurry up, since you didn't let me hasten the ordeal."

It was then that he recognized the gleam—the exact one that had prompted his hesitation. The look she'd given him, it'd been… *flirtatious.*

No wonder he hadn't been able to pinpoint it at first.

Braced by the heavy wooden headboard, he chastised himself before returning his attention to her prone form. It was a strangely tender feeling, having her lie beside him and beneath the covers. Though to her it was completely natural. Or, at least, outwardly that's how she appeared.

She was curled up on her side and still facing him, one arm tucked under the pillow and the other under her head. Her hair had escaped the high-tied knot and framed her profile with unfettered waves, while her respirations idled in a slow and even pace, further drawing his gaze to the pearled chain constricted by the dip of her breasts.

"Shouldn't you head upstairs? Before someone notices you're missing?" His reluctance was palpable; howbeit, no one could say he didn't at least *try* to do the right thing.

Chivalry wasn't dead, but it was sure as hell a challenge to maintain.

"I haven't slept up there in ages," she confessed, and her lips couldn't have curled up anymore if she tried. "Whenever I do visit, I'm usually up late into the night working and eventually doze off on the couch. Or in here, seeing as it used to be my father's study."

What the fuck was he supposed to do with that information? What would Lucien have done? Never mind, he knew *exactly* what Lucien would have done.

But he wasn't so sure that he wanted to be that guy again, even if presented with the opportunity. Just the sound of his given name—as she spoke it those few times—left him feeling distant. Like the person she was referring to was someone else entirely.

Would she have been able to so effectively disarm the man he once was? he wondered. Though, if he were to be completely honest, the question itself was rhetorical. Considering he knew with an unequivocal certainty that, that same man would have enthusiastically walked into her trap and closed the door behind him.

He had no doubt that this girl would be the end of him; however, as he was now, he knew he held a much higher chance of survival.

TESSA

Corey would have accused her of being completely out of her mind, she told herself.

If she'd asked, her target would have relinquished his entire story. Right then and there. Though professionalism had not been her sole reason for avoiding the subject, she would still have argued with her partner. She would have reminded him that the most precise truths were those offered unprompted and adventitiously. And just as often as not, they were insinuated rather than audibly spoken. What was true for her day job translated seamlessly into her personal life as well. Therefore, she would admit that her intentions with Sterling were not entirely executive-based.

If at all…

She wasn't lying. She'd meant it when she said that, in this moment, what had happened previously didn't really matter. Because it hadn't mattered. It didn't matter. The only thing that did was the realization that she was cradled next to him because she wanted to be; there was no other ulterior motive. And she feared that posing dually loaded questions would have changed that.

It was generally assumed—if not implied—that the journalist should be well-versed in basic intimacies, considering Tessa relied on not only her guile but also the subtle nuances of seduction. Though she couldn't really fault the misplaced conjecture, in actuality, she barely let her targets touch her. And under no circumstances did she go home with them.

Not anymore anyway…

No, the crucial part had always been to leave them wondering. Wanting. Obsessing over what they couldn't have. Or what they thought they could. It had been a long time since she had interacted with any male outside of these intended marks—as baffling as that may have seemed. But these career pursuits had always been her main focus; *that* and the fact that she found very few individuals worth more than the passing pleasantry.

Thus, lying beside this man was both intimidating and freeing, as was the fact that she had both nothing and everything to lose at once.

STERLING

Her posturing had been spontaneous and independent of her normally composed and premeditated behaviors—quick but not any less catlike —as both her presence and stature bestrode the man beneath her. Upon impact, her knees pinning the slight V-shaped dip of his transverse muscles, Sterling's eyes closed with a vocalized groan. They opened as she released each button of his dress shirt before sliding the material down off his shoulders and onto the floor.

The tips of her fingers played along the sculpted outline of his exposed upper body. His clavicle, to his sternocostal, to his deltoid. As if they were memorizing the well-defined details. Necessity, rather than narcissism, had cut and broadened the architect's physique whereas endurance had molded it.

The gentle exploration had ended with her hands flat and paralleled on his bare chest while his palms tucked into the bend of her knees. Counteracting her initial leverage, he utilized this sudden gravitational vantage point to tug her forward, her mouth meeting his. He lightly cupped the side of her face, the kiss fluctuating from soft to animalistic.

Her initial appraisal had been accurate; there was no question about which parts of him were fully functioning. If only his legs had been as cooperative, he would have already flipped her onto her back and shown her just how right she had been. But the reality of the situation left him completely at her mercy. He could only give her what she took, offer what she embraced and accommodated.

The suppressed whimpers and moans she was emitting were enough to drive any man crazy; however, it was the back-and-forth grind of their clothing that edged him towards madness. Cursing under breath, he tilted his head back against the headboard willing the resounding *thud* to knock the sense back into him while he attempted to steady his respirations. And yet, his efforts would remain fruitless as she continued her pointed assault on his ability to rationalize.

She nipped at the base of his jawline, grazing her teeth along the stubbled contour before meeting his ear with shallow pants. *"Dis moi ce que tu veux..."* The sound was as carnal as it was incoherent. "Tell me what you want," she repeated, dragging her nails across the skin bordering his waistband.

His capacity to formulate thoughts or articulate any further was all but fragmented as he hissed the singular word. "You." Had she been testing him—despite the stuttered, faltering response—it appeared as though he passed; that is, if her reprisal were any indication.

She unfastened his weighted belt buckle, next focusing on the top button and zipper of his pants. "You were never going to be able to sleep like that," she whispered, wrenching the leather strap through each loop in a single directed flick of her wrist and chucking it onto his crumbled shirt. "You should have let me take it off *before* you came to bed, *chose têtue."*

Upon achieving her unrestrained and self-imposed access, Tessa's hand dipped into the open pocket of the tailored fabric while her gaze fluttered upwards, piercing his own. She gripped the uprisen bulge between his thighs. Palm pressed excruciatingly tight, she taunted him into increased submission. Her gestures were slow, methodical, just enough to stir the flame but not nearly enough to satiate it.

He searched for some hint of similar instability, aching for the slightest testament that would denote her reciprocation. A man haunted by self-doubt, he sought any sign willing to confirm that this femme fatale burned as hot and as hungered as her harshened command would suggest. Nevertheless, when he encountered Tessa's shared intensity—her eyes flickering between appetence and combustion—he balked.

"*Fuck…*" Swearing with baited exhale, he momentarily halted her touch. "You know you are damn near *killing* me, right?"

"*Mon ours,* I can assure you that is not my intention. Then again, what is life without *la petite mort…?*" Unburdened by discretion, she recaptured his lips, hers feverishly sealing the promise that hung in the air.

TESSA

The control she held over Sterling was almost as gratifying as the rhythmic rise and fall of his hips beneath her. Without regard for propriety or consequence or even the fact that they knew less about each other than she cared to dwell on, Tessa unsheathed the man.

She took shameless pleasure in just the sight of him: exposed, throbbing, and raw from her embrace. Though unclear whether it had been by instinct or intimidation, he pulled away, stilled, and waited for her next move; while the usually patient journalist had no interest in building the suspense a minute longer.

Despite how tempting her view, she mused, cocking an eyebrow at the thought.

Had he still been wearing his necktie, this would have been the part where she yanked it forward and closed the distance between them—a small reprimand for having created their separation in the first place. However, lack of a proper leash be damned, her pet couldn't evade her predatory crawl nor *she presumed* would he care to. Regaining sufficient proximity, Tessa enclosed her arms over his shoulders. His chest taut, hers heaving. Before mounting the man in an impassioned display of dominance.

The sudden rush of heat and friction where it'd been needed most left them both gasping. Desperate and breathless, she rode out the pulsing ache at her core. There were no thoughts, no second-guesses. All forms of logic and reason were dismissed as the pressure sharpened with every staggering grind of her pelvic bone. Even as her toes grew numb, her flanking thighs both tense and trembling, Tessa remained too far gone to consider the post-climatic aftershock her body would endure. As her energy waned, his hands—which nearly encompassed the entirety of her waist—hastened the tempo with each additional thrust.

When she finally reached her peak, he kept one palm firmly in place at her hip, the other shooting upwards to muffle her cries. Slinking over the stimulative edge, Tessa bit down on the meat of his knuckle in a half-hearted attempt to quiet herself. The sinking sensation of her teeth into his flesh heightened his own release, which culminated in an unrestrained growl. And almost as if her allegorical strings had been cut, the journalist collapsed onto the security of the architect's chest, his arms innately clutching her there.

STERLING

Short-winded and fighting for air, Sterling couldn't help but think how the expression *a little death* had never been more fitting.

He'd looked death in the eye. He knew death. Surrender. And this… This was jarringly close to it. Where most would say *fuck you* to that final submission, the man had spit in the Grim Reaper's face and said, "Fuck me," instead. And she'd complied.

CHAPTER 11
THE LOOKING GLASS

STERLING

IT'D BEEN a year since he'd met the girl he would easily consider the love of his life. And nearly a year to the day before he would marry her. Looking back, had anyone told him this was where he would be, he would never have believed them.

But this girl… she was unlike anyone he'd ever met and he couldn't seem to get her out of his head. Like a bad habit he just couldn't shake, an addiction he'd no intention of breaking. Their engagement had been spontaneous—one he hadn't planned. Instead, the thought had hit him suddenly and without warning.

He couldn't live without her. He didn't want to…

And so, he'd spit the question out before logic or reason could argue with him otherwise. *Be my wife?* It hadn't necessarily been phrased as a request but it hadn't been a statement either. It was more open-ended than that…

She was the exact opposite of everything Lucien had been raised to look for in a future spouse. She defied him at every given chance, countered his every decision, and inspired him to blindly dive towards so much more than he thought himself capable. She was the spark that seemed to set his world ablaze and he voluntarily watched it burn.

Even now, as he repositioned his tie, he could hear her humming in the background as she readied herself for their dinner with her parents. And he couldn't stop himself from grinning over the joy that simple, soft vibration elicited from him.

"Careful, keep smiling at your reflection like that and you'll have a fate no better than that Greek nymph," she warned from her perch at the threshold of the bathroom.

She was beautiful...

But to say it or think it wasn't enough for him. The three words weren't enough to even begin to describe her. They were minimalistic in comparison to her presence. After all, beauty was such a trivial concept. A label given to a painting, a piece of jewelry, a distant landscape, and all the other things the world chose to disparage and gawk at. She wasn't one of those things and while he couldn't deny the fact that he was driven to stare at her; it wasn't out of the need for a visual inspection—it was in wonderment and awe over every aspect of her entirety. And yet, in the current state of his primitive brain, all he could come up with was:

She was beautiful...

"It's *you* I'm smiling at," he retorted, staring at her mirrored image reflected back at him as he continued to button his suit jacket and adjust his cufflinks.

"Hm... I find that rather unlikely, considering you have yet to even turn to look at me." Her expression was bemused, her tone mocking.

"I don't need to look at you to be so utterly captivated." He paused and tapped his index finger against the hollow of his temple, maintaining the reflective eye contact. "Your image is perfectly ingrained up here, darling." She crept up behind him, flinging her arms around his neck and draping them across his chest; her lips pressed close to his ear as she kissed the sensitive skin along his nape.

Breathing in the scent of his cologne, she sighed. "Save the charm for someone who's likely to fall for it, Lucien."

"I did..." was all he said before he pulled her from behind him to capture her mouth with his. She tasted as sweet as she had that very first night they'd been together and every night since.

"All right, enough, you two lovebirds," Charles interrupted, obnoxiously motioning at his invisible wristwatch. "I refuse to be held accountable if we're any later."

Almost as though their reaction had been choreographed, Charles was met with a synchronized pair of eye rolls before each exited the master bedroom.

"On that note," he continued. "I'll take my own car." With a captain's salute, he turned on his heel, refusing to glance behind him at the imaginary holes being burrowed into the back of his head in the form of friendly fire.

———

Pleasantries and well-wishes were exchanged across the table, while all parties sought to soothe the circulating tension by glaring at the bottom of their empty liquor glasses. Charles was his usual carefree self, eager to entertain and content with all focus narrowed in on his every word. And for once, this was more of a relief than a bother for the couple, especially considering it filled the frequent, uncomfortable intermissions. The evening had been rather uneventful, a formality really, however still somewhat awkward.

Her father, widowed just six months prior, was already remarried. Though their nuptials may have seemed sudden, the ordeal wasn't entirely unexpected. Her mother had been ill for quite some time, and in truth, the woman had been *long gone* prior to her physical passing. This was the first time everyone had gathered together since the funeral and fast-paced vow exchange. Thus, the discomfort was palpable and it eased into a sensation somewhere between mourning and celebration—a sort of emotional purgatory.

Regardless, Sterling would take a million more evenings such as this, if it meant spending them beside the woman currently in the driver's seat. He closed his eyes; the air was cool against his face as they traveled down the highway and towards their vacation home in the countryside. Charles remained behind at the restaurant, hoping to liven up the stiff interactions that had prevailed over the course of the meal, while they made a quiet escape out the side door. Neither had any interest in prolonging the experience. And adding more alcohol to the mix only seemed to stir unresolved contentions.

No, it had been a far better decision to end the night prematurely and in the best spirits possible, all things considered, Lucien concluded.

He struggled to stay awake; but he feared that he had one too many glasses of brandy with dinner and part of him was still fighting to maintain his state of consciousness. While he'd been hesitant to allow his bride-to-be control of the steering wheel, he was now thankful for the luxury of the passenger seat and the reprieve the elongated blinks granted him.

The roads were remarkably empty and the radio lulled him into a further state of restfulness. Before he even knew he was sleeping, Lucien began to dream of this girl and the life he hoped they would have. He dreamt of their future home and the possibility of children. And he dreamt of all the intangible niceties he never before thought possible. Until meeting her.

It was while his mind sunk deeper and deeper into this meditative trance that the vehicle began to swerve.

Lucien couldn't remember what he heard first: the slamming of the brakes and the shrill echo of tires screeching, the shattering impact of the car slamming into the hillside, or the devastated sobs beside him…

The isolated sounds seemed to jumble together, neither forming a cohesive sequence nor escaping to distinguish themselves individually. It was as if his neurological system had altered its wavelengths and could no longer decipher the subtle differences in time. He couldn't perceive variations between what he heard, felt, saw, or even smelled.

But blood—*he tasted* the blood. It was metallic and raw and seemed to pulse in his mouth. It was thicker than he recalled the liquid being and coated the back of his throat.

He didn't know if minutes, hours, or even days had passed—as he internally stumbled in and out of the near-drunken haze. At first, he'd felt an unimaginable sense of warmth, not unpleasant but not exactly reassuring either. It was a tingling sensation, both thermal and wet until that ache transformed into a near existential agony.

His outstretched hands attempted to gain bearing amidst the composite of rock and foliage, but every muscle fiber fought in opposition of furthering his movements. The shooting pain seemed to emanate from the entirety of his being with no discernable root cause, as though he himself and his mere existence were the very source. All while his fundamental drive for self-preservation was collapsing steadily and giving way to acceptance.

He accepted death. He welcomed it.

Desperate for oxygen, his nerve endings screamed with each sputtered intake of air as crimson tinted his breath upon discharge. He paused between respirations and swallowed the expelled blood clots, simultaneously ignoring his stomach's desire to evacuate its contents. The world around him felt both intrusively close and apathetically distant. And he was no longer certain what was real and what were hallucinations as he struggled to orient his physical body with his surroundings: who he was, where he was, and what day it was…

"No, no, no, no. Please, no…"

They may have been his words—possibly mumbled inwardly or gasped outwardly—or they may have been hers. At the time, they held no recognizable ownership; however, they were unequivocally present in some form or another. He had no memory of any verbal exchange in those suppressed moments. He could only hope that he'd said something worth saying. That, at the very least, she understood what she meant to him and what he had been thinking in the seconds immediately before…

All the noise.

The throbbing was starting to subside; though in truth, he would have chosen the pain over the inevitable numbness that would come to replace it.

Feeling something was far better than feeling nothing.

For Lucien, there was no greater realization than that. He'd always thought that death was meant to ease the suffering of a dying man, and yet somehow the fear of his approaching mortality only increased his burden. When his vitals began to plummet and his breathing grew more laborious, he knew *then* that—just as intrinsically as he had known he wanted to marry her—he would have done anything to stay alive. For her. And done that same thing ten times over, to feel her touch rather than the coldness he was succumbing to.

Willing his eyes to open, it wasn't blackness he saw. Instead, it was *nothingness.* There was no more accurate of a definition, no better way to express it. However, after a few additional strained breaths, his vision focused. And the looming shadows morphed into tangible images.

The irony was not lost on Lucien as he stared at the iridescent glass in the shattered side-view mirror. The evening had ended unnervingly similar to how it had started. Huddled against his larger frame, Tessa's reflection stared back at him.

Tessa, the girl he couldn't stop thinking about. The girl he couldn't stop dreaming about, even as she was forced to watch him take his last breath…

CHAPTER 12
THE MAVERICK
SIX YEARS PRIOR

TESSA

HER FIRST TWO thoughts had been: *What the hell had she gotten herself into? And how the hell was she going to get herself out of it?*

Cursing under breath, Tessa shifted her weight back and forth just long enough to realize her wrists were crossed and bound behind her. The throbbing in her head pulsated in rhythm with each inward gasp of air. The atmosphere itself was stale, *dusty,* and flavored by death and rot. Or rather, what she could only assume those things would taste like. Licking her bottom lip, she could feel the swelling as well as the gash present there; however, continuing to run the tip of her tongue along the inside of her mouth, she noted that all her teeth remained intact.

"Dieu merci pour les petites choses..." she huffed. *Thank God for the little things.* Even as young as she was, she wasn't a crier. Not usually. And not in instances such as these. Though—and of this she was certain—had she in fact been one, *now* would be the time for it. In the absence of tears, she had been taught to act out of instinct and logic rather than emotion. Ironically enough, the answer to her internal dialogue was her failure to adhere to those same teachings.

What she had gotten herself into was an underground power

struggle between two different criminal organizations: the Russian *Bratva* and the Italian Mafia. On the other hand, how she was going to get herself out of it had yet to be determined.

————

The mission had been simple: infiltrate one of the high-profile crime families, unearth any hidden or obscured details behind Salvatore Ragetti Junior's death, and get the hell out of there. Perhaps *simple* hadn't been the correct adjective; it may have been more accurate to say that her instructions had been *straightforward.*

She and her partner were given the lead on the upcoming feature in *The New York Time's Magazine,* centering on the unsolved murder of the fallen west coast mob boss. The anniversary of the supposed robbery-gone-wrong was around the corner, and her editor was hoping to spark new interest in the notorious case. *That* and, of course, increase profit margins. Anything and everything lurid always sold more papers, even if the information was vague and repetitive. It was what the public wanted—a glimpse into the immoral world that remained just out of their reach.

And Tessa was determined to give it to them.

Before she had even graduated college, Tessa had been working as an embedded undercover journalist. She was handpicked early on in her career because of her charisma, decisiveness… and, most of all, her ability to charm her way out of trouble. Whatever situation her use of words and wit couldn't overcome, her exceptional boxing skills would.

Until she'd met one man; a man who would not only shatter her confidence but ruin her career before it'd even started. A man who neither her intellect nor her left hook was ready for.

At the time, the most prominent syndicates on the east coast were the Agostinos and the Morettis. Sebastian "Bash" Santoro had been filtering information from the lower-level soldiers in the Moretti Family. Cold-hard cash was an easy way to loosen lips with these 'yet to be made' men, especially considering how ill-regarded the familial patriarch seemed to be amongst his own crowd. However, the Agostinos were an entirely different story. Their men were intrinsically loyal, well-vetted, and couldn't be bought—the crew's esteem had been earned rather than enforced and no amount of dollar-signs seemed to be able to diminish that type of allegiance. No matter how hard the journalists tried.

The little bit of knowledge Bash had been able to siphon out helped devise Tessa's next plan of action. The weak link in the organization was the youngest Agostino brother, Marco. The kid had a proclivity for skirt chasing and it seemed to take only a few bats of an eyelash and a nice pair of legs to grab his attention. And Tessa just so happened to possess both. Because the boy seemed to run through women so quickly, there was rarely enough time for a proper background check before he was onto the next girl. She just needed to hold his attention a little longer than his usual conquests, just enough time to flesh out a lead, and then she would disappear as quickly as the last piece of arm candy.

That had been her intention anyway.

What she hadn't prepared for was how working so closely with Bash would eventually affect her. This would be a mistake she promised herself she would never again repeat.

She couldn't remember the exact moment she had fallen for her partner; all she *could* remember was that the feeling was there before she could stop it from formulating. The late nights, the forced proximity, and their shared professional drive ignited the heated infatuation between them. It wasn't until years later that she would come to realize she had been the intended mark all along, and the affair had never been mutual.

———

After weeks of planning, it only took a few minutes of sitting at the bar —her legs bare and crossed and hair pulled high and tight while revealing a neckline too perfect to not be sculpted—for Marco to notice her. In part, because he had an eye for beautiful women. But the other part was because Tessa just seemed to have that *something*, that *allure*, that attracted men like flies to honey. And the younger Agostino heir was all too willing to be captured.

Part two of their modus operandi meant *keeping* him there. This task took a little more finesse than just looking pretty. With such a ruthless and domineering lineage, what Marco hadn't been accustomed to was hearing the word *no*. And Tessa long ago theorized that, much more than the prize itself, men hungered for the chase. The sort of bait dangled just out of reach.

If bait was what the boy needed, then bait she would be…

As effortlessly as she'd whispered all those pretty French words in his ear, she would turn on her heel, peer over her shoulder, and reject him. She became the jigsaw puzzle he just couldn't piece together. And that kept him fixated.

However, the problem arose when that *fixation* spilled over and onto the other organizations with much more nefarious intentions; those individuals who began to see the coupling as leverage and a rather large bargaining chip against the Agostinos. And that… *that* had been the first mistake that had led to her downfall.

The second had been trusting Bash…

An undercover partnership was one that required an unquestionable amount of interdependence—one that not only involved the utmost discretion but also impacted matters as significant as life and death. And Tessa had relied on her partner as much as she relied on herself at the time. Bash assimilated comfortably with the patrons at the *Danza* nightclub, both owned and operated by the Agostino Crime Family. He was assigned as her eyes and ears should her cover be blown and her safety be jeopardized. Wearing a wire or any sort of recording device was too risky; therefore, he was the only thing that stood between the journalist and the back of a trunk.

Or so she'd thought…

Instead, when push had come to shove, the son of a bitch had walked away without even a glance backwards as the large Soviet hitman had snatched Tessa from the back room and thrown her into the vehicle before driving away. Leaving her where she presently sat, beaten and tied to a metal chair in some dilapidated warehouse outside New Jersey.

Fuck New Jersey. She spit at the thought, the resulting puddle tinted pink.

The Russian men had falsely come to believe that she meant more to the Agostinos than she really did, and the fuckers now hoped to use that to their advantage.

Though the sting of betrayal crawled beneath her skin, Tessa forced the bitterness into the depths of her stomach. She left it to burn and bubble there, to ferment amongst its own acidic nature until there was room enough for it to boil over and finally be of use. But while she waited for that rage to manifest itself, she didn't have time for self-pity or loathing; she had to focus on survival first.

And she did survive. Better yet, the journalist conquered and overcame.

The intricate details of her escape never came to light. She didn't share them with a soul; she didn't tell a single person what exactly she'd endured during her sixteen hours in captivity. However, she'd emerged far more stalwart, stronger somehow. She hadn't allowed them, nor the deception she'd faced, to break her. *Because there was a difference between being battered and being broken*—a proverbial mantra she believed she'd read somewhere and she began repeating over and over again internally. Or perhaps it had been the devil himself that had whispered those words in her ear. But that was an entirely different story and one for another day…

Regardless, the saying had resonated with and empowered her.

———

Injuries be damned, she finished her article—a piece entitled <u>Wise-Guys Finish Last: *Who Whacked the West Coast King?*</u> And it was published front and center in the following month's edition.

Picking up the freshly printed paper from her local newsstand the morning of its release, Tessa was met with the final stab she would ever allow to penetrate her heart. All mention and credit to her name had been erased. In the biggest, boldest, Times New Roman font stood the accreditation: *by S. Santoro.*

But it hadn't been there, in the middle of that sidewalk, where she'd surrendered to her fate and to leaving that city forever. Fumes dancing from every pore, Tessa stormed full speed to her office building. And crumbled-up magazine in hand, she flung the article down on the desk of her chief editor in full view of her colleague, ex-lover, and partner—a single man *all* one and the same. As Sebastian sauntered into the room, it took every fiber in her being to keep Tessa from smacking that smirk from his mouth. Both men stared at her as though they couldn't begin to comprehend what the problem was, as though *she* were the crazy one. Neither could decipher the string of French obscenities that preceded her next words.

"This… this was *my* story. I wrote it. I *bled* for it and not even an acknowledgment!"

Their off-kilter replies would haunt her, even six years later. "Darling, your name will never be published. It's cute though, to think you are that naïve," Sebastian mocked, before pinching her cheek like she was a child and only there to entertain him. "We chose you because of that pretty face of yours. And that ass doesn't hurt either. But, sweetheart, leave the writing to us men."

Despite being made a fool of, at that point in their exchange, Tessa may have been able to save her career had her retort not been a fist firmly planted in Bash's jaw. But the feeling of her knuckles making precise contact with that man's glass chin was worth more than any amount of recognition the field could offer her.

Ironically, they'd been right about one thing. Her full name would never be published. Because moving forward, she would be known under her abbreviated pseudonym; however, she would never be able to "leave the writing to the men" as they had so condescendingly suggested. The challenge just spurred her on, drove her every action, and made her resolute to prove them wrong.

That would be the last time she ever saw Sebastian Santoro, Marco Agostino, or the New York City skyline. None of which would she ever come to miss or regret leaving behind.

Nevertheless, her new code of conduct had been indoctrinated that day. Bash became both the first and last romantic interest to ever get that close to her heart—though, without reciprocation, she knew it wasn't love she felt. Having seen what her parents had between them, Tessa would never dare to call it that. She meant it when she claimed that Jack was the one man to ever create permanence in that hollowed-out cavity in her chest. Furthermore, in the six years to follow, her ex-partner remained the only person to ever share the intimacy of her bed. No one had earned that privilege. Not after the atrocities she'd endured in that warehouse…

Until Lucien…

CHAPTER 13
THE ACE-KING
THE PRESENT

STERLING

CONTRARY TO WHAT his subconscious had just revealed, to what his brain was screaming at him to believe, to what some part of him was wanting to be true… in that side-view mirror, those eyes weren't *Tessa's*. That haunting stare had never been *Tessa's*. Because the girl wasn't there; she'd never been *there*. Not before. Not during. It wasn't until long *after* that night that she'd begun to obsess his thoughts.

The nightmare itself hadn't startled him awake. He'd grown accustomed to its repetitive nature, to gasping for air in the middle of the night, as if he were back in time and his lungs were once again pitted and desperate. He'd even learned to suppress the phantom muscular contractions that incessantly tore through his nerve endings—the same nerve endings that, once his eyes fluttered open, lay still and lifeless. Dead and defective.

As if God himself were taunting him.

Instead, it was the fact that his mind had materialized *her* in what had always been Madelyn's placeholder, the one safe haven where his first love was still *his*. Even if he knew how the dream would end, how the actual events had long ago come to fruition, it was the peaceful moments just *before* that he'd always cherished.

This sudden change... he didn't know what to make of it.

Had he been able, he'd have run, fled in the middle of the night like the bastard he was beginning to believe himself to be. However, that wasn't an option so he allowed his pangs of consciousness to eat away at him in the shadows of the darkened room.

She wasn't his. She belonged to someone else. He kept chanting it internally. Madelyn was married... to William. A man with the ability to walk her down the aisle, to sweep her off her feet and dance beside her, for as long as she would have him.

Then why did he feel so... *guilty*? Was he going to mourn her loss for the rest of his life? Was he supposed to? Or was this knee-jerk reaction, this irrational dread, really just his own gratuitously self-inflicted need for some sort of... atonement? Better yet, why was he so grief-stricken in the first place?

The woman, though out of his reach, was alive and well.

Were these feelings just an outlet for his self-pity? A preoccupation with and regret over all the what-could-have-beens? She had moved on and was happy. Perhaps even more so than she ever would have been with him. That being said, why did everything now still feel so utterly... *wrong?*

Or was it that it felt right?

And rightness was an emotion long since forgotten by Sterling; it was such a distant memory in fact that the architect couldn't even tell the difference between the two anymore.

The girl began to stir next to him, seeming to seek out the warmth his body emitted before sighing and once again succumbing to the restful quietude.

When she dreamed, her expression softened, her brows unfurrowed, and that ever-present smirk of hers fell into a natural pout. As though all the worry she carried throughout the waking hours slipped from her shoulders, and for the time being, she didn't have to pretend so hard. Because pretending seemed to be how she got through the day-to-day: pretending she was okay, pretending she knew everything, pretending she didn't care one way or the other. But she did care.

Perhaps she wasn't so different from him after all.

Her touch grounded Sterling, calling his spiraling thoughts back to the present—to *the here and now*—while his unrelenting panic began to subside. Gently, so as not to disturb her, he combed his fingers through the ends of her hair. He wondered what her story was; he knew there was so much more to it, to what made this girl tick.

Would she tell it to him? And would he ever share his own?

TESSA

Whereas most people looked peaceful whilst they slept, this man appeared plagued. Tormented. His teeth were clenched and his jaw ticked with the slightest movement. It was as if whatever new hell he was facing escalated tenfold during the time his mind should be resting. Her heart—the same organ presumed to be nothing more than dead space and dust—ached at the sight of this inwardly angled and self-guided torture.

Placing her hand to the center of his chest, Tessa watched as he stilled with the weight of her palm, as if his thoughts could be unburdened by the slight gesture.

It wasn't until several moments later, at the sound of the heavy pocket doors shifting, that they were simultaneously stirred from the comfort of the sheets. The would-be intruder seemed to be perplexed by the antiquated locking mechanism, choosing instead to shake the firmly rooted panels. Irate footsteps stomped back down the hall, followed by an onslaught of unintelligible and mumbled expletives that could only belong to none other than Charles Fox.

Sleeping in the SUV all night likely had the poor man waking up on the wrong side of the steering wheel. Tessa laughed to herself. "And here I thought Charlie would understand how a skeleton key works by now," she jested.

"Do you honestly think that man steps foot in those old, rundown homes? Can you imagine the screams, should the pretty boy come face to face with a cobweb?" Sterling retorted, while the pair chuckled in unison.

"Then who does all the detail work and measurements?" Her tone suddenly more direct, Tessa stretched and faced the man beside her, the bedsheets still strewn haphazardly across her chest in some semblance of intended modesty.

"I do."

STERLING

He couldn't hide the edge to his voice. Despite avoiding her gaze, his delivery had been just as sharp, just as pointed. It wasn't out of embarrassment that he'd evaded whatever reaction he knew she would instinctively formulate upon hearing his claim. But rather, he didn't want to see the questions or doubts that he feared were lingering in her eyes. He hadn't yet shielded himself against the skepticism. Not from her. Not yet.

Steeling his nerves, he clarified, "I get what I can from the ground-level; for the remaining, I rely on my research and photographs."

Her smile grew and her face lit up. *"Ça alors! C'est incroyable!"* Her spine straightened as she gasped. "That's incredible…"

She cocked her head to the side and began scrutinizing the intricacies of the room. Perhaps trying to speculate how the architect himself saw the world from where he sat. Wrought by his own sense of internal conflict, Sterling couldn't tell if her movements had been deliberate or subconscious.

As if she could somehow feel the weight of his introspection, she stopped and smiled before returning his tentative stare. "I just can't imagine… It must require so much determination and discipline, preserving homes such as these. Not just anyone has that level of passion and respect for the history in these walls. Each decision impacts what'll be left behind, what story is told to those who will live here next." Taking a moment to reflect, she sighed. "I'm sorry. I probably sentimentalized that a little more than I intended. It's a bad habit of ours—*writers*—we like to overindulge in the idealistic. Overcomplicate language and how we express ourselves."

All he could do was nod in response, realizing that every word that fell from this woman's mouth left him speechless. There were only two possibilities: either she was one of the few people to understand him, inside and out, or she really was a far better actress than he'd given her credit for.

And he wasn't entirely sure which option would be more dangerous.

———

"So, who was that guy in the towel anyway?" Charles asked, his demeanor nonchalant, as though there was nothing abnormal about discussing half-naked men at the breakfast table. Sterling nearly choked mid-chew, while Jack clamored the silverware in the sink with a little more gusto than necessary before turning to face the inquisitor.

"What guy? In what towel?"

Shrugging his acknowledgment, Charles continued to poke the proverbial Papa Bear. "Tall. Blonde. Abs painted on like some sort of Greek Adonis and wearing a towel about this size *here*." He lifted the napkin in his hand to help exemplify his elaborate depiction. "He answered the door when we stopped by *your* apartment." First gesturing his fork towards Tessa, Charles then proceeded to inhale his plate of scrambled eggs.

If Sterling could only kick his so-called confidant from where he sat, the man's shins would have turned a dark shade of purple by this point in the interrogation. He'd already explained to Charles that Corey had been the same individual who'd crashed Madelyn's wedding. Therefore, this loaded line of questioning had no real gain other than to incite tensions between those now present. To that end, he had no clue what his friend was hoping to accomplish here…

As if she just realized the context of the conversation, Tessa's head shot up; she slammed her hands down onto the counter with a force greater than her small frame would imply she was capable and rose to her feet. "That son of a bitch!" she huffed, though neither man quite understood the intensity or direction of her sudden mood-swing. Grabbing her cell phone, she appeared to be sending-off multiple frenzied text messages while muttering to herself between gritted teeth. "If I find a single one of my new towels out of place, I swear to God I will castrate him."

Though her grumblings did little to diminish her two houseguests' confusion, realization instantly coated Jack's face as his shoulders relaxed and bounced up and down in a silent chuckle. "Oh, you mean Corey." Mr. Owens attempted to clarify his relief. "You should have mentioned it was *him* from the start. Sure hope he kept his hands out of her Häagen-Dazs this time." He turned, shaking his head. "Or that boy is in for a world of hurt…"

————

One week. He'd spent nearly the entire seven days joined at the hip with this girl and yet it felt like a lifetime. They'd fallen into a comfortable routine, each holed up in the study: Tessa working on her laptop for most of the day as Sterling switched between his computer and his various long-distance calls. Even in the silence, her presence had a way of soothing him.

Unlike anyone else could.

After that first night, Tessa moved all of Charles's belongings into her old bedroom. Across the hall from Jack's. Her father outwardly ignored the implications altogether while Sterling's counterpart huffed and puffed his way up the old creaking staircase, none too pleased with his new sleeping arrangements.

Each night that followed, she'd curl up against Sterling's side, her head on his chest. As though she'd molded herself into place over years' time.

Like she belonged there.

The architect chastised himself at the notion that anyone could feel something so strongly for someone so nearly a stranger. He knew better. He *should* know better.

But then she'd walk into the room again and he could feel his heartbeat pounding in his throat, his mouth would become uncharacteristically dry, and he would have the incessant urge to tug at his collar—like, out of nowhere, the same loose-fitting fabric was somehow strangling him.

The aftermath of her presence left him disoriented, and he'd *forget* to *remember* what he *thought* he *knew*. She would smile at him, as if the interaction had been preemptively scripted, and Sterling would accept that what he knew was absolutely nothing at all.

Ironically, that concession was freeing. Like a game he'd already accepted and planned on losing. It didn't matter what the next card was; regardless, the man was always going to fold.

CHAPTER 14
THE QUEEN'S BISHOP

TESSA

ONE WEEK. Somehow, in only seven days' time, the man had begun to break down the concrete walls she'd constructed over the course of the last six years. Brick by metaphorical brick. However, Tessa refused to let that insight fully sink in and settle. She overlooked the crumbling foundation, her free will in shambles, and hid behind the security of her hometown, as if her emotional fortitude could regenerate of its own accord and her heart would be none the wiser.

But it knew.

Without the buffer, she took on the role of a girl infatuated, besotted… and, more importantly, not the least bit broken. She took on the persona of… *herself*. And, for once, the disguise fit perfectly. Her expressions had been real; her laughter and enjoyment had been real; even her moments of outward vulnerability had been real. Though, should anyone have asked her, she would have denied it. She would have argued and said it was all part of the character she was playing and the story she needed to portray.

And that sentiment would have been a bald-faced lie.

But it was over. Her bubble had been burst, and reality sank in as she stepped over the threshold of her apartment, where she thought she would feel relief and instead felt hollow. Like it wasn't the barriers themselves she was missing but something much deeper. That piece of herself that she thought she had left behind in New York.

Dropping her phone and keys onto the entryway table, Tessa sighed, flung her leather bag on the floor, and kicked her shoes off before jumping back with a start.

"Forget about me already?" Corey leaned against the counter, his bulky arms crossed in feigned annoyance. Had it been anyone else, his glare would have been imposing, but to Tessa it was more comical than anything.

"Of course not. You just startled me. That's all."

Her blatant dishonesty evoked an amused eyebrow raise as he pulled her in. Squeezing once, he released her from the welcoming gesture. She padded barefoot into the living room, tossed herself onto the familiar cushioning of the sofa, and sprawled across almost its entire length. Plopping down next to her, Corey lifted her legs and folded them back over his lap as he reached for the remote and muted the television.

COREY

"How's Jack?" He paused. "And Em?"

"They are… as well as can be expected." Her expression suddenly somber, the journalist directed her sharply bladed stare at Corey's profile. "Did you know about her English?"

He winced at the accusation underlying her question before attempting to shift the dialogue. "And how's the boyfriend?" Though he was relieved that she willingly took his bait, he would have preferred if she hadn't done so while aiming a pillow solidly against the side of his face.

"I know what you're doing, *mon chou*, so don't think for a second you've won." She raised a threatening finger in his vicinity. "You're just lucky I don't want to talk about it either. Regardless, we need to get back to work if we're going to make the deadline. I've done all I can with what little we have so far."

"Right, and when are you gonna tell him?" he prompted, unsure if this new topic of conversation was any safer. Although, if he were being honest with himself, he knew it wasn't.

"About what?" She diverted her gaze and inspected her cuticles as if she had the ability to simulate ignorance at this point. Her performance may have been credible with someone, but that someone wasn't Corey.

"*Tess*, about how he's the subject matter of the article you're writing." Sucking in a deep breath, his nostrils now visibly flared, Corey tapped his forehead with the palm of his hand. "You're telling me that you sat next to him all week. Typing away on your keyboard, taking notes, and composing your draft versions, *slept next to him* each night—all with no intention of confessing what you're up to? This won't play out how you think it will. You're smarter than that. You need to tell him about the story and face the consequences, *or* pass it on to someone else. We still have time to find another angle and make print."

"I'm not—I won't—give up *my* story. For *anyone*," she hissed; the daggers in her eyes had now fully ignited into two unwavering emerald flames. "I will *never* let someone come between me and my career." She didn't finish the thought, nor did she say the word audibly. But like an omen, it hung in the air and Corey could infer the unspoken meaning.

Again. She would never let someone come between her and her career... *again.*

Pushing the matter wouldn't get him anywhere. He needed to steer the disagreement in a more amiable direction, appeal to her reasoning. Tessa was always one to gravitate towards logic, and Corey could only hope she would see it here as well.

Lifting his palms in mock surrender, he admitted temporary defeat. "I get it, TK. I really do." He hoped the use of her nickname would somehow soften the blow of his next thought. "But hear me out. Anything you use moving forward—if told in confidence—will taint *whatever it is* you have going on between you two. I know you like the guy. You can't even tolerate *me* in your personal space for an entire week..."

Rolling her eyes, Tessa tapped him with an open fist. "That's because *you* root through my freezer, *mon chou*. But that's all irrelevant. Because I didn't—nor do I plan to—get anything from him in confidence," she affirmed. Noting his obvious confusion, the journalist attempted to clarify. "You were right about one thing: I *am* smarter than that. So, we're changing the focus of our operation. We thought Lucien was the story. But he's not. The real story is the Beaumonts. It's

Madelyn and why the engagement was called off without a press release. Which means..." She pulled her legs back, tucking them under her while grasping the top of the sofa frame, subsequently doubling her height like a predator about to trap her prey "...you need to dry-clean your tux. We're going back into the field."

"Tess..."

She raised a hand, effectively cutting him off mid-sentence. "We're going to embed *you* this time. And I'll be *your* eyes and ears, darling." Appearing quite pleased with herself, Tessa pinched his cheek. "There's a charity event at the same venue as the wedding. *In two weeks*. Both the Beaumonts and the DeLacys will be in attendance. It'll be the perfect opportunity for you to get nice and comfortable with Madelyn's closest, most pompous confidants. A few rounds in, and jealousy will flow as freely as the champagne. All you need to do is stay sharp, look pretty, and catch it, *mon chéri.*"

"And what makes you so sure your boyfriend won't be there?" This time his taunting was met with a jab of her elbow.

"*Careful...*" She directed an outstretched finger at him. "But to answer your question, Lucien doesn't go to those kinds of things—he hates them almost as much as I do."

"You have it all figured out, don't you?" Sighing for what felt like the dozenth time since she walked through that door, Corey shook his head when his rhetorical statement was met by the curl of his partner's elongated, self-contented grin. The woman was impossible.

Fingers-crossed, he could only hope everything would work out as seamlessly as she seemed to think it would.

TESSA

But she didn't have it all figured out. Nope, not in the least bit.

Tessa had no idea what she was doing. This—whatever it was—was completely out of her realm. And everything was always so much simpler within those confines of normality. However, she wouldn't let Corey see this sudden, uncharacteristic lack of confidence; in fact, she wouldn't let anyone see it. See her insecurities.

It would just be another mask she'd have to wear…

Until it wasn't.

———

She didn't like this feeling.

The thought was childish, so she could only imagine how it would sound should she give it a voice. But she didn't like it nonetheless. She didn't like how the sanctity of her own apartment now felt cold. Or how the contentment her enormous mattress once offered was suddenly so *isolating*. And above all else, she didn't like how she actually… *missed* him.

She willed her overactive brain to sleep, to push aside the bullshit, but all she did was toss and turn. Staring at the blank-white ceiling,

Tessa reprimanded herself. For being so foolish, for being weak, and maybe even for the enjoyment she found in *being* both of those things.

It was then that the vibration of her cellphone and the illuminated screen caught her eye. She glanced at her alarm clock as an innate sense of dread enveloped her. Realizing that it was already several minutes past twelve, the only thought that came to mind was the saying: *nothing good ever happens after midnight.* It wasn't superstition that had her on edge; it was the understanding that one of these days the late night call would be about her mother. And having returned home, every unexpected "ding" reinforced that reminder. She could handle anything thrown her way.

Anything but that…

Fumbling for the buzzing device, Tessa swallowed her apprehension; and, as she did with most of her unpleasant and unwanted emotions, she ignored them. She punched in her four-digit code before staring at the message now glowing in the darkness of her bedroom. She couldn't help but grin as the three simple words seemed to mean much more than the obvious.

UNKNOWN:

Good night, Tess.

She didn't need to look up the number to know who it was from.

For a man who seemed so sure of himself in most things, the brief text proved Lucien was as hesitant as she was. A fact that was somehow both endearing and disconcerting. The usual decisiveness that drove Tessa's ambition was divided between what she knew she should do and what she was certain she shouldn't—but really, really wanted to.

After a few more moments of inner conflict, it was the devil on her shoulder that seemed to win out. And so she responded before she could change her mind.

TESSA:

Good night, Lucien.

Within seconds, a reply hummed in her open palm. She smirked at the reminder she'd entered into her contact list—in place of his name—before opening the message.

HE'LL RUIN YOU:

Shouldn't you be sleeping?

She grinned, her retort burning the tip of her tongue and biting into her lip before manifesting on her device screen.

TESSA:

I would be. If my phone wasn't buzzing in the middle of the night.

Although she'd fallen asleep before receiving his response, the next morning, Tessa awoke to a nearly dead cell phone battery, a pending notification, and an ambiguous promise.

HE'LL RUIN YOU:

I'll make it up to you.

CHAPTER 15
THE FALL HAZARD

HE WAS AN IDIOT.

The thought spiraled in Sterling's subconscious as he read and reread the message he'd so carelessly typed out the previous night. And not just typed out, because the masochistic bastard that he was had doubled-down by pressing send. He must have been a sucker for punishment. It was the only plausible conclusion.

Otherwise, he couldn't explain why he was making promises he wasn't entirely sure he could keep. He could argue that his response had been impulsive; it wasn't all that beyond the realm of belief. But the truth of the matter was that nothing drove his actions. Other than his urge, his want, to do something more for her. To see her smile. And more than that, to see it directed at *him*.

He should have been sorting through acquisitions and ensuring his client's deadlines were being appropriately met; but instead, the architect was once again tapping his fingers on his desk, lost in thought over this woman. There had been plenty of red flags tacked up when it came to Tessa Owens. Plenty of indicators that he was in too deep and too soon.

The tabloid writer was a hazard to his habitual and long-standing efficiency. And yet, work ethic and sound judgment be damned, it would be an exhilarating way to go... That was one thing he was sure of.

Sterling found himself grinning like some basket case for no reason, the curl of his lips manifesting at just the thought of her. Her wit was sharpened and more invasive than any blade, and it struck its target with the precision of a master swordsman. So sudden and so piercing that the penetration was gone before he knew it was even there. Until he felt the prevailing sting.

And then... then there was the way she always seemed to come out on top—both literally and figuratively. That woman always found a fucking way to win. He would never admit that to her, and yet, it was clear she already knew.

Despite his curiosity as to what exactly she was saying, it wasn't with those purred little pet names that she'd succeeded; nor had she bested him with her usual well-orchestrated measures. No, the games, *those* he saw right through. And tore down as quickly as she built them up.

It was with her authenticity that she had finally conquered the man. Something that was buried so deep inside her that getting a glimpse— one in which she herself didn't realize had seeped out—was utterly addictive. If she only knew how incredible that side of her was, he wasn't sure she would be able to hide it as thoughtlessly as she did.

She seemed to plan out her every exchange to the most minuscule detail; as though the interaction had already taken place in the confines of her mind before its execution. She had an endgame, a countermeasure, and a backup plan. Every word. Every phrase. Every small gesture perfectly choreographed how she wanted and for what she wanted. She had a taut grip on those puppet strings. *She* was in control.

But when she wasn't, when that mask fell, when her smile actually made it all the way up to her eyes... *that* was true beauty.

Admittedly, at first, he thought it was the chase that aroused his interest. That once that playful round of "cat-and-mouse" had ended, the thrill would die down. And he would be back where he'd started. Engrossed in his work and brooding—as Charles would call it. But it hadn't tapered off. Not in the least. The more he learned about her, the greater the mystery seemed to deepen and the more questions he had. Until he was certain he needed to know everything about this woman. Every last detail and it still wouldn't be enough.

He found himself wanting to send her random messages throughout the day and then he would obsess over waiting for hers in return. Even though he could sense her hesitancy and how her mind continued to overthink each word she typed out, he could always tell she was as eager to hear from him as he was to hear from her.

He was distracted during his quarterly review meetings, his projections, and his investment plannings. He could feel himself intermittently glancing at his phone between pauses, absentmindedly scanning his screen for notifications.

He should have been focusing on his latest undertaking: the restoration of a 19th century, five-thousand square-foot Victorian—one he had been fighting alongside the historical society to preserve rather than tear down for a series of duplexes the city wanted to expand. The project may have been a pro bono charity case, but it was one he couldn't turn his back on. The house itself needed extensive work but after all it had survived, it would have been a crime to allow it to fall to ruin. However, instead of sketching out the required architectural restructuring, Sterling was daydreaming about a pretty girl and all the pretty things she liked to whisper to him.

A sudden *thud* jarred the architect from his trance.

"Here are the blueprints you wanted checked out of archival." Charles slammed the heavy, yellowed, leather-bound documents onto the desk before noting, "Staring at your phone again, huh? Man, do you have it bad."

Glancing upwards, Sterling had only been half listening. "Have what?" he mumbled before unknowingly side-eyeing his phone for the umpteenth time. "I haven't done the sketches yet. How can they be bad?"

Charles shook his head, chuckling to himself, and plopped down in his usual chair. "No one mentioned anything about sketches, *Luci.*"

"*Do. Not. Call. Me. That.*" Sterling growled, his hatred for the childhood nickname finally rousing him from his compulsive preoccupation with his cellular device.

"There he is! The man of the hour. Finally back down to earth with the rest of us." No matter how absent the audience, Charles was somehow always able to put on a one-man show. He stretched his arms out, far-flung and open, before dipping his head to his nonexistent crowd of onlookers.

"What are you going on about now, *Foxy*?" Sterling retorted with his cohort's equally cringe-worthy grade-school moniker.

"Though it was never my first choice, can't deny the accuracy there." It was likely that no matter the intent, the well-fluffed ego of Charles Fox could find a flattery in any gibe. He leaned back, his wide grin and wider wingspan spread across the top of the seat, emphasizing just how much he believed that statement to be true. "But enough about me. Your—let's call it *fondness*—for a particular tabloid writer. I'd much rather discuss that."

"And *I'd* rather not." The response was curt, to the point. End of discussion. But, of course, the discussion did not end. Not there and not with the current company in attendance.

"Luci, my dear, dear friend, we're sensing that your concentration has been a little... *adrift* lately." There was in fact no collective *we*. Charles knew it. Sterling knew it. And Charles knew *that* Sterling knew it. However, the charade continued anyway. "We're concerned that you may not be able to put one-hundred percent of your efforts into this new project. Maybe we should just subcontract."

"*Sub-what?*" The question was hissed between a tightly clenched jaw and gritted teeth. "I've spent months drafting this proposal, buried in these damned legalities and all the red-tape and bureaucratic bullshit, and you want me to do what?"

"Exactly my point, Luc." It was one of the very few moments where Charles's voice would become solemn, the flair and revelry thrown aside and only the man remaining. "You've been drowning yourself in venture after venture, building after building. For years. And now, finally, you have something—*someone* to distract you and you don't even know what balance is. Let alone how to obtain it. So, maybe it's a good time to figure that out. Take a break, let go of the reins. God knows you have the bank account to do it."

"While I appreciate your concern, *Chuck*, I just took a break. An entire week actually. If you recall. A break we both just returned from."

"With all due respect, that was not a break. Sitting in the same room with the girl as you work on a remote brokerage deal is not a vacation. Nor very romantic, I might add. And while I have your attention, I suggest you watch a romcom or two—take some notes."

"What's more romantic than being buried up to your arms in purchase agreements and insurance titles?" Sterling shook his head before placing his index fingers against his temples. "You just wouldn't get it. Having her there was enough. And she had her own work to distract her. It was… relaxing. It was a break from my thoughts. From all the noise. But you *have* given me an idea…"

"Somehow I doubt it's a good one." Charles sighed. "Please tell me you aren't going to drag that poor girl down here and have her sit in your office on the regular. She's pretty to look at and all, but torturing you is one of the few highlights of my day. Not sure I want to share the task."

Sterling's grin grew tenfold before he replied, "I promise that won't be the case."

However, for some reason, Charles seemed wary that whatever his friend had planned wasn't much better.

CHAPTER 16
THE FINE PRINT

TESSA

COMPARTMENTALIZATION. It was a tactic. A skill set. A second nature. That the journalist had cultivated into a true art form over time.

With practice, Tessa had developed this uncanny ability to manipulate her emotional state. She could submerge those feelings she wanted to ignore the most, tamp them down, and leave them to decay. A feat that would be impressive if the psychological aftermath didn't include the exceedingly unhealthy coping mechanisms that followed. However, it was for this same reason that she could effortlessly fall into character; she could be whatever facade someone wanted her to be at the time, whatever twisted version of herself that'd been imagined.

Somewhere, beneath it all, was the broken girl. The one who would never climb out to the surface again because she was buried under so many layers of dirt, earth, and sand that surely she had already succumbed to its weight. The girl with the story too salacious to be printed. Too damaged to be spoken aloud—who, with any luck, had decayed and rotted away so that nothing was left but her faint imprint and an ethereal stone epitaph that read:

Here lies the foolishness that once was. And would never be again.

But who Tessa was today, this was an entirely new identity. One waiting to be named and labeled, so the mask could be catalogued amongst the others already tucked away in her privately owned arsenal. Then again, this version may not have been as foreign as she'd initially thought. It seemed to fit in a way that was uncharacteristic yet oddly familiar. It was like a stranger's face she was certain she'd seen before. But only in passing.

She berated herself, her first logical question being: *what had changed?*

Of course, the only viable answer was: Sterling. He affected her in a way that was so seemingly unnatural she felt severed from her innermost person. As if she were wearing someone else's skin and forced to embody it like it was her own.

However, a far more disturbing question hung in the air. It floundered about like a complex equation not as readily solved, no matter the numerous attempts she made to recalculate it: Why did this role feel so inexplicably customized, with each and every perceived vulnerability pinned and sewn in place? And how could she possibly feel like something so unequivocally synthetic otherwise *belonged*?

———

"...What's the progress?" The voice was piqued, slightly barred, and clearly growing more impatient.

"Progress..." The repeated word rolled off Tessa's tongue like it was alien to her, its definition unknown and unclear.

"Yeah, P-R-O-G-R-E-S-S. Now, for the second time, TK, what's your progress on the undercover feature? Are ya even listening?"

Nope. She. Was. Not.

A sudden, aptly timed kick—exerted from beneath the conference room table—jolted Tessa from the clutches of her mental fog. However, the unexpectedness of the strike propelled the flattened pen cap from the confines of her jaw and onto a yellow-lined notepad, where it presently sat. Unfazed by the resulting puddle of saliva that was now wrinkling the previously crisp pages, the journalist glanced down once before shrugging her shoulders.

"For fuck's sake. Do ya have a story? Or not?" Composure was not the man's strong suit, neither was subtext.

No, Frank Fitzgerald—beloved Editor in Chief of the largest magazine currently in distribution in the local metropolitan area—was affectionately called "Fitzy" for a reason; the moniker derived from not only his last name but also his propensity for adult-sized tantrums. A fact that became more evident when the man slammed his fists on the pile of paperwork in front of him.

"The teasers need to be embedded in the next issue or we won't have enough time to generate buzz before publication. I don't pay ya to sit there and look pretty. I pay ya to write goddamn articles. No bullshit, what's the status?"

"You know damn well anyone can write, Fitzy. You don't pay me to write. You pay me because I'm fucking good," Tessa corrected, rising to her feet as if she had been instantly tugged then tethered up and out of her chair. Her palms flat against the veneered surface, the journalist leaned closer—her eyes now level with his—before continuing. "And if we're arguing semantics, you pay me because I deliver, I don't disappoint, and most of all, because I fucking sell. But if all you want is a writer, by all means, you have your pick." She gestured to her tight-lipped colleagues. "Feel free to reassign my column."

Satisfied with the impromptu tirade, Tessa stepped off the proverbial soapbox and reclaimed her seat while the older man muttered to himself incoherently. She waited, deliberately inflicting a few more fleeting moments of silence, just long enough to make the entire room uncomfortable.

"We'll make the deadline. Just the same as always. This time isn't any different," she affirmed, her inflection pronounced and her arms crossed.

"Fine. Good." Though he clung to his ballooned posture, the editor's expression had weakened along with his deflated tone.

It wasn't like Tessa to conduct herself in such a disruptive manner, not in the office and certainly not amongst her other team members. Similar discussions had always occurred behind closed doors and with an even temperament—well, from her anyway. The red face and puffed-out bravado was the Irishman's preferred uniform, as was a standard accompaniment of foul language.

But not her. No. It was not normal for the girl to emote so recklessly and without careful forethought.

While it was true that his comments had pissed her off, she couldn't deny that the outburst was far more theatrical than she'd intended it to be, and not entirely directed at just Frank. Self-doubt and guilt seemed to be festering in the pit of her stomach, prompting a reactionary combustion as soon as her latent fears had been drawn to the surface.

She wasn't a failure. She never had been. And underachieving sure as hell wasn't a trademark she was willing to assume in any foreseeable future.

She had to provide the marketing director with a title or tagline by the end of the month. If she missed the deadline, then by the time her feature made print, her target audience would be unreachable and disinterested. Poor publicity meant poor sales, and she'd worked too hard and for too long to fall into that category.

Steeling her resolve, Tessa realized the bottom line was becoming that much more apparent. She needed to ensure that Corey was successful at the upcoming charity event. There was no wiggle room or capacity for delay. Without a longer thread to unravel, the journalist would have no choice but to stick to her original plan, delve further into Sterling's family, and drop the Beaumont angle altogether.

As a point of contention, Tessa despised the overuse of exaggerated statements. But this time it felt appropriate because she'd never before found herself this lost, without a narrative to tell. Throughout her career, it had always been by some unknown and intrinsic force that every one of her articles had ultimately written themselves.

Her love affair with word play and subtle symbolism had been long-standing, a feverish passion that was ignited with each and every keystroke. It was unbridled and unrelenting. It demanded release and couldn't be contained, no matter how hard she tried. With or without her consent, the text would materialize from beneath her fingertips and onto the computer screen.

But not now.

Now, in place of her usual literary arousal, the only picture that seemed to paint itself inside her head was yet another memory she wanted to forget. Over and over and over again, the scene played out. A recurring and unrelenting loop. As if it were on an internal film reel rather than a single stilled image that she'd captured and he'd deleted.

She was haunted by the look on Sterling's face and the regard in which he'd held that woman, who in turn was held by someone else. It was as though realization, acceptance, and regret had all hit him at once. Before twisting and turning. The resulting onslaught both unrecognizable and unwanted by the same man who'd created it.

So, where had she gone wrong?

Like every assignment before, her established protocol had been followed to the letter: she had gained entry, allowed her gut to take the reins, secured her mark, and was inevitably driven to raw inspiration. And like every assignment before, her instincts had been dead-on. Accurate. But this time, in this instance, the story it told was far too close to home to ever be written. She could no longer guarantee that anything she put down on paper would fall within the realms of journalistic integrity. Because the entire process was now skewed, biased, and indiscernible.

She'd been ambushed and ensnared in a self-imposed web. A trap she had artistically woven in suggestion and subterfuge. But instead of cutting ties and walking away, Tessa had allowed one prolonged interaction with one seemingly irresistible man to somehow become her defeating mechanism. And worse yet, she knew it was of her own doing; it had been her very own design.

If she hadn't stopped. Or rather, if she could have stopped…

If she didn't engage. Or if he hadn't engaged…

If she didn't need to prove herself. If she hadn't hunted him down. If he hadn't needed to do the same. Or if she didn't dare him to, want him to, need him to…

She was beginning to realize wherein lay the problem. Compartmentalization only worked when each of the *compartments*—each alter ego—remained separate and isolated. However, Sterling had crossed over into several facets of who she was. Or at least who she needed to be in the moment: professionally, socially, and intimately.

This sudden unease, this discomfort, it was an identity crisis. It was psychological and emotional seepage at its fundamental level. All she needed to do was regroup, reconfigure, and rebuild. She had to place this man in his very own cognitive box. She had to define and label him; but most importantly, she had to keep him there.

Or else her world—and everything she'd come to know and understand and find security in—would implode…

———

Tessa hadn't even noticed that the meeting had ended or that the office was silent and vacant. It wasn't until her phone began vibrating along the polished conference room table that she was stirred from her thoughts for the second time that day.

She shoved her decapitated pens and scribbled-on notebooks into her bag before reaching for the pulsating device. As if her mental fixation had conjured the man himself, she paused when Sterling's nickname lit up and flashed across the screen.

Internally, she remained at war.

Part of her smiled—a warm, fluttering sensation invading her core at just the prospect of hearing his voice on the other end of the receiver. While the remaining part struggled, her decisiveness fluctuating between panic and provocation. She was unsure if she should curl up in a ball, cover her ears, and ignore the possibility of having to face further emotional turmoil. Or if she should systematically press end call. Erase the man, erase his number, erase the distraction altogether.

It was simple. Her options once again whittled down to: fight, flight, or freeze. So she made the only conceivable choice, the same choice she always made. Except once. But this instance was nothing like the last time, or so she told herself.

"Lucien." Her voice was soft, nearly sweet, but not fake. "I'm glad you called. We should probably talk…"

CHAPTER 17
THE RULE OF THREE

STERLING

"WOW, she's breaking up with you already?" Charles shook his head before stepping over the threshold to enter the office. Circling the desk, he placed his hand on Sterling's shoulder and continued. "That's rough, buddy. I'm sorry."

"What are you going on about now?"

"Oh no! It's worse than I thought! You're in denial!" Charles plopped down in his favorite chair, his arms crossed and expression somber.

"Apparently, I'm missing something. So why don't you explain it to me, O' Wise One." Sterling's tone was as blatantly mocking as the gesture that followed. "I doubt I can stop you anyway. So please, Chuck, go on." He waved his hand with the same flair one would use to introduce the next act in a theatrical production—which, to be fair, wasn't that far off from the truth.

"You must be smarter than you look, old chap!"

Sterling was starting to wonder if he should be concerned, seeing as his intelligence was constantly in question. He wasn't sure what was more worrisome: the possibility that he was emitting an air of stupidity or the idea that Charles and Tessa were rubbing off on each other. He didn't like either option. His mind aimlessly wandering, it took several minutes for the architect to realize his friend had begun speaking again.

"...so you see, it all started with the birds and the bees..."

Sterling interrupted his cohort mid-sentence. "Yes, yes, I'm aware. Can you skip the basics and get to the point, please?"

"Right..." Charlie nodded before leaning in closer. "So anytime a woman says *we need to talk.* What she really means is *we need to talk about whatever it is you did or didn't do and why I'm dumping you for it.*"

"That's ridiculous. She just agreed to go away with me this weekend—wait a minute. How did you know she said that we needed to talk?!"

"I was listening on the other end, of course..." Charles affirmed, sinking back into the seat and rolling his eyes. "Who uses a landline in this day and age? I don't know why you would make a personal call on the conference phone anyway."

"Chuck, you do know that creates more questions than answers. How'd you even know it would be a personal call?" Sterling narrowed his gaze. "How often do you listen in on my business line?"

His partner's only response was silence and a wider grin.

TESSA

For someone seemingly conflicted moments earlier, Tessa had agreed to spend the weekend with the supposed source of her contention without requiring much coaxing on his part. It was against everything her internal defense mechanisms had taught her.

The only person she should rely on was herself.

It had taken years for her to develop the sort of comfort level she now had with Corey; and it was only after he had secured his place as someone who was more like family—than anything else—that she had finally allowed herself to trust him. And yet here she was, face flush and heart aflutter like a girl with a teenage crush.

But she wasn't a girl. She was a fucking full-grown adult. A woman with responsibilities and a career and priorities and all the things that *girls* were expected to sacrifice (along with their dignity) for the men in their lives. Which was precisely why she didn't entertain them—relationships, that is. Sexual or otherwise. That, and because she'd never been quite the same after everything that had occurred in New York.

She didn't understand why things had escalated so quickly with Sterling. Or why, after so many years of avoiding intimacy, being with him and being with him in *that* way had been primordial. She freely admitted she hadn't been thinking. Same as the first time he had kissed her in his office. Or maybe she had kissed him…

Even now, the exact details of their interaction that day and the event itself remained a bit hazy. It was the same as every time she seemed to engage with that man. She didn't think. She reciprocated. She felt...

Actually, what she felt was still a paradox.

She was no fool. Not Tessa. Not ever. At least, not in any way she would care to admit. She didn't believe in fanciful notions like instant attraction or love at first sight. Those were stories told to little girls who dreamed of white knights and princesses in towers. And nothing like the real world. Fairy tales were dangerous and could taint the sensibilities of a more easily swayed mind. And leave a young girl waiting to be rescued. Tessa didn't need to be rescued. Not by Sterling. Not by anyone.

And yet, there was something... something that kept her from fleeing. Something that kept her coming back for more. Something that both eased and quickened her trembling. He didn't look at her, or through her, and yet he *saw* her.

That sounded cliché. But she could think of no other way to describe it.

The reasoning behind the sudden change in her behavior would have been more apparent had she been ready to face it. But now was not the time. The journalist was not prepared to delve that deep into her psyche. Not yet anyway. Not today.

Yes, avoidance felt much better than the intricacies of her erratic decision-making. Avoidance kept her from having to remember and relive; it safeguarded her. And with Sterling, she set the pace. She was in control. And should she change her mind, with Sterling, she could run.

This was different than the last time. *It had to be, right?*

She'd been young then, foolish even, and weak. That word echoed in the back of her mind. Weak. In so many ways, she'd been weak. But that wasn't who she was now. She'd conquered those demons. She'd risen above the labels that those men had placed on her. She had her moments, she would admit. She had her doubts. But, God, was she a force to be reckoned with.

Her inner monologue—the very story she told herself about herself

—was all that mattered. Not what anyone else thought of her. Because the only validation she needed was her own. No one else could tell her what she was worth or how much. Hers was the only opinion that held significance. Everyone else's changed as quickly and as wantonly as the weather. And was often based on what she gave them or could give them down the line.

As to what any of this had to do with her current predicament, she really hadn't the slightest idea; however, what it did remind her was that she shouldn't let her past insecurities dictate her current choices. Despite her fears, Sterling was not Bash. He was not any of the other men she had previously encountered either; the kind of men who had undermined, demeaned, or underestimated her. She was in control and he didn't fight her for it; nor did he act as though that fact impinged on his masculinity. In fact, he seemed to enjoy that spark in her. He seemed to ignite it. Incite it. Just so he could see it burn that much brighter. He challenged her. Not to win. But because he enjoyed the game as much as she did. The end result was of no consequence.

She felt safe with him. Safer than she felt with nearly anyone else. And not safe in the way that most would think. She didn't need a male counterpart to secure her physical well-being; her father had ensured that much. Rather, it was the type of security that meant, for a brief moment, she could put her guard down and just breathe. She didn't have to plan or think or be on the defensive. He didn't need anything from her. And outside of her ensuing article, she didn't need anything from him either. Not his money, not his name, not his approval—she had earned those on her own.

And so, as mentioned before, the decision had been simple. She *wanted* to spend more time with Lucien. And answering him had been natural. Because at the end of the day, after everything was said and done, she was a fighter and she would fight.

Even if it meant her opponent was herself. Her doubts. And the prize was her own happiness.

CHAPTER 18
THE ACQUISITION

TESSA

THE HOUSE WAS like something out of a dream. Maybe not everyone's but certainly Tessa's. You could see that at a time the home was loved. And that, at another time, it wasn't. Treated much like mankind treated each other. Some taking care; some barely taking notice. The structure was old, tired. But not dead. There was still some semblance of a spirit there, something alive, waiting to be either tended to or extinguished.

It creaked and groaned with each step she took, while the paint chipped and peeled and fell. Much like tears. Light reflected and blinked back off the stained-glass windows, somehow still preserved at the house's highest peak. They flickered in the sun as if speaking to her. Telling the journalist that life was still there; though buried, it could be kindled and salvaged. The splintering wood of the porch begged for reprieve underfoot as Tessa inched closer to peer inside.

She gasped in a mixture of awe and anguish. Not many would see the beauty beneath the graffitied walls and crumbling plaster. But then again, most were blind to begin with. Nowadays, the world wanted things quick, manufactured, convenient. And this home was anything but. It was a labor of love. The carved wood took time, care, precision. The glass tiles were hand-blown and colored organically before the design was patterned piece by piece. In their prime, these kinds of homes embodied their residents, with personalities as unique as those who lived there. She caressed the sill as though she were uttering a silent promise.

It will be okay. You will be okay.

The family who built it may have been long gone, but the spirit of the home would live on and remember them. And so would she.

As if forgetting the present company, Tessa forced back the nailed-in plywood barricading the broken window panes before granting herself entry, one leg at a time carefully flung over the ledge and into the vacant sunroom.

Once upon a time, the residence had been grand, she concluded, taking note of the opulence of the remaining brass chandelier. The emptiness seemed to call to her; it beckoned the journalist up the decimated staircase—one she should have assessed before mounting upwards but of course did not—and over towards the banister which presented a panoramic view of the entryway below.

This was something the city could never offer her. Not to this scale.

From her perch on the second floor, Tessa noted the woven design of the original parquet flooring. The shifts from dark to light hardwood offered a checkered aesthetic, both rich and riveting from her aerial vantage point. But the image that caught her off guard, as she tried to stifle the quivering in her throat, was the man she saw entering the double-paneled Eastlake front doors.

The utterance wasn't that of surprise. They had driven there together after all. Rather, her sharp intake of breath had been caused by the innate increased pounding in her chest, one that seemed to involuntarily quicken each time she saw *him*. The grin he offered as he stared up at her earned him one and the same.

"Tell me we can keep it, *mon ours*," she jested.

"We?" Though Lucien raised a single eyebrow in question, the curl of his mouth didn't falter. Tessa's lean on the banister laxed as she propped her head up by the bend at her knuckles. She tucked a free strand of hair behind her ear before tracing the curve of her neck, resting her remaining hand loosely by her bolstering elbow.

"What? Too soon for such a grand gesture?" She laughed. "Seriously, though, Lucien..." The musing nature in her tone dissipated as her heels tapped their way down the staircase.

STERLING

There it was again, parting her lips and landing on him like a single word could somehow singe his skin. Creating a bridge of permanent scar tissue that seemed to imprint each letter in its wake.

Sterling hadn't even heard the rest of her commentary; he was so shaken by her repetitive usage of his given name the architect had no choice but to ask her to reiterate.

"I said... tell me you're going to restore her." Tessa looked up once more before continuing. "It's marked for demolition but tell me there's something you can do. You wouldn't take me here otherwise, right?" She didn't wait for a response; instead, she crossed the threshold into the parlor and wistfully marveled at the architecture. "This place has a story. I can feel it. What I wouldn't give to dissect it. To write about the history that filled this home, breathe life into these walls. Those are the stories that deserve to be told the most. The ones that no one tells."

"I'm glad you agree." He followed close behind her, his head tilted when he prompted, "Then why don't you write them?"

Once again, she distanced herself. A step. A pause. And two more. "Mhmm..." The sound of her voice was more like a hum, equal parts longing and loss. "Stories like that don't sell papers... or magazines. The general public doesn't want to read about the character of a home; they don't give a damn about the people who built it either. They like the seedy, the salacious, the rich, the infamous." Tessa turned to face him. "They like to read about men like you—or families like yours, at least," she was quick to clarify.

"And what do you know about me? Or my family for that matter?" Sterling snapped, though his tone didn't seem to faze her.

"I know the type."

"Have you ever tried to write something else?" He stifled his resentment, choosing to focus on the task at hand. Though she seemed withdrawn from the conversation, *he* wasn't done with it. Not yet. "Maybe people will surprise you."

Maybe he would surprise her.

"I have. Tried, that is. I was going to do great things. Write great things. Life-changing things. The sorts of things men like you would notice."

Men like him. There it was again. And what kind of man was that? The rich kind? The broken kind? The foolish kind? He could only imagine her choice of adjective…

"And…? What happened?"

She stopped her pacing, dusting her fingers along the brittle mantlepiece before rubbing them together as though deep in thought. "Hmm…"

She was humming again. He took note of the sound, of her sudden posturing.

"The usual. I was young, naïve, ill-prepared for the male-domi-nated career field—the politics behind it all. I guess you could say my hands were tied. In a manner of speaking…" she professed, as though her phrasing were chosen purposefully, her meaning laced in subtext.

"You… give up? Accept defeat? Somehow I doubt that."

"What can I say? Knocked down seven, get up eight." The state-ment was just above a whisper, meant more for her own ears than his, he concluded.

"What was that?"

"Oh, nothing. Just something my father says. It means you have to get knocked on your ass every now and then, in order to learn how to get back up. So, yes, I was down for a bit. But not out."

"That sounds a little more like it." Sterling nodded. "However, I still think you should give it another try. Writing something you're passionate about..."

"Ha! Passion doesn't sell print, Lucien." Her sarcasm landed with every word, her jaw tight and her teeth clenched. "It's easy for you to say. The spoon you were raised with is as silver as your last name. I, on the other hand, had to bleed my way to where I am. I get it. My assignments aren't to your liking. Your elitist standards." She threw an arm in the air as if to further emphasize her point. "And, yes, I know they're vapid and meaningless a majority of the time. But when they aren't. When I can dig in, sink my teeth into something real and unexpected. When I find that detail that no one knew was there and I bring it to light. When I'm in the field and see what everyone else in the room is too blind to see for themselves. *That* is true satisfaction. That is fulfillment. That is the validation that not only am I good. But I'm damn fucking good."

"You trying to convince me or yourself?" he quickly countered.

Silence. The air was deafeningly silent, and for some reason, that seemed to bother him more than any cleverly designed quip she could have lashed out at his expense. Where before the quietude between them had been comforting, now the intensity of it prickled his skin.

"Are you trying to start an argument with me today? Your responses seem much more on edge. Like you're intentionally digging at me, Tess..." He reached out and grabbed her hand; though covered in dirt and dust, he held it between his own and sighed. "Is it true what Chuck said? Are you here just to break things off with me?"

"That's awfully presumptuous, *mon nounours*." The lilt to her voice had returned, her smile lighter. Genuine. "That would mean you both think we are together in the first place." She finally allowed her gaze to meet his, searching his face as though he held the answer to some unresolved question.

He didn't. Or at least he didn't think he did.

But whatever it was that she saw there caused her to soften before turning her frame and straddling the architect in his chair. The kiss was just a brush of skin to skin. Not burning. Not passionate. Not frenzied or animalistic. He cinched his hands around her waist, the only choice he thought he had to keep her from fleeing. Because that was what this felt like. Like a goodbye before she ran.

"I can't help but think that you're pushing me away," he admitted out loud.

"I just… I may be… I… I honestly didn't plan on it though." Her confession seemed to hang between them. Nonsensical. Unexpected. Meaningful and meaningless.

"Tell me to leave you alone and I will. You should, you know?" He sighed before repeating, "You should tell me you don't want this, or me, or what little in life I can offer you. You should tell me not to kiss you again. Not now, not ever. Not here—" His lecture was interrupted by her mouth crashing into his and offering everything the prior kiss had been lacking.

"You should stop talking, Lucien," she chided. "Or maybe I really will break things off."

He smiled into her lips before bouncing her words off his own tongue. "That's awfully presumptuous, Tess…"

TESSA

She hadn't planned on the man being so straightforward. Nor had she planned on him calling her out on her bullshit. Instead, if she would have guessed, she would have prepared herself for another game.

Games, she was ready for.

The truth? Not so much.

She would fully admit that she had been "digging" at him as he had called it. She had been steering the conversation in an uncomfortable direction—one that was likely to lead to an argument. However, he hadn't taken the bait. And worse yet, she hadn't even meant or wanted to argue with him in the first place.

It was instinctual, she concluded, to treat every scenario as though she were armed for battle. Though Sterling seemed to be the one man that could delicately remove each piece of armor, leaving her open, exposed, and vulnerable. Adjectives as foreign as the pet names she whispered into his ear.

You should tell me you don't want this, he'd said.

And he was right. She should. It would have been the safest, smartest route to take. But it would have been a lie. Because she did want *this*, and more so, she wanted *him*. One look into the eyes of the man who freely surrendered to her—even though he could match her wit, even at his own expense—and she knew. She knew that what she should do had little effect on what she was going to do.

The house he had taken her to was his most recent investment purchase. And he'd somehow known that she would appreciate it as much as he did. While he was confined to the first floor, she was able to fearlessly ascend each staircase and assist in obtaining the necessary measurements he would use to begin his preliminary drafts.

Ballgowns, stilettos, and jewelry: none of it compared to the feeling of the dirt, dust, and grime beneath her fingernails or the gratifying ache of manual labor. Despite his warnings, Tessa crawled across the rafters in the attic, sweat and sediment clinging to her every pore.

It was a challenge after all, she thought to herself.

She even attempted to make her way along the roof and into the partially crumbling chimney, but her hips had been too wide to venture farther. Though this was likely for the best, considering it appeared to be a death trap all its own.

"That's a good look on you!" Sterling called out, as Tessa lowered herself onto the ground from the dormer's edge and jumped to the grass in order to cushion her fall.

She knew her hair was probably wild, her makeup smeared, her face peppered by residual ash; however, she couldn't help but agree with the sentiment. The filth spoke to a hard day's work; one she was proud of. Brushing a layer of soot off her hands and onto her jeans, she trekked through the unkempt flower beds towards her onlooker.

"It is, isn't it?" She laughed, lightly grasping his tie and tugging it forward, sullying both it and his dress shirt in the process. "It's a shame you're so overdressed."

"This was a new suit, you know?" He chuckled in response. And, as if his words evoked a dare, Tessa's grin widened as she painted her fingertips down his throat, loosening his collar before marking his lips with a kiss.

"You can afford another one. These are priceless," she urged, holding up her carefully annotated dimensions while keeping them just out of the architect's reach. "Don't you agree?"

"More than you know, Tess. More than you know."

CHAPTER 19
THE MASQUERADE

TESSA

"AND WHY EXACTLY CAN'T I just wear a wire?" Corey huffed.

Sounding much like a giant man-child, Tessa noted to herself.

"Feel free to ask my last partner. If you can find him…" she retorted, her ominous tone stifling any further complaints he thought to muster outwardly. Though he appeared to be grumbling to himself in the mirror nonetheless. "I'm not sure what you're so nervous about, *mon chou,*" she continued. "This isn't any different from picking up women at a bar."

"Yeah, well, the bars I go to don't exactly cater to these types of women." He adjusted his bowtie, tugging on the fabric as if it were a noose before throwing his hands in the air and rolling his eyes. "And neither do I," he added.

"What you cater to has little to no bearing; it's not about you, remember?" Tessa glided across her apartment floor, her mask now firmly in place and her fictitious arsenal fully stocked. "It's about them: what they want you to be, who they want you to be, and how they want you to be. They'll already have the image subliminally painted in their minds. You just have to embody it, darling."

Her gown was red. The kind of red that, upon first glance, one would associate with refinement and perhaps debauchery. The kind of red that was meant to catch the eye. Her purpose was not to blend in but to deliberately stand out. To be forgettably unforgettable. While the color itself would solicit stares, little else about the journalist would be memorable. She would be the woman in the red dress and nothing more. Likewise, there'd be no question as to whether or not she concealed a recording device; the fit of the material made it clear that there was none.

No, there was nothing between the clinging satin and her sculpted form. Not even undergarments.

A fact that anyone in proximity would be able to easily determine as well, Tessa assured herself as she smoothed her hands against the bunching lines at her navel. Though they would be tempted to wonder.

She'd fitted her counterpart in an all-black tux—contrast found only in the gleam of his gold cufflinks, light hair and eyes. In actuality, the extravagance of his attire was of little consequence. It didn't matter if the women there thought he had money; they had their own after all. And yet, they weren't looking for husbands either. No, a lover is what they really sought. Someone to warm their expensive silk sheets for a few hours, or nights, or days. Depending on their current proclivity.

And that was the kind of man Corey needed to present, a man who was easily projected into that fantasy. Nameless. Faceless. The bulk of his trousers was, more than likely, the only discerning factor. And as much as she didn't like to look at him that way, *bulk*—she would admit —Corey had. That being said, she'd tailored his suit to further advertise that feature, and Tessa wasn't the least bit embarrassed about doing so.

"All's fair," she hummed aloud as she crouched down and straightened his seamline. When her hand unintentionally crept upwards towards the apex of his pant leg, Corey quickly grabbed her wrist and turned his hip.

"Okay, I think they'll get the point. You can stop tenderizing the man-meat already," he grumbled.

"Now you know how it feels," she rebuked, steadying herself on her heels before adjusting her cleavage. "Not so fun, is it, *mon amie?*"

———

The journalist couldn't shake her sudden feeling of déjà vu as they entered the same reception hall with the same chandeliers and the same silverware, an undertaking that would undoubtedly be outfitted with the same pompous patrons. Though one patron in particular would be missing; and that would be the same patron Tessa actually cared to see again. But tonight was not about that man.

Well, mostly not about him, she told herself.

Her freshly manicured hands delicately planted within the crux of Corey's arm upon entry, Tessa observed how even the serving staff, security team, and hired photographers were all distinctly familiar from the event prior. Though, the vigilance over the comings and goings of those in attendance was far more lax this time around—bearing in mind, this was no socialite wedding. She paused at the staircase landing that descended into the largest ballroom in the hall. And repositioned Corey's lapel.

"This is where we go our separate ways, *mon chou,*" she instructed. "Remember: you're here to look pretty. A nice, muscular bite of arm candy for these women. Nothing more. They don't care about your opinion, so don't offer it unless it's to agree with theirs. However, if you find yourself in a sticky situation, act as though your *life* depends on it."

Because it just might. She didn't say that part aloud, though. She didn't want to traumatize the kid.

Tessa reached up and dipped Corey's chin to ensure he met her gaze at eye level. "Repeat the code. LIFE: Listen. Insult. Flatter. Evade." She'd slightly altered her usual bit to cater to a female target, but the intention was much the same. "*Listen* to whatever bullshit your snobby lady friend sputters. *Insult* everyone and anyone who isn't her. *Flatter* excessively but not wantonly—make sure the compliments count. And *evade, evade, evade.* If you don't know the answer to a question, change the subject. Ideally, you can refer to one of the other letters. Got it?"

He nodded, though his widened pupils emitted the fear she'd hoped to squelch.

"You've got this. I have faith. Look at you," she ribbed. "You're almost as irresistible as I am. Sic 'um, tiger."

COREY

She had a way of always making everything sound so easy, he groaned inwardly. Then again, for Tessa, it was always just that easy.

He never felt this unnerved when she was the decoy. He had stepped into this same room several weeks ago without a second thought about how much was riding on the slightest interactions. He was her eyes, making sure she didn't get into too much trouble; and if he was being completely honest, he was just extra muscle really. But now, with the weight of added responsibility on his shoulders, he felt as though he were suffocating.

The pair had spent the last week reviewing their potential marks—the list of women most likely to spill everything dark and dirty about Madelyn DeLacy. And there were several options for the choosing. However, they'd settled on two primary targets.

The most logical starting point was Abigail Harrington. She and Madelyn were almost never photographed out in public separately, and research suggested she was the closest thing to a confidant for the blushing bride.

Then, of course, the next obvious choice was Susanna Beaumont, the infamous step-mother. She was rumored to have eased her predecessor into an early grave, and the supposed gold digger was only a few years older than Madelyn herself. If there were skeletons locked away in a closet somewhere, surely one of these women had the key.

Corey had already lost sight of Tessa in the sea of blurred faces; though he guessed that was probably her intention to begin with. She would likely keep watch at a distance, ensuring there were no external distractions, including herself.

It didn't take long for Corey to spot Ms. Harrington. The only thing louder than the woman's taste in gemstones was the piercing sound of her voice, and worse yet, the obnoxious cackling that followed.

The instructions he'd been given were clear: first and foremost, he was not to approach the blithe brunette. No, Tessa had been sure to counsel him on how making initial contact was the most important step. How the exchange must appear natural and unsolicited, as if it had been the mark's idea all along. Instead, he was to pay attention to every other female patron in Abigail's proximity, social crowd, and general age group.

Be noticed, but don't look like you're trying to be noticed, he repeated Tessa's words in his head. The woman sounded like a damn fortune cookie. Granted, he had to admit it didn't take more than a few minutes for Madelyn's lady-in-waiting to unabashedly saunter to his side.

Her skin was coated in expensive perfume, her breath peppered by expensive liquor. She wasn't even trying to conceal her intentions as she twirled the string of pearls that draped deep into her neckline around her fingers and leaned across the cocktail table separating them. Corey had seen Tessa mimic similar actions. But, with this woman, it just seemed… *crude.* Her gestures abhorrently unrefined.

It was a lesson he'd learned early on, during similar assignments: money was not synonymous with class. He'd discerned that the difference was in how the two women carried themselves. Whereas his partner emitted an air of sophistication and confidence, he noted that his current cohort seemed to be looking for hers at the bottom of a champagne bottle. And clearly, she hadn't found it; however, the predicament did make for loose lips.

Next, he was to steer the conversation towards Madelyn but was told that his remarks must remain neutral.

Follow Abigail's lead, Tessa had cautioned him. *If there are latent resentments, they will speak for themselves. But if further prompting is needed, issue Madelyn or her family a trivial compliment. Abigail will likely argue otherwise, which will open the door for the more depraved details.*

And just like his mentor had predicted, an opening seemed to present itself, after a congratulatory "cheers" was given to the DeLacy couple in celebration of their current wedded bliss.

"They appear to be enjoying married life," he whispered softly against the overly indulgent brunette's ear, while alluding to the raised glasses.

"Yes, because for darling Maddy, appearance is everything," Abigail hissed, finishing what was left of her overpriced bubbly beverage and reaching for another.

Corey masked his surprised utterance with a cough before hesitantly coaxing, "Trouble in paradise?" His tone was light-hearted. Inattentive. Disinterested. Though it didn't seem to matter. The woman's bitterness had already risen to the surface and manifested itself in the form of a scowl.

"You wouldn't know the half of it," she scoffed, her index finger gesturing towards William DeLacy. "She was engaged to *his* cousin, you know... Head-over-heels in love with the guy; that is, until he didn't represent that perfect image anymore." Hiccups punctuated each sordid statement as Abigail edged closer and lowered her voice. "A shame, too, that man was worth more than the occasional jump in the sack—speaking of..."

Corey stilled as the socialite's hand snaked beneath the tablecloth and began to trail up his thigh. She was losing focus; he needed to redirect her before the situation got out of hand.

Quite literally. He gulped as he attempted to disengage the fumbling fingernails without staunching her word flow. He lifted her wrist to his mouth and brushed his lips along her quickening pulse.

"Tell me more," he urged playfully. "I mean, who doesn't love a good dirty story before bedtime?"

Her face flushed at his veiled implications and her eyes darted across the room. "Of course, you didn't hear this from me, sugar."

Another pause. Another hiccup. And another drink.

"You want to talk about appearances? Ha! Miss Prim-and-Proper spent her entire wedding night in a drunken stupor, crying over that banker's boy. *The one who got away.* Can you believe it? After marrying the man's fucking cousin? When everyone thought she'd been whisked off on her picture-perfect honeymoon and bedding Tall-Dark-and-Handsome over there, she was actually hugging a toilet bowl and spilling every last detail about her supposed 'first love' to anyone in earshot."

Abigail huffed, her torso pressed against the tabletop and her breasts nearly spilling out like an unspoken offering.

"You see, this whole time we all assumed *she* had dumped *him* after the car accident. Poor guy would never walk again. And with a name like hers, there are certain *expectations*. It was understandable. Suffice it to say, the Beaumonts could not be without an heir. But, no! Turns out, she had been the one driving the car and two sheets to the wind at that! Blood alcohol level through the fucking roof. Not so perfect after all."

The woman sneered and continued, her speech increasingly slurred.

"Her *daddy* covered up the whole thing. Luci took the blame so poor little Maddy could avoid rehab and jail time. They have no tolerance for that kind of thing in Europe, no matter how deeply lined your pockets are. Lover boy eventually cut things off with her. Something about wanting a better life for her than he could offer, or so she claimed anyway. Both families kept everything a secret all this time. Shows you how corrupt the Swiss are. If that happened here, it would have been in every headline. She would never be able to show her face again. Instead of standing up there on her porcelain pedestal with a ring the size of a tennis ball. She must have a golden crotch, that one, to have two men in that family so thoroughly whipped. I don't even understand how she could hide this from me..."

An abrupt hitch in Abigail's throat marked her sentiment. Corey tensed, struggling to maintain his composure while simultaneously hoping to postpone her influx of tears for at least a few minutes longer. Then, as luck would have it, the woman's choked chorus of intermittent sniffling began to gradually subside with each new tip of her glass. Nevertheless, the aftermath—an unreasonably exaggerated intake of air—served to only further obscure the already long-winded, alcohol-laced narrative.

"...six years old, you know, we've been friends since we were six years old!" Abigail bemoaned. "And she didn't say a fucking word to me! About the accident. About the broken engagement. About any of it! So much for friendship... Daddy Beaumont must have paid a pretty penny, to keep that story under wraps especially after they returned stateside. Poof! It was like the whole unpleasant experience never happened. Hm..."

She paused, as if only now just realizing something.

"Considering there hasn't been a single mention of Luci either over the years, my guess is they worked out some sort of deal. A tit for tat. Luci got to have his privacy; his family got to make sure not a word about his *situation* leaked to their high-rise investors. And in turn, she... she got to keep her *squeaky-clean* reputation. Now that I think about all that fiscal back-scratching, I can't help but wonder if the new hubby was part of the deal. One bankrolled heir in place of the other. Appearances, though, right?"

Shit. Corey grimaced. *Shit. Shit. Shit.*

CHAPTER 20
THE MAN BEHIND THE MASK

TESSA

WHETHER OR NOT HE realized it, the man was a natural.

Tessa grinned into the rim of her whiskey glass as she regarded Corey's carefully orchestrated proceedings from afar. That girl had flocked to him like a fly to honey.

Or should she say a honeypot? Tessa mused. It had been just as she had predicted, and yet, it was still a sight to behold. While one of her skill sets included the ability to read lips, she couldn't quite make out the specifics of what was transpiring between the two.

But she'd known Corey long enough to be able to interpret his body language. Whatever information he'd gotten, it was good. And precisely how good was written all over his face. She could tell by how, for the briefest moment, his spine had stiffened, an involuntary spasmodic display of his initial shock. By how his jaw squared, as a result of lightly grinding his teeth when he concentrated too hard. And by how he had reached to rub the back of his neck, likely trying to resist his urge to loosen his bowtie.

Now, she could only hope that he remembered the escape tactics she'd laid out for him, before that poor drunken creature tried to drag her partner into a darkened corner somewhere and have her way with him. Then again, at the rate that the woman was throwing them back, she wouldn't be able to stand much longer anyway.

Which made for a solid Plan B.

———

The wise thing to do would have been to keep walking, where the reckless one was—often and arguably—the most fruitful. Or so Tessa had the tendency to tell herself. The thrill of the unknown was what seemed to keep her upright, seemed to keep the blood pumping in her veins and the air filtering in her lungs.

At this point, walking away was no longer an option.

The journalist had every intention of following the evening's previously established protocol. Every intention of meeting Corey at the designated spot and hightailing it out of there as quickly and quietly as they'd first entered the room.

That was until she overheard the conversation behind her. And, in testament to how curiosity had killed the cat, she couldn't resist the opportunity to inch a few steps closer. At first glance, the two men would not have appeared out of place, while Tessa's gut screamed otherwise. Their attire was ostentatious—overtly so—and while they had sought to camouflage themselves with indifference, that same evident posturing hinted towards ulterior motives.

They were... forgettably unforgettable. She mulled over the irony.

Listening intently, in addition to English, she was able to make out: German, Russian, and a peppering of Italian. Though there may have been a few others she couldn't quite distinguish, partially due to all the white noise and partially due to their poor pronunciation. They were multilingual, howbeit, they certainly were not experts, she'd gathered.

In particular, the men sought to distort their French Creole accents to sound more Parisian. And yet, their attempts at altering aside, their distinct dialects indicated they were American-born and presumably from the south. Her guess was Louisiana, and if she were being specific, she would have placed her bet on New Orleans. They seemed to effortlessly switch from one vernacular to the other without fumbling. More than likely, this technique was used to ensure their anonymity and, by that same token, their agenda.

As if simultaneously sensing her interest as well as the weight of her gaze, the free-flowing chatter was replaced by a pair of reciprocated glares in her direction. She wasn't sure how, but she'd been spotted. Panic at this point would serve no purpose other than to further raise their suspicions. So she steeled her resolve, as the older of the two men excused himself from his associate before turning to approach her table.

He was attractive in his own right... if sleazy had been her preferred type.

"So, it seems you've picked up on my tell, *mademoiselle*," he remarked, his breath uncomfortably close to her ear. "Would you like to know yours?"

"I'm not sure I know what you're referring to, *monsieur*," she rebuffed. "However, you are welcome to explain it to my husband when he returns."

As if he couldn't stop himself, or perhaps by reflex, the stranger's expression turned mocking. "Let's not play these games, sweetheart. There's no conning a con man. You're not married. And we both know it. However, I can waste your time if you like and list the half-dozen reasons why I know this for a fact. But you don't need me to do that, do you? Because you can recite them all yourself without my help, *no*?" He grinned, responding as though Tessa's silence had been an open invitation for him to join her.

It was not, she huffed internally.

She wanted to be angry at the man. At his intrusion. But if she were being honest, she could only be angry at herself. She was better than this. At least she had been better. Until recently. Because, recently, everything felt so completely muddled, her emotions uncontrolled. And, as a result, her other senses seemed to be as well.

"Come now, *cher*," he pressed. "I could smell the *voodoo* on you a mile away. Why work separately when we can work together?"

"Your accent is slipping, *mon amie*. Then again, you must know your efforts are wasted on such a crowd," she noted, before motioning towards the waitstaff and ordering a double. "While I admit you have made tonight much, much more interesting, I fear I must leave you to your present company." She gestured to his cohort just as her drink arrived. Placing the glass in front of him, she stood and nudged his chin upwards with the tip of her polished fingernail. "For your troubles," she purred, briskly pivoting on her heel before she did what she should have done from the beginning. Walk away.

Insult. Flatter. Evade. Evade. Evade…

"Philippe Hebert," he called out. She didn't pause. Or turn. Or give any indication that she was still listening. But she was—listening, that is—when he remarked ominously, "I want you to know my name for when we meet again."

COREY

Fucking godsend.

Those were the words that came to mind when the hired photographer loomed closer, fortuitously catching the attention of the drunken socialite pawing at Corey's waistband. Her appetence for the public eye had been enough of a distraction that the woman had immediately dropped her hands from raking along his chest. One need synchronically replaced by another, Abigail seemed incapable of shying away from the cameraman. Or her thirst for attention, for that matter.

Like a dousing of ice-cold water, each new flash had a sobering effect on Miss Harrington. She didn't bat an eyelash as Corey buttoned his jacket and hastened towards the exit. When he finally felt as though enough distance separated *him* from *her*, he paused to glance back over his shoulder. And chuckled. Either the woman had yet to notice he left, or she'd noticed and didn't care. And he was perfectly apathetic over whichever the case may be.

He had more important things to worry about than how easily forgotten he'd been. The evening's culmination left the journalist torn. His most pressing concern was how he was going to relay the information that had been divulged to him, and how Tessa was going to feel about it. The result of his little venture turned out to be a double-edged sword. They had a new story. Better yet, a scandal.

If proven true...

It *was* fucking career-defining, it was about the Beaumonts, and it was exactly what Tessa had wanted. However, it still centered around Sterling. The same man whose exposition she was trying to circumvent, the same man her counterpart knew she didn't want to betray, and the same man that Corey had been slowly watching her fall for. Even if she wasn't able to—or maybe didn't want—to admit it.

He still couldn't quite figure out what kind of story she thought she would get with all this. Or how she thought she would be able to skirt around any mention of the man ill-fated to a wheelchair, considering her angle focused on the broken engagement. Corey couldn't wrap his mind around it. Any of it.

It didn't make sense. She wasn't making sense.

He hadn't been able to determine if she was blind, whether it be knowingly or unknowingly, to the unavoidable negative outcome should she continue down her path and not pass on the feature piece. In its entirety. Or if she was really just that cocksure. That hopeful... maybe... That she could find something else. Something *better*. Something that let her have her cake and eat it too.

He didn't like the sickening sensation that was gnawing in the pit of his stomach, telling him how everything would come to fruition. And how that fruition would ruin the girl who'd become like a sister to him. A sudden chill crawled up his spine and settled at the base of his neck as he realized what his gut was actually saying. She wouldn't just be ruined; she would be ruined in a way she didn't even know she could be.

She would be numb.

She would close herself off to all emotion, sever whatever ties she perceived as weaknesses, and succumb to the only thing in life she could control. Her career. Because that was what Tessa did. What she felt she had to do, he surmised. There were things he knew she hadn't told him. Things that made her so cautious or at least made her think she had to be. Things he feared she would have to face before the silence destroyed her.

———

It wasn't until the twenty-minute mark had passed that Corey began to feel anxious. He checked the time on his phone, tapped the screen after a few more breaths, and rechecked. There were no missed calls. No texts. Nothing.

This was completely out of character. Tessa never missed a check-in. Not in the entirety of the going on six years they'd been working together. Even when the trail was hot or she was distracted, there was always a signal. Something that told him she was safe.

Corey glanced down at his device, almost as though he thought he could will it to vibrate. Again, it sat in his palm, soundless and idle.

"We have to go." The hand on his shoulder left him startled, while in contrast the hushed voice behind it offered a reprieve. "I've been compromised."

"The Beaumonts?" he questioned, locking his arm in hers before ushering her down the back staircase and into the parking garage.

Tessa shook her head. "No. I don't know who they are, nor do I care to wait around to find out."

CHAPTER 21
THE NOSEDIVE

COREY

"IT'S ALL TRUE." Tessa paced back and forth over the low-piled carpet in her living room. If it had been possible for her to wear a path into the fibers, she likely would have by this point. "At least, it all appears to be true from what I've been able to gather," she clarified.

"And how do you know?" Corey goaded.

His concern for her and her sanity had intensified over the last few weeks. And it had grown at a rate that was very much congruent to her increased obsession with discovering the truth. He recognized that saying it out loud would come off as sounding cruel; however, for Tessa's sake, he'd wanted her to be taken aback. Or hurt. Or angry. Or second-guess herself... Or maybe even cry, for reasons she'd yet to figure out. He wanted something from her. For her to react to something. So that he knew that at least she was acknowledging her feelings, no matter how chaotic they may have been.

But after the pair had exchanged and compiled the intel they'd each obtained from their encounters that night at the charity event, Tessa hadn't reacted. Not to the freshly imparted knowledge about her lover, nor to the lingering threat of being made. Not even, perhaps, to the fear of being tracked down. On the contrary, she was stoic as ever.

Consumed by the new angle. She appeared to be on autopilot, her impassivity only tempering when she happened to be in the architect's presence. It was as if all her efforts to keep her mask in place were reserved for that man and that man alone. As if she was split into two parts and only half of her, Sterling's half, could emote.

It seemed to be the only time she would smile earnestly anymore, he realized.

"From the accident report and medical records I had faxed over," she responded.

Though, frankly, Corey'd forgotten he'd even asked the question. "After all the effort that was put into the coverup, they just sent everything over? No questions asked?" He crossed his arms, a single eyebrow raised in a gesture of outward disbelief.

"I may have had to stretch the truth… *a bit,*" she conceded. "Logically speaking, though, there's no reason for them to suspect that anyone would be looking into it after all this time. No one was killed in the wreck. The only property damage was personal. And there was no insurance involvement. No claims. The case was closed. People move on. Retire. *Die.* Whoever's hands were greased is more than likely long gone, the money long spent. And, at this point, they can't be bothered to care."

"If you say so…" Despite his statement, Corey was unconvinced. "And you know the Harrington recounting is accurate how? You can't tell me the Beaumonts weren't smart enough to ensure nothing in the accident report was contradictory to the story they wanted to tell."

"I called in a favor… from Lane," she continued.

"You called my sister?" he croaked, unable to disguise the shock in his question. "Wait… Why does the department suddenly owe you a favor?"

"I never said the department owed me anything, *mon chou.*" The nonchalance in her voice was beginning to irritate him.

"I don't understand…" The realization hit him harder than her fist ever could. "You can't mean… Why does my sister owe you a favor? What'd you two do!"

"I'm sorry, but you'd have to ask her yourself." Tessa shrugged. "As Lane likes to say, *chicks before dicks.*" Tessa ignored his distress, her sole focus on the information at hand. "Anyway, Lane reviewed the files and compared the injuries sustained to the photos taken at the scene and the damage to the vehicle. She said, without question, it all aligns with our theory that Lucien was the passenger, not the driver." Again she paused, clearing her throat. "You know, you shouldn't be so hard on your sister. What's good enough for the goose is good enough for the gander. She doesn't give you shit about what you have to do for your job, so you shouldn't give her shit about what she has to do for hers."

"So now *you're* giving *me* life advice? That's rich." Corey laughed. He didn't know how else to respond.

"And what exactly is that supposed to mean?" Tessa halted her incessant pacing, her trance broken.

"Really?" he barked. "Like you don't know, Tess? Seriously?"

Silence.

"Fine. You wanna pretend like you don't know what I'm talking about, I'll take the bait. How can you honestly still be thinking about writing this fucking article?" Corey raked a hand through his hair, scratching his scalp in indecision.

If he didn't know her better, he'd insist his cohort was playing him. Ironically, he would have almost been happier if she had been. *Almost.* It would mean that at the very least, she was self-aware. But he knew her mannerisms. He knew the real Tessa. And by the look she gave him now, he knew she really had no fucking clue.

She spun on her heel and resumed her pacing, as if confirming that very fact. "I'm not *thinking* about writing anything, *Cormac,*" she snapped.

He didn't like the way she enunciated the word 'thinking' and he really didn't like the way she had called him by his full first name. He couldn't remember the last time she'd done that, but if he were guessing, he would have said it was during the initial few months they had started working together. Before she began to trust him.

"...I don't get it." He frowned.

"I'm not thinking about it because I already wrote it. The draft is on Fitzgerald's desk, waiting to be green-lighted."

"You have got to be kidding me! What the hell, Tess!" Heat traveled up the back of his neck and tinted his ears. "Since when do you turn in articles without me? And what's the point of these files anyway? Why did you even call me over here to review them? And don't say professional courtesy, because you sure as hell don't have any of that, do you?"

She was pushing him away and he didn't understand why, or if she even understood herself. She hadn't stopped moving, nor had she attempted to make eye contact.

"You're overthinking it. You know how it is, how it's always been. I get the urge to write and I write. Just the same as every time before, as every other assignment and every other mark. And these files..." She gestured towards the towering pile on her coffee table. "I've only had them for a couple of days now. I was just waiting on a few more loose ends, a few more fact-checks before it's all finalized and good for print. I've always handled things on the back side. I don't get why you suddenly care so much."

"And *I* don't get why you don't seem to care at all," he retorted, his tone harsh and his eyes narrowed. "I can't believe you. I can't believe you're actually doing this. I've been waiting for some common sense to smack you upside the head, and apparently I've waited too long. The only mark in this whole disaster-waiting-to-happen is you, Tess. The only one you're fooling is yourself. And I can't stand by and watch you do it."

"You're being ridiculous." No rumination behind the statement. It was case and point. Matter of fact.

"Me? Ridiculous. Have you looked in the mirror lately, babe? Because you're losing it. You're obsessed with this story, nearly as obsessed with that man. And what's most troubling is that you are obsessed with destroying everything. It's like that's your end goal. The whole incident... they covered it up for a reason. And while I agree that the Beaumonts weren't trying to be altruistic and really give the guy his privacy, *his intentions* at the very least seem selfless. He obviously cared for the woman. You saw how protective he was over her at the wedding. He didn't look like a man slighted or out for vengeance. And if it's true—what the Harrington woman said, that he ended things with her so she could have a better life—you can't fault him for feeling that way. How do you think he's going to react when you blow up his world? When he finds out you've been lying to him? Betrayed him? Tess, he's never going to forgive you for that. And I can't say I'd blame him either..."

"If he doesn't, he doesn't." She shrugged, her posturing cold. Distant.

"Bullshit. I know you care. What I don't know is why you're so set on ruining the first outside human interaction you've had in years."

"What are you talking about? I have plenty of human interactions. That's all I do, *babe.* I *interact.* It's part of my job, remember?" she attempted to rationalize.

"Ha... no, what you do is act not interact. There's a difference. What do you have that's real?" His tone boasted a hidden challenge, one he knew she had no chance of winning.

"That's not fair. I have plenty that's real. I have you. I have your sisters. I have the team and Fitzy."

"What you have," he countered, "is work."

"And you don't!" She was getting desperate, grasping at straws, he noted. "You work just as much as I do."

"No one works as much as you do, Tess." *It was true.* "I go out. I have friends *outside of the office.* I have my family, nieces and nephews. And, one day, maybe a wife and kids of my own. And what will you have?"

"Fuck you. So what? I'm focused on my career. More women should do the same. You're sadly mistaken if you thought I was ever going to play the part of someone's little housewife." The last word rolled off her tongue like a curse, as if she could taste the indignity of the supposition.

"I never said I wanted you to quit your job and suddenly become fucking Suzy Homemaker, for fuck's sake." *Now she sounded just like his sister,* he thought to himself. "Just that family life is important too. Balance is important." His frustration was evident, his normally complex vernacular replaced with variations of the word "fuck."

"I have my parents. I have a family life," she argued.

"Yeah? Really? You have a family life all right. So much so you didn't even notice how bad your mom was..." He regretted saying it.

The same moment the words left his mouth, he regretted saying them. But regret didn't keep them from being audible.

"Get out." The directive might as well have been a slap to his face. It stung.

"Tess... I—" But the apology was left to die in his throat, stifled by the repeated phrase.

"Get the fuck out." She was assertive but calm.

Too calm, he feared.

"I'm sorry. I shouldn't have said that—" He stopped at the threshold, turned to glance over his shoulder, and he knew... He knew she was barely hanging on. The restraint she was showing outwardly was like everything else. A mask. And it was slipping. She was slipping, and all he wanted to do was catch her. But Corey had crossed a line, and the look she gave him now told him there was no stepping back over it. Not until she was ready to let him.

"Get out!"

And then it slipped... No, it crashed. *Shattered.*

Every piece Tessa had been holding in place slammed to the ground as she shoved him out the door and into the hall. Corey stood there for a moment, hand pressed against the frame. He could hear her as she fumbled with the lock before she sank to the floor. And he could hear her as she muffled her sobs into the fold of her knees. He'd fucked up. Instead of grabbing hold of her to keep her from plummeting over the edge, he'd inched her backwards and pushed her head-first.

He'd sent her spiraling...

CHAPTER 22
THE CLIMAX

TESSA

OKAY, *she may have had to stretch the truth a little more than a bit...*

Had she wanted to be transparent, she would have told Corey what she'd really done in order to obtain all the documents in those files. She wouldn't have held back that, to her benefit, she knew that French was the second most commonly used national language in Switzerland. German was the first; and though she was no linguist, she would have reminded him she wasn't half bad at that either.

She would have admitted that she'd posed as a medical assistant, claiming that the records were needed for Lucien's continued care before she'd faxed over the forged release form. She would have commented that it had been surprisingly easy to do, all things considered. And that the hardest part had been the waiting. Because had she been honest with her partner, she wouldn't have failed to mention that —despite the thirty-day grace period—with a polite nudge, shameless pleading, and implied urgency the request had only taken a week to be processed. Though she'd waited two to share the information with her other half.

And lastly, she would have confessed that she didn't know why she felt so compelled to lie to him about everything. But she had. And she did.

Tessa slumped against the door and cradled her legs to her chest. This was what she wanted, right? To seek comfort in her work. And in herself. No one else. To be reliant on just herself and no one else. To be tied to only herself and no one else.

Then why did she suddenly feel so… *alone*?

———

The voice had been screaming at her long before Tessa was able to place it. Surprisingly, when recognition did finally hit, the voice was her own. Or rather, it was her common sense. The logic that warned her this was a bad idea and the reasoning she had the propensity to ignore. She shouldn't have left her apartment. And she most certainly should not be standing at his front door with her finger hovering above the doorbell, contemplating whether she should press it. Or not. But here she was.

Standing. Hovering. Contemplating.

"Do you want to come in? Or is lurking out there all part of some devious plan of yours, Miss Owens?"

"How did you know—"

His laughter cut in before she could finish the question. "The flood lights and motion-activated cameras have been going on and off for a few minutes now," he explained.

She looked up and then back down at the intercom. "Oh, right…" Her breath was heavy, her words just above a whisper. "Lucien, can I come in? Please…"

STERLING

He rested his cheek against the top of her head. The familiar scent of her hair and the weight of her body pressed to his was comforting. More so than the smell of fresh drafting paper, than the pressure of a sharpened pencil between his fingertips. It was a stammering realization, but a true one nonetheless.

"I'm starting to feel like maybe I should invest in a red suit. Let the facial hair grow out a bit and buy myself a team of reindeer," he teased. "If word gets out, you may be facing a crowd next time you're looking to stop by. Then again, the wait'll be worth it—I can just picture it now, Charlie in an elf costume. I'd pay to see that." While his tone was meant to be lighthearted, Sterling was worried about how he'd found her on his doorstep. It wasn't like Tessa to be so hesitant, nor was it like her to wordlessly curl into his lap.

"Are you complaining?" she retorted, her lips slightly curled at the sides.

"Not in the least bit, love. Merely an observation. Besides, it saves on the heating bill. And I must say you look much better strewn across my legs than one of those old nursing home blankets." He chuckled, tucking her hair behind her ear before tugging her under his chin.

"Don't say things like that." Her response was followed by a backhand to his chest.

"Things like what, love?" he hummed into her ear.

"Self-deprecating things, things you think will make other people feel better at your expense."

"But what if it's not about other people? What if it makes *me* feel better?" he offered, though his stare was distant now, his posture slightly tensed.

"Do you? Feel better?"

"Sometimes... sometimes I do," he mused. "Especially when it makes you smile."

"It doesn't make me smile. I don't like it."

"You liked it enough to be attracted to me. To be here now." His argument was weak. Even he knew that much. But he argued all the same.

"No, I was attracted to your bullheadedness, *mon nounours*," she corrected. "To the fact that you caught me off guard. That you challenged me."

Sterling had yet to learn what the nickname meant. But she said it to him often and always in a way that seemed more tender than anything else. He wondered if the meaning would be lost in translation. Perhaps, in this instance, the ambiguity outweighed the knowledge.

"*Was*, you say? And what about now?" he cautioned, unsure if he really wanted to know the answer.

"*Now* I'm attracted to this." She clung a little tighter to the fabric of his shirt. "To everything. To the real you, Lucien."

"But not to my jokes?" He raised an eyebrow while his lips quirked.

"No. I unequivocally hate your jokes," she confirmed. "Seeing as you're such a prudent businessman, I advise you to invest in better ones. Maybe Charlie can help."

———

At this hour, the white paint always appeared to be tinted an almost pale blue, the same color as the light that reflected through the windows and onto the ceiling. But it wasn't a nightmare that held

Sterling captive and blinking up at that familiar spot where the coffered grids crossed and intersected above his bed frame. It was the huddled, pliable form of the woman next to him that kept him from his sleep.

Something haunted her; he recognized that look in her eyes. It was the aftermath of trauma. And it was the very same look he saw in the mirror each morning. He just wished he knew what it was that troubled her.

He sighed and nudged her deeper into the crux of his shoulder as he continued that same train of thought.

More than merely identifying the cause, he wished he could rid her of it. Though, even if he could, he knew she would not be inclined to accept his help. He grinned at that fact, as frustrating as it was.

He adored this beautifully broken creature and all the complexities that she seemed to embody. She was a breathing contradiction, with the aptitude of a vixen and the vulnerability of someone as deeply flawed as he was. And she'd somehow given him back a part of himself he'd long thought dead. What that part was exactly was hard for him to verbalize. To put a label on.

However, it was tied to the way she looked at him. The way no one had been able to look at him since the accident. Without pity, without horror, without lamentation over everything he could have been. Should have been. And wasn't.

It had to do with the reason she was here with him now. Because she wanted to be. Because she found comfort lying beside him. Because out of everyone's doorstep she could have been on, it was his she chose. Seeking nothing more than this right here. She didn't ask for favors or for strings to be pulled. She didn't want his money or connections. And she cared for him despite his bloodline, not because of it. She sought only the warmth of his body and his arms wrapped around hers. It was that feeling alone that allowed her to drift off while simultaneously leaving him to his thoughts.

Because as good as sleeping sounded, watching her finally at peace was better.

He must have fallen asleep at some point in the middle of the night, because his eyes flickered open to the smell of breakfast and a half-clothed woman straddling him. Granted, he could think of far worse ways than this to be woken up.

Her hair was loose and wild—a rare occurrence—and it skimmed along his stomach, then his chest, before stopping at his cheek when she bent down to kiss him. He brushed the dusting of powdered sugar from her nose with his thumb, licking it clean while he struggled against his urge to discover if the rest of her tasted just as sweet.

"Don't tell me you cooked?" Though from the aromatic smell of her, a perfume peppered by cinnamon, he already knew the answer.

"I woke up starving. I must have forgotten to eat yesterday," she confessed. Her stare was distant for a second, quickly flashing to normal by the time she looked back down at him. "We need to do something about that kitchen of yours. Everything is so... *healthy*. Not a carb in sight."

"I have a cook, you know. He could have made you whatever you wanted." Over the last few months, Sterling noted that Tessa had an insatiable sweet tooth. While sugar had never been a weakness of his, the girl seemed to be able to consume her body weight in a single sitting.

"Yes, well, you know what they say: when you want something done right... Besides, the man took one look at me and ran off with his eyes covered. I think your staff may be afraid of me. What kind of stories have you been telling them?"

"Ah, yes, could be that," he postulated. "I'll admit I gave everyone fair warning about your antics. Though I can't help but think that it may have something to do with your current state of undress?" He motioned to the partially buttoned dress shirt she'd borrowed and the pair of perfectly toned legs barely hidden beneath it. And grinned. "You probably gave old Gus a heart attack, love."

"Perhaps." She lifted a shoulder in a half shrug. "But what sense is there in getting dressed just to take it all off again?" Her shared smirk turned sinister.

"I thought you were hungry?"

"Oh, I'm famished..." she hummed. Though, by the gleam in her eye, he knew she was no longer talking about breakfast.

Agile.

This woman was fucking agile. It was the only word that came to mind when he watched her. Her movements were nearly aerobatic, as she removed her shirt with one hand and his boxers with the other. He never felt more important, more like the man he used to be, than when she admired him the way she was now. Like he was everything she could ever want. *That* was what the flutter of her eyelashes and her labored breathing told him, that there was nowhere else she'd rather be.

And if it was all just a lie, it was one he chose to believe.

When she mounted him, it was as though nothing else... no one else mattered. Not the use of his legs, not the wealth and power behind his family name, and more importantly not any of the other failures that haunted him. He didn't want, care, or feel any of it. Just her.

She both dulled his pain and enlivened all sensation better than any drug or alcohol or therapy ever could. It didn't matter how much his joints cried and ached at the end of the day. Her hands on his chest, her nails digging into the flesh there, and the way she threw her head back and bit her bottom lip—the combination assuaged his every muscle into complacency. While the little whimpers she emitted with each back-and-forth motion aroused his need to satisfy her. More so than himself. He had to bring her to that point... the moment when her voice grew husky and she blurted out his name as though it were a prayer rolling off her tongue. And when she finally did say it, she collapsed against the thud of his heartbeat. While her panting continued, an even match to his heaving breaths, her aftershock lulled him into his own satisfaction.

It may have been the adrenaline talking. But as he lay there, her body settling against him, he was overcome by the sudden awareness that he had never felt this way before. Not with anyone. There was nothing that compared to this woman in his arms or to the emotions she elicited. It wasn't about the sex.

That was great, of course. Unparalleled.

No, this was something more though. Something different. Something he wasn't sure, until this very moment, if he'd ever even experienced in his lifetime. Despite what he'd told himself and everyone else in the past, this was new. And as the trembling began to ease itself, he realized it wasn't about any chemical reaction either. Because, as if reality hit him all at once, like an uppercut to his jaw, Sterling discovered he loved her.

He loved this woman. And there'd never been anyone else. Just her.

CHAPTER 23
THE WRITING ON THE WALL

TESSA

"YOU LOOK like you're trying to solve world hunger over there." The familiar gruff inflection did what it always seemed to do to her, jarred Tessa from her ruminations while simultaneously evoking a candid smile. "And from the way you're staring into that cinnamon bun, my guess is that you plan to conquer it one pastry at a time," Sterling posited, as he approached her at the counter, her elbows pointed and head down.

He reached out, grabbed her waist with one hand, and scooped her up and onto the warmth of his thighs. Sending the platter of rolls she'd just frosted tumbling after her. Tessa crossed her arms, with an air of annoyance she was unable to maintain, as she broke out into full-bodied laughter.

"I was going to eat those, you know?" she chided, sucking the tops of each of her fingertips until she was certain nothing sugary remained.

"I'm sure you were," Sterling agreed, though his tone suggested a hint of sarcasm. As she lifted a piece she'd salvaged to her lips—the only piece that hadn't bounced along the floor tiles—he swatted it loose. Before quickly shoving it into his own mouth. She blinked back at him, her shock evolving to indignation and then back again.

"I can't believe you just did that..." she huffed.

"Believe it, love." Eyes daggered in challenge, he admitted, "And I'd do it again—" The last word hadn't fully formed in his mouth, halted by the dessert flying out of Tessa's hand and splattering on his freshly shaven face. In a similar fashion, it was Sterling whose eyes now fluttered back at her in disbelief, his eyelashes caked in the liquified sweet cream.

"And so would I," she retorted, her own antagonism just as prominent, her posturing just as combative. However, when she raised her arm to fling another pastry in his direction, he caught her by the wrist. He enacted a small amount of pressure at the base of her thumb, forcing her grip to slacken and the offending cake to crumble to the floor. Once she was empty-handed, he drew her captive palm upwards and gently parted his lips along her exposed and quickening pulse line. The ghost of a kiss.

"Tess, I—" Whatever the admission was, Sterling swallowed it back down as footsteps invaded the kitchen.

Glancing up from his phone and surveying the chaos of the room, Charles snorted. "Is this some kind of sex thing?" He looked at the pair, each now plastered with a thick coating of frosting.

"Have I ever told you that your timing is impeccable?" Sterling responded, ineffectually wiping a white glob from his brow while Tessa shook her head and attempted to stifle her laughter.

"...because if this is some kind of sex thing, I can come back later..."

"What is it, Chuck?" Sterling rolled his eyes, quickly turning his chair to face the interloper. "Come out with it already, please."

"There's been a last-minute addition to your calendar. A two o'clock." His cohort's grin widened as he continued. "I see that you are... *preoccupied.* However, the caller said the work would be of personal interest to you and..." He read verbatim from his cellular device, "That the matter was of utmost urgency."

"I should go anyway." Tessa nodded, and everything that had been genuine and expressive was gone. Her mannerisms were once again controlled, backpedaled, and latched in place. Her stomach clenched as if of its own accord, as her breakfast threatened to travel up her esophagus and project onto her shoes. Her gut was telling her that something about this didn't sit right. Her every instinct screamed it; but her every instinct had been wrong lately. And she couldn't even distinguish if her sudden unease was warranted at the moment.

"Don't…" The singular request came out more like a plea. Sterling grabbed her hand before she could turn towards the bedroom. "Do you have an assignment due or anything?"

His question made her heart sink this time. She didn't want to think about the reality of what she had done and what it was about to do. This was supposed to be her escape, the place she could run away to.

"No." Her statement was as involuntarily dry as her mouth. "I turned everything in already. I haven't been issued anything new… just yet." She chewed on her words. Either Sterling didn't notice, or he had grown used to her shifts in mood.

"Then stay," he insisted. "The meeting will take an hour, two tops, if they bring specs to review." He tugged at his collar.

He was nervous about something, she observed.

"I mean, I'd love for you to sit in. It may give you a little insight into the bigger picture I have planned down the line. Once the Victorian is finished."

She nodded, though she herself didn't understand why she'd agreed. Her initial explanation would have been that she was just curious. She wanted to know what it was about this particular scheduling change that left her with a sense of dread. However, if she were to take an in-depth analysis of her motives, she would have realized that she'd stayed because she'd wanted to.

———

"So what does this project have to do with any of my personal investments?" Sterling enquired, his fingers tapping impatiently.

"No idea." Charles shrugged. "The chap who called said you'd know when he got here. Made a big *to-do* about how well-known his name was… Can't say I have ever heard of him though." He paused, then seemed to suddenly remember. "He did mention that it had something to do with your growing interest in more international ventures—oddly enough, I couldn't quite place the accent… But it was definitely foreign."

Tessa muffled her gasp. *It couldn't be…*

A knock sounded on the office door. A gesture that was somehow self-important, pompous, and obnoxiously loud. Charles grimaced—almost as if he could hear Tessa's thoughts and thoroughly agreed—then shook his head before standing to greet whoever was on the other side.

"Luc—" Charles's polite introduction was severed by the visitor's sudden entrance.

"Cousin!" The man approached with familiarity and an open wing-span. "You should have told me you'd be joining us, *cher.*"

No wonder Charlie hadn't recognized the accent, she mused. It was as god-awful as she remembered.

"*Philippe.*" The name felt acidic as it left her lips. "You know full well we aren't cousins, *mon cher.*" She corrected both the inaccuracy of his statement as well as that of his poor pronunciation. Tessa had yet to figure out what his endgame was here, but she knew she didn't like it.

"Well, distant cousins…" he seemed to explain with the twirl of his hand. "Twice removed and all that." He pivoted, veering his attention to Charles seated in front of the desk and Sterling positioned behind it. Tessa could see each of their wheels turning as Philippe continued. "But if you would like, *ma chérie,* we can all get straight down to business."

His phonetic adjustment had been uttered with a purpose; and it was one that was meant to be mocking.

"As I was telling this *lovely lady…*" The con man stalled. "By the way, she gets her looks from our side of the family. But that's neither here nor there. Back to business, right? I was telling Tess about my upcoming endeavors abroad—when was it?" He tapped his foot and tilted his head, implying as though he couldn't recall the date and time that they last saw each other. The threat was veiled but it hung there all the same. "*Cher,* be a dear and refresh my memory, won't you?"

Tessa shot up from her chair, her gaze narrowed and as equally foreboding as her opponent's. "Actually, if you could please give us a moment in private." It wasn't a request, and it was directed at the only two men who actually belonged in that room.

"Ah, yes!" Philippe agreed. "Let's catch up on family matters first. Gentlemen, I'm sure you don't mind." He placed a palm on Tessa's lower back as he guided her towards the door. "How is your dear mother?"

Her toes raked along the floorboards in response to the barred remark. "Excuse us," she called out over her shoulder; though she didn't dare turn to face them, for fear that they would see how rattled she had become. "Lucien. Charlie. We'll be in the drafting room… catching up. We won't be more than a few minutes."

She could feel the weight of their concern against her back, however, she refused to witness it head-on. Instead, the journalist callously chose to further quicken her exit. As they turned down the hall and past several open doorways, Tessa allowed her grip on the man's wrist to express her irritation. Her hold twisted and jerked in angles that were not meant to provide comfort. When she located the farthest room on the left, she swung the hinges sharply and tugged Philippe behind her.

"A rich boyfriend, I see." The curl of his smirk told her what his rhetoric had not.

"What do you want?" At this point, she wasn't sure how this encounter would pan out. So she loosened and flexed her muscles in preparation for a fight, in the event it all came to blows.

"What do I want? That's what you ask? That's obvious, *cher*," he sneered. "I'm surprised you didn't ask how I found you instead." One step. Then two. And three. He was closing in on her, campaigning to edge her towards the far wall. "Don't you want to know about the trail that led me to you… about all the little bread-crumbs you left behind? You know, if I could find you, someone else could too."

Four. Five. Six.

"You can lie and say it was done with precision, some half-brained scheme meant to lure me here, but your eyes betray you."

No matter what he said, she didn't look away. Nor did she respond.

Her concentration solely focused on counting. *Fifteen paces*, she surmised. She had fifteen paces before her back would hit the wall.

"But since you asked," he continued his tirade as most villains did, whether or not someone was listening. "I want in on whatever scheme you have going on here. If not, I'll tell your boyfriend all about how and where we met. He doesn't know about your little outing, does he?"

Shit.

"And would you like to know who told me this tidbit of information? You did," he goaded her.

She paused, losing count. It was ten. Or was it eleven?

"Well, your face did," he taunted. "Just now, when I mentioned him. There's that tell of yours, *cher*. You know, we'd make a good team. Much, much better than you and Mr. Wheel-of-Fortune."

Thirteen. She had to be at thirteen by now. Right? Wrong…

Fuck. The emitting force was much greater than Tessa had anticipated, her back solidly pressed against the wall. She'd been shoved there with enough exertion to leave her now breathless and winded. His form towered over her as he held her in place, his intent clear. There was no escape. And still, she didn't falter. Not an ounce.

In size, he outweighed her by a near hundred pounds, but with her targeted willpower, she was certain she could outmaneuver him. Just as she had intended. It wouldn't take much more than a duck and a side-step to loosen his grip. He wouldn't expect it, *surprise* the ever-present weapon added to her arsenal of quick wit and indomitability.

But then… then, he did the one thing she hadn't seen coming.

Clutching her face between his thumb and forefingers, he imprinted his grip, his nails nearly digging perfect facsimiles into each of her cheekbones. He clamped her jaw so tightly that she swore the shape of her skin would never return to normal. The room was deafeningly quiet—she could sense every minuscule, nerve-racking movement—and yet she couldn't stop it from happening. She felt her heart in her throat, where it sat, choking her more determinedly than he ever could.

It wasn't the pressure of his crushing embrace that shook her. No, not even the stench of his heaved respirations dampening her flesh could elicit a response. Her expression was stone, chiseled stoicism masking the rage that boiled beneath the surface. What finally ignited her outburst was the aggressive puckering of his lips crashing down on hers.

There was no way for him to predict it…

There was no way for the man to know what that simple unsolicited gesture would invoke. Not that he didn't deserve it. He most certainly did.

However, it didn't change the fact that her reaction was far more incensed and frenzied than any one person should have been humanly capable. Especially one of her stature. She was like a creature possessed. And to some extent, she was. Because the moment his mouth touched hers, she was no longer in that suffocating room. She was back in the warehouse, back somewhere outside the New York City limits. She was the living, breathing poltergeist of the girl still captured there. The girl that everyone, including herself, was certain had died.

And that girl was angry.

She didn't think about her next movements; in fact, she didn't think about anything at all. Each and every blow was as if it were by instinct, her body acting out in a way it was predestined to do. The imagery almost beautiful if the aftermath wasn't so god-awful and bloody. Her mind, having long since filed away the trauma, couldn't register what the rest of her was physically doing. Even as her knuckles gaped open, too raw to self-lubricate anymore, she didn't stop. She didn't feel.

She just kept striking over and over and over and over again.

Until some unknown presence seemed to be pulling her back by her arms and off the prone figure—a figure she'd found herself straddling. As she stared down, she stilled, her vision finally returning to the here. To the now. And to the battered body of the man on the ground. A man she'd beaten to a pulp. The same man whose face had returned to its true form, no longer an apparition of the past that still haunted her. Or the memories she'd thought were entombed by lock and key and allowed to rot away to nothing.

Outwardly, she was numb. The pulsing of her broken left fist vibrated up her arm and to her shoulders, and yet she felt no pain.

Despite her visible shaking, the only ache she could recognize was that of her psyche, which seemed to have unequivocally and inexplicably shattered, her mental state as noticeably fractured as her offender's facial features. She didn't know when it was exactly that she had collapsed to her knees only that, that's how she suddenly found herself.

Disoriented. Dissociated. Distraught.

There was no sign of the controlled, calculated woman she was thought to be. In her place, curled into a heap of crisscrossed limbs and gore, resided but a shell of a person. Somehow broken, even after all these years. Or maybe especially after all these years.

Through the shuffling of distant silhouettes and the muffling of distant voices, Tessa was frozen in place. Nearly catatonic. That was until she felt herself being tugged against her captor's chest. The scent was familiar, comforting, and safe. And as though it were second nature, she sighed, drawing her breath in deeper before expelling it to coat her lungs. A gesture that seemed to soothe her every nerve ending.

Had she been a crier…

But before the thought could take root, tears ushered from the crux of her eyes and streamed down her cheeks. Except they didn't stream; they gushed in ugly, gut-wrenching sobs as she buried herself closer into the man's torso. Cradled like the most precious, delicate thing that he'd ever held. Like she was made of glass and too much pressure would crack her, while too little would prompt her to slip through his fingers as if she were sand. A lifetime of unshed emotions dripped from her chin and soaked into the fabric of his shirt. Her body trembled as she gulped in air between each of the choked, unrelenting wails that materialized from some unknown depths of her innermost person.

He didn't speak. He didn't question her or demand an explanation. Though the tightening of his grip spoke for itself. *He wasn't going to let her go either.* He combed his fingers through the matted, sweaty strands of her hair and rested his chin on the top of her head. It wasn't until she shuddered with exhaustion and no longer had the energy or the tears left to cry that his voice finally broke the silence. And it wasn't until she heard it that the recognition washed over her.

"Tell me, Tess…" Sterling whispered, his body still sheltering hers —a physical barrier in place of the one he could not offer her mentally. "You don't have to. Not ever, if you don't want to. Say the word and I'll promise not to ask you about it again. But I need you to know… I need you to understand… I'm here. And you can tell me what happened to you…"

CHAPTER 24
THE BIG APPLE
SIX YEARS PRIOR

TESSA

BY THE TIME she was tall enough to reach a bag, Tessa had learned to take a punch. And not too long after, she'd perfected how to avoid one. Though, that lesson didn't seem to apply to her current situation. No, at the present moment—bound to a chair with her arms behind her back—avoidance wasn't much of an option. But preparing herself for the inescapable sting of the man's fist meeting her flesh, *that* she could do.

Each time he pulled his arm back, his muscles tightening in antici-pation of inflicting another blow: she steadied her breathing, loosened her posture, and braced for impact. She had to keep her jaw clenched, tongue rooted, and mouth shut while simultaneously tucking her chin and presenting her forehead instead. This posturing ensured that the contact would be mutually painful each time he struck her, his knuckles meeting solid cranial bone rather than the delicate, easily fractured features of her nose and orbital cavity. Lastly, she remem-bered to dip her shoulders in the same direction as the opposing force, allowing his fist to roll off with the least resistance and, in turn, the least pursuant damage to her soft tissue.

He was growing both tired and bored; tired from the effort needed to inflict her punishment and bored with her lack of response. He was the kind of sick fuck who indulged in the whimpers and cries of frightened little girls. The kind of monster that held no qualms about beating women and children; in fact, he was the kind of man that seemed to get some sort of depraved satisfaction from the entire ordeal. And right now, he stood in front of her very *unsatisfied*.

Though her ears were beginning to hum from the repeated hits to her temple, Tessa could still hear him shouting at her in some sort of hybrid language. A mixture of both Russian and English. To which, she would only respond in French, half to confuse the man and half because she found gratification in insulting him in terms he couldn't comprehend.

However, her enjoyment was short-lived, as was his patience for her continued antics. She could sense that he finally had enough. See it in the flickering in his eyes, the tick in his clenched jaw. She didn't have a plan—other than staying alive, of course. Nevertheless, she had been stalling. Buying time. Until she was able to formulate a means to get away.

She understood that whether or not he got the information he wanted, her time was limited. He was either too uninformed or too stupid to realize that she didn't have anything he wanted to begin with.

She wasn't who he thought she was. Or nearly as important. If truth be told, she couldn't even guarantee that the Agostinos would notice her absence, let alone barter for her return. And once he—or whoever he worked for—discovered this little tidbit, Tessa was as good as dead. If not worse. After all, she knew there would only be two outcomes in this scenario. She would need to escape, or she'd die in this warehouse. She doubted men such as him would have any other use for her. And if they did, she knew she would prefer death over those possibilities anyway.

She stilled, her eyes drawn to the darkness looming over them, and her hair began to stand on end. They weren't alone…

There was no way for her to know for sure but she could feel eyes on her. On them. It was that same kind of chill that traveled down your spine when you could sense you were being watched. That feeling that somewhere out there someone was looking down on you. And she didn't know who was more twisted, the man beating her to a pulp or the person watching him do it... However, judging by the salacious grin on the figure currently in front of her, it didn't really matter who was worse. Either way, this was the moment of truth.

He stalked over to her, appearing ever the proud predator despite the fact that his prey was tied down and presented to him like a gift for the taking. No man should have had pride in that. But this one certainly did, further proving he wasn't much of a man to begin with. She was beaten, bleeding, and bruised but she wasn't out for the count. She just needed to play her cards right. She needed to remember every lesson her father had ever taught her. Because at this moment, there was no better time for implementation.

With much more vigor than was necessary to restrain a battered hundred-pound girl, he released her bindings before dragging her off behind a wall of pallets and out of view from whomever's eyes she was certain were still watching. She didn't fight him. She knew she needed to both conserve her energy as well as ease him into a false sense of security. He had to believe she was more broken than she currently was.

Once they were far enough away that he seemed comfortable with his backdrop, he threw her down onto a makeshift bed; it was really nothing more than an old dirty mattress and a wrinkled sheet. She shivered at the thought of what had likely occurred there. At the thought of what may still occur there. But outwardly, she didn't recoil. Tessa pretended to be dazed, somewhere between consciousness and unconsciousness.

Even as he pawed at her clothing, tore the zipper of her dress, and removed her stockings—she didn't react. Instead, she listened to her surroundings. Making note of any footsteps in the foreground, the subtle creak of any doors, and the likely distance between them. She returned her focus to her carefully measured breaths, ensuring that he found them shallow enough to believe she was still knocked out. She blunted the sickening feeling that crept up her neck, knowing full well what was about to happen. And that she would have to allow it, couldn't fight it, until she had an opening.

Preparing for the inevitable—steeling herself mentally, physically, and emotionally for what was next—couldn't stop the devastation that washed over the journalist as the man dropped his pants, kneeled down over her, and forcibly inserted himself into her body. She held back her urge to whimper. She held back the tears that she refused to let leave their ducts. And she held back the wave of nausea that threatened to spur from the pit of her stomach. His movements were rough. Vile. Disgusting. And as if violating her lower body wasn't enough to get this sick fuck *off*, he reached up towards her mouth.

Clutching her face between his thumb and forefingers, he imprinted his grip, his nails nearly digging perfect facsimiles into each of her cheekbones. He clamped her jaw so tightly that she swore the shape of her skin would never return to normal. The room was deafeningly quiet—she could sense every minuscule, nerve-racking movement—and yet she couldn't stop it from happening. She felt her heart in her throat, where it sat, choking her more determinedly than he ever could.

It wasn't the pressure of his crushing embrace that shook her. No, not even the stench of his heaved respirations dampening her flesh could elicit a response. Her expression was stone, chiseled stoicism masking the rage that boiled beneath the surface. What finally ignited her outburst was the aggressive puckering of his lips crashing down on hers.

And the secondary double-edged penetration of his tongue snaking passed them. In a flurry of movements that were much quicker than should have been humanly possible, especially for someone of her small stature, Tessa's eyes flew open. And with deadening accuracy, her jaw clamped down and onto the smaller of the two intruding foreign bodies with as much strength as she could exert. Her teeth sunk into the meat of the twitching appendage until they had sawed themselves through, severing the gory pinkened clump of tissue and taste buds from its stem.

The man's system had shocked him into a silent scream, nearly a growl that rumbled in the back of his throat. But the sound didn't quite emit itself from his vocal cords. Instead, blood spurted from his mouth, pouring down over his chin like a pot boiling over. There was no other way she could think to describe the foaming substance discharging from his bottom lip and onto her chest. She shoved him off her as he curled up on his side and choked, gurgled, and gasped for air. His dignity was as open and on display as his undone fly.

Tessa stared down at the floundering figure. In accordance with her heart, her eyes were fixed in a gaze that was both dead and cold. She watched him flail, attempt to beg, and struggle to breathe —all without a single inclination towards remorse. He'd already killed whatever decency she had left in her soul as assuredly as she planned on leaving him there to die. But before she turned her back on him for good, she left her attacker with one more parting gesture. A swift kick to his groin as she spat at him, her saliva tainted pink by the remnants of his blood still embedded on her teeth.

Then she cracked her neck from side to side and sprinted into the shadows cast by the nearest assemblage of cargo pallets before tiptoeing towards the sound of the hinged creaking. She needed to find the opening and she surmised this one provided her most likely escape route. Slinking through the doorway, Tessa held her breath and clung close to the walls.

The corridor had a small room—or maybe a staircase—to the left but directly in front of her was the exit. It was only a few steps out of reach. That was all that stood between the journalist and her freedom. But she soon discovered that those few steps… were precisely a few steps too many.

Appearing from the opposing aperture, and blocking her only outlet, was a taller, much wider, and more menacing figure than had been her first opponent. He grabbed her by the shoulders. His grip wasn't gentle but she wouldn't have called it violent either. Or perhaps, in actuality, she'd grown numb to the violence. Too desensitized to tell the difference anymore.

And too detached to really care.

Whatever the reasoning, she didn't back down. She didn't crumble. Even as she stared defeat in the eyes—eyes with no discernible color—

it was only blackness and intent she saw there. As to what his intent was, however, she hadn't quite figured that out yet.

What she did know was that this man was not her savior; there was no doubt in her mind that he was another Russian mobster. Another member of the Bratva. The tattoos on his knuckles told her as much. And his heavily laced accent when he vocalized his warning moments later solidified her theory.

"You. Are. Dead." He spoke harshly and with conviction, though the threat sounded just above a whisper.

Despite the trauma, despite the unmistakable pounding of her half-dead heart, Tessa couldn't hide her true nature any more than a leopard could hide his spots. She smiled a frighteningly swollen, purpled smile. Like something out of a horror flick and much too grotesque to be true to form, nature, or even living.

"*Pas encore, je ne le suis pas.*" *Not yet, I'm not.*

"*Prekrati eto der'mo.* Stop. The. Shit. Speak English. Understand?" He enunciated each word as though it were an additional assaultive strike to her already afflicted and discoloring flesh. "You. Are. Dead," he repeated, tightening his hold on her with one hand while brushing the blood from her cheek with the other. His actions were as conflicting as his aggressively softened tone.

"I'm perfectly alive. But I can't say the same for your friend." Her retort slipped out much easier than it should have, like silk dancing along her tongue. She knew that at the very least if she was going to die tonight, she was taking one of them with her.

"*Zatknis'.* Shut up, girl. Don't make me say it again. YOU. ARE. DEAD. Leave. Change your name. Disappear. Tessa Leroux is dead, *ponyat'*?" *Understand?*

"She can't be dead. She never existed..."

He paused at her admission, as if taking a moment to mull over the information she'd so suddenly divulged. "*Sukin syn...* Son of a bitch, so it's more *pizdets* than the Italians know. But *mne pokhuy.* I don't give a fuck. Right now, I just need you to run. And run fast. Before I change my mind. Whoever the fuck it is you are pretending to be, she died in this warehouse tonight. The *Bratva* killed her. But it's your choice how convincing I need to make it."

"I want my ring back," she hissed the demand between bloodied teeth, her spine steeled despite her lack of a bargaining chip.

"Your life is on the line, girl. And you're worried about a trinket. A piece of jewelry?" The man laughed, though the sound resonated anything but humor. "You're lucky he didn't take the whole finger. Now go or I'll take more than a souvenir."

With those parting words, he offered her both a promise and a warning. And Tessa realized that while he might not have been the devil himself, in that moment, he sure as hell looked like it. There was something in the mobster's voice that told her that he didn't want to hurt her. But if she argued with him… if she fought him… if she forced his hand, he would.

Wanting had little to do with it.

So, for once in her life, she didn't fight. She didn't argue or attempt to negotiate. No, on the contrary, she fled. Though she had believed what he told her, and that he would make good on his threat, that was not why the journalist left New York. However, it had been a good enough reason to not look back when she finally did.

———

When the adrenaline wore off and her impulses were no longer anesthetized by the need to survive, Tessa's shock morphed into self-loathing. She wasn't the same girl she had been. The one who'd walked into that nightclub, fearless and uninhibited. The one who'd looked the most dangerous of men in the eye and refused to flinch, even as common sense screamed at her that she should run. The one who'd risked facing the targeted onslaught of the criminal under-ground just to get a better story. No, that wasn't her anymore…

She could never be that same girl again. Her constitutional being, her frame of mind, her entire sense of who she was intrinsically had been forever altered.

A surrogate, a creature blackened by disgust and anguish, crept forward in Tessa's stead. She wrapped her daggered claws around the voice of logic and reason—the voice Tessa relied on hearing, even if she hadn't always chosen to listen. And like a noose dropping before pulling tight, the imposter silenced the sound into submission while claiming her rightful place at the forefront of the journalist's mind. The proxy, now firmly positioned at the helm of Tessa's subconscious, guided her arsenal of subliminal warfare, humiliation, and stigma while drowning what remained of the woman's confidence and indomitability in a sea of questions that seemed to bear no answer.

Because it shouldn't have happened.

It wasn't one of the potential outcomes, she told herself. As though she believed doing so would change what couldn't be changed. Why hadn't she seen it? Predicted it? Prevented it? If she couldn't see it, how could she have stopped it? The strategy was simple: designate every action a reaction, every offense a defense.

She glared at the image in the mirror, failure staring back at her in the form of smeared makeup and dried tears, and shook her head.

Every possible measure had been covered, then countered…

Except the one that mattered, her own voice echoed back. The one that would have preserved her self-worth. Her dignity. She just couldn't seem to grasp that fact. She couldn't wrap her mind around it. She couldn't absorb what she couldn't dissect and understand. The reality that there was nothing she could have done differently. Because even though it shouldn't have happened, it did.

In the deep abyss of Tessa's psyche, where she hid her unwanted emotions, she enlisted her hatred to stand guard. It resided as a single soldier, alone and left to battle the sting of her ever-rising hindsight and the self-inflicting voice that lashed out and called her the very thing she had fought so long and hard to deject. The thing she had sought to dispute and disembody. To diminish and defeat. The phantasmal voice that seemed to make its sole purpose to remind her that she was the manifestation of vulnerability. She was just a girl and…

She was weak.

In that moment, in the moments prior, and in the moments where she'd trusted anyone besides herself, she'd proven just how much so. She hadn't been strong enough, smart enough, or quick enough. She'd allowed the Russian to violate her. To use her body just as easily, just as submissively, just as wantonly as she'd allowed her former partner to exploit and defile her heart.

Tessa could hear her father's voice in her head, his instructions when she took to the ring and he taught her how to take a blow before delivering one twice as potent, and realization ate away at her insides.

Because when push came to shove, she hadn't fought. She hadn't even made it to the ropes. She'd succumbed to her own weight class. She'd tried to play possum with the eight-count, and in the end, like a well-delivered uppercut to a glass jaw, she'd lost anyway.

CHAPTER 25

THE LIVING DEAD GIRL
THE PRESENT

Sterling

SHE HADN'T TOLD him what had happened. She didn't seem able…

Instead, she relived it in a way that seemed to separate the woman she was from the girl she had been. Like two sides to the same coin that refused to acknowledge the other even existed. The images, the emotions, each sequence of events was narrated as though some distant being had been observing her. And it was that same being who was now recounting the tabloid writer's backstory as it had played out in front of her all those years ago. Her voice had been devoid of all sentiment. The rage he'd seen firsthand was extinguished, the torment neatly tucked away, where he assumed she thought it belonged.

He didn't know what to say to her. What could he say? That he understood?

He didn't. And he never would. Never could.

That he was sorry?

If he knew anything about the woman in front of him, it was that she didn't want his pity any more than he wanted hers.

That he loved her? That he wanted to… needed to know that that man was really dead. That he would spend every penny of his fortune to locate and dig up the grave just to see with his own eyes what was left of that piece of shit. That if in fact he hadn't met his end by Tessa's hands, Sterling wanted to hunt that man down himself and make sure that fucker knew exactly what it felt like to be tied down and beaten into submission. And worse...

Yes, of course, that would be the perfect response. If he was looking to imply she was just as helpless as her attacker had made her feel in that moment. She didn't need or want him to do any of those things for her. Or in her name. That much, Sterling knew.

It took little effort to list all the words he was certain were precisely the wrong ones to say. However, what was right, what would ease her suffering, *that list* evaded him. He tried to think back to after his accident. He tried to consider what he had wanted to hear when faced with the worst moment of his own life. And came up short. All he could remember was everything he hadn't, everything that seemed like empathy but came across as disappointment instead.

He supposed there was no correct answer.

Saying something, saying anything, would be self-serving. With the intention of unburdening his own conscience, his own distress, rather than any of hers. Because there was nothing he could ever say that would dull the ache of what she had been through. And so, he remained silent, his outstretched hand still in hers, his fingers itching to squeeze tighter while fear and hesitation kept a single muscle from moving.

Her fist—the same one that sat bruised and billowed, despite her brain's refusal to acknowledge the pain—opened and closed as though by instinct. As though the sting and crunching of bone grounded her to the present while her mind drifted to the past. Common sense urged him to bring her ice to alleviate the swelling; whereas his intimate knowledge of the woman cautioned him that if left to her own devices, she would likely run.

Another stalemate, where both action and inaction were equally detrimental.

TESSA

Steady your breathing. Loosen your posture. Brace for impact.

The instructions played over and over again in her head, as she repetitiously flexed the knuckles on her left hand.

Jaw clenched. Tongue rooted. Mouth shut, she reminded herself.

The grinding sound of her joints seemed foreign, even as the pulsing heat traveled up her wrist to her chest and back down again. She didn't recognize the sensation of pain. Just the wet, sticky coagulation of torn flesh as it clung to bone. And the rhythmic thuds that confirmed she was still breathing. With each inhalation, the air around her was tied off and strangled, except for her inner monologue and the synchronized palpation of her heart that followed.

She'd lost count of how many times she'd recited the combination. Similar to how—like a first-time ring fighter—she'd lost count of her paces. She'd been unprepared, a boxer caught cold on the ropes. She'd given him the upper hand, lowering her mitts just long enough for the popping feint that jabbed into a sucker punch. A psychological hit (verses a physical one) but a landing blow all the same. And she didn't like that feeling, the unease that told her she'd learned nothing in the six years that'd passed. She was that same girl. Nothing had changed. Not a thing.

She was still weak.

The altercation with Philippe had reiterated that sentiment. She may have bloodied the man beyond recognition, but he'd gotten under her skin. And surface wounds were far easier to heal.

If she hadn't killed him.

The shock of the statement rattled her. She hadn't known when to stop. What was more troubling was the understanding that she wouldn't have if someone hadn't forced her to do so. She would have continued to slam the crackling meat of her fists against whatever part of him was within her reach. She would have remained unresponsive and entranced. And she would have likely added another body to her count.

Her gut lurched at the thought. She felt the caustic burn of bile as it rose and pooled in her throat. She was going to be sick.

"He's bad, isn't he…" Though she formed the phrase like it was a question, she spoke as though it were fact. "He's not… I didn't… did I?" There was no time for a response. "I need my phone. I need to call Lane. I have to go to the police. I've killed a man…" She paused before correcting herself. "*Two men*. I've killed two men…"

STERLING

She was frantic. Feral. Clawing at the bedsheets before turning her attention to his nightstand and the drawers of his bureau.

"Where is it! I need my phone," she pleaded, her voice a mixture of panic and desperation. Both agitated and distraught. "I need to go." The declaration was nothing more than a whisper as Tessa glanced from Sterling to the open doorway. He could see her thought process. Her intentions were as clear as if she had spoken them aloud.

If she left now, she wasn't coming back. Not to his home. And not to him.

He wanted to edge closer, and yet he knew he needed to do so without forcing her to feel cornered. He approached her like he would an injured bird. He was afraid she would flutter away just as easily too.

"Tess, it's okay." He reached up to brush his hand against her cheek, but quickly removed it when she flinched. His brows furrowed. "You didn't do anything. You don't *have to* do anything but rest. He's— well, I'm not going to sugarcoat it. He's fucked. But the son of a bitch will live. And everything else is being handled. So please, love, lie down."

Her retort, akin to joyless laughter, was as transparent as the hostility that bristled beneath it. "Handled? Ha… handled?! Handled, like you *handled* everything for Madelyn. Is that what your plan is?

Throw money at the problem? Take the blame yourself? Pretend it all never happened? Thank you, but no. I can pretend just fine on my own. And without *you* having to *handle* anything." She stepped back, ensuring there was an appropriate amount of distance between them.

"What do you even know about that?" The phrase wasn't uttered with curiosity; he hadn't had time enough to be truly curious. It had been more of an impulse, an automatic reaction driven by shock and bewilderment.

"I know everything, Lucien. Every fucking sordid detail of what you did to protect that woman. Is that your plan now too? To protect me? I don't need you to protect me. I've protected myself before. Just fine. Without anyone. Without you."

He shook his head. "One thing at a time, Tess. No, I'm not trying to control this situation for you, just stating the obvious. Let's look at this logically. We don't need to do anything, *because* he's not going to report it. He'll want to keep this as quiet as possible for two reasons: one, his pride. He doesn't appear to be the type of man who'd want to openly admit he was taken down by a woman half his size. And two, he'll want to keep his con going. He doesn't want a paper trail and he sure as hell has to have a record already. If he reports anything, it'll mean his head too. It was self-defense. *He* assaulted *you. You* protected yourself. You're a…"

He didn't want to say *victim*. It tasted sour. And he didn't like the word *survivor* any better. The terms just felt inauthentic, overused. She'd been assaulted. Raped. But Sterling couldn't bring himself to speak those words aloud either. They made his skin crawl, the labels as superficially inaccurate as being called *crippled*. Nothing could ever verbally encompass what she'd experienced, what made her who she was today, while arguing otherwise only cheapened it.

"You're… suffering from PTSD," he chose to say instead. "No judge in the world will prosecute you, but if you still want to go down to the police station tomorrow, I'll escort you there myself. But right now, you need to rest."

"So you know about his con…" Once again, she presented a question that wasn't really a question, he noted.

"Yes," Sterling sighed. "At least part of it. I'm sure there's more to it. More you're not telling me. However, I would rather hear it from you than some dirtbag blubbering between broken teeth." He paused. "But not now. And not tomorrow…"

He wanted to know. For fuck's sake, he needed to know. Everything. Who this man was. How he knew Tessa. What they were each looking to achieve. And whether they'd been working together. Those were just a few of the unanswered questions floating in the air. But not like this. Not when she was barely hanging on.

It was frightening because it didn't seem to matter what the truth was. He realized he would still love her anyway.

To be fair, deep down, he'd always suspected there was more going on behind the curtain. Behind her façade and the games she played. He'd already determined that she wasn't the sort to just let things go. Meaning, if he'd been using his common sense, he would have looked further into why she was at the wedding in the first place. He would have asked her what story she was currently working on and how it related to him or his family. And he would have gotten those answers long before inviting her into his bed. But Sterling had chosen to be willingly blind. Because he didn't care to know for sure. He only cared for Tessa. And the way she made him feel. Especially about himself.

Though that sounded selfish now…

She pivoted, turning her back on him. And, for a moment, he was certain she would run. But instead, her posture weakened and her shoulders slumped. "It shouldn't have happened. All the training… it should have prepared me. I could have taken him if I'd acted quicker. But I… I let it happen. I didn't fight back until it was too late."

He didn't know which instance she was referring to specifically, considering he'd yet to learn all the details of what had transpired between her and the battered con man. Or if she had intended it to be a mixture of the two. But frankly, to Sterling, it didn't matter.

"Tess, look at me. *Look.*" He waited for her to oblige before continuing. "You're absolutely right. It shouldn't have happened. To you or to anyone else. But that's the *only* thing you're right about. There's no amount of training that could prepare someone for something like that. There's no textbook answer. I know that's terrifying for you to hear."

She shifted with unease but he didn't hesitate.

"Because saying there is or was a way to prevent it means you had —you *have*—control over the situation. And oddly enough, you find comfort in that. In the fact that there's something to prevent that from ever happening again. It keeps you from being afraid. If you can control every little aspect of your life, every interaction and every emotion, you feel safe. It's not so terrifying. And you can pretend to move on from the one situation where you had no control whatsoever. But I'm sorry to tell you, love…"

He shook his head because he really was sorry. He wished wholeheartedly that all of it—*any of it*—would have been able to take her pain away.

"None of that is going to work. You think you're living in a world you control, but in actuality, you're living in a state of constant fear of losing it."

He watched as a barrage of emotions traveled across her face before she settled on her preference. The one she seemed to carry with her as a last-ditch defense. Anger.

"You think you know everything, don't you?" she seethed. "That you have all the fucking answers?" She paced. It was a habit of hers, he'd come to realize. Almost as if she needed the monotonous movement to anchor her.

"No, Tess, it's quite the opposite actually." He maneuvered himself to block her path. And warily gestured his fingertips towards her again.

This time she invited his touch, sinking the side of her face into his palm. It was a reminder to them both that neither was the enemy. Or the opposition. It was a reminder that each was equally unsure and broken and cautious. And it was a reminder that despite the uncertainty, it was worth it. He wasn't sure who'd sighed, but the release of air brought him back from his thoughts.

His lips twitched into a near smile as he confessed, "The second I met you, it hit me. The fact that I know fucking absolutely nothing. Not a goddamned thing. Except that… the only time I feel anything is when I'm in the same room as you. Good. Bad. Amused. Enraged. Anything other than numb, *indifferent*, is sparked only by you, love."

She closed her eyes. "What am I supposed to say to that, Lucien…"

He pulled her into his lap. Though pleasantly so, he was surprised when she didn't fight him. Instead, she curled against the warmth of his chest willingly, as if it had been what she wanted all along. But wouldn't admit, let alone ask for.

"You're not supposed to say anything. You don't *have to* say anything. I didn't mean to say it in the first place, if I'm being honest. Hell, I don't plan to say half the shit I do when you're around. But it seems to happen anyway."

"I know the feeling, *nounours*," she murmured into his neck before finally giving in to exhaustion and falling asleep in his arms.

CHAPTER 26
THE GUARD DOG

STERLING

HE DIDN'T KNOW how much time had passed before he had no choice but to move her. He only knew that it had been long enough for his desensitized thighs to begin to ache. She'd barely fluttered an eyelash as Charles assisted him in positioning her on the bed and under the covers; the architect had thought about bandaging her hand and quickly decided against it. He couldn't care less about the blood staining his sheets; he just didn't have the heart to disturb her again.

Half of what she'd told him about New York had seemed far-fetched. Implausible, really. But he didn't doubt the validity of her story, as much as he wished that he could. Nothing but sheer torment could have caused what he'd witnessed. And it was this same torment that seemed to haunt her for years, erupting and devastating her hard-pressed exterior in an accumulation of today's events.

Sterling had determined that she should stay with him. At his house. Where he could somehow make sure she was recovering. Or starting to recover. Or attempting to start to recover. Or at the very least, that she was *considering* attempting to start to recover.

Though what she should do was very different from what she was likely to do, he conjectured.

That insight, while maddening, brought a curl to his mouth. He couldn't help but absolutely adore her for it. For her tenacity. For her fortitude. For her ability to gouge her way into his chest cavity, grab onto his heartstrings, and twirl them around her fingertips as if it had been no feat at all. If only he could profess as much aloud.

But this was not the time, he attempted to reiterate to himself.

She was emotionally vulnerable and influencing her in any which way—adding more baggage to her shit pile—would be egocentric on his part. And she deserved far better than another self-serving prick in her life. No, Sterling refused to be that guy.

He glanced over at her slight form, her long dark hair the only thing visible over his comforter, and suddenly remembered there was another issue at hand. Her knowledge of and possible involvement with Madelyn.

The implication, the very idea, that those two worlds had or would or may need to collide made him shudder. It nearly tore Sterling in two. The man he'd thought he was, the one who would do anything to protect Maddy. No matter the cost to himself or anyone else. No matter how presumptuous and utilitarian it may have been. And the man he had become with Tessa, the same man he barely recognized in the mirror anymore. Because this present man was somehow more worthwhile, freer, more content. This present man, for the first time in his life, felt like he was enough. Just as he was. Not because of what he had the potential to offer. And not because of what he never could.

Forcing these two parts of himself to meet—to come together—was not an internal battle he was prepared to witness, let alone one he believed he would win. Though, at this point, what other option did Sterling have?

Fuck. He wrung his hands through his hair, matted with sweat and longer than he usually wore it. *This had turned out to be one hell of a shit day,* he remarked inwardly to the silent room and to no one else in particular.

———

It was early the next morning when Sterling awoke to the sound of the shower running. He glanced over at the analog clock still glowing in the shadows cast by his tightly drawn curtains. Cinching the bridge of his nose between his index and forefinger, he saw that 05:00 a.m. glared back at him.

"Fuck," he exhaled.

He'd slept maybe an hour, and his joints seemed to jeer and contest with every breath he took. He hadn't even felt her leave his side. Though, with Tessa, he should have predicted it. He didn't know if he would ever be lucky enough to have that woman stay put.

Once again, the thought of her blatant obstinance provoked his laughter—because, admittedly, he wouldn't want it any other way.

He draped an arm over his eyes, fighting his urge to roll back over, to get just a few more minutes of sleep. Despite his chair, Tessa had never gone easy on the man. Hearing the sound of her bare feet on the bathroom tile, followed by the loud shattering of what he could only assume was his shaving mirror, Sterling grinned. Because nor did it appear as if she planned to start doing so today.

———

She scratched her heels back and forth over the veneer, etching her trail into the hardwood flooring as she crossed from one side of his office to the other.

"You would escort me there yourself," she spat, and as if to further reiterate the statement, she gestured first at him and then herself. *"Your words, not mine."*

"Please, can you just sit for a moment and let me explain?" Sterling raked his hands over his face. He must have been insane to think this would have gone any other way. Daring to look up, he cringed as her head snapped to the side, her gaze shooting daggers in his direction.

Yep, he was crazy, a fucking madman to say the least. Perhaps lack of sleep had driven him there, he debated. But he'd spent the last twelve hours contacting every resource at his disposal, and for fuck's sake, she was going to fucking listen. *Or something like that, right?*

Right... he seemed to answer himself sarcastically while her defiant posture corroborated his conclusion. Because there was no way in hell she was sitting down.

"Right." This time he said it aloud. "Well, before you decide to run out of here and into the confines of a jail cell, can you please just take a look?" He handed her a plain manila envelope. "There's no record. No reports. Tess, there's no mention of any such crime in New Jersey or New York or Pennsylvania, for that matter. I've checked. We've all checked. I've had every detective, every PI—hell, every news outlet that answered their phones in the tristate area—reviewing open case files. How are you turning yourself in for a crime that for all intents and purposes doesn't even exist?"

"I don't understand..." She paused mid-stride, dropping her eyes to the bundle of paperwork she was holding—somewhat tighter now—and then back up again.

"Either they covered it up or that man is still alive. And from everything I've been able to gather so far, my guess is the latter." He motioned towards the envelope she was clutching and nodded. "There's a picture..."

Although she sought to remain stoic, he observed a slight tremble in her hands and again, albeit wordlessly, he offered her a seat. She sunk into the leather material before hesitantly pulling the black and white mugshot out from between the other documents. The sudden sharp drawing in of her breath was the only visible sign of recognition she displayed.

"Tess, you didn't kill him," Sterling explained. "Slavi Chelovek. He's a lower-level enforcer in the Russian mob. Factor in certain physical attributes, and the fucker was easy to track down." When her eyebrow raised in question, he added for clarity, "It's rumored that the bastard doesn't speak because *the devil ate the man's tongue.*"

Tessa's spine subconsciously uncoiled at the turn of phrase, as though some part of her relished the vilified analogy. "But all this time... I..." Her voice was wistful. "I assumed... But he's still out there..."

Quickly realizing his mistake—that instead of comforting her, he'd merely heightened her distress—Sterling continued. "If that's the case, then for whatever reason, he's not looking for you. Let sleeping dogs lie, Tess. Bringing this all up now will have no benefit."

His sentiments fell on deaf ears. The journalist was in a daze; she wasn't listening. "He said I was dead…" Her expression was vacant as she stared through him and out the stretch of windows on the far wall.

"Tess, it was just an idle threat. They won't come for you here. I'll upgrade the security systems. Increase my staff. Whatever you need."

Assuming she agreed to stay with him, he mulled, not wanting to think otherwise. Not wanting to consider that she may still walk out that door and he may never see her again.

"No, *he* said I was dead…" she corrected, as if repeating the words would hold a deeper meaning to him.

It didn't. They didn't.

"Tess—"

Her attention bounced back. "No, Lucien. You're not listening. He said I was dead. He told them all I was dead. He told Marco I was dead. That's why he never looked for me, why none of the Agostinos ever looked for me."

Sterling froze, unexpectedly jarred by the utterance.

Had she wanted them to? He couldn't help but feel a twinge of jealousy as the infamous Mafia Prince's name rolled off her tongue. Had she felt something for the kid? The same kid who was surely a man by now. Had it been more than just an act for her? Did her theory that the boy likely thought she had died all those years ago suddenly change everything for them?

He wanted to ask all these questions. He wanted to know exactly what she was thinking and feeling. But her mental state was far more important than his own, her well-being far more precious than the frailty of his male ego.

TESSA

It was true.

Despite thinking she'd killed the man, despite all the time that had passed—the years that she had been forced to carry that burden—he was still out there. And still very much alive. She didn't know if she was more relieved or frightened by that knowledge. By the knowledge that she *wasn't* a murderer.

Though, she was equally startled by the abrupt realization that both criminal organizations would have needed to accept the narrative. Especially one that ended with her supposed demise. The possibility had never even occurred to her until this moment, probably because the journalist tried her best not to think of it at all. And yet, it was like clarity had rushed up and struck her across the face.

If her attacker was indeed alive—*Slavi,* Lucien had called him— then in retaliation, he and his constituents would have had no choice but to target the Italians. Or face appearing weak in the eyes of the men who already held a tighter grip on the city. Regardless of Tessa's significance, likewise, Marco's family would have been expected to make a show of force. To shed reactionary blood at the insult. For someone daring to lay hands on what was deemed their property.

It was the way things were done. It was the founding principal of that world. And it was what kept those key power players still in power. Still playing. This would have meant all-out war in the streets of New York.

Thus, the only plausible conclusion was that someone had intervened. Someone—and she suspected she knew exactly which someone —had ensured that both parties, both sides of the criminal underground, were equally placated. However, what Tessa couldn't fathom was why he'd chosen to do so...

What had the mobster gotten out of the deal?

She hadn't told Lucien about the second Russian, the one who'd so emphatically suggested she leave the city, that she remain dead. The one who both threatened and safeguarded her. Nor did she intend to. It was better he didn't know that detail, she'd concluded. And she was thankful she had.

If the architect wanted her to *let the sleeping dogs lie,* then she surmised she shouldn't disturb her guard dog either.

CHAPTER 27
THE CAGED CANARY

SHE WAS MILES AWAY. Lost inside herself and her inner workings. Again.

Like she had been since the morning prior. But at the very least, she hadn't run. Not yet anyway. Though Sterling was afraid to question, to even think why that might have been. She was like a bird whose wings had been clipped. She wanted to fly away—the intent was there—but the ability to do so and the fear of falling was holding her back.

This comparison left him wondering if she would ever be happy being caged. Being tied down to a man such as himself. The very idea of it felt like a disservice. Like a weight this incredible creature didn't deserve to be ensnared in and tethered to. And as quickly as the realization had hit him, that he truly loved this woman, he recognized how selfish of a pursuit it would be.

And what kind of life it would mean for her.

Sinking into his own dark thoughts, Sterling hadn't even noticed that Tessa was looking at him. Not until the look turned heated and unrecognizable.

"You aren't going to ask me, are you?" The accusation vibrated with a purpose. She wanted a fight, he suspected. It was Tessa's go-to when things began to feel uncomfortable or whenever she got too close to feeling something real. She would shove him away and force him to pull her back in.

However, today he didn't know if he had it in him to fight back. To further prune those metaphorical feathers of hers. Today he may just have to let her go. Fly.

Dance, he considered, as though he were thinking about Madelyn all over again. His mind lost to the memory of when he realized he could never offer his once-fiancée their first dance.

He shook his head and sighed. "Ask you what, Tess?" He glanced up from his computer screen. He hadn't been productive over the last few hours anyway; he'd just been staring at the list of unanswered emails as she sat in equal silence. Where once the soundlessness that fell between them had seemed natural, presently it was anything but.

"About my article. About why I was at the charity event. About how and why I know what I know?" she clarified, her eyes ablaze, though not with the kind of passion he'd grown accustomed to. The kind he preferred to *this*. To her wrath.

Ah, so that was it, he posited.

She'd been expecting an interrogation and was tired of waiting for it, whereas Sterling had been internalizing his questions and avoiding the topic altogether for *her* benefit—or so he'd assumed. But obviously, he'd been mistaken. However, he'd already concluded Tessa was more of the *damned if you do, damned if you don't* type. And whatever he would have done would have been precisely the wrong thing to do. That inkling of familiarity pushed back his doubts, even if only for an instant, and his expression softened.

"I was going to ask, love," he reaffirmed. "I was always going to ask. I need to. But I didn't think it was the right time." He gestured towards her bandaged fist.

Her resounding laugh was fake and forced. "Why? Because you presume I'm as weak as the lot of them? You think I can't handle whatever it is you plan to throw at me? That I'm delicate? That I'll wilt, right?" She stood as if a fire had been set beneath her. "Ask me, damn it! Get your fucking answers and stop treating me like I'm so irreparably broken. If I wanted your pity, believe me, I have my ways of getting it. I can easily throw myself at your feet, distraught and doe-eyed, and you'd be none the wiser."

Her words were meant to sting, but they didn't. She wasn't fooling him, as hard as she seemed to try. He saw the truth behind them. He understood them. He knew them. *Intimately.* At a time, those very words had been his own. And with that appreciation, no matter how hard she lashed her tongue in his direction, it didn't hurt.

"Okay, Tess," he responded, more as an indulgence than to appease his own curiosity. "Tell me then, what is it that you want from my friends? From my family? I know it isn't money. I know you don't care about my name…"

She snorted with more feigned amusement. "And which one is she?" Tessa hissed.

"She… who?" Sterling countered, his brows upturned. He really hadn't the slightest idea as to what she was getting at…

His outward display of confusion incited the rage that had been boiling below the surface—the same anger that had been waiting for her avoidance and denial to subside so it could uncoil and strike out. She searched the room but didn't appear to find whatever it was that she was looking for.

An escape? Something to throw? Something to break? He could only guess.

She shook her head before again facing him. "*Madelyn*, Lucien." The name dripped from her lips with the same disdain as the most exacting expletive. "Which one is *Madelyn*? Friend or family? And I'll even give you a hint. Neither. The answer is neither." The insinuation left him dumbstruck, and so she continued. "And do you want to know why? Why she is deserving of neither endearment?" Though it was a question, she didn't leave time enough for an answer. "Tell me I'm better off without you. Tell me you have nothing to offer me. Tell me we're over, Lucien. Tell me!"

He felt those same heartstrings she held so taut between her fingers wrench forward and tug. Ready and waiting to be severed.

"Tess—" As much as he told himself that it was the right thing to do, he wasn't sure he could.

"Tell me, damn it!" She urged.

"Okay... If that's what you want," he conceded. "It's over, Tess... We're over."

"No." She spun on her heel, her arms crossed, her expression resolute. "See how easy that was? It's a simple word. Two letters. I'll even spell it out for you. N-O. *No.* It doesn't matter what you say, because you can't make me. It takes two—two people to end a relationship. It's not that you left her; it's that she let you." She turned away again. "So why do you still care so much..."

The last statement had been rhetorical, uttered to the surrounding space itself rather than anyone in particular. But the heavy office air was just as unsure as Sterling was, when it came to how to respond. And therefore, neither he nor the emptiness called after her when she climbed onto his bookshelf, grabbed a picture frame from the top ledge, and threw it against the wall. Her gaze shot downward as if to inspect her handiwork. To confirm that the impact had in fact shattered the glass. Before she stepped back to the floor and stomped off and out of the room.

He knew what photograph she'd inflicted her wrath upon without even having to glimpse the carnage of broken glass that littered the hardwood. Because Sterling himself had been the one to toss it up there in the first place, not long after the same girl who'd destroyed it had first stormed into his life and out his office doors.

It was the one image of himself and Maddy he'd kept over the years. Everything else had been tossed, damaged, or stowed away. However, he supposed the bigger question was how Tessa even knew it was up there in the first place. He could only assume, after observing how quickly she'd located it, that what she had been looking for moments ago wasn't the picture itself but a way to reach it.

Damn that fucking woman, he growled to himself. He wasn't sure how it was even possible...

She'd been the one lying. She'd been the one with a hidden agenda. She'd been the one with ulterior motives. And yet, somehow, Sterling was left feeling like the asshole at the end of it all.

She was good—he'd give her that. Too fucking good for *his own good.*

TESSA

"Es putain de pathétique," Tessa spat at the reflection glaring back at her in the mirror. "You're fucking pathetic."

She wanted to throw her fist through the same wall the picture frame had dented, but as she stretched her knuckles beneath the ACE bandage, she knew it wasn't one of her better ideas. Besides, she seemed to have no problem getting her point across without having to further injure herself.

Then again, what exactly *had* been her point?

Envy was not a color that suited the journalist; however, the green vixen was rearing its ugly head in the pit of Tessa's stomach, controlling her actions as if she were the puppet, jealousy the puppet master.

As of late, her behavior had been petty. She knew it, even if she hadn't been able to stop it. She knew it even as part of her hadn't *wanted* to do a damned thing about it. And she knew it even as the other part of her had refused to consider it. Her controlled world was in utter chaos and she both hated and craved the upheaval…

Worse yet, Tessa wanted nothing and everything to do with the man that seemed to be the catalyst. She wanted to run away and she wanted to be chased. She wanted to scream and she wanted to cry. She wanted to never see his fucking face again, and she wanted to see it every fucking morning, asleep and beside her own. None of it made any sense. Her very thoughts made no fucking sense.

Though she would never admit it, she had purposely dropped Lucien's antique shaving mirror the morning prior, after reading the inscription on the back: *with love always, Maddy.* She hadn't thought out her intentions. She'd just done it. As though her grip had been animated from some external force—a force that had instructed her to watch the blasted thing fall and bounce along the tile floor.

She'd waited for him to yell at her, to mention the sentimental value behind the gift. But instead, he met her with a half smile and a shake of his head. He'd pulled her into his lap and away from the hazardous shards of glass that scattered along the bathroom floor. And she both hated and loved him for it.

No. She closed her eyes at the poorly chosen turn of phrase. She didn't. She couldn't, right? But even as she told herself otherwise, deep down, she knew the truth. She loved him. And it was tearing her apart from the inside out.

She sunk to her knees and onto the same cold tile that had been the final resting place of that god-forsaken mirror—now clear of the pursuant damage, as if the incident had never even occurred—and she stilled. She had no one anymore. She, by her own hand, had driven them all away, inciting altercation after altercation to avoid the vulnerability of ever needing them. And yet, she found herself not only needing them but truly wanting them all the more.

"Tess..." She looked up, but the voice was not derived from the man she had hoped it would be. Noting the disappointment that shone in her eyes, Charles added, "He would have come himself but I think he's still leery of your good aim."

"So he offered you up as the sacrificial lamb in his stead?" She wiped at her running mascara and chuckled, despite her disheveled appearance.

"Oh, no," he retorted with a wink. "I volunteered. Who knows? I may just get off on that sort of thing. Unlike Luci, I've never been one to turn down a little rough play." Crouching to meet her eye level, Charles extended a hand. "Come on, killer. I know where Gus hides all the good stuff."

CHARLES

Charles stared at the strange girl currently positioned across the counter from him. Strange and brilliant. In a way he hadn't seen before. Yes, strange, brilliant, and so unbelievably damaged.

Much like Luci, he thought to himself.

And yet, something about her had begun to slowly piece his friend back together. Where tragedy most often begot more tragedy, with these two, it somehow seemed to act as a salve. Likely because no one seemed able to understand them better than they were able to understand each other. It shouldn't work, he knew. It should have been disastrous. But it wasn't, and he would be a fool to think otherwise.

Then again, he was used to playing the fool. It was easier to watch others when all eyes were on you. It was easier to read the room. To decipher everyone's endgame. But now was not the time. He needed to drop his comedic mask, if only for a moment, or risk the calamity of Lucien facing yet another broken heart—both of the man's own doing. But still, self-destructive or not, Luci deserved happiness in his life. Even if it had to be shoved down his throat.

Of course, Charles wasn't stupid. Despite being Tessa's most vocalized proponent, it wasn't like he'd trusted the girl at first glance. In fact, when it came to most things, he didn't trust her as far as he could throw her. She could hide her every emotion except the one that poured from her eyes every time her gaze fell to Lucien. Ironically, neither of them appeared to realize it—how so unequivocally infatuated each was with the other. Instead, they were surrounded by insecurity. Immobilized by self-doubt.

Dumbasses, the lot of them. He laughed and shook his head before finally speaking his thoughts aloud. "She was never right for him, you know."

CHAPTER 28

THE SIMPLE WORD

CHARLES

CHARLES DIDN'T WAIT for his words to sink in before continuing. After all, she should have known by now that he would be eavesdropping.

"Luci was a different person back then. Hell, he was a different person after the accident. And now… now, I'd like to think he's a different person again. A better one." It was a rare form for Charles: his smirk faded, his eyes darkened, and his expression somber. A form he found as uncomfortable for Tessa to endure as it was for him to embrace. "Before the accident, our boy had never faced a challenge that money and status couldn't surpass. As horrible as it may sound, what happened to his legs… it was probably the best thing for him. It was something Luci had to face internally and externally. Something he had to do alone. It purged him of all the fake relationships in his life, forced him to make his own way."

He shook his head and thought back to a time when they'd both been different men. Before that night, before the crash, Charles would not have been the kind of friend who would be having this conversation. Who would have had any conversation that bordered so close to this level of sincerity. But seeing the aftermath of the wreck—the shattered glass, the cinched metal, all that blood—it's the kind of thing that sobers you. It urges you to realize your own state of impermanence and how, suddenly, everything is subject to change. How one minute you could be throwing back shots with a man you've known since childhood, a man on the rise, and the next you could be staring at that same man seemingly lifeless. Except for a series of inconsistent, shallow breaths you willed to be more than a figment of your own imagination.

Charles shuttered at the image, at the memory, and continued.

"Sure, I wish Luci had—or could—recognize that for himself, rather than tuck everything away. It may have taken him a long time to get here, but as an outside observer, I can tell you that man is smitten with you, dear. And not like I've ever seen him, certainly not like he was with Maddy. I do think he cared deeply for her, but part of it seemed to be out of sheer expectation. She was the type of girl he was supposed to marry. There was no thought process behind it; it was how things were done. However, with you, he has tried everything in his power to resist his impulses, and only finds himself further drawn in. She was the expectation but you, dear, you are the exception. One we do out of duty; the other we do despite it. Which one would you rather be?"

She shook her head and tapped her teaspoon against the sides of the porcelain cup, the rhythmic clanking acting in the place of the pacing her seated frame would not currently permit.

"Pretty words, Charlie. But lest you forget, I'm an expert in pretty words." She stared across the kitchen at nothing and no one. "And unfortunately, they're as empty and hollow as the tone in which you offer them to me right now."

"Hm, perhaps I've given you more credit than you deserve." He grinned, the playful lilt returning to his voice. "Because that's either naivete or blissful ignorance talking."

"Charlie, I'm really not interested in games right now… please…"

"Says the woman holding the dice."

Whether it was shock or annoyance that shot Tessa to her feet, Charles had yet to determine; however, he wasn't about to let her run off so easily. His thumb and forefinger caught the base of her wrist and clenched just slightly—the pressure enough to stop her from fleeing, but not so much that it would cause her discomfort. She hesitated, her eyes flicking back in his direction, before she returned to her seat and sighed. Or perhaps it was more of a huff. Like a child who'd just been scolded into submission.

"What do you want from me, Charlie." It was one of those questions that wasn't a question in the slightest. Therefore, he ignored it the same as if it hadn't been spoken and proceeded as if their conversation had never paused.

"Why do you think that the only enjoyment he finds is in his work? He's shut himself off from anyone who tries to get near him. Locking himself away in those dilapidated buildings, and at the risk of his own bloody health. It's not because he is as driven and as dedicated as he leads you to believe. No, he uses it as a shield to keep everyone at a distance—even me." He seemed to realize in that moment.

"I don't understand. He's always had an infatuation with architecture. This wasn't a career path he fell into, Charles." *Yes, Charles. Not Charlie.* "For God's sake, he's a fucking artist. He takes numbers, insignificant measurements, and transforms them into this." Tessa gestured to the open air. To the original, carefully curated barnwood beams. To the exposed brickwork. To the hardwood floors, which had been salvaged from a home that he could not. To each and every small detail that Lucien had obsessed over and had personally appraised.

"Hm, an artist, you say? I suppose so. But with his skill set, the bastard should be drawing up high-rises and skyscrapers. With his name alone, he'd win each and every bid in this city—fuck, in any city. But instead, he chooses the charity cases. The rundown structures that no one else wants. And he pours his heart and soul into them. Sure, he does have respect for preserving history; that's not a facade. But it goes so much deeper than that. Those broken buildings... he sees himself in them. Forgotten, unwanted, unusable. A mere shadow of what they used to be. In another life."

Charles shook his head. The truth always cut a little deeper when spoken aloud, and the full brunt of it seemed to level his shoulders and darken his tone.

"It's the same outcome every time: the immediate pride is replaced by the loss you can see in his eyes, almost as if he were expecting that in fixing the homes, he would somehow be fixed too. Then he moves on to the next project, the next repair, and the next disappointment. Because he will never be one of those homes; there is no fix for him. And until he realizes that there is nothing to fix in the first place, that his state of self-declared unworthiness—just because he is a different kind of man than the one he thought he was born to be—that it isn't a flaw. That it's part of who he is now. And that he deserves to be as adored as those remodels of his... Until *that day* comes, he will keep repeating the pattern over and over and over again."

"You act as if what he's done here is insignificant. As if it's all just been a placeholder until what? He finds a wife? What's wrong with putting your career above everything else? You say he chooses me despite his obligations, despite his long-term goals. I don't think keeping him from his life's work—something he's sweat and bled into —is a good thing. It's what he's always wanted to do. And now you're telling me he's distracted because of me. *And that's supposed to be a compliment?* He shouldn't have to choose between his accomplishments and whoever's warming his bedsheets. One of those lives on indefinitely while the other is fickle. One will stand tall long after his libido's had its fill and he's come to his good senses. And I've come to mine."

"You don't get it, do you? He loves his work, sure. But it was never his life's passion. It became that so he could keep himself from ever being passionate about anything or *anyone* else. Because he'd given up on ever having more. Hell, even hoping to have more... He constructs physical walls to fortify those long-standing emotional ones." Charles sighed. "Fuck, it's depressingly poetic when you think about it, Tess. Hm, it's funny though. He led *you* right on in, didn't he?"

"What do you mean?" she stammered, her eyes narrowing in on the man in front of her.

"The Victorian. He's never brought anyone to a jobsite before, let alone passed those walls..." Charles knew better than to let the significance hang in the air, fearing the girl may choke on the meaning. Instead, he changed tack. "He's resumed his PT, you know. Since meeting you." He didn't dare make eye contact, his gaze locked on his tea as he sipped. "You'd think he would have been more intent on his progress with how strenuous those renovations can be. But Luci's refused to do his required weekly appointments for years now, choosing his own regiment and forcing me to spot him. But more *recently…*" His gaze darted towards Tessa while he inflated the last word with emphasis. "Every Wednesday—like clockwork—he's been following the prescribed routine. And not being much of an ass about it either."

Her lips curled and her chest bounced with her subdued laughter, her resolve broken before the realization finally set in. "His two o'clock…"

Charles nodded. "Yep, his two o'clock. In the downstairs gym. I'm actually surprised you haven't asked about it sooner." He smirked, raising a single eyebrow, before again avoiding her glare and washing down another gulp of lukewarm liquid.

"So he's been lying to me. About where he's going? What he's doing?" she countered.

"Darling, your every word is peppered by lies and half-truths. Of which I'm certain are countless. You can't begrudge the man for keeping a few of his own."

TESSA

Well, fuck…

She should have had a clever retort, but her own state of reticence mocked her instead. Her heart had been torn from her chest cavity, dropped on the table in front of her, and fileted open. And neither her brain nor her mouth could process the relevance of it all. If truth be told, she wasn't sure what was more disconcerting, her lack of wit or the sudden depth of Charlie's character. Both facts left her crawling in her own skin, her toes dancing beneath the table and aching to barrel forward.

Flight. She was fucking better than flight.

She couldn't understand why facing Sterling was so much more terrifying than any physical altercation. She would give anything for Charles to just reach out and gut punch her. To force her to focus on something other than the reality of her unease. Ironically enough, that's what it felt like—a fist slamming into her abdomen, leaving her breathy and wordless. She hadn't been accustomed to this kind of fear in a very long time; or at least, if she had, she hadn't acknowledged it. And she didn't want to acknowledge it now either. But there it was, floating in front of her. Each little liquid letter spewing from his mouth and thickening the air, causing her to gasp upon inhale. When all she wished she could do was spit some back.

She chewed on this internal dread, rolling the self-destructive thoughts around her tongue as if she were cleansing her palate and preparing to dine on antagonism. Yes, she was still itching for a good fight. She stood, smiling through her throbbing cheeks, the meat of which she hadn't even realized she had been gnawing on. And dipped her head towards Charles, signaling her exit.

There was no point in pretending she had dialogue for him when it was clear he knew she did not. And this time, the suddenly somber wisecracker didn't care to stop her.

———

"Only a monster would call that non-dairy bullshit dessert. I don't know what it was, but it certainly wasn't ice cream." It was as good of an entrance as any, Tessa had decided.

It wasn't. It was childish, undignified. Arbitrary at best, and overly guarded at worst. However, her impromptu bout of juvenile regression was a problem for another day.

Sterling glanced up from the paperwork she knew he wasn't reading as she tore through the office door.

"I... um... okay," he stuttered, his head slightly craned to the side while his eyebrows knitted in confusion.

Without full cognizance of even her own intention, Tessa slammed her palms down onto the flat surface of his desk. She needed to speak before the look in his eyes left her dumbfounded for the second time that day.

"If it comes down to a story or you, I'll choose the story every time. Without hesitation. Without a doubt. Without a tear shed. I won't let anything or anyone stand in my way. Not you, not my friends, not family, not even myself. Just ask Corey." The mention of her partner's name stung as it left her lips, much more than the erratic journalist cared to admit. "I'll run off without question, without notice, without permission—though you should know better than to think I'd ever ask it in the first place. I won't play hostess, nor will I ever entertain the notion of being someone's perfect little housewife. This is who I am intrinsically. It's not a phase. I'm not some spirited girl looking to be tamed. I'm not someone who 'settles down' or follows suit. Or fits the mold. I break it. I crumble it. I shatter it. Do you understand?"

"I… yes, of course. Tess, do you really think that's what I want? For you to morph into some imaginary ideal that I have swimming in my head? Do you really think that little of me?"

She didn't know if it was Lucien's expression, his tone, or the combination that pierced her heart. Regardless, her shoulders slumped despite her willing them to hold form.

Tessa closed her eyes on an exhale. "I think that little of everyone. Everyone wants something, Lucien. You're no different and neither am I," she confessed.

"And what is it that you want?" His voice caressed her, soothed her, while his thumb reached out to do the same.

"Honestly, I don't even know anymore. But it's something. And it's not playing house. It's not giving up my dreams, and it's not meeting anyone's expectations of what it is I am supposed to do. Who I'm supposed to be."

"Fair enough. However, I do know what I want, Tess, and it's simple. I want you. Exactly as you are. This maddening—no, *infuriating* woman who's absolutely impossible to understand half the time and so incredibly readable the other. A woman who simultaneously drives me up a wall and then effortlessly lulls me back down. This utterly captivating creature who monopolizes my dreams and invades my nightmares. In a way I never imagined possible. You throw things at me. You break stuff on purpose. You act as though you own every room you enter—and somehow you do. You assimilate into any crowd but stand out like no other. You are passionate and intrepid, and yet hold back emotion as effortlessly as you dispel it. You're a goddamned paradox, and fucking hell if I don't love you for it."

"Take that back!"

"Which part, love?"

"That word, that part! All of it! None of it…"

"No. It's a simple word, or so I've been told." Her name parted his lips on a sigh. "Tess, I'm not asking you to change anything. Run off. Go chase that next story. Whatever and wherever it may be. And I'll be here waiting for you, my eyes glued to my phone even as you leave my texts on read, more than aware that you do it just because you know you can."

"I… why?" It was the only response that came to mind, the only viable question.

"Because I want to. It's as simple as that." He shrugged.

CHAPTER 29
THE OVATION

TESSA

WORDS WERE powerful as often as they were meaningless. They could incite fear or leave you feeling hollow. It all depended on the speaker, the intention, and how deliberately the pen was wielded.

Words like *Wednesday*. There was very little meaning behind that word for many people, but for Tessa, it left her curious.

And maybe not just curious, perhaps a little apprehensive as well. She should have known that Lucien was lying to her. Or at least sensed that he was hiding something. Instead, the man had this way of completely putting her at ease. Of removing any and all doubt—at least as long as she was in his presence. Because when Tessa was alone, with just her thoughts and innermost insecurities, self-doubt was all she ever felt. Sickening, mind-numbing, soul-shattering doubt.

So, yeah, she had secrets of her own, she supposed.

She'd waited until a quarter to three, giving the man a false sense of security before bursting through the heavy wooden double doors.

STERLING

"Huh."

He heard the hum of her voice before he could even register that the doors had flung open. And his heart sank. It was one of those moments in time. The ones that were unavoidable and you knew as much; however, the dark claws of denial sunk into your chest and you hoped above all hope that somehow you would be the exception. That living in the now would help you sidestep the truth. But there was no evading it. Reality.

———

"Luci."

"Stop calling me that!" It was funny—though certainly not in the haha way—how the sound of Maddy's voice, which was once comforting, somehow grated his ears as of late. Everything from "before" seemed to do the same. It reminded him of what he used to have, of what he'd never have again.

"Fine, Sterling, happy now? I'm not sure why you insist on going by your goddamn last name all of a sudden." She ignored his moods. She stood by his side and supported his slow-moving recovery, yet it served to only irritate him further. Maddy continued rambling as though Lucien hadn't just barked at her. "I spoke to Dr. Mattsson. He said you took two steps yesterday! That's

amazing! We should have you fitted for your tux soon. It could take months for Andre to get the measurements right." She hummed to herself, and her ever blossoming optimism was nothing short of maddening.

"What? You called my doctor?? What happened to patient confidentiality? How dare he disclose my medical information." Sterling was still getting used to the chair, therefore a slew of expletives followed when his wheels unexpectedly tangled in an abrupt curl in the area rug. *"And get this fucking piece of shit out of here, for fuck's sake."*

Ignoring his comment regarding her decor choices, Maddy remained single-minded in her reply, *"I'm your wife! Your next of kin. That's what I told him anyway."* She seemed all too pleased with herself when uttering that last part.

"You are not my fucking wife. You're not even my fiancée. We've talked about this! Goddamn it, Madelyn."

"Stop being ridiculous, Lucien. You are not running away from me. We just have to get things back to normal and then you'll see—"

"Back to normal? What the fuck do you mean back to normal! Things are never going back to normal. Look at me!"

"You blame me, don't you? That's what this is all about. Isn't it?" She pivoted to face him, her eyes dilated by unshed tears. Because Sterling was certain she had cried them all and there was naught one left.

"You know what? You're right." He verbalized the very fear that had been eating away at her hardened exterior, no matter how hard she tried to tuck it away. *"I do blame you. And I'm not crawling down the fucking aisle. Not with you. Not with anyone. Do you hear me?"*

———

He hadn't meant it. Not a word. Hell, if he thought he even had a chance at making her happy, he would drag himself through that church by his teeth. But this wasn't what she wanted. He saw it in the way she looked at him differently. In the hope that painted her face the first time she saw him take a step. Hope that things would get *"back to normal."* Hope that all this would be a distant memory. But there was no hope. The doctors had said as much. This was as good as it was going to get.

A few insignificant steps here and there.

Sterling would never walk again. Not like the man he was, not with his head held high. All he had in him was a shuffle of feet. He looked no better than a colt fumbling about on newborn legs.

God, if it wasn't for that fucking hope. If she could accept him as he was… maybe. Maybe one day he could get over his insecurities. But, no, that hope that moistened her eyes, it told him this wasn't what she wanted. More so than her words ever could. She didn't want to spend the rest of her life as a caregiver for a man who was now only half of one. And so he did what he had to, to push her away.

Even if it meant making her hate him.

He'd apologized after his outburst. It was true that he wanted her to move on. For her own good. But he also didn't want her living with the guilt. There was no reason for them both to be miserable after all. He didn't want that for her. He wanted her to have a life and he wanted to give it to her, even if it wasn't with him. And so, he let her go. It was the right thing to do. He apologized but made it clear that they'd never be together.

Not now. Not a year from now. Not ten. And she needed to accept that.

As much as he tried to forget her over the years, forget the life that was stolen from him that night, it was her eyes that somehow always haunted him. He saw them in his dreams. Staring back at him, reflected in the mirror, and forever breaking his heart.

The same way Sterling had shattered hers.

———

And all those emotions, so dishearteningly similar to the ones he'd felt five years ago, flashed through him again at seeing that same goddamned sparkle in Tessa's eyes. The same hope he'd been secretly fearing to see from the moment he met the woman.

"Get out…" Sterling didn't know if he was directing the command at Tessa, or the man still gripping onto his shoulder and forearm while guiding him around the room like an infant learning to toddle. And apparently neither did they, since each remained steadfast in his presence. "I said. Get. The. Fuck. Out." This time, the words bit the tip of his tongue even as he dispelled them. But she didn't move.

That girl's backbone could put a goddamned steel rod to shame, he thought to himself.

"Sir?" It was unfair to put Joe in this predicament.

Sterling's legs were shaking from both rage and exhaustion, his labored response resounding as barely a whisper. "Just take me to my chair, Joe. You're dismissed for the day. Thank you for your time."

The physical therapist dipped his head, before brushing past Tessa and shutting the doors with a *clink* that seemed to echo louder than usual in the tension-fueled office.

"Tess…" Her name was issued with a growl. "I already know what you're thinking and you can stop. This is it. There's no getting better. This is as much as I'll ever be. So, stop."

It was the truth. Nothing had changed. Those few steps… A *man*—for lack of a better word—with the capabilities of a two-year-old. No, less so. Because two-year-olds grew up and Sterling never would.

"Stop setting yourself up for the inevitable disappointment." His tone was seething, regretful, and something else—what he really meant was *him*. Stop setting *him* up for disappointment.

"Funny, seeing as that's not what I was thinking at all." Her omission caught him off guard. It was haughty, condescending. And, as always, it was followed by the raise of her brow.

"What do you mean? If not…"

"I was thinking that you must have liked having me on your lap, considering you've had the strength to push me off this entire time."

He didn't know how to respond to *that*. So, instead, he repeated the demand that seemed to slide off his tongue near effortlessly. "Tess, you've done your good deed. You've humored a broken man. Just go." It was far easier to push her away than face the eventual rejection he knew was coming. But it wasn't rejection or obedience that greeted him.

In the time that it took him to exhale, Tessa had diminished the space between them, landing a knee on each side of his pulsing thighs.

"So you've figured it out?" When his only inclination was to raise his own eyebrow, she clarified, "That the easiest way to get me to stay… is to tell me to leave." Again, she paused, her teeth marking the pliable flesh of his ear. When she seemed to get the reaction she intended, she pulled back.

As much as he was able to disarm her when she was at her worst, she could inexplicably do the same when he was certain he would not concede. When he was certain he needed to turn her away. And that was where she differed from Madelyn. *In spirit*. In tenacity. In her ability to twist and bend him to her will. And how she made him want to do it.

"Lucien…" The word parted her lips on a soft moan as his hands sought to both push her away and drag her closer. Logic, lust, and something more were constantly at war in her presence.

"Why do you insist on calling me that? You know very well if I wanted you to use my first name, I would have given it to you when we met." Though he intended to berate her, the softness with which he spoke suggested some small part of him liked the sound of it.

"Why, you ask…? Well, the answer is simple. I like the way my tongue caresses the roof of my mouth when I say it." She accentuated the click of her tongue as her hips held him hostage. "Why do you insist that I don't?" She repeated his name twice more when he refused to look at her.

"After…" He gestured to his chair, unable or perhaps unwilling to say the word *accident*, almost as if it tasted sour had he done so. "An older man, in the hospital, one who knew damn well he was never leaving that bed. Not alive…" Sterling hesitated. He'd never relayed this part of the story, his story, to anyone. And here he was, about to tell a woman whose sole purpose was to tell other people's stories. To make money off their tragedies. But the words came spilling out anyway. "I was at my worst then…"

———

He could smell the alcohol from where he was seated, the stench nearly as overwhelming as the odor of rot. Rotting flesh, rotting trash, and rotting souls. It was the last one that sickened Lucien the most, however. Because no matter how often the nurses came in to bathe him, the scent clung to his skin like a parasite embedding itself in his chest. An added weight that only sought to feed the crushing bitterness that resided there.

"Hey, boy." The old man was calling for him again. It was becoming routine. "Boy, get your ass over here, would ya?"

There was no point ignoring him either. The blue blood's patience had a tendency to run out long before the elderly fucker's vocal cords ever tired. "Lucien."

"God bless you." The long-term resident was fucking with the new guy again.

"No, that's my name. For the millionth time. That brain of yours working or should I tell them to pull the plug already, old man?"

Seeming to ignore the question altogether, Gerald—whose name Lucien did remember but refused to use until the sentiment was returned—gestured a shaky hand to his right. "Look out the window."

Humoring the man, though he wasn't entirely sure why, Lucien closed the distance between himself and the sill and peered out at the cemetery adjacent to the hospital wing.

"Tell me what you see?"

"Grass?"

Gerald smacked Lucien upside the head. "Stop being a smartass, boy."

"Fine. Graves. I see a bunch of fucking graves."

"If you're going to act like 'em, I'll treat ya like 'em. Don't know any of their first names either."

Sure enough, as Sterling continued to stare at the stone markers, the only letters he could make out in the distance were the bolded surnames chiseled across the tops.

———

"He used to tell me if I was going to act like I was already in the ground, then he was going to treat me like it. Said he wasn't wasting his time learning the first name of a dead man. I've been Sterling ever since. Reminds me things could be worse, I guess. And it lets me be someone else. I was brought into that hospital with one identity but I left with one of my choosing. It was easier that way. For everyone. To let that other version of myself die."

At first, when she didn't speak, Sterling had assumed he'd said too much. He hadn't known Tessa for more than a few months and here he was… unraveling his deepest, darkest, most grotesque truths and setting them out in front of her. A buffet of his insecurities for her to feast upon should she so choose. Therefore, when she finally did respond, her assessment was not at all what he was expecting.

"Why do you keep thinking I want to fix you? I met you exactly as you are. Didn't I? I don't know who you were before, but I honestly don't think I'd like him very much. He sounds sort of like a dick."

After the shock had subsided, Sterling laughed. "You're right. He was. But still a good-looking guy, if I say so myself."

The gyration of her hips was the only concession she offered; though the heat between her legs told him, at least physically, she agreed. And that attraction was mutual. He couldn't think, not rationally anyway. No, this woman owned him, perhaps more so now that he had purged his innermost thoughts for Tessa to do with as she pleased.

"Goddamn it, Tess."

"Stop fighting me," she countered, as if she could read his mind as effortlessly as she played the rest of him.

Despite his waning energy, her fingertips awakened his every nerve ending. And struck the man dumb. Too dumb to protect him from himself. Though he tried to fight the hold she had over him, the sensation of her grinding against his thighs shut his brain down just long enough for his heart to speak.

"You don't get it, love. I stopped fighting this the moment I fell for you. And I lost long before you knew you won."

She froze, perhaps as stunned by the weight of his sentiment as he was by the fact that he'd accidentally given it. It wasn't exactly a declaration of love, nor those three overly used and cliche words themselves, but he could tell she knew damn well what he meant. And Sterling was shocked when she didn't run, instead choosing to swallow his confession with a press of her lips.

"Tess, I'm trying to talk to you." The attempt was meager, but it was an attempt nonetheless.

"And I'm trying to avoid talking at all costs," she admitted.

"All costs, huh? Is that what you call this?" He gestured to her hands as they slid beneath his shirt.

"You have no idea what this costs me…" Her revelation was as disconcerting as it was ominous. Still, she didn't run. That in itself was progress.

And Sterling couldn't help but think that perhaps baby steps weren't insignificant after all.

CHAPTER 30
THE HEART OF THE MATTER

TESSA

IN ACTUALITY, it wasn't hope the journalist had felt when she'd first seen him stand. It was fear. As selfish as it sounded, she didn't want him to get better. She was honest when she said she liked him exactly as he was. He was safe. She could run. And he couldn't chase her. Until maybe he could. And it was that thought that made her realize what she had been doing all this time…

Running.

Where Sterling should have been another story to her. An end which justified the means. Somehow he had become more. And instead of analyzing her mark objectively. She had been in a perpetual spiral of overanalyzing quite *un*objectively, of avoiding that realization at all costs. And the end result was a story void of any sort of journalistic integrity. However, the only other option was worse—pulling the article ripped her of her *own* integrity. Her self-worth. So she had avoided the reality of what either path would mean for her.

Having made up her mind, Tessa stopped at her office to ensure her story would run before she stopped doing that herself.

Running…

From the world, from the truth, from her past.

What she hadn't expected to find was the man (one of many) she'd been running from. His eyes were soft as he stared back at her, his shoulder in its usual position, planted against the doorframe. He always had this way of observing her as if trying to untangle the web of contradictions that somehow made her both fascinating and infuriatingly complex. And instead of appreciating his admiration, she'd pushed him away. Like she'd done with everyone, anyone who tried to get close to her.

"Hey there, TK." Corey propelled himself from the threshold, but only chanced two steps in her direction. "I'd say *long time, no see.* But, considering how we left things, I'm assuming that's the way you wanted to keep it, huh?" As stoic as she tried to present her exterior, even Tessa would have to admit those words stung. When she didn't reply, he nodded towards her bandaged knuckles. "What happened?"

She shrugged, slamming her desk drawer shut before turning to face him. "Nothing. I just hit the bag a little too hard."

"Did the bag have teeth?" He knew better, and she knew he knew better. But still she lied. Somehow, it had always been easier that way. To only tell people what you wanted them to know, securing the truth close to your heart, where it couldn't be used against you.

She didn't answer him. What was the point? She would just spew more bullshit and he would call her out about it for a second time.

After a few more awkward moments of silence, he spoke up again. "Well, since you're here... I might as well tell you in person." For some unknown reason, Tessa's heart began to beat faster, as if physically foreshadowing whatever Corey was about to say next. "I've been thinking about it and you were right. About putting your career first. And it's time I do the same..."

He paused and the only thought that ran through her mind was: *he's leaving me.* It was an odd fear to manifest, considering she had been the one to force him out. But it plagued her nonetheless. He then dropped himself into the chair closest to the door as if guarding her only escape route should she try to flee. Now, that fear turned to panic. She felt trapped, like the walls were inching forward and boxing her in. Either he didn't notice her distress or he chose to ignore it, continuing to explain instead.

"Fitzy's sending me to New York. Giving me my own story. Since you made it clear you'd never step foot in that city again, he asked me to follow-up on that missing journalist from back in the day. The one everyone thinks was a mob hit—Fitz mentioned you knew the guy. Sebastian something..."

All it took was the mention of that city, that fucking name, and Tessa's world crumbled around her. She gasped for air, but the weight, the distress, would not allow her lungs to expand. There was no other way to explain the sensation of drowning, of suffocating, while cognizant of the fact that there was nothing tangible keeping her head below the proverbial water.

"You can't. No." She forced the words out, despite choking on them. And used the only card left in her deck. "If you care about me at all, leave it be. Please..."

Because the journalist knew exactly what happened to Bash, or at least she could assume, with what she was sure was a high level of accuracy. And her fear had nothing to do with the *Times* and every-thing to do with the Agostinos. Tessa didn't know what would happen to her, what would happen to Corey, if he went digging up the past she'd knocked over the head and buried—figuratively of course.

It was bad enough that Sterling had been snooping around the Russians. She couldn't put her best friend in danger too. She wouldn't.

"Seriously?" He shook his head before throwing her own words back at her—the ones she had spoken so effortlessly that day at her apartment. *"You're being ridiculous.* What's good enough for the goose is good enough for the gander, am I right? You said it yourself: the story comes first, Tess."

"Please..." She fell to her knees. It was pathetic but lately she felt like everything about her was. She thought she knew the consequences of her actions, had it all figured out, only to find that she couldn't be more clueless. Corey dropped down beside her, pulling her into his chest with a sigh. "Leave this one alone," she begged.

COREY

"I thought you always said the truth was more important…" He braced his chin on the back of her head, as she sobbed against his shirt. He'd never seen her cry before, never seen her walls drop so completely.

Heard it, maybe.

Assumed it, probably.

But never saw for himself.

"Not this truth…" she countered, and again he sighed.

"I'm sorry, dear, but you don't get to weaponize the truth while simultaneously bending it to your will. It's one or the other." Tessa refused to look up at him or even acknowledge the point he was trying to make and so he continued. "I'm not going to New York. I made it all up—I learned from the best, mind you. Tess, I would never, ever, ever, choose a story over you… Don't you get it? If that means I'll be remembered as a shit journalist but a great friend, well, I can live with that. I was just trying to get you to understand. To understand what you're doing with your life. With Sterling. Before it's too late."

He knew his deceit hadn't sunk in because she had yet to push him away. Though he also knew it was only a matter of time before her temper was unleashed.

"He's just a guy, Corey…"

Was she trying to convince him? Or herself?

"Yeah, well, I'm sure there are still people out there who'd look at you as just some girl. And we both know how wrong they'd be…"

"Who was it?"

"Hm? What do you mean?"

"Who told you to lie to me? This wasn't you…"

He smiled at her accusation. She was right. He could never be so devious on his own. Hell, if it wasn't for her own good, he wouldn't have even chanced it. In fact, he was still waiting for her to kick him in his balls. When he didn't answer right away, she threw an elbow into his gut.

"Laney," he grunted out his sister's nickname.

"That twat… What happened to chicks before dicks?" After another moment of silence, Tessa asked more to the air than anyone else. "What am I going to do, Corey? I already ran it…"

"I know you did. And I don't know, Tess. I really don't. But I have no doubt that if anyone can figure it out, it's you. You love him, don't you?"

"No."

"Liar."

"Yeah, that's what everyone says. It's what I'm good at, right?"

"See, that's where you're wrong. You're good at anything you set your mind to. You just haven't chosen anything else recently."

"I can't face him. Not after this."

———

Tessa waited until Corey had stepped out in search of a fresh cup of stale coffee from the break room, before drawing her phone from her pocket and hitting the name in her contact list. She took a deep breath, holding it in her lungs until the voice on the other end picked up. And she spoke as soon as she heard the recognizable sound that meant the call hadn't rung out.

"Do you still have that contact—the one you told me about?" The journalist paused for a response, then quickly added. "Yeah, I'm ready… I'm sure… I suppose you're right. It's time… Thank you. I'll be there."

Tessa powered down her cellular device, shoved it into her pocket, and exited out the side door when she heard Corey's footsteps making their way back down the hall, likely with two cups of the cheap stuff in tow.

STERLING

"What you do in your office is up to you. However, you put a whole new meaning to the term physical therapy." Charles grinned back at his friend, whose face was clearly postcoitally flushed.

"Funny." Sterling didn't even look up when his business partner had entered with the usual clever banter the man was known to offer.

"I know I am, aren't I?" Like the cat who ate the canary, Charles plopped himself in his usual seat facing the rectangular desk while Sterling slammed his laptop closed.

"I know you are awfully proud of yourself, but you had no right to intervene. That setup had your name written all over it."

"Hmm, and here I thought getting laid would finally help with that whole dark and broody thing you have going on." Charles flicked his wrist in an up in down motion, the gesture aimed at the tragic figure in front of him.

"You're right… about *that* anyway." Sterling nodded, his shoulders dropping, and as quickly as his anger had been roused, it subsided. "It's hard to stay angry at you when she's around."

"So you admit it. You're happy?"

"Of course I am. Look at her… look at what she has accomplished. And she doesn't need a damn thing from me."

Though Tessa wasn't physically in the room, both men could sense her presence. Sterling felt like his former self again. But then, nothing like that self at all. Like a self he could have been—shouldn't be—but a self he liked. A different self. A better self.

In enlivening the reclusive architect, the tabloid writer had managed to invigorate the air around him. And he felt lighter, though he would admit that the release of sexual tension had helped ease the burden he frequently carried on his shoulders.

That is, until Charles spoke the words both were thinking but only one of them dared to say.

"Except that story…"

"That's not why she's here…"

"You're right. I don't think that's why she's here either. But you do, or part of you does. That voice in the back of your head is screaming it —and that's exactly why you haven't pressed her about what she's been working on. You're afraid of what she might tell you. You're afraid of what she's after. And you're afraid that she's just like everyone else."

Sterling didn't need to agree; the observation was far too accurate to need a verbal confirmation.

"There's only one way to find out. Stop with the secrets. Both of you." Charles sealed his advice with the tap of his knuckles against the solid wood of the desk before standing and making his exit.

———

For someone who had suddenly seemed so worldly, doling out life lessons like he was a goddamn human fortune cookie, Charles was speechless when Sterling tossed the crumpled note at the showman's face, knowing that even the best advice was worthless when given a day too late.

Because when Sterling had shut off his office light, traversed the hallway leading to his bedroom, and opened the door, what he'd expected to see was the woman he'd just cut his chest open for and hand-delivered his heart to. Instead, he found an empty bed, the ghost of her perfume, and a handful of sentences scrawled across a monogrammed notepad—words barely adding up to a sentence. Hardly a complete thought.

I'm sorry. It was always real for me. Even when it wasn't.

—Tess

It was about the story. It had always been about the story for her. She had warned him as much, and yet he'd hoped. Foolishly, he'd hoped. And what's worse, he'd given her that perfect touch of tragedy. That selling point that was known to draw the reader in. It was going to be front-page news.

His image. His family. His ultimate heartbreak. She'd used him for it all.

And none of it mattered. Not a single betrayal, because he still loved the woman. And given the chance, he'd also forgive her.

Fuck, if that wasn't a knife to the heart…

EPILOGUE:
THE BEGINNING OF THE END

TESSA

THE SUN WAS SETTING *over the city's skyline as she parted the blinds to peer out the window, dust drifting with the movement before settling on the sill. The room itself carried the odor of stale cigarettes and staler dreams —the kind that had decayed long before the occupants had crossed the threshold.*

Tessa shot her gaze from left to right, taking in the brown atop brown interior while noting the irony of the tomb-like atmosphere. Yes, this was ambition's final resting place. And least of all spared: hers.

She'd grown tired of waiting for the older gentleman to greet her, so she'd slipped back into his office and, finding little of interest, perched herself against the cool glass and dwindling daylight.

He entered as if he'd been expecting her presence in his personal space, before crossing the distance and situating himself behind his desk. "Come in, sit down. May I offer you some water? Coffee?"

She rolled her eyes in response. She'd heard the click of the recording device, and clearly she was already "in" the room. There was little need for the bravado.

"No, thank you." She was finally able to choke out the unnecessary— however seemingly polite—refusal. Then, with a curt nod, she slipped onto the

grief-weathered chair in front of her, the faux-leather material groaning in time with her movements. As her counterpart removed a pen and notepad from his desk drawer, she leaned forward as if she were looking to reposition herself. But instead, she clicked the PAUSE button, halting the tape. "I'm well aware of what you're doing. And I don't take kindly to having my privacy invaded."

"Miss Owens, I had no intention of doing any such thing. If you'd let me proceed, I was in the process of seeking your permission. This is as much for your benefit as it is for my own. To protect us both." He chastised her as a parent would a child, and she was beginning to second-guess her decision to meet with the would-be paternal figure. "One professional to another," he continued as he gestured to her regressed posturing—her crossed arms barricading her against the emotional onslaught. "I'm sure you have your way of doing things. As do I."

A puff of air parted her lips before Tessa's internal debate ended with a concession. "Do as you must," she offered with a wave of her manicured hand.

Resuming as if the intermission had never taken place, he compressed the button with his left index finger, and the tape shifted back into gear. The whine of the mechanism, which had first alerted her to his deceit, once again carried over the silence in the air. "Before we begin, I have to advise you that our conversation is being recorded. And I must obtain your verbal consent to proceed. May we continue?"

She didn't trust his intentions. Nor his word at the moment. And while there was shared honor among thieves, was it the same for liars? She supposed not. Lies went down much easier; they were sweeter and far more palatable to digest.

Because if there was anything at all that liars shared in common, it was the knowledge that the harsher the truth...

TO BE CONTINUED...

THE SWEETER THE LIES

BONUS CONTENT:
THE FOX'S TALE

CHARLES

"Hold up, wait. What happened?"

"Were you paying attention to anything I just said?"

"I was! But you talk so fast!"

"Then you'll just have to keep up. Repeating myself takes away from the ambiance." Charlie flicked his wrist, as if to gesture towards a stage that only ever existed in the man's mind. However, the one thing the dramatist hated more than being interrupted was losing his audience altogether. "Fine. What's the last thing you remember?"

"…something about a wedding…?"

"Are you bloody kidding me?" *Crickets.* "Whatever," he huffed. "I was always a sucker for an encore." Charlie shifted back in his seat, crossed a leg over a knee, and cleared his throat. You could almost picture the spotlight zoning in on the man and his theatrics. "The beginning it is… Tessa Owens, the beautifully brilliant bitch that she was, was tasked with finding a story. But not just any story—*the* story. And, instead, she found herself a man. Cliché, I know. But what can I say? Everyone deserves to get laid now and then."

Especially a guy who hadn't gotten laid in years. But Charlie decided to leave that part out.

"Anyway, they had this whole enemies-to-lovers, will they/won't they thing going on. To the point you just wanted to lock them in a room and force them to figure their shit out—that's actually not a bad idea. I'll keep that one in my back pocket for later..."

"Charlie..."

He grinned with the wave of a dismissive hand before continuing once more. "Right... keeping on track. The cat and mouse game ended at Daddy Owens's house, where unbeknownst to me, they finally did the deed—thank fuck. And everything seemed to be hunky-dory until my girl got cold feet and left poor Luci high and dry. Did I mention her best friend is a dude? And by dude, I mean Michelangelo's inspiration for David in modern form. Complicated, am I right? Can't make this shit up even if I tried. So my boy couldn't get over his issues and was overcome by jealousy. Who could blame him? Someone is bound to catch feelings when they both look like that."

Charlie leaned forward in his seat as though he were about to divulge the biggest secret. "Now here's the real kicker. Tessa had more secrets than we thought—the chick was not only mixed up with a couple of con men, she also had ties to the goddamn mafia! Which understandably left her on edge and forced my hand. I mean, meddling is what I'm good at. What I do. Why stop now?"

He shrugged. "So I maneuvered a couple of chess pieces on the board, hoping to force the two to come to terms with their issues, and my plan seemed to backfire. Tessa ran off, Luci sought comfort in the bottle, and here I am waiting for the next shoe to drop..." Charlie sighed before leaning back in his chair once more.

PROLOGUE
THE SOURCE

"DOES HE KNOW?"

"Which part?"

Tension thickened the air like black smoke, though it was somehow harder to choke down. While the girl's precocity could be charming at times, at the moment, he could think of several other choice adjectives and none of them were as complimentary. Flaring his nostrils with a huff of forced air, he pressed the bridge of his nose with his thumb and forefinger before speaking. She enjoyed taunting him, feeding off the prickling of his skin as if it were a life force of its own. Therefore, indulging her would be counterproductive.

"Miss Owens..."

"Is this really necessary?"

Answering a question with a question. It was an avoidance tactic. He knew it. She knew it. And each knew the other knew it. "Would I ask you otherwise? Do they—does anyone—know he was your mark?"

"How the hell am I supposed to know what you would do?" The retort was gritted between her hard-set teeth but he heard it all the same. Anger this time. When flight didn't have the desired effect, she'd reverted to fight. "I suppose he knows now, at least some of it. Considering how I left things... Does it matter? It's not like the story is printed under my name. Nothing ever is..."

"As if that's any sort of comfort? Did you even realize who you were messing with? The money they have! The connections!"

"Don't you lecture me. Don't you dare. I know full well the consequences and what it cost me. What it continues to cost me. But we all make choices, don't we? We carve out our own paths, and backtracking does little more than hinder our progression. So what's the goddamned point?"

"You tell me? What IS the point of self-reflection? Of reviewing our past mistakes, so that our future course is less offtrack?" When she didn't respond, he pressed further. "And... did you have feelings for him? At any point during the assignment?"

"No, of course not." She spun on her heel as if the very idea propelled her forward. "Do you think I make it a habit of crossing professional boundaries? He had something I wanted, and I got it. End of story."

"I see..."

"Are you insinuating I deserved this?" Anger was perhaps too weak of a word for what the woman was; she seethed. And she was goading him. She wanted to argue. More than that, she wanted a physical altercation. He could see it in her eyes. But she couldn't fight her way out of this one.

Not this time.

CHAPTER 1
THE DEVIL IN DISGUISE

STERLING

YES, despite the fact that moments ago he'd been kicking her out, ordering Tessa to leave, he couldn't stop himself from chasing her. It didn't make sense. Then again, nothing did when it came to this woman. A woman he'd only known for a few months and yet had somehow embedded her talons in the depths of his soul. A woman who, unlike his first love, he couldn't let go.

Because his first love, he'd come to understand, had never been that at all…

Though Sterling had spent years pining over Maddy, he realized it wasn't the woman herself who left him wanting; it was the idea of her. The idea of what she was to him and what he was *with* her. He realized he'd never really been pining for *her*. Selfishly, he'd been pining for the life he thought he'd have with her. And that's where the two women differed the most.

If he was going to accept the fact that she was leaving him, he needed more than a few lines scrawled across a piece of paper. He needed to see her, to hear her say the words, to believe they were true. He didn't care that the cost was his pride. He'd lost that the first time she'd seen him struggle to crawl into bed. He lost it the moment he'd lost everything to her.

That being said, as he pulled up to her apartment building and witnessed her standing outside in the arms of another man, the myriad of emotions that struck him like a condemned man facing a firing squad were at the time unrecognizable. Jealousy, of course, but it wasn't until he'd downed his fifth glass of Scotch that he was able to dissect that there was more to it than that.

Yes, jealousy was the easiest to name. Sterling had been jealous of the fucking blonde Adonis from the moment he'd first seen Tessa walk away on the man's arm at Maddy's wedding. Back then, the architect had been far too bullheaded to admit it, but clearly his affection for the woman had a way of disarming even the strongest of his personality traits.

If it had just been the green-eyed monster that plagued him, he could move past that. That emotion was superficial and easily shed. Even if it was his best default setting.

However, the louder voices, the deepest fears, the ones he was still trying to drink away were those that told him how idealistic the pair looked together. Tessa in the arms of that other man. A name that still bothered him to utter out loud.

There was that jealousy again.

He knew better; he knew the relationship was platonic. When Tessa was in his bed, Sterling knew that anyway. But having left him, that statement was far harder to swallow, the image of them together on the sidewalk worse still. She looked like she fit perfectly beside him. She didn't have to look down at him, or ensure that the building was wheel accessible before entry. She wouldn't have to call ahead before making dinner reservations to ensure the doorframes were within compliance. She wouldn't have to dedicate her life to being a caregiver before the age of thirty. She could have children with someone like Corey…

There was so much she would have to give up to be with Sterling, and despite the words she'd spoken about liking him the way he was (before she'd left him anyway), she didn't truly understand what that meant. What it might mean in the future. She couldn't. And the architect couldn't fault her for that.

Maybe it *was* jealousy after all. Just not in the traditional sense. It was jealousy over the kind of life the other man could offer her, a life that had nothing to do with money and everything to do with normality. Tessa deserved normality. She deserved to be taken care of, not the other way around. So, yes, he was jealous of Corey. Sterling was jealous because he would give it all away, every cent, if it meant he could stand by her side and hold her like the other man had today.

Therefore, it hadn't been anger that had compelled him to instruct his chauffer to drive away, after witnessing the two embracing on the sidewalk like two protagonists at the end of a romantic film. It had been his deep-seated affinity for the girl, which had caused him to choose her well-being over his own.

As if history were repeating itself.

Fuck.

He slammed his glass down on the kitchen counter, the expensive crystal nearly shattering in the process. Not that he would have cared if it had. After breaking things off with Maddy, Sterling had felt nothing. Too numb from the trauma and the cocktail of pain meds. But now, with Tessa, he felt everything. Even as he tried to dull the ache. Alcohol had brought him to the lowest point in his life, and here he was again, seeking its comfort. He'd avoided the stuff during his recovery, partaken rarely since then. But, tonight, the burn lessened the twinge in his heart. He didn't care what tomorrow would bring, nor did he want to throw himself into his work. If he couldn't feel her next to him, he wanted to feel nothing instead. Or, at the very least, try to feel nothing.

———

When the article was thrown down on his desk a week later, Sterling wasn't even surprised. Nor was he bitter. However, he hadn't found the numbness he'd sought either. It was jealousy that continued to ebb in and out, haunting his already tortured soul. Jealousy directed at the one man who seemed to have everything Sterling lacked. It wasn't rational. He knew this. He knew the emotion was misplaced. But that knowledge did little to assuage the sting. It was easier to be mad at

Corey, easier to blame the other man rather than himself. And, above all, it was easier to be angry than it was to be heartbroken.

For the tenth time that morning, he skimmed the headline. <u>From Debutant Darling to Drunk and Disorderly: A Billion Reasons for DeLacy's Deceit</u>. It'd become a feeding frenzy after the initial article, and everywhere the architect turned, it was either his name or Maddy's acting as the media's cannon fodder. He swept his arm across the desk, tossing aside the black and white words that seemed to taunt him from the page. Despite the distance, the print continued to plague him from its nest on the floor.

It was like the woman had never existed. He couldn't even seek the comfort of reading her name printed alongside his own, as deranged as that observation sounded, because she used a fucking pseudonym. Other than the toiletries Tessa had left behind, it was as if their paths had never crossed. He raked his fingers through the unkempt and overgrown knots currently occupying the top of his head—far different from the usual trim cut he sported—and cursed the world, and God, and himself.

He knew. He'd *known*. From the moment he'd laid eyes on the woman, he knew she would be his downfall. And here he was, somehow unprepared for how truly far he'd plummeted.

Twenty minutes later, Sterling found himself outside her apartment, though he hadn't remembered the drive there. And after an additional five spent staring into the grain of the wooden door, he knocked. No sooner had the hinges begun to creak, than he'd realized the gravity of his mistake. Because fate continued to be the type of twisted bitch that loved to mock him to his face. And, in doing so, he was met by the only person who obsessed his thoughts nearly as much as Tessa.

As he glared at the man, hoping his stare alone could manifest flames, he heard a soft voice call out from behind the towering figure. And though he couldn't make out the words that were spoken in the form of a purr, looking at the man's state of undress, it didn't take a genius to realize exactly what he'd interrupted.

For a moment, Sterling was conflicted. He was delusionally relieved by the familiar sound, at the idea of being this close to her again. And at the same time, he was enraged, despaired, and frozen by the materialization of his innermost fears.

"You love her. Just admit it already." Those hadn't been the words Sterling had originally planned on divulging, but they were the ones that fell from his lips nonetheless.

"You're absolutely right. I do. Wholeheartedly."

COREY

It took a beat for Corey to realize the meaning behind the question, or rather the *accusation*, meeting him at Tessa's door. And so he was certain his silence acted poorly against him. He also knew he should choose his response carefully; however, where was the fun in that?

Might as well give his accusers what they wanted.

"You're absolutely right. I do. Wholeheartedly." He paused, allowing the admission to sink in before attempting to tamp down the fire behind the other man's eyes. "But not in the way you're implying and not in the same way you seem to love her." Corey took a step back, offering Sterling entry with the gesture of his arm and a shake of his head. "I love her like I love my mother. Like I love any one of my seven sisters. Sometimes more, others less. But never outside *that* level of familiarity. And here I'd thought you were a more observant man."

"I don't understand." Though he spoke, Sterling was scanning the room for Tessa's presence.

"Clearly. And I know what you're doing, but she's not here. She hasn't been since…" Corey didn't finish the statement, which would have ended with "since she left you." Instead, he allowed the knowledge to thicken the air.

After several awkward minutes, the source of the female voice made herself known behind the sparsely dressed Irish cowboy, who seemed none too shy when it came to answering the door half-naked. The girl was, at most, in her early-twenties. And when she giggled, her age appeared a quarter of that. She seemed to understand some unspoken cue, and rather than introduce herself, she continued to wrap the bedsheet around her torso and escape to the privacy of the restroom.

STERLING

Sterling rolled his eyes. It must have been a sick sense of optimism that had led him to first believe the sound that now assaulted his ears had belonged to Tessa. Optimism or masochism. Which, he wasn't entirely sure.

As the architect maneuvered himself into the shared dining room/living room area, Corey held out a bottle of water as any good host would. It was odd being in Tessa's space. Throughout their entire relationship, Sterling hadn't spent more than a few moments outside her door. So, entering the apartment was odd indeed. Odd and strikingly intimate.

The interior was sterile, the walls practically bare outside of the occasional family photo. It was almost as if she left the space as she did most things. Dispensable. Able to be dropped on a whim. However, she couldn't help but sprinkle the same pops of yellow she would use to accentuate her daily attire. She was drawn to the color and it showed in her otherwise gray, impersonal decor choices. The architect took note of how not a thing was out of place (other than the large man now standing in her living room) further showcasing her need for control in all aspects of her life.

Returning to reality, Sterling focused on the source of his obsession, rather than his present surroundings. "Do you know where she's been? Where she is now?"

Corey didn't answer, instead countering with a comment of his own. "I'm surprised it took you this long. Figured you would have been here as soon as the story made print—you have seen it, haven't you?"

Sterling sighed. *Seen it? Of course, he'd seen it. And every article since.*

Reaching into his breast pocket, he tossed the crumbled pages onto the counter. As they had been for the last few days, the words stared back at him, smirking at his distress. If that were even possible.

It seemed like an eternity had passed before Corey spoke up again, but really it had been no more than a minute or two. It appeared as if the man didn't know whether to laugh or yell, therefore, his voice came out more as a half-hearted, ironic chuckle. "*That* is not her article. You have no fucking idea, do you?"

CHAPTER 2
THE RECORD

SHE SHOULDN'T HAVE BROKEN into the office. Then again, that could be said about many of the choices she'd made recently. There were so many things Tessa shouldn't have done, and regret was a poor bedmate. So she chose to not have any. Regret, that is. She needed to hear *it* herself, not just from her own mouth but as an outside observer.

Her fingertips traced along the PLAY button. The device was archaic; it still used cassette tapes. However, somehow, that was fitting. She did always have an appreciation for antiquities. And, nowadays, they reminded her of Sterling, the man she thought of with fondness and regr—

No, she promised herself she wouldn't use that word.

Deciding that she wanted to only face one demon of the past in this moment, Tessa finally elicited the pressure needed to set the recording into motion, her eyes following along with the typed transcript. After a few minutes of static, the voices began to project through her headphones:

. . .

Q: Come in, sit down. May I offer you some water? Coffee?

A: No, thank you.

Q: Before we begin, I have to advise you that our conversation is being recorded. And I must obtain your verbal consent to proceed. May we continue? [PAUSE]

A: Yes.

Q: Great. So please, for documentation purposes, can you tell me your full name and current age?

A: Tessa Kolette Owens. I'm twenty-six years old.

Q: Thank you, Miss Owens. I'm happy to meet you, however, I am sorry for the circumstances...

A: Yes… thank you.

Q: I have reviewed your paperwork. But, in your own words, can you tell me what brings you here today?

A: The story of a lifetime.

Q: Can you be more specific?

A: My lifetime.

Q: I'm sorry, but I must ask again. Can you be more specific?

A: [AUDIBLE SIGH] I was kidnapped, raped, and nearly murdered. Hmm… it's funny… I've never said that out loud before. To anyone. Not even myself. It feels dirty to say those words. It feels like saying them gives them some sort of [PAUSE] power.

Q: They're just words, Miss Owens. The only power they have is the power we ourselves give them.

A: Exactly. And what you say now, it's the same. Your words have meaning because you say they do. No other reason.

Q: You're deflecting the conversation. We don't have to do this, you know? We can reschedule? There's no pressure to proceed.

A: No, let's get this done.

Q: Okay, I have some forms for you to fill out. You will need to sign here [PAUSE] and here before we proceed. Please note, Miss Owens, this is your choice. Do not feel obligated to sign anything under duress.

A: I bet you say that to all the girls.

That had been enough, more than enough, for today anyway. The journalist quickly slammed her index finger down on the STOP button, before ejecting and pocketing the tape. He really should update his archival system to the 21st century—without an electronic backup, he had nothing more than his notes, his scribblings to fall back on.

Not that it mattered at this point. What was done was done. However, Tessa couldn't help but seek out this little bit of satisfaction, knowing that her story, her voice, was still her own. That she controlled its final resting place. Because it had always been about control, hadn't it? That's what everyone else had insisted. All her fears, all her self-destruction and manipulation had been about regaining that little bit of control to counteract what she'd subconsciously felt she'd lost all those years ago.

Though, regardless of how much self-realization she unearthed, a part of that was still intrinsically her. It would always be her. And she would always seek out the comfort she found in these little acts of regaining control. Of dictating her own path. And *that*… that made her smile a little bit. She hadn't lost herself; she'd found it. She was still finding it. She had embodied it and owned it. The good, the bad, and the grotesque. All of it. Her flaws didn't make her weak. They made her human. And human meant she was allowed to feel, rather than try to avoid vulnerability at all costs. This was what she'd discovered after facing only one of the many demons from her past…

COREY

His physique was nothing to be humble about; however, lifting dead weight was very different from working out at the gym. Combing a hand down his face, he had no choice but to reach out to Charles. Though Corey didn't know the man well, the assclown was listed as Sterling's emergency contact in his cell phone.

After reading Tessa's article, Tessa's actual article, her ex (or was he?) had drunk himself into a stupor. Corey hadn't even noticed the fucker had a flask tucked into his suit jacket, until he was already two sheets to the wind. He must have started early in the day. That, or the guy's tolerance just wasn't what Corey was used to, being a good Irish Catholic boy and all.

The pounding on the door, rapid and impatient, alerted him to Charles's arrival. The usual jovial expression that seemed to accompany Sterling's counterpart was noticeably lacking. Not that Corey would blame him. The conversation had been awkward to say the least, especially considering the redhead he'd picked up in the bar was still making herself scarce in Tessa's spare bedroom.

That's what he got for trying to have a life of his own, or so he told himself.

"So, remind me again exactly what happened?" Charles the

showman was gone and in his place was the concerned best friend of a broken man.

"Help me drop his ass off in Tessa's room and then we can exchange bedtime stories." Both men glared at the figure slumped over in his chair before plopping the architect, clothes and all, onto the queen-sized bed piled high with accent pillows.

———

The Maverick—Chicago's highly prestigious literary source—employed the top, most influential journalists in the Midwest. The content ranged from political interests and embedded newscasting to lighter topics on health and beauty. But no column was more sought out by writers and readers alike than the "Spotlight" feature, whose frontrunner for the past few years without interruption had been TKO, otherwise known as *The Knockout* columnist. The guy was a legend among men, and *she* was neither a guy nor a man…

Because she was none other than the city's own Tessa Owens, never claiming to be male but assigned the gender nonetheless. And *her* article (the real one) was currently clutched in Charles's hands as he took in the same information that had driven Sterling to drink. Her identity was obvious; at least it should have been if the man had pulled his head out of his ass and asked the questions he'd been so afraid to face, and she had been just as afraid to freely give. So, instead, both had assumed. Assumed the worst of each other. Assumed one was nothing more than a Tabloid writer and assumed the other would never accept the truth.

"Kolette," Corey answered the question that Charles had been thinking to himself. It was obvious in the way his brows furrowed. "Her middle name is Kolette. It's not too hard to see why she chose TKO—well, that and her left hook."

"Her parents actually named her that? Gave her those initials?" If you knew Tessa's parents, this was not as incredulous as Charles made it out to be.

Corey laughed before responding, "You met Jack. You should know the answer to that. Though, I don't think Em knew the significance when she agreed to the name."

After pouring himself a drink of his own, Charles loosened his posture and began to read more than the pseudonym, which had first grabbed his attention. <u>A Sterling Legacy: From a Silver Spoon to a Silver Lining.</u>

"I don't understand?"

"As is the theme of today's events..." Corey shrugged.

"But there's no mention of Maddy or what happened *that* night... Did she sell the story? The photos? Contact the press and go into hiding?"

"Fuck you. If Tess was going to tell anyone the story, she would have told the world herself. You honestly think she would take a payout? *That* is her story. *That* is what she wanted to say. And those... those aren't even the photos she took. They're similar but they aren't the same. Those look professional, definitely not from a cellphone camera." As soon as he uttered the words, he knew. It all clicked and Corey knew. The photographer from the wedding, the same photographer who'd been lurking the night of the charity event, the same photographer who'd been in earshot for the entirety of the drunken confession. "How ever the fuck the other media outlets discovered your friend's little secret, it wasn't from Tess and it sure as fuck wasn't from me. Which is probably why the fucker did a little drunken soul-searching—guilt will do that to you."

CHAPTER 3
THE BLUFF
A FEW WEEKS PRIOR

TESSA

TESSA HAD IMAGINED some dramatic scene, the sort of thing where she would bust through the door and shout, "Stop the presses!" The machinery would screech to a halt and a heavyset man with half a cigar and a bowl cap would step in her way before spitting out some colorful 1950s lingo such as, "Not so fast, little lady." But this was real life and that's not exactly how magazines were run anymore; though Fitzy was not too far off from the iconic image in her head as she turned the knob to his office and flung the door against the beaten-down rubber stopper that remained the sheetrock's only saving grace.

The older Irishman didn't have a hat or a cigar, but a cigarette parted his lips and a slew of discarded Styrofoam coffee cups crowded his desk as if they were a prized collection he was seeking to amass.

"I'm pulling my article." Tessa slammed her hands onto the only clear space in front of her, her nails digging into the veneer of the cardboard-like surface. The stickiness of the spilled cream and sugar did little to dissuade her as she stood shoulders wide and palms spread. She was met by a half chuckle, nearly a grunt, before her counterpart realized she was serious.

"Funny, TK, but stick to journalism. Comedy ain't really your thing, darlin'." He took another puff of his cigarette before drilling the butt into the overgrown, soot-tinged ashtray, which was no more than an unkempt graveyard for crumpled tobacco ends. A tribute to how gray his lungs were likely tinctured over the years.

"And comebacks don't seem to be yours. Don't make me repeat myself, Fitz." Tessa maintained her stature, daring the editor to argue, to force her to pull her metaphorical punches—her still-bandaged hand had enough of the literal ones. For now anyway. She was itching for a fight with someone other than those closest to her. Someone she could sink her teeth into and tear away with a piece of flesh still embedded in the space between her molars. Without the least bit of regret weighing her down.

Her posturing forced the man to open his coat pocket and, whether out of habit or discomfort, withdraw another cylindrical white tube from the packaging to replace the one he'd just obliterated. He lit the end before inhaling as if the concoction of chemicals included a hint of courage.

"I think you fail to realize some things, Miss Owens. One, it ain't your article. You submitted it. *That* makes it mine. Two." He held up a second finger as if to ease Tessa's ability to count. "Unless there's been a title change 'round here, the only one fixing to kill a feature is yours truly. And I'd have to be daft to even consider it. That story is pure fucking printed gold." He crossed his arms before continuing. "What's this all about? You fishin' for a raise or some shit?"

At this, the towering journalist had to throw her head back and laugh. She lowered herself onto the upholstered chair in front of him and crossed her ankles on top of the ledge of the desk, one sneaker bracing the other. Leaning back, she mimicked his relaxed posture, before a slow grin curled the corners of her lips.

"You really want to play this game, Fitz? How long have you known me? I don't need a dick between my legs to have bigger balls than you do, *darlin'*." She paused, letting her words thicken the air. Then, tilting her head to the left and raising an eyebrow, she continued. "However, if you want to make this about money, let's do just that. Print the story as is, *my story*, because sure as shit, *mon amie*, till the day I die and long after, that story is mine. But, by all means, print the story. And the moment you do, I walk out that door and take the offer from the Times. They called again, just last week, mind you."

"Bull-fucking-shit," he grunted, though she could tell by the tremor in his throat that he wasn't entirely sure if she was bluffing. "Nothing those pricks offer you will get you to step foot in the city again. You've said as much yourself."

Her grin dropped to a small smirk, a subtle indentation to the hollows of each cheek. "Try me." Then silence, nothing other than the rhythmic inhale and exhale that flared her nostrils and the rapid heaving of a man who smoked one too many Newports, filled the room.

"For fuck's sake, girl," he huffed. "What in the hell do you expect me to do with a blank headliner? Throw a coin into the wishing well and pray for some good luck?"

"What's more promising than the luck of the Irish, eh?" she quipped before tossing a folder over the stack of cups and onto the narrow opening in front of him.

"What's all this then?" Fitzgerald glared down at the file before squinting his eyes back up at Tessa.

"Like I would ever leave you hanging, *mon petit râleu*. That." She gestured to the papers now fanning the older man's features as he thumbed through the neatly typed composition. "Is your missing feature. The digital copy is in your inbox. You're welcome." Tessa stood, pivoting on her heel before calling out over her shoulder. "New York real estate is expensive. Don't force me to call in those favors, Frank. I'd hate to waste that kind of leverage just to prove a point."

He shook his head, momentarily pausing her progression through the door. "This isn't what your readers are expecting. They'll see it as a bait and switch, kid. Ya sure you don't want to print under a different name? Save your reputation?"

Tessa froze, steeling her spine and raising the drop of her chin. "The readers want my writing; that's my writing. Take it or leave it. We agreed on a story about that family and I gave it to you."

"I know that's how you see it…" he prodded.

But the journalist was quick to obstruct his flow of words, widening the space between the door and herself. "I see things how they are.

Don't you ever doubt that," she affirmed before slamming the tempered-glass frame shut and allowing her steps to echo down the hall.

Switching the headliner was a risk. However, risk was never something Tessa had feared, or at least not in any sense she was willing to admit. This moment was career-defining, possibly career-ending. Either way, it'd been her choice to make and it was one she would stand by.

It was true. She swore for more reasons than she cared to list presently that she would never return to New York. That being said, she was not one to bluff with no follow-through. She would ignore every nerve ending screaming at her otherwise, pack her belongings, find an obnoxiously overpriced studio apartment in the city, and cash in on the standing offer she repeatedly rejected on a monthly basis from the pigheaded copy editor who had once deemed her worth no more than the height of her skirt. And she would do it all on the grounds of sheer principle and to prove, despite so many thinking the opposite, that her word held merit. That she meant what she said and she didn't brandish empty threats.

The knowledge was hard to swallow but she would not back down. That's what this world wanted, a pretty doormat, someone to bend to their will, for the benefit of those self-imposed alpha males. The ones who sought to bark louder, and the ones with little actual bite. Tessa would not cower. She would not tuck her tail between her legs and she sure as hell was not afraid to snap her jaw a few times more than necessary, if it meant getting her point across. This was a fact she had seemed to forget over the past few weeks, and one she was seeking to remember.

She'd determined, as if suddenly self-aware, that society was cannibalistic. The thought of it was dark, taboo. But true nonetheless. Everyone was guilty of it. Hungered for it. The taste of flesh between our teeth as we bit into our fellow man and tore away part of him. For our own benefit. It was a realization that had haunted Tessa more recently. The way mankind seemed to nourish itself, whether it be ego, the need for validation, or purely for sport.

Her readers were guilty of it as they licked their lips, thirsting for the next sip of gossip they hoped to find between the pages. And Tessa, just as much so as she fed off the self-worth the sponsorship supplied her, with each magazine purchased and click of the mouse hovering over SUBSCRIBE.

She'd recognized that we each took a piece from each other, often ripping off far more than we'd given in exchange. In the wake of this societal human sacrifice, we left our fellow man broken: emotionally, spiritually, physically. It was eye-opening, the concept that we rarely took time to observe the aftermath, to truly know those we fed off. We'd already stolen what it was we sought before discarding the remnants. The broken shards. And that's what she had become. What Lucien had become.

Though, there really was so much beauty in imperfection. In the flaws that made them both consumer and the one being consumed. If only either of them could step back long enough to see past themselves. To see past what they thought they wanted and find what it was they actually needed. But until that time came, Tessa could no longer participate in that vicious cycle, to continue to feed off humanity, just to try to replicate what it was she was missing in herself.

CHAPTER 4
THE JOKER CARD

PRESENT

STERLING

FOR A SECOND, waking up to the hint of her perfume, Sterling thought the last few weeks had all been a dream. *A nightmare.* Like those that had plagued him over the years. But it was only a second before the throbbing in his head and the ache in his chest told him what he already knew. Reality was far worse than anything his sleep-deprived brain could conjure up. Because, instead of waking up to the ethereal creature whose voice remained no more than a whisper haunting his subconscious, it was a deeper octave that greeted his pounding temples.

"Rise and shine, Sleeping Beauty. Your Prince Charming hath arrived!" Charles swung the door open, neither cognizant of nor concerned by the impact of the brass knob hitting the unprotected drywall.

Sterling cringed as the sound seemed to vibrate from his ocular bone to his toes. Though he could recall the events of the night before, they sat on his chest, feeling both distant and all too palpable—as if they were somehow the memories of a stranger, who had unwittingly deposited them into Sterling's mind by mistake. As if any minute that person would come to reclaim them…

———

What was that saying? Something about never drinking with an Irishman? The exact phrasing eluded Sterling, but it didn't make the words any less true. The first glass had warmed his chest while the subsequent four had left him with an uncomfortable chill—the sort of numbness that was no longer appealing.

The conversation had been civil, at first anyway. Sterling had been in control of his facilities after the incident at the front door. But the longer he sat across from the man, his actions fueled by both alcohol and unresolved emotions, the harder it became to subdue his lingering insecurities. The accusations seemed to manifest as if of their own accord.

Sterling could blame the whiskey, the sedation of his sensibilities and propensity to manage them. He could blame the useless lumps of meat, which by all appearances remained physically sound and yet mocked him each morning when the slight tingling dulled to an unremarkable nothingness. He could blame the man who occupied Tessa's apartment as often as she seemed to occupy Sterling's own mind. But all the pointed fingers would do little to alleviate what troubled him.

Even knowing as much, the question was spat amongst the heavy, intoxicated breath that filled his mouth before grinding against his teeth. And the taste overstayed its welcome; it was bitter. "Have you slept with her?" Despite feeling the words bounce off his tongue before reverberating against his eardrum, Sterling himself hadn't even realized he'd spoken.

Thought it? Yes, more than once over the course of the night. But his own voice sounded foreign, tinged by a brokenness that crippled him far more than an accident ever could.

"Not yet. You barged in here, remember?" Corey rose his glass to his lips before emptying its contents in a larger than necessary gulp.

Everything about the man was larger than necessary, especially his ego. It was a strange thought but it manifested all the same.

"I'm sorry?" He wasn't. It was, however, polite to say so—and as was true to his breeding, Sterling tried at the very least to remain polite.

"The redhead. Can't for the life of me remember her name..." Corey punctuated the statement with a grin, suggesting he hadn't even asked it.

"No. Tess. Have you slept with Tess? For fuck's sake. I don't care about the

redhead…" The shake of his head. The roll of his eyes. The heavy sigh. None of it verbalized the response Sterling needed to hear. "Before, after, during? At any time?" he prodded.

"No."

"No, what? To which part?" It was an obsession. The urge to know. To not know.

"No, you don't get to ask me that. No to that part. You don't get to come into her home, and ask THAT. I don't care who you are."

"Exactly, HER home. Why are you here? Why are you always fucking here?" It wasn't his place to say as much, and yet Sterling claimed it all the same. He'd been reduced to irrational, juvenile impulses, to floundering attempts to control that which he could not. Like a sailor refusing to acknowledge he was drowning.

"I believe we already went through this. I have seven sisters."

"And?"

"AND one bathroom." This explanation seemed to only leave Sterling all the more confused, so Corey decided to elaborate. "If you ever had my mother's cooking, you'd understand why moving out is not an option. So, whenever Tess is out of town, here I am. My home away from home." The younger man shrugged as if the answer had been obvious all along.

———

There was no use in continuing to dwell on his foolishness, or so Sterling concluded as he pinched the bridge of his nose in an attempt to relieve some of the pressure thrumming between his eyes. The reprieve was only momentary as Charles began to speak again, somehow louder.

"Shit, I may not have thought this through. Does the prince *have to* kiss the princess to wake her? Or was that the frog one? I'm not up-to-date on my fairy tales." Charlie seemed to mumble to himself for a moment before continuing. "Whelp, you're not really my type, *but* I'll give anything a try once." He shrugged, then bent over his prone, less-than-amused companion.

Sterling had been so lost in thought, he hadn't even noticed the nonsensical prattlings of the man beside him. "Can you stop acting like life is some giant joke?" Whether the attempt was made or not, the architect was unable to stifle the irritation boiling beneath the surface at his friend's no-more-grating-than-usual histrionic performance.

"Ah, says the man who's been living in his own perpetual Shakespearean tragedy."

"Fuck you, Charles, seriously. You have no clue what the hell you're talking about. It's always been a spectacle to you. Is that all that I am? A fucking sideshow? Something to amuse you between intermissions? The tragic character, as you say?"

"Really? Is that the level of self-loathing you're at now? Where you question *my* motives? You can't walk. It sucks! But this *woe is me* bullshit is getting old, my friend." It was the first time Charles had let his frustration slip out in anything other than jest. "I'm not the enemy, Luci. For fuck's sake, I never have been. But if you're looking for a villain in this narrative, just like every other goddamn cliché, you need not look further than in the mirror. Do you know what it is like to watch you self-destruct? I'm tired of watching you wither away. Of watching you continue to punish yourself for something that happened five fucking years ago. You've been dragging your feet. Doing everything you can to sabotage yourself. You have a second chance at life, and not one that's been laid out for you. Not one that's been planned for you, but one that is completely serendipitous, one that you can make your own. So stop being a pussy and do something about it."

Those weren't the words Sterling had wanted to hear, nor were they the words he'd expected. However, like most unsolicited sound advice, they were the words he needed.

"I…" The argument died in his mouth before he had a chance to counter. "You're right. That's exactly what I should do. End this."

"Lucien, that's not what I meant. Tess…"

"No, not Tessa, Maddy. You said it yourself. This… everything… it all centers around what happened that night. It's been a domino effect ever since."

———

It didn't take long for both Charles and Sterling (with a little help from Corey) to piece together how the Tabloid articles had come to be. Or rather, it was a theory anyway, one with substantial evidence that only needed the final experimentation in order to be conclusive.

And so, Sterling found himself positioned outside the towering manor estate of his once-upon-a-time, would-be bride. He felt their eyes, the stares, before he saw the camera flashes and he knew this was as idiotic an idea as his presence at her wedding had been. Yet, much as the time before, he found himself here anyway. He was already front-page news. What was one more blow to his reputation?

While his internal ramblings began to wear away at the architect's resolve, the front door crept open. The wisp of a woman barring the threshold appeared slighter, gaunter than when he had last seen her. As her pale-blue eyes locked on to his darker ones, no introductions were needed. It was as though two fallen soldiers haunting the same battlefield now drew lines in the sand. The reality of their downfalls suddenly recognizable where previously it had been overlooked, purposely ignored in hopes that burying the truth would mean altering it.

But there she stood—the truth—her mere existence like a vise to his lungs.

"I know what you did. I just don't understand why you did it, Madelyn. After all this time…"

———

He didn't know what was colder: the unwelcomed stares of the staff and the quick emptying of the parlor upon his entrance, or Maddy's expression as she sought refuge in the gleam of her polished fingernails.

"Where's my cousin?" Sterling offered what he thought would be a safer topic of conversation; she chose to ignore him, however, and responded to the question he'd initially posed at the door.

"I… I don't know why I did it." Maddy had yet to make eye contact and Sterling himself wasn't even sure what *it* was exactly. He just knew she had done *something* to set this media circus into motion. The architect was hoping she would elaborate but instead his ex-fiancée changed tack. "I just couldn't live with it anymore, Luci. I couldn't live with the guilt. I know Daddy—I know *you*—said it was for the best but it never felt that way. Why should I have this storybook life like nothing ever happened? When you... you..."

"When I *what*?" he spit the words back at her. He knew what she thought of him. He saw the pity. He saw it from everyone... *almost* everyone.

"When you threw away everything." She didn't bother to look up as she choked the words out between a pair of plump pink lips.

"Is that what you think happened? I chose this? I threw it all away?" He gestured to his legs, to his chair, to *Madelyn*. Her head immediately popped up, as if the fire he once thought had extinguished had suddenly been reignited. Because he'd found the kindling.

"Didn't you?" She narrowed her eyes at him.

"Yes, Maddy, I chose to be fucking crippled. I said why the fuck not be the goddamned invalid son of a family who's only ever cared about image? That's exactly what I wanted."

"No, what you wanted...." she clarified. "What you've always wanted... was to be your own man. Even as you walked on the path paved in front of you, you couldn't help but veer off course. The life you and Daddy thrust on me was never one you wanted for yourself. That's why it was so easy for you to walk away. If you think otherwise, if you dare tell me otherwise, you're only lying to yourself, Lucien."

"Walk away? Ha, nice choice of words. I can't walk away from anything. Or have you forgotten?" He gritted the sentiment between his teeth.

"Stop that. Stop diverting the conversation to self-pity. You're better than that."

"Now you sound like Charles."

"Well, I'm glad one of you has some sense after all this time."

Though the remark was smart, Sterling could hear the familiarity behind it, the affection that still lingered there. He chose to ignore it, much as she had done with the mention of her husband. "I didn't want to *walk* away, Maddy. I thought I was doing what was best. For both of us."

"For you. Not us." Once again, she corrected him. "There was no us. Remember? There could have been, there would have been. But you decided for me that that would never be an option."

"That's not true. I wasn't the same person. I'm not the same person. I don't even know that man anymore."

He didn't even like that man anymore, he'd come to realize.

"Well, you should have let me decide which version of you I loved. I never got that chance."

"How? How could I give you that chance when all you wanted was to get back to normal? To act as if nothing ever happened. To return to wine tastings, and tux fittings, and fabric swatches. To choose hors d'oeuvres and place settings."

"I… I was wrong, but I felt you slipping away… and I thought... I thought if I could just get you to marry me, before I lost you, that I'd have a chance to get you back. I'd have time to remind you that you loved me once." The reply left Madelyn's mouth like a confession. They were words that seemed to tether her to the past, words that would not allow her to move on to the future. Words that had never been spoken between the two, because the shortcomings of youth, the pressures of societal confines, and sheer stubbornness had barred her from doing so. And as much as he hated to admit it, Sterling had his own words, his own reluctant admission.

"Maddy, you were suffocating me. Every time I looked at you, all I saw was what I couldn't give you. What I would be taking away from you."

"And, instead, you took away the only thing I ever wanted."

"I… we were both wrong. But that doesn't mean it wasn't for the best. You were right. I wouldn't have been happy in that life, the role William fills so much better than I ever could, with or without my legs. I care for you. That much will always be true. But I'm not the man you think I am. And I don't think I ever was."

"I know…" she conceded. "I wish I didn't. But I do."

"It took two of us, you know. To *walk* away. If you didn't want it as much as I did, all you had to do was say so."

"Perhaps you're right. The wedding, the pressure of it all… Maybe, subconsciously, it was easier to accept. To see you as the villain. Instead of looking at myself."

"*Perhaps* it was easier for both of us." The reality of which seemed to just as suddenly strike him.

"I was never your happily ever after, but someone is, aren't they? That's really why you're here. You're conflicted. I can see it on your face, Luci." It seemed, after all this time, this woman was still able to read Sterling almost as easily as the architect could read a room.

CHAPTER 5
THE TRAGIC HERO

TESSA

THERE WAS something about the click of the button that was way more satisfying than the click of a mouse ever could be. Or so Tessa believed anyway, as she absentmindedly pressed the plastic key of the tape recorder, flicking it on then off again, before removing her headphones. This had become her new obsession; she always needed something to fixate on, somewhere to focus all that restless energy. These tapes had become her something, whereas dissecting herself had become the end result.

She began to study herself, same as she would a mark. Listening to her personal narrative as though she were an outside observer allowed Tessa to shed her emotions, like a second skin, and analyze her brain's inner workings.

What made her tick? What were her motives? What did she want?

She couldn't be alone with herself, let alone anyone else, without first determining this.

The answer seemed elusive; however, Tessa was not one to throw in the towel so easily, not when she had a few more rounds left in her. And she sure as hell was not down for the count. She was somehow both weaker and stronger than she had initially assumed herself to be, and that realization made absolutely no sense. How could she be both, yet neither? How was she victim *and* victor?

When she had those answers, she could return to her old life, or create a new one—of that she was certain. Until then, she would find solace in these tapes, in her own internal monologue and the ghosts of her past.

COREY

As he sat in the confined space—*confined* because the sheer cost of the leather that upholstered his seat was more than he likely made in a paycheck and that fact was suffocating—Corey felt like a side character in someone else's narrative. He'd begun to feel that way a lot lately; however, he reminded himself that that had always been his role. To support Tessa in her professional endeavors. And nearly from their first night out in the field, he'd agreed to do the same with those personal. She was more than a coworker to him, more than his partner; she was the friend he hadn't realized he needed in life. One who, like his sisters, both vexed and endeared him.

Up until the most recent events, Tessa had been the backbone of their symbiotic relationship and the catalyst for their rising career paths. That being said, Corey was willing to be what she needed now. Even if it was no more than a shoulder to help bear the weight of her trauma, or an advocate for her less-than-stellar decision-making.

Corey might have had a special connection with each one of his seven sisters, but there was something different about how he felt about Tessa. Something more than platonic but not quite romantic either. There was an unspoken respect. A protectiveness, despite the fact he knew she didn't need protecting. He supposed it stemmed from how much she resembled Laney, younger than his partner by less than a year. With his sister, he had this innate sense of fraternal possessiveness. But with Tessa, it was replaced with wonderment and awe. He could watch her in her element, free of the familial bonds that seemed to burden him otherwise.

He worried about how their relationship would be forced to transform *if* and *when* either of them found themselves in a long-term relationship. Therefore, the devil on his shoulder questioned why he even found himself in this room.

The man clearly had a thing against Corey—the jealousy was palpable. Yet, as any true friend would, he had to put Tessa's needs first. And in some odd way, she needed this man. He'd forced her to face everything she'd been running from over the years. The things she refused to bring up in conversation, even with Corey. And while they were painful, ignoring them had only caused more damage than good.

So, if being here, in Sterling's office, meant an end to their friendship but a beginning to her actually living, it was a sacrifice Corey was willing to make. After all, he was certain any woman who took one look at his partner would be putting him in a similarly uncomfortable predicament. It was unlikely for a female to believe there was nothing between them.

Good thing he wasn't looking for anything more than a one-night stand. Though that was a plight for another day. Corey's love life wasn't the one in shambles at the moment.

Before his thoughts began to wander to the redhead who'd yet to have the pleasure of warming his sheets, Corey was interrupted by the anticlimactic clearing of Sterling's throat—a near repeat of how the man's knocking had interfered with his bedroom antics involving that very woman in question. He didn't know how long the architect had been positioned in front of him, nor did he really care. He may have been a proponent of the relationship between the two; however, it didn't mean the obvious discord didn't go unnoticed. Nor was it any less irritating.

He should take it as a compliment. He laughed to himself. The fact that he was seen as a threat to the would-be, had-been suitor. But more than anything, it was bothersome, infuriating actually, how blind the architect was to the truth and how misplaced his resentment was. It seemed, no matter how many times Corey expressed the neutrality of his friendship with Tessa, the man sitting across from him just couldn't fathom the notion, as if it were impossible for two people of opposing genders to rely on each other for anything other than sexual gratification. Admittedly, the pairing was rare, though not nearly as unattainable as society sought to implicate.

"Would you like—" Sterling began to offer.

Sucking in a breath, Corey decided there was no better time to cut the bullshit and figure out why exactly he'd been asked to meet with the same individual who seemed to despise his mere existence. "What I would like is to know what the hell I'm doing here. You don't like me. I tolerate you. So why pretend?"

"I never said—"

Raising a hand, Corey once again severed the architect's attempts at civility. "It doesn't need to be said, Sterling. You've made it quite obvious how you feel about my interactions with Tess. How ever ridiculous your allegations may be, I'm here out of courtesy to her alone. I owe you nothing. *Nada.* So, save us both the gratuitous small talk and just spit it out. What do you want?"

"I don't dislike you," Sterling admitted, although begrudgingly, while avoiding the question altogether. "I just don't like the way you look..." Taking note of Corey's raised eyebrow, the architect gritted out the last two words, the tick of his jaw punctuating each syllable. "... with her. I saw you with her... outside her apartment. Before she went... wherever it is she went."

"And?"

"And..." When faced with unrestrained candor and a lack of decorum, Sterling appeared to lose his ability to appropriately communicate; therefore, he struggled to adequately construct his sentences. Or so Corey surmised from the man's continued fumblings. "I... well..."

"You saw me play the part of her husband at the wedding. What's the difference? It's my job to have her back, to be the one she turns to when things feel out of control. If you want that to be you instead, you better man the fuck up and act like it. And if you think you can force her to go to you by taking away her other options, then you don't know Tess as well as you think you do. Your role as her partner, as a man, is to make her choose you despite those options not because of a lack of them." Corey shrugged. "You might be able to afford a fucking island of your own, but good the fuck luck isolating our girl. She loves people. She needs people."

Sterling remained tightlipped, seemingly unable to refute Corey's searing admonishment. But not yet willing to agree with it either. And so, the self-proclaimed mama's boy decided to soften the initial blow.

Transitioning from aggressor to confidant, Corey leaned forward. "I'll give you a moment to let that information sink in, and do with it what you will. In the meantime, let me ask you something, Mr. Obser-vant." Sterling stiffened his mandible and flared his nostrils at the sarcasm while his counterpart smirked. "Since you've been so keen to watch Tess and me together, have you ever taken note of that cute little pet name she calls me? The term of endearment that parts those plump lips of hers like a purr." He was purposely taunting the fucker but it was as if he couldn't help himself. He watched as Sterling unintention-ally gripped a drafting pencil and split the wood with the pressure of his thumb. "Whelp, in case you haven't had the pleasure, let me do a little translation for you. Unless French was on your transcript next to equestrian lessons and water polo?"

"Enough." The singular word was interjected with the vibration of a closed fist bouncing off the polished wood between them.

"I'll take that as a no." Pushing back from the ledge of the anti-quated desk, Corey sank into the stiff cushioning of the chair and framed his chin with his thumb and forefinger. "As I was saying, that name she calls me, it translates to some sort of vegetable—a cabbage if I recall correctly. I know… it's sexy, isn't it?"

"Right, and so what's your point?"

"My point, Richy Rich, is that Tessa's words are her best weapon. They aren't random, nor without forethought. She's affectionate towards me, as a mother is to a child, or a sister to a brother. But the words she chooses for you, the ones I've only ever heard her use towards you—not a mark, not to someone inconsequential—they are the same ones used by her mother towards Jack. Whether she realizes it or not, I couldn't tell you. But knowing Tess, observing her over the years, I assure you that means something. Not just something. Everything. And it's the only reason I'm here today. Because sure as fuck it's not for my own benefit."

STERLING

The tension in the office had grown exponentially before dissipating into a cloud of uncertainty. No doubt Charlie was off listening somewhere with a bowl of popcorn and a recording device, focused on the drama as if it were those telenovelas he watched not so secretly.

If Sterling could get out of his own head, pull the blasted thing from his ass, he wouldn't have allowed the blonde playboy to so effortlessly provoke him. However, when it came to Tessa, sense, reason, logic, it was all shoved aside and replaced by impulsivity. Foolishness. He'd asked the man to meet him here with every intention of getting straight to the point, and yet he had done everything to avoid it. To avoid asking for help. The end result outweighed his pride, or so he reminded himself for the hundredth time.

Now that he was sober, Sterling thought it best to tamp down his accusations and focus on the matter at hand. Getting her back, whatever it took. Whatever he had to do. That night at the apartment, though the exact events are still hazy, he'd learned from Corey that Tessa had not returned to her hometown. She'd made it clear to her partner to keep her impromptu departure from her parents; she hadn't wanted them to worry on top of everything else they were already dealing with. And therefore, her whereabouts were up in the air. The girl had work and she had Sterling—*had* being the formative word when it came to her dejected lover—that being said, there was little else tying her down. She could be anywhere. With anyone.

That thought alone evoked a complexity of emotions: jealousy, apprehension, concern for her well-being…

He could throw money at the problem, much as he'd done when he'd watched as she fell to pieces in his arms. But he knew that would do little more than push her away. No, he needed to find her without pulling those strings his family was so used to orchestrating in order to solve all of life's complications. He needed to be a better man.

"I… I have to find her. Is there anything you can tell me?"

Raking his fingers through his recently trimmed hair, Corey huffed out a breath before responding. "Look, all I know is that she cashed in her vacation days—six weeks, I think. She didn't give me anything else." Pausing, as if contemplating whether or not to offer more, the journalist shook his head before pulling out his cellphone. "Against my better judgment, I'll send you my sister's contact information. If anyone can find Tessa without risking bodily harm, it's Laney. Keep in mind: she is my *sister*. Fuck around, let me hear that you even looked at her wrong, and if she doesn't kick your ass, I will."

"And what exactly is it that you think I'd do to your sister? What sort of impression have I given you?"

"No fucking clue. But you seem to have this weird obsession with me, not that I blame you. So who the fuck knows what you'll do when you meet me in female form? Our genetics are flawless after all." Corey grinned, brushing imaginary lint from the fabric of his shirt, then hit send on his phone screen.

CHAPTER 6
THE CONFIDANT

STERLING

THERE WAS something otherworldly about the quietude his home afforded him in her absence, as if it too had been gutted the moment she exited the door and refused to return Sterling's messages.

The loss notched away at his sanity, each tick of the clock carving deeper and deeper into the remnants of his psyche. It wasn't healthy; he knew this. But knowledge did little to assuage the puncturing to his chest. Acceptance was the only ammunition against his obsession. Acceptance that this was how it would feel without her and determination to alter his current circumstances.

The architect had divulged what little information he had obtained from Madelyn to Corey and Charles, explaining how the reluctant bride had shared details of the collision with her best friend, with both the hope and understanding that it wouldn't take much for the other woman to pass the story along. Corey suspected that the photographer from the wedding—who'd also been present at the charity gala—had overheard and sold the commentary (in addition to some wedding photos) to the highest bidder. It was during this exchange that Sterling had consequently come to realize just how Tessa had learned about the accident and the specifics involving his ex. There were so many moving parts, so many chips, which in turn had to fall exactly as they had in order to bring them all to this point in time.

Yet, here they were.

The buzzing from his cellular device shattered Sterling's concentration as he stared idly at a blank computer screen. He'd texted Corey's sister, a message that was nothing more than a series of illegible ramblings, and she responded with a singular phrase. An address. The architect didn't know what the location would provide him, a mere meeting place or perhaps the woman he sought in her entirety, though he thought it best to rein in his eagerness. And not hope for the best. He couldn't face more disappointment, not now.

It took less than an hour for Sterling to find himself staring at another closed door, willing there to be answers rather than questions behind it. He raised a hand more than once and allowed it to hover above the buzzer. Much like Tessa had the night she'd run to him seeking solace, though that felt like a lifetime ago instead of several weeks. That thought had his index finger thrusting forward and announcing his arrival with an irritating hum.

Moments later, the hinges swung inwardly, and at the threshold stood a figure that somehow forced his heart to beat again while simultaneously halting it in his chest.

"Tess..." She wasn't a sight for sore eyes. No, that sentiment was far too overused and could never do the woman justice. She was oxygen to a man who had been starved of air. A life-preserver to a man who'd been drowning in self-pity. A balm for a man whose ache was far too deep for any medical professional to treat.

"Lucien..." She spoke his name in turn, as if the exchanged greetings said more than either of the two could verbalize. However, where he crumpled beneath the weight of her gaze, she remained stoic. As though she were waiting for his reprimand. And as if she also needed it too, she added, "I'm assuming you've seen the article."

"I have."

"And?"

With her bitter prompting, Sterling reached out and tugged her down and against him. To where he needed her the most. In his arms. Her legs dangling over the bend in his, she fell willingly as much as she fought against herself to oblige. When their lips met, the reunion was at first hesitant. Unsure. Before the heat forced each to the brink of their shared restraint and deeper. To the place where actions spoke louder than words ever could.

There was no apology, though Sterling could taste her anguish over the decision she'd made. And in exchange, he offered her no reprieve. No admonishments. No questions as to why. He knew why. And he honestly didn't care. He was that far gone, that far removed from the place where the *why* would offer him the same sort of comfort that having the weight of her against his chest granted him.

TESSA

And Tessa, she was drawn to him like a moth to light, uncontrollably and twice as deadly, because it wasn't just her tangible body at risk of setting the rest of her aflame but her sanity as well. Her metaphorical wings... her freedom itself was in danger of being singed. And he clutched her tighter to him, as if he could feel the burden of her reticence.

"I love you."

Those words haunted her, more so when they parted his lips now as if they somehow solved all their problems, and were harder to issue than an apology. It wasn't that she had never used them before. Obviously, Tessa loved her family. Her friends. She'd even spoken them romantically. But only once. Then they grew sour on her tongue. Nearly impossible to offer back and not feel as though her skin were crawling. As though she were... dirty. Yes, they gritted like gravel between her teeth. The texture solid and unappealing.

"I don't like the way he touches you..." The sound emitting from her colleague's throat was closer to a growl than anything else.

"And who's that?" She refused to play his game, instead initiating one of her own.

It was her fault really. Tessa knew better than to get involved with someone in the workplace, especially given the task at hand. Men fell too easily to jealousy. It was as if they couldn't help but grab rulers and position them at their dicks. She rolled her eyes. Because that was what the fairer sex wanted, a bunch of grunting, ill-equipped misogynists. Then again, she wouldn't have such an easy assignment if it weren't for her target's inability to make direct eye contact—his gaze forever planted on her neckline.

"Tess, don't be coy. I'm not a fuckin' mark." Sebastian was pacing now, wiping the perspiration from his brow with a hand glued to his temple.

She observed his obvious distress, smiled, reapplied her lipstick, and deposited the black and gold tube into her clutch. "Coy? I'm not exactly sure what you mean..."

"Then perhaps you need a new fuckin' dictionary." He stopped walking just long enough to toss the book in question across the mattress towards her vanity chair.

"Clever," she huffed, twisting her body to face him. "This is just a job, Bash. You know it, and I know it. The only one who doesn't know it is Marco."

"Exactly my point!"

"Exactly MY point!" She threw his words back at him.

"I just think you should turn this story over to me. For your safety. I—"

"And what would you do with it?" she countered before he could finish his idiotic comment. "Go after Sienna?" The mafia princess was an expert in the tech industry. Sebastian wouldn't make it through an initial background check, let alone into the woman's bedroom. They both knew as much without ever having to verbalize it. "I didn't think so... Marco is our best option and I'm not sure you're his type." Tessa raked her eyes across her partner's large masculine frame, scanning him from head to toe, and emphasized her point with a lift of her brow.

"Then at least print the story under my name. So no one comes after you... I'm worried, Tess." His pinched expression did little to calm the storm brewing in either's chest.

"I didn't use my real name, and you know damn well I'd never turn a story over. I don't scare that easy, Bash."

"I hate standing by and just watching... You have no idea..." He high-lighted his sentiment with a slamming of his fists. "He acts like he owns you."

"He's an Agostino. Right now, he does. This is what we do. This is embedded journalism. I'm whatever and whomever he wants me to be. And when it's over, I'll still be me. And you'll still be you. It's playing a part. That's all."

"But I love you, Tess... I don't want it to just be you. And me. I want there to be an us."

"I love you too. And there will be an us. But this is my career, and no matter what, it will never be just us. It will be us and whomever else I need to be to get a solid lead. You knew this when you met me, Bash."

———

It had been their last exchange before that night. The night she'd been taken by the Russians. The same night that same man had turned his back and deemed her as worthless as the words he'd offered mere hours ago. Perhaps that had been Bash's form of reprisal for her blatant refusal to *be a good girl* and *do as she's told*. Or perhaps she'd never meant anything to him at all.

Lucien cupped her cheeks. She'd been so lost in the past she'd completely forgotten her present and how an insignificant blip in her timeline should no longer occupy her thoughts. Looking up, Tessa froze as he repeated the utterance she'd hoped was again confessed in error.

"Tess, I mean it. I love you."

If he was probing for reciprocation, Cupid had chosen the wrong target. She had none to grant him. And in its place hummed an acknowledgment.

"Say it back, love. I need to hear you say it."

"I can't." It wasn't a lie. In fact, it was as close to the truth as the journalist was willing to get.

"Good enough." He smirked. "*I can't* is far better than *I don't*."

CHAPTER 7
THE DEUTERAGONIST

TESSA

LANEY'S CHOICE of decor was similar to the woman herself. Fiery, though she shared the dark-brown hair of her mother. And brash, garnering your attention but not in a way that was overall unpleasant. Her color palette was vibrant—someone who knew what they wanted and cared little for outward opinions in the matter—with splashes of dark-emerald green paired with darker blacks and highlighted in metallic golds. In contrast, her furniture was a light, near gray hue, which bordered on a shade of lavender. The walls depicted a crime scene of black and white family photos, each lined up and strung together as meticulously as the law enforcement professional would identify and tag a piece of evidence.

No, it wasn't haphazard. That wasn't the visualization. Instead, it was sporadic but oddly intentional all at once. A chaotic mind somehow reined in and wielded. If only Tessa could do the same. Paint colors seemed to be a point of contention for the broken woman when it came to her own space, the spattering of color hitting the pure white drywall and replicating a commitment she just couldn't bring herself to make.

Each time she stared down at the cardboard color swatches, the red seemed too red, the blue too... blue? But the nothingness of a satin pearl was remarkably comforting, like the padded walls of her own mental prison. Tessa told herself that her decision to leave her apartment bare was out of practicality; however, the more she thought about it, the more her intention veered towards fear of attachment, of being tethered to a singular place. She hadn't made it a home but rather a makeshift dwelling, until the urge to flee crept up her spine and embedded itself in her temporal lobe before manifesting into a sudden bout of apprehension. If she couldn't relinquish herself to a singular tinted gallon can of Valspar, how could she ever do the same with one man? While the comparison seemed like a stretch, the symbolism was relevant nonetheless. After all, what better way to define humanity than a sum of all its choices?

Like the choice the journalist had made to turn her back on Sterling and slam the door...

"Wow, I need a cold shower and I was only in the audience." Laney chuckled as she crossed the small space that separated her from the common area. As much as Tessa knew how to play the game, Laney knew how to watch the pieces. And the power of observation had its advantages.

Tessa clutched the textured pillow against her chest, as if the padded fabric could shield her from the interrogation that was likely to ensue. She felt—she *appeared*—several years younger than her birthday candles would attest.

"How do I face my demons when they are all either dead or think I am?"

The question hung in the air for a moment, before Laney replied with a truth she herself seemed to know all too well. "The only demon you have to overcome is the one you see in the mirror. The rest are inconsequential."

Tessa couldn't face him, but more so, she couldn't face herself if she did. She couldn't face the person she became in his presence and she couldn't face how instantaneous the transformation—from someone she knew to someone she couldn't recognize—seemed to be. She needed to figure out what was real, who was real, which version of herself was true to form. And she couldn't do that with Sterling around. She didn't trust herself to remain clear-headed and impartial when all she wanted to do was fold into the comfort of her internal bias. Into the comfort of *him.* When she came out on the other side of this, if he was still waiting, then she (whatever part of her was left anyway) would decide where to go from there. And if the person who'd punctured her heart deserved a piece of it.

She wasn't foolish enough to believe that being with any man—this man—would somehow resolve the internal conflict she'd been battling for the last few years. She wouldn't suddenly heal because he loved her. In fact, if anything, they were toxic together. Because each sought to hide from their insecurities rather than face them head-on. They used each other as an escape, an excuse to continue the eternal path of avoidance. No, Sterling was not the solution to her deep-seated turmoil, but he was a catalyst. He'd forced her to feel things she preferred to ignore and in doing so she realized, perhaps a little too late, that she was stronger than her fears. Better than her self-doubt.

"Why do you always do that?" Laney drew Tessa back from her thoughts.

"Do what?"

"Retreat inwardly instead of talking to me. It must be one of those only child things, preferring imaginary friends to the ones in front of you."

Or perhaps just a tad bit of trauma response, a quiet observer might add.

"I'm not sure what you're trying to imply. Sounds a lot like you're accusing me of running away. Which is exactly what I'm not doing, remember, Lane?" Tessa huffed and rolled her eyes. She was already being compared to a child, so she might as well act the part. This was supposed to be a reprieve, not an inquisition.

"Look, I'm all about you stepping back a bit from work, from your apartment, from my brother, even from the hot guy pouting in the hall-way. *But,* and I say this with the best of intentions, do you think it's time you went back? To at least one of those things. Maybe start to integrate into some semblance of normalcy again? Albeit, with a little more balance in mind?"

Tessa laughed, but not out of humor. The sound was more of a release of emotions, none of which she could identify at the moment. Everyone had turned on her in some form or fashion.

Everyone but Sterling, her internal dialogue argued. He'd remained steadfast in his pursuit, even knowing the truth. Most of it anyway.

STERLING

The woman was mad, nonsensical, impossible to please. And fuck if he didn't love her for it. Not that any of it was advantageous at the moment. Especially as he stared at the opposite side of the door, barred from what and who he wanted. He was at an impasse. He hadn't expected her face to be the one to greet him, though he wasn't complaining. But of all the outcomes running through his mind, that—*this*—hadn't been one of them.

His mouth still tingled from where hers had been seconds ago, and his fingertips itched to pound against the white paneling once more. To force her to hear him out. Though he had no idea what was left to say; he'd laid all his cards on the table. And the house had taken the win. There was nothing left to bet, no chips to toss in and pray to Lady Luck. He'd lost it all.

His sanity. His pride. His sense of self. But not his heart. No, the godforsaken organ was crushed instead.

But she hadn't denied it. Her feelings for him. And that foolish blip of hope was what kept his darkness at bay.

CHAPTER 8
THE PROPOSAL

FOR A FEW DAYS ANYWAY. But as those days turned into weeks, the remnants of hope diminished like sand in an hourglass.

It was as if the entire encounter at the door had been nothing more than an ambitious daydream, one meant to quench his inner demons before easing Sterling back into the nightmare that was his existence without Tessa. Rationally speaking, it didn't make sense. He'd survived before the damned woman had slinked her way into his life; he should be more than capable of doing so long after. That was if rationality had anything to do with the matter. And it certainly didn't.

"Sulking again, are we?"

Sterling had forgotten Charles's presence. It was becoming a common occurrence. The architect would withdraw into his own thoughts midconversation, usually when something had sparked a memory or random emotion. He'd lost count of the number of weeks that had separated them. And yet, it was as if no time had passed at all. He could still smell her.

Oh, right, he'd been asked a question…

"I don't sulk." He reached through the chaotic pile of proposals, blueprints, and sketches on his desk. "I was... calculating measurements."

His counterpart smirked, crossing an ankle over a knee. "For what?"

Sterling's hair rose on the back of his neck, almost as if he could feel *her* presence. Like the girl haunted his halls. And now, he was certain the breeze carried the familiar scent of her perfume. Was he going mad? "For... for the brownstone on 8th, the one with termite damage."

Yeah, that sounded right.

"You mean the project we completed last week?"

Or not...

To be fair, it wasn't Sterling's fault. After Madelyn, he'd been able to throw himself into his work. He found a sort of sanctuary there. And he rarely thought about his old life, not until he was alone in bed at night. And by then, he was too exhausted to dwell on it. But Tessa? She'd crawled into the confines of his mind and dug in, polluting his every thought. And his nerve endings were on sensory overload, unable to rid themselves of her grasp. Like her arm remained deeply seated in his chest and every time the organ tried to beat, she clutched it tighter. Until he was suffocating in his own skin.

Fuck, he could even hear the string of French expletives that had once vibrated his walls.

His office door flung open, the handle flying against the drywall and embedding in the plaster, which now needed to be patched. He had to be dreaming. A nightmare maybe? Had he fallen asleep in his office last night? And this was his subconscious's way of fucking with him. It seemed more than plausible. Likely even. Given the fact he'd begun drinking more than usual again.

"You..." The apparition hissed the accusation before stalking forward and slamming a single sheet of paper down in front of him. An email. An email addressed to her boss at The Maverick. An email, addressed to her boss at The Maverick, and written by Sterling. "I don't even know what to say to you. This is beyond what I thought you capable of. A new low, Lucien."

He blinked. Twice. But the image in front of him didn't change. He didn't recall writing it. Not that an absurd idea in that realm hadn't crossed his mind on more than one occasion. But to follow through with it? No, he wouldn't have…

Would he?

He didn't respond, instead opening his outbox to see the digital version staring him in the face. Last night… What had he done last night? He'd worked late; he pretended to work late at least. Really, he'd been holed up in his office, accompanied only by his self-pity and a bottle of 30-year Glenfiddich. Where was that bottle? Had he finished it?

He glanced to his right, then his left, where the empty container mocked him from his wastebasket. He'd been thinking about her last night. That much was true. Then again, when wasn't he? With this in mind, Sterling pulled up his bank statement and the corresponding wire transfer.

Fuck…

"Look, Tess…"

"No, you don't. Don't you dare '*Look, Tess*' me," she seethed. And rightfully so. "You contacted the magazine, my magazine, Sterling. You inserted yourself into my professional setting. You had no right. You can't force your way into my life. Not like this. It's… it's not—"

"Fair…? Really? Is that what you're going with? That's childish, even for you, love. Life's not fucking fair. You should know that far better than I do."

"I wasn't going—"

"Yes, you were. We both know it, so cut the crap."

Her only response was a series of French invectives she gritted between her teeth before raising her head and staring him in the eyes. "You think you can just throw money at your problems and everything is solved. It's like your goddamn default setting, Lucien."

"Default setting? Really? As if you're any different? What is it that you do, Tess? Huh? What's your conflict resolution? Oh, right, you run away! From your problems, from your friends, from me, from your goddamn career even!"

"I've never run away from my job—not ever."

"Hah… That's the one you choose to address, love? Fine. Then what about New York? What about now?"

"Don't you bring up New York. That was different and you know it. And now? I'm not running now. I'm working on something—"

"Oh, I'm well aware of what you're working on. Remember? Can't fucking escape it. Just look outside the window!"

"You have no clue what I'm working on."

"Only because you won't tell me. You won't tell anyone. Everything has to be this lone ranger act. Tessa Owens against the goddamn world."

"Really? Like you're one to talk? Who do you let in, Lucien? Who the fuck do you have?"

"You, or so I thought."

"Don't."

"Don't what, Tess?"

"Don't do that. Don't turn this around on me."

"I'm not turning anything around, love. I know you came here to fight. I know a part of you needs that. And fuck if I don't love that fire in you. But, at the end of the day, I'm not looking to win. Not against you."

"I…"

"Marry me." The words fell out of the architect's mouth before he himself knew if he meant them; however, they tasted right.

"What?"

"You heard me."

"Are you insane?"

"Likely, yes. Look at me, Tess, really look. I'm miserable without you. Marry me and I'll fight with you every day. I swear it. Give in to me and I'll give it all to you, love."

"Were I to dignify this sudden bout of madness with an answer, it would be a *no*. However, I will consider this a clear misunderstanding. Or maybe you've just had a bit too much to drink."

Sterling watched Charles in his peripheral, waiting for more unsolicited advice. Some sort of comment or counterargument. But the man remained silent, leaning against the bookcase and staring at his cuticles while listening intently. Every time he agreed with a slung insult or well-delivered verbal dig, he'd raise an eyebrow and subtly shrug a shoulder as if saying: *she has a point*. Without saying anything at all.

Returning his focus to the woman in front of him, Sterling reached into his drawer, grabbed his flask, and slammed it on the desk. "Oh, would you like some? Here, take a swig."

"If you think this is over, it's not."

That statement had him grinning. "Truer words have never been spoken."

"You smell like a goddamn brewery, Lucien. It's not a good look." It was meant to be a jab, but even Tessa couldn't mask the concern underlying her tone.

He smirked. He couldn't help himself. "Everything is a good look on you." However, he knew it was the wrong thing to say when she closed the distance between them and dumped the contents of the flask over his freshly polished antique desk. Though even her blatant irritation didn't sway him. "If you wanted me to lick it off you, all you had to do was ask, love."

She seethed, the air forced through her lungs and out her mouth before she spun on her heel and slammed the door behind her. "Tomorrow morning, 8 a.m. Don't be late," she yelled the vague instructions down the hall, with little care if he could actually hear them. Or so it seemed.

He wanted to argue with her. To say he knew her far better than she knew herself, but what he knew more than he knew her soul was the fact that she needed to get the last word in. So he let her.

Sterling's gaze shifted, landing on the only other occupant in the room.

Charles shrugged. "Don't look at me. I'm much craftier when it comes to my meddling." Then he slipped into the open chair and crossed an ankle over his knee, resuming his favored position before addressing the giant elephant filling the space between them. "So, is that like your go-to move now?"

"What?"

"Spontaneous proposals?"

"I... no, I just... um..." The architect stuttered over his words, recognizing his pattern. He was controlled in everything, everything other than his emotions. Somehow, when it came to the women in his life, he wore his heart on his sleeve and little thought went into his words and proceeding actions. He did and said what felt right. When it felt right. Because it felt… *right.*

"Yeah, that's what I thought." Charles shook his head and pushed to his feet, exiting the office with little more than a dismissive wave of his hand.

CHAPTER 9
THE HEADCASE

"HE'S FUCKING WITH MY JOB..." Tessa stared out the window of the familiar office, the room that was somehow becoming a second home to the girl too lost in her own head to properly observe the world around her anymore.

"Is he?"

This was the game they played. The back and forth. Most days it felt as though she were talking to herself. She wasn't sure she saw the point of continuing the charade. Of pretending like any of this was fixable. Of continuing to live in the past. It was easier to ignore it. To bury everything deep and let it fester. She spun on her heel. Her favorite emotion at the helm.

"Are you fucking kidding me? Of course he is!"

"I mean, a follow-up piece makes sense? And considering he's refused all other media outlets, the magazine would be crazy to turn it down." The older man stared back at her from the rim of his lowered glasses, his hands neatly folded one over the other. "Think about it, Ms. Owens. This could be exactly what you need. A little familiarity, not much pressure—the public will eat up whatever you put out there —and a distraction. Something else to focus on."

"Him, that's what I'll be focused on. And he'll be focused on me." She shook her head and returned her gaze to the city skyline. "Once again, my work will suffer. I'll be forced to walk the line of professionalism. He isn't good for my sanity. And I'm not good for him."

"And you're certain? If you're certain, then I agree. Pass the job on—"

"I will do no such thing." As quickly as the words left her mouth, her stride matched the speed and landed the girl by the desk and into the vinyl chair. "I'm doing the job. That was never the question. I need you to tell me how it's possible. How do we finish what we've started here, without his interference? Without Lucien getting into my head."

"Your head? Is that what you're worried about?"

She reached forward and stopped the tape. "I know what you're doing… and I'm not playing into your hand. We're done here."

———

The dark sky loomed above them like something out of a nightmare. Ominous. Foreboding. A clear sign that her demise was imminent in some fashion or another. However, nothing could prepare Tessa for what lay ahead. Or whom…

The man was both her ultimate temptation and saving grace. And she had yet to learn what to make of that. How to cope. But what she didn't know she could fake—it was what she was good at after all. Pretending. And so, she placed one foot in front of the other, pretending her heartbeat didn't pulse in her throat or thrum in her ears. That her palms didn't itch nor her breathing hitch at the sight of him. She painted on a smirk and presented false confidence. Wearing the emotion as if it were an invisibility cloak. Hiding all her self-doubt and uncertainty. While presenting that picture-perfect image of composure.

Though, with each step, it was getting harder and harder to maintain the facade.

She could hear nothing above the pounding in her chest. Not the crunching of the gravel, the hissing of the wind, or the words welcoming her from a distance. Not until she stood inches away from the figure that was both her salvation and demise.

"Tess," he breathed her name as if it were a plea. Though she wasn't sure what for. Perhaps the same sanity she was lacking.

She'd been so entranced by the man that she'd forgotten to take in her surroundings—a mistake that could mean the difference between life and death. At least in most scenarios. Tessa's gaze flitted upwards, scanning the construction zone, before once again landing on her onlooker.

The Victorian appeared nothing like it had during their first visit. And yet, it was notably the same as well. Preserved. Restored. Revitalized. As if it were a box of puzzle pieces that merely needed patience and finesse to manipulate it back together. As if the black and white photos of its past had seeped into the present, reclaiming its original grandeur.

The interior of the house was like stepping into a history book. Similar to watching a silent movie lit up in techno color for the first time. It spoke to Tessa—a part of her anyway—ushering her forward as a predator would seek to capture its prey. That's what this was after all. A trap. A distraction to lure her in, ease her in to contentment, before caging her against her will.

Melodramatic? Perhaps.

But not too far from the truth. She was stuck, her wings plucked by the spider that had so effortlessly captured her in his web. Whether physically or metaphorically made no difference. Not when it came to her greatest weakness. Falling for the right man at the wrong time. Or was he the wrong man at the right time?

The answer didn't really matter. It didn't alter their reality.

The silence was deafening, yet the journalist couldn't find the courage to fill it either. It was easier to be lost in her own head, in a world of her own making, rather than face the truth staring back at her through the eyes of the only other person in the room.

As if he could sense her apprehension, or perhaps his own, Sterling cleared his throat and approached her like a hunter would a wild beast. Cautiously. Deliberately. While teetering on the edge of excitement at the promise of that final blow. "I'd ask what you thought, but truth be told, I'm hardly prepared to hear your answer." It was his attempt at brevity.

Stifling her growing unease, Tessa allowed the honesty to pour from her lips. Because the home deserved nothing less. "It's… beyond words—perfect. Better than I could have imagined it, Lucien." She leveled her gaze to meet his. "You really are an artist in your own right."

Her compliments had a way of cracking open his rib cage and baring his soul, somehow serving Tessa a piece of him ripe for the picking. Or so the depths of his pupils seemed to tell her. He smirked, because he genuinely wanted to, tilting his head to observe her reaction. "While I appreciate the ego boost, much of what I do is oversight. The contractors are the ones with the skill sets. The hands-on finesse."

"And you're the one with the vision," she countered. "Don't sell yourself short and don't fish for compliments. Neither practice is appealing."

"Does it matter? Whether or not I'm appealing?" Sterling quirked an eyebrow as he trailed behind her, her heels clicking on the freshly polished hardwood and echoing in the hollow space of the barren entryway. They served as a barrier between them, the high-fashion shoes a reminder that she was to be professional, and her entire demeanor screamed as much. She dressed as the image she wanted to present, like an actress donning a costume, allowing herself to fall into whatever character reflected back at her in the mirror.

Her steps punctuated the lull in their brief conversation, before Tessa paused to glance back at him over her shoulder. "I suppose it matters to some."

"And to you? Does it matter to you, Tess?"

Her upper body rose and fell with the visible sigh as her spine stiffened, signaling both a surrender and a quiet acceptance. "I'm here to work, Lucien. Can we not…" She pivoted to face him before gesturing between the two of them. "…do this? I would appreciate it if we could focus on the task at hand… *please.*"

It was the last word that spoke to him. It was the only word that held any real emotion. She was pleading with him, begging for a reprieve, for something else to focus on. Distract her. And that much he understood. He could relate to. And so his response was a curt nod of his head before he shifted back and spun towards the parlor. She wasn't far behind him as he continued the uncomfortable tour.

Several long, awkward moments of silence passed between them before Sterling finally broke the tension. "I'm not going to tell you what to write."

"What do you mean?"

"Treat the house like one of your marks. Observe it, dissect it, and find your story. I'm not here to stifle your process or creativity. It would be a disservice to your… art."

"Is that meant to be a dig?"

"No, love, that's not meant to be a dig. It's meant to set you free. To do as you see fit here, with me and the story."

"But the email—"

"Tess, I don't even remember writing the goddamn email. Though I won't apologize for it. Because I'm not sorry. I'm not sorry you're here right now. I'm not sorry you're the one showcasing this project. And I'm not sorry for doing everything in my power to see you again. To be part of your life. However, I don't want to interfere with your work or what you seek to accomplish for yourself. No matter how much I wish it included me. So, you have free rein. Do, write, and act as you please. In everything. I'm happy to sit on the sidelines. I just want you to know I'm here… waiting."

"Lucie—"

"*Sterling…* You have your barriers to maintain and I have mine. I thought they'd come crashing down in your presence, but it seems there were large enough blocks for me to piece them together again."

She nodded once, a curt gesture meant to symbolize both agreement and acceptance. Though neither emotion felt right.

CHAPTER 10
THE OTHER WOMAN

"FUCK..." Sterling crushed the cotton sheets beneath his grip, balling the material into the palm of his left hand.

He wanted this. God knew he needed it. The release that had been pent up since the moment she stormed into his office. Even more so as she poured the liquor onto his desk, staring him down in the process. And though she wasn't present, he could still hear her voice. Her scathing tone. Smell her shampoo, a mix of lavender and mint. Feel her breath as she cursed him to high hell. Her hand... Even though it wasn't hers that now stroked him up and down to the rhythm of her heaving chest, or at least how he remembered it. He'd pretend it was her, as wrong as it was.

And, fuck, he couldn't help but wish it was her...

Tightening her fingers around the base before tugging upward, the gesture both punishingly abrasive and soft. Grazing her nails across the tip, teasing him simply because she could. Because she held that power over him, over his every muscle and corresponding reaction. Repeating the sequence of events until he wanted to beg her to end the slow torture while wishing it would continue indefinitely. She would bring him to the brink of pleasure, watching him succumb to her devices, and pull him back again, allowing him to teeter on that edge without plunging over.

Then, without warning, she would trail her mouth down the planes of his chest to his prominent oblique muscles, her lips parted just enough for her tongue to dart out and moisten her pathway before flicking along the vein now pulsing with anticipation.

Yes, he could almost feel it. Feel her.

The brush of her hair cascading like a waterfall, a curtain obscuring those green eyes that no doubt danced with both mischief and self-assuredness. The weight of her chest pressed against his thighs with just enough force to keep him from thrusting forward. The pleasure-inducing bite of her nails as they sank into the sensitive flesh above his pelvic bone, offering both control and purchase.

There was no sensation in the world that could compare to the meticulous application and withdrawal of her lips. The precision of her movements. As if she knew his body better than he knew himself.

These present strokes were uncoordinated and sloppy. And nothing like those of the woman obsessing his subconscious. His eyes sprung open before glaring down at the hand wrapped firmly around the base of his cock. The wrong hand. Far less delicate and appealing than the one he envisioned moments ago. Much larger and more masculine too.

"Fuck," he growled to the otherwise empty room, before tucking himself back into his pants and yanking at the zipper quicker than common sense would advise.

He'd thought a little self-gratification would serve as both a distraction and a tension reliever but all it had done was send him spiraling, while creating an additional ache in his nether regions to complement the one in his chest. It was of no use. The woman had all but ruined him. And fuck if he didn't both love and hate her for it.

The morning came, though he never did, and Sterling found himself in the usual puddle of sweat brought on by restless sleep and familiar nightmares. He considered texting her, but thought better of it.

Tessa Owens didn't like being chased, though she did like being caught off guard, as was made apparent by the first night they spent together. She was a hunter in her own right; she enjoyed the game. The back and forth. If only he could figure out a way to give it to her, to ignite that spark he saw in her eye whenever she got a taste of it. Better yet, if only he had someone she wanted… Since he himself was obviously not enough.

To say he was wound up when he arrived at the Victorian would have been an understatement. Sterling's insides were coiled tighter than a compression spring. He'd promised Tessa he'd leave her to her own devices. Let her roam the building alone and as she pleased for the next week. And he'd meant it at the time. However, it was no longer *that* time.

He could tell he'd startled her. She pretended otherwise but he saw the tension in her spine before she pivoted on her heel and landed him with a solid scowl. *Work boots today,* he noted and approved. He felt the heat of her words long before they filled the air. Her aggravation tightened her jawline. It pinched her perfectly petal-like lips and flared her nostrils. Her left eyebrow danced momentarily—the action subtle, inconsequential, but not—and her pupils dilated before narrowing in on their target. All this transpired in seconds, though in her presence, time was irrelevant. Meaningless. And meaningful.

"What are you doing here?" She punctuated her question with a swift crossing of her arms.

Right… what was he doing there? He was annoyed, wasn't he? Frustrated? It was much harder to think when she glared at him that way. Harder to breathe and quite honestly function. But then he remembered his fight drove hers, his irritation ignited her rage, and better yet, his indifference elicited her passion. Nothing was simple. Never easy. Like a cleverly choreographed dance, where neither participant knew the outcome. And so he took the lead.

"It's my property. I didn't think I had to ask your permission to be here." He smirked at her frown.

"That's not what I meant and you damn well know it. I thought we came to an agreement."

Sterling shrugged before leveling his eyes at the woman in front of him. "I changed my mind. You more than anyone should know what that's like, Tess." He hissed her name, despite his best efforts to remain calm.

"So we're back to this, are we? I thought we could be professionals, stop revisiting the same subject matter. Over and over and over again, Lucien. It's like a goddamn broken record! Has no one ever told you no before? Do you understand the meaning of the word?" She continued her tirade, spinning on her heel with her arms waving in the air. "The entitlement must run rampant in your blood. There's no other explanation!"

"Entitlement? Really? That's where you're going with this? Back to the *I'm too rich to understand the poor* girl? Are you in that much denial? Or just that desperate to justify your actions?" The accusation left his mouth in a rush of scalding air, burning his lips as he delivered the blow. "Rationalize it all you want, love. Tell yourself everything is for the best if you must. But it doesn't change the reality of the matter. It doesn't change what I know to be true." He paused, raking a hand through his unkempt hair before peering up at her in a way that somehow bared his soul. "I've caught you every time you thought you might fall. I've held you when you insisted no one else would. And I'm not looking to dangle that over your head or make you feel weak. I was honored to be that person for you. Because I know you don't drop your walls with just anyone. So to walk away, to act like it was nothing, I... I can't wrap my head around it. I can't push past it or accept it. I need to know. To understand. What are you doing, Tess? What have you been doing? And why does it involve pushing everyone away?"

"I'm working on something." She said the singular sentence like it told him everything, when in reality it revealed nothing.

"What? What are you working on? Is it someone else? A guy?" He knew the question was childish but that knowledge didn't stop him from asking it anyway. He needed to know, even while recognizing that the answer would do little to solve anything.

"What? No, not that it matters. We aren't together."

"Then just fucking tell me. What the fuck are you working on? What can't you tell me? Why all the secrecy?"

"Myself." She spat her response. "Goddamn it. I'm working on myself."

"I don't understand."

"No, you wouldn't, would you? Because it always has to be about you. To the point that you're blind to everything else around you—

trust me, I know. And that's why this, us, will never work. It doesn't matter how much you hope it will, how hard you fight, or long you refuse, together we are oblivious to reality. To the real world. And that's just no way to live. Not in a bubble."

"That's nonsense. That's you trying to convince yourself you need to be miserable in order to feel alive. *Trust me, I know,*" he parroted her words right back at her.

"No, that's me being realistic. You're so set on being right you can't even consider the possibility that you're not. You can't see what a disaster this will be."

"And you're so set on it being a disaster, you won't even consider the possibility that it could be something great. Prove me wrong, Tess. If you're so certain that you're right, prove it. Because, right now, all you have are a bunch of theories with no trial and error. No data."

"I… can't…"

And, once again, *I can't* was so much better than *I won't* or *I don't want to.*

"You're right on that one. You can't. Because I'm not wrong, Tess. I know it as certainly as I know I need air to breathe." He meant it. He meant every last word as it came tumbling out of his mouth like a wayward priest in a confessional. But the weight behind his admission wasn't heavy enough to keep her from walking away. For a second time.

Part of Sterling felt validated. Because he knew if Tessa had a rebuttal, she would have had no issue tossing it his way. While another part of him realized it didn't matter because the end result was the same. He was here and she was gone.

CHAPTER 11
THE RIGHT CALL

TESSA

SHE COULD FEEL his eyes on her back, boring into her flesh like a soldering iron through a piece of thin aluminum. Peeling away at her layers and gripping the innermost parts of her. *Gripping* and then twisting, so that she could feel his pull in the depths of her chest. Walking away from this man felt like walking away from a piece of herself. And everything inside her urged her to turn around, to run back. But if there was anything Tessa was an expert on, it was ignoring her most basic impulses.

So she tugged back on the invisible strings tethering her to the one man she wished she didn't have to resist. And placed one foot in front of the other. Again and again. Till his silhouette diminished in the distance. The only thing she could hear was the thrumming of her own heartbeat as it pounded in her ears, pulsing in her temples in an attempt to drown out her thoughts. By the time she realized she'd distanced herself from the property by nearly seven blocks, the sun was beginning to set, her car a distant memory.

She should turn around, call a cab, do anything but keep pushing forward. However, that was the only thing she seemed to be able to do. Push forward. Keep moving. Never stop. And definitely don't look back. Looking back meant reflecting on things you couldn't change. It meant regret. And it meant second-guessing your life choices. But, most of all, it meant falling into old habits. Like mixing business and pleasure. Like loving a man you needed to avoid. Like being open and vulnerable and risking everything you'd worked so hard to attain.

And that. That was terrifying. A shiver chilled the base of her spine and snaked upward before brushing across the tiny hairs on Tessa's neck. She was being watched. She knew it. She knew it like she knew it in that warehouse, and the comparison settled in her gut before crawling up her throat and lodging itself in her gullet. To the point she could feel herself choking on air.

But it wasn't air. It was the hand that had slinked around her head and pressed into her mouth before yanking her backwards into the adjacent alleyway. She didn't fight him. She knew better than to expend her energy before assessing the situation. She needed time. A moment to think, to plan and counteract.

"What are you doing here?" she hissed the question as she narrowed her eyes, and recognition replaced the uncertainty.

STERLING

He should have gone after her. That was what he should have done. No, that was what he wanted to do. What he should have done was give her space. Leave her be and not push her to give him what she wasn't willing to offer. Right?

His inaudible ruminations were answered by the audible ringing of his phone. *Though everything was always so much clearer in theory,* he reminded himself as he slipped a hand into his jacket pocket and withdrew his cellular device. Tessa's name screamed at him from across the screen, freezing the architect in place before common sense urged him to answer it.

"Hello…? Tess?" Sterling prompted tentatively, as if fearing she would somehow reach through the other end and choke him with her reply.

He was met by silence and shuffling. He should have known better than to assume she would actually be reaching out to him for anything more than a daily beratement. But something kept his ear glued to the receiver. Kept him wordless and listening as the shuffling faded away into the background and voices filtered through.

"Oh, I think you could make a guess, *manmi,*" the unknown speaker snarled in the distance, his accent thick, unrecognizable, yet oddly familiar.

Tessa cackled—Sterling knew the sound, could find it in the dark if he needed to—before responding in a cold, methodical tone. "Save the sentiments for your friend. The games too. I'm sure he can remind you how well I play with others."

"None of that now, pretty girl. Phillip is one to *voye flè*. Not me…" The man seemed to hum his words, carrying them with a lilt while deadening their intent.

"*Parfait*. Something we can finally agree on. What is it that you want? And why wait so long to seek me out?"

"Want? What do I want?" He seemed to laugh in her face. "What does anyone want? Some good wine, a full belly, a pretty woman to warm my bed… oh, and the fucking money I was promised."

"Promised by whom? Certainly not me. Perhaps you should find that person and ask them. I'd love to help you… What was their name again?" While the question was asked in obvious jest, there was subterfuge laced in her intent. Sterling knew it even at a distance. He could hear it in her delivery. In the way he knew her lips parted, almost breathlessly to distract from her unease, from the way he was certain her nostrils flared minutely, subtly, indicating her distress. To anyone who knew her well enough to notice it.

"*Mon cher*," the man breathed the endearment and Sterling couldn't help but picture him breathing Tessa in too. Enjoying her scent in an effort to establish dominance as well as her perfume because, as a member of the male species, you couldn't help but take her in. In every way possible. "I thought you didn't want to play? If you have a question, don't be coy. Ask it." The last two words came out as a growl even from afar.

"How did he know about my mother?"

"Aw, pretty girl, didn't you realize you were the mark all along? It was our job to know everything. To lure you into our confidence. To get you to turn on your boy toy. To learn everything there is to know about you. That was until you fucked it all up for us, and now it's all on my shoulders. And my employer is, well, less than thrilled."

"I—but why? Who? Who hired you? The Russians? The Italians? Who was it?"

"I don't know any Russians, *cher*. And we ain't got nothing nice to say about the Italians. So ya may want to rack your brain a little harder. Who d'ya piss off?"

The better question was who hadn't she pissed off? No, it couldn't be... He was presumed dead.

"Bash?"

Sterling froze. There was something about the way Tessa uttered her former lover's name that left the architect gagging on his next breath. But regardless of how he was feeling at the moment, he knew he had also heard enough. Because he knew who was speaking on the other end of the jumbled call.

He'd promised her she was safe. That she wouldn't have to worry about the con man making an untimely appearance. And yet, here he was—or at the very least an associate of his—seeking her out when she was most vulnerable. And there was not a goddamn thing Sterling could do about it with his legs confined to this chair. He couldn't chase after her. Couldn't follow her down the poorly paved streets. Couldn't do much more than listen on the other end and count her breaths, ensuring they were still there.

He racked his brain for some sort of solution, anything beyond his body's psychosocial reaction to freeze, before lifting his work phone to his ear and dialing Charles. The nosy son of a bitch picked up on the first ring.

"The business line, interesting choice. But, by all means, give me the dirty de—"

"Enough," Sterling severed Charles's obnoxious banter before the man had a chance to fully form his smirk. "I need you to help me find out what Tessa's been up to..." The architect could hear his best friend's eye roll through the receiver, nearly feel the weight of the man's scowl. But he pushed forward anyway. "It's not what you're thinking. She's in trouble. I... I overheard her talking—"

"Right..." Charles elongated his reply with an exaggerated puckering of his lips, forcing the word out through his clenched teeth.

"Chuck!"

"Fiiiiiine. What do you need me to do?"

"Meet me back at the Victorian. She ran off but her car's still parked out front."

TESSA

She'd spoken the name hesitantly, as if saying it allowed would cause the man to materialize. However, she couldn't help but wonder if Sebastian Santoro was more than just a ghost haunting her psyche. Had the man gone into hiding? Was he hoping to torture her now in some misguided attempt at revenge. To ruin her life, after he'd sunk his own reputation. Or were the rumors true? Was the coward dead and buried?

"Nope..." His lips popped as the smug bastard uttered the singular response, both relaxing Tessa's spine while sending her thoughts spiraling. "Honestly, your guess is as good as mine. Haven't met the guy. Doesn't really matter who he is as long as the funds hit our bank account."

"So you've been fucking with me. You don't even know who it is. It could be anyone! It could... be... anyone..." she repeated that last part softly and more to herself than the man in front of her. The same man nonchalantly picking at his cuticles as if her life didn't hang in the balance. He replied with a shrug. And Tessa ground her teeth to the nerve, considering her response carefully before speaking it aloud. "How about I make you a better offer?"

The sick son of a bitch's mouth curled into a Cheshire grin that would make Lewis Carroll envious before he drew in a long breath and replied, "I'm listening…"

CHAPTER 12
THE PUNCH LINE

STERLING

SHE WAS GONE. Vanished like a fantasy emerging in the daylight hours, leaving her car behind without any indication as to when or if she was coming back. And Sterling couldn't help but wonder if this man had anything to do with Tessa's initial disappearance from his life. He didn't believe in coincidences or chance meetings—his first encounter with the woman was evidence enough of that—however, he couldn't deny the shock and hesitance he heard in her voice. As if Tessa hadn't expected to see the man and feared his intentions... Unless that was all part of the act.

It was possible.

He knew as much and better than to doubt her capabilities. But his gut told him otherwise. That he shouldn't assume the worst of her. Though he also knew that neither option mattered. She seeped into his pores, charged his nerve endings, filled his lungs with every breath he took. It was deadlier than an addiction. He was obsessed. And worse yet, he recognized that fact and had no intention of fighting it.

He called her. Texted more times than he cared to admit to anyone outside his cellular provider. And he was met by radio silence. He used the excuse that he was concerned for her safety. And he was. That much was true. But he was also self-aware enough to realize it was more than that.

Sterling needed to know what this man wanted, who hired him, and what any of it had to do with Tessa's extracurricular activities and sudden refusal to see him. He was certain it was all somehow connected. He could taste the subterfuge, feel it coursing through his veins. He didn't have all the pieces from the box, just a few scattered corners that he knew when slotted together would form the bigger picture. And once he knew what he was dealing with, he could figure out a way to surpass it. Like measurements on a blueprint, he merely needed a solution. When you couldn't find a way through a problem, you had to come up with a way around it. A bypass. You didn't trash the entire project. No, you traced over it, erased and resketched lines, until the end product was better than your original plan. This thing with Tessa was no different. At least that's what he was going to keep telling himself.

He was lost to the light-blue glow of his computer screen, staring but seeing nothing, when the swing of his office door from its hinges drew his eyes upwards, landing on the olive-green irises of his obsession. Tessa appeared disheveled and breathless as she clung to the doorknob, her expression obviously pained as she regarded him from across the room.

"Ster—"

"Tess—" They began to speak at the same time before Sterling lifted a hand, gesturing for her to continue.

"I... I apologize for... leaving things the way I did. It was unprofessional and I—"

"Tess, love, can we cut the bullshit? Please. It's exhausting. We're far beyond any line of professionalism, and I'm not looking to backpedal. If nothing else, will you at least drop the pretense and consider me a friend?" He meant it. He was exhausted. But that didn't mean he was giving up, just that he knew when it was time to return to his corner of the ring for a brief moment of reprieve.

Metaphorical gloves lowered, Sterling allowed his gaze to trail up her midsection before landing on her face. And he knew the moment she saw his earnestness because hers reflected back at him in the way her features softened. In how her jaw unclenched and her brow relaxed.

"I, um, I'm not sure how to do that, Lucien. But I really don't have another choice at the moment." The admission burned her throat. Sterling took note of how sour it appeared to taste on her tongue, and he could hardly imagine the magnitude of whatever problem drew her to his door.

Tessa closed the distance, approaching his desk void of her usual bravado. She didn't want to be here. That much was clear. It was evident in every step she took and more so when she lowered her body into the chair in front of him and sank back into the cushion and into herself, appearing far smaller than her inflated ego was known to project. She sighed, folding her arms across her chest and drawing his eyes downward—despite his best efforts to maintain civility—before she amassed the energy she seemed to require to speak again.

"I… I'm…" She cursed under her breath, clearly fighting an inner battle far outside Sterling's depth of knowledge. "I need your help. A favor, I guess…"

Ah, that was it. What was so hard for her to voice. A need. A want. Dependency. It was the woman's kryptonite. Her greatest fear. Yet here she was. Coming to him. It had to mean something, right? Otherwise she would have attempted manipulation in place of a simple request.

"Okay, what kind of favor?" He kept his expression neutral, his voice tepid, fearing that tipping the scale any which way would send her running.

"I'm good at my job. You know this, Lucien. I have so many resources at my fingertips, so many favors I'm just waiting to cash in, and I'm not afraid of getting my hands dirty. Of getting into the meat of things, the grit. Of working hard to get what I want…"

"Tess, you didn't come here to recite your CV. Out of everyone in the room, I've never been the one to doubt you. Just tell me what you need." He solidified his response with a nod of his head. It was a social cue, a tactic used to subconsciously lull the second party into a sense of contentment. Concession. A nonverbal *yes, go ahead.*

If Tessa knew what he was doing, she didn't point it out, simply sucking her lip between her teeth and sinking them into the swollen meat. She must have been doing that often. Chewing on her lip while she chewed on her thoughts. Or so Sterling told himself, hoping the plumpness of her mouth wasn't due to something else. Something far more salacious and less anxiety-driven.

"Tess, it's just me. No one else. You can tell me what you need. I swear it won't leave these four walls. No one else will ever know—"

"Except me!" Charles sauntered in with a grin rivaling a crescent moon, and Tessa's face immediately brightened. She was either that blatantly happy to see his counterpart, or that guarded, that trained, that her mask fell into place on instinct and without making conscious effort. And Sterling wasn't sure which conclusion gutted him more.

"Charlie..." She hummed his name somewhere deep in her throat —somewhere Sterling longed to be.

He shook his head of those thoughts. It wasn't like the architect to be so carnally focused. So single-minded. He was usually much better at containing his baser instincts. At shoving them aside for practicality. Then again, nothing about this woman was the least bit practical.

Charles sank into the chair at her right, acknowledging Tessa with a dip of his chin before turning his grin on his associate. "As you were." He raised a suggestive brow, urging the two to continue as if his presence wasn't an intrusion. Because, in Charles's mind, it wasn't.

The journalist shook her head, her posturing seemingly both more relaxed and more defensive, while Sterling narrowed his glare in her direction. He watched as Tessa's chest rose with a deep inhale, as she straightened her spine and spoke with intent.

"Right, well, as I was saying, *mon ami*." She grinned, her choice of endearment clearly intentional. "Despite everything I have at my disposal, what I don't have is any insight into banking. Neither do my usual contacts." Sterling could only assume she meant Corey's sister. But with Tessa, there was no way to say for sure. "So I was hoping you would be able—and willing—to reach out to some of yours. Verify if there is any way to determine where a wire transfer originated. A name. An address. Anything. All I have is a reference number with no means to locate the sender."

Sterling opened his mouth, as if to speak, but Charles beat him to the punch line. "Is this a matter of business or pleasure?" The under-lying implication was evident to all parties.

"Neither," she replied. "Though I'd consider it personal. He knew things, Lucien." She returned her gaze to his as she addressed him. "About me... about my mother... and now I've just been made aware that someone else was paying him to do it."

"Who's him?" Charles interjected.

"No one of consequence, as far as I know. However, he was there that night, with that con man, the one who followed me here. They were partners, I assume. Though I'd never seen them prior to the charity event..."

"That doesn't mean they haven't seen you, though," Sterling added.

"I don't think—no, I suppose you're right. I can't honestly say how long this has been going on. Only that I assumed it started then."

"The reference number, you have it?" Sterling prompted, and she nodded. "Where?"

"Screen shots, sent via email."

"I'll need to see your phone, dear," Charles instructed before his counterpart could say otherwise.

"Why?"

"To trace the IP, make sure the information is legitimate and that this guy isn't just fucking with us."

Tessa nodded again, unlocking the screen to her cellular device before passing it to Charles. "You have an hour. Then I need it back. I have actual work to do."

"As do I, sweetheart. Remember, you're the one who came to us." Charles grinned through his retort, one side of his mouth pulled up into that permanent condescending smirk of his. She rolled her eyes but didn't correct him. Something about Sterling's counterpart seemed to affect Tessa in a different way altogether. Almost as though the more he tried to get under her skin, the more she enjoyed his company.

With a superfluous bow, Charles sent a wink Sterling's way before exiting the room as dramatically as he'd entered it. The man was up to something. Sterling knew it. Though now wasn't the time to question him. Not in front of her. The woman eyeing him with undefined emotion. The kind meant to remain neutral. However, he couldn't help but discern a hint of… *something* pulsing just beneath the surface.

"So… how is your mother?" Sterling asked the question not to break the silence. And not because he needed to do so in order to initiate conversation and fill the air with something beyond tension. But rather because he actually wanted to know the answer.

"Why are you asking that?" Tessa's posture immediately stiffened, and her eyes narrowed in on him as if she were trying to uncover some underlying nefarious intention.

Sterling leaned forward on the desk still separating him from the woman who had placed much more than furniture between them, piercing her with his gaze like she'd long ago pierced his heart. "Because I care, Tess. That's all. No other reason."

She shook her head, whether it was at him, his question, or herself was unclear in the moment. "Right. Well, she's much the same, or so I'm told. Though I doubt my father would tell me anything otherwise."

"True. The man does have his own way of doing things…" To that, Tessa smiled. Because Sterling was putting it mildly. Phrasing it politely. Jack Owens didn't just do things his own way. He did them the only way. The right way. In his mind at least. And the architect was more than aware of where the military veteran's offspring got her stubbornness from. "Should she need anything…" Sterling began, though he had a feeling his sentiment fell flat. "I, ah, know my fair share of doctors."

"I appreciate the offer, but I'd rather not talk about it at the moment. If you don't mind." She closed herself off, her legs crossing in unison with the way her arms returned to their tight positioning, folded over her chest.

He wanted to shake her. To remind her that she was in her safe place. That it didn't always have to be the strong-willed journalist against the world. One woman fighting mankind. Tessa Owens versus humanity. However, he didn't have the energy to argue with her. Not now. Not when she looked as exhausted as he felt.

CHAPTER 13
THE OTHER MAN

"WHERE IS SHE?" Charles leaned against the doorframe, his hands tucked into the pockets of his neatly pressed slacks and his gait suspiciously lax. Even for him.

"Resting… I don't think she's been sleeping well. If at all." His counterpart lifted a singular brow, and Sterling was quick to add, "Don't. Get your mind out of the gutter. I'm not in the mood."

"When are you ever?" Charles's retort was delivered with a chuckle.

"And yet it doesn't stop you," Sterling reminded his friend on a growl.

"Touché." The indomitable jester pushed himself from the ornate antique casing that welcomed you into the office space and stalked forward, his steps measured and precise—his delayed pacing meant to further irritate the beast of a man he sought to meet on the other end of the room. Or so Sterling could only assume. "You should be nicer to me, you know?" He sat himself on the edge of the desk, instead of sinking into his usual chair, forcing his cohort to stare up at him.

"Really? And why is that?" Sterling huffed out the words, though he wasn't certain he wanted to know the answer. Charles liked to play games, almost as much as Tessa, and the architect was more than ready to tip the board and send the pieces flying.

"Because I uncovered what our girl's been up to."

"My *girl*," Sterling was quick to correct, and Charles waved his hand as if to dismiss the sentiment. "I'm afraid to ask, but how did you manage that?"

"Why do you think I took her phone, you twit? It's not like I know anything about banking. That's all you. I went through her call log. Circled back to see which numbers were most frequently in use. Then reverse-searched to find the caller's location."

"And what is it? Has she been seeing someone?"

"Yes, but not in the way you're thinking…"

"And what other way is there?" Sterling slammed his fist on the solid wood desk top, both his hand and chest pounding. One with a physical ache and the other with an agony much more intense. Blood rushed between his ears as his thoughts went into overdrive. "Fuck! Really? Who is he?"

"A doctor, Luci." Charles shook his head. "She's seeing a doctor, you nut."

"Got it. She crossed a goddamn cripple off her list and now she's moving on. Fucking brilliant!" He couldn't think straight. He could barely think at all. As much as the truth had been right in front of his face, there was something different about hearing it. Something visceral as the realization sank into his veins and infected him from the inside out. The heat flashed through the tips of his fingers, traveling up his arms before running up his shoulders and throat, and plunging back down to the lowest part of his spine where he couldn't feel anything. And then numbness took over. A coldness that solidified around his heart and held the organ captive.

"Don't be an idiot." Charles broke him from his trance, though not from his harsh reality.

"Right, because she prefers them smart with medical degrees," Sterling spat the retort, disgusted with himself and the woman of his contention.

"What? No. Listen to yourself, Luci. He's a sixty-year-old man, for fuck's sake!" Charles shot up from the desk and began pacing the diminished space in front of it.

"Ah, even better. He's already got one fucking foot in the ground."

"At this point, I don't know if your lack of knowledge when it comes to women is supposed to be laughable or endearing?" Charles stopped midstep, eyeing his friend like the halfwit he clearly thought the man to be. "You aren't even listening to me. You're twisting whatever words you think you hear until you've contorted them into something resembling your greatest fears. Self-fulfilling prophecy and all that nonsense."

Sterling paused, as if finally absorbing his counterpart's words. As if comprehending them for the first time since the other man had entered the room. "What are you saying?"

"That she's in therapy, you twat. She isn't seeing anyone other than her shrink. From what I was able to gather in under an hour. However, you have about fifteen minutes before she barges in here looking for this." Charles tossed Tessa's cellular device into Sterling's open palm. "So chop-chop. Better hope you can do something with that reference number in the interim."

"Why didn't you write it down and give it to me earlier?"

Charles grinned, backing over the office threshold with his hands raised in surrender before calling out, "Because it's much more fun this way." Then he slammed the door milliseconds prior to the recognizable thumping of a solid object against the only barrier between them. Sterling could hear the unmistakable chuckling followed by the thud of footsteps as the son of a bitch fled down the hallway.

As if this day could get any worse, he mused, unlocking the phone screen and scrolling to the email in question.

It took everything in him not to snoop; though he doubted he would find anything of substance unless Tessa wanted him to. He was certain she wouldn't have handed over her phone otherwise. He jotted down the transfer number before tossing the device into the seat cushion opposite him, the action so quick it was as if the plastic had burned his fingertips. He didn't need any further temptation. It was better to just pretend the goddamn thing didn't exist.

Several phone calls later and, with barely a second to spare, Sterling cashed in his last favor. The name that stared back at him from the sheet of drafting paper, where he had scribbled it down in a frenzy to meet the hour deadline, haunted his subconscious more readily than any other poor life choice. It sent a chill up the back of his neck and crawled into his skin, crippling his ability far worse than that accident ever had his legs. The air around him was thick. Too thick to take into his lungs. And too thick to keep his heart beating. So, instead, it remained suspended midpump, as though time itself stood still.

The clacking of heels approaching the office door forced a new breath of air down his throat, and his nostrils flared with the deep inhalation that finally allowed his blood to pump once more. She called his name as she entered the room but Sterling didn't quite hear it. Just saw the movement of her plump lips as they formed the word.

"Did you find anything?" she seemed to ask. However, the tone of her voice told him it wasn't the first time she had spoken the question.

"Ah… yeah," Sterling responded in an attempt to shake himself from the haze. "I got a name…"

"Okay…" She drew out the singular word. Then, noting his continued silence, she prompted, "Well, what is it?"

He glanced down at the annotation on his desk, though he didn't need to. He knew it all too well. "Rem E. Steele. But it wasn't him…"

"What do you mean?" Her eyebrows narrowed in confusion, and he couldn't blame her. He wasn't exactly being forthright with the information.

"It wasn't him. Because he's dead…"

"How do you know?"

It was a logical question, though he wished she hadn't asked it, since the only response to tumble out of Sterling's mouth was the last thing he wanted to admit to the woman he hoped to win back. "Because I killed him."

CHAPTER 14
THE BURIED TRUTH

STERLING

TESSA'S EYES scanned the room as if she could somehow spot any possible listening devices. Then she lowered her voice to a whispered hiss as she asked the question Sterling really had no answer to. Not now anyway. He wasn't ready to delve that deep into his own psyche at the moment. He had other matters to settle first.

She inched closer—he was surprised she wasn't running—repeating herself, though he'd heard her clear as day the first time. "What do you mean you killed him, Lucien?"

"Exactly that." His reply was both simple and factual, as he accompanied it with a shrug of his shoulders. "He's not the one looking into you. I saw him placed in the ground myself."

Tessa slunk into the chair opposite him, her gaze fixated on the nothingness directly in front of her as she stared off into the distance. Her lack of a response was unsettling. Then again, death seemed to surround this woman. Meet her at every turn. "So…" she seemed to huff out. "Whoever it is, they're hiding behind an alias."

"Something like that…" What Sterling didn't say was that he knew exactly who that someone was. There was no doubt in his mind.

"And they must know you, or enough about you," she deduced. "To know that name would affect you. Almost as if they wanted you to find them, but why?" Her glare landed on him like a pair of freshly sharpened daggers, though he should have expected as much. This was her wheelhouse, her area of expertise. While she figured it out quicker than he'd hoped, the outcome was inevitable. The woman was no better than a dog with a bone and she'd keep digging until she found something—he knew the irony of that thought would come back to haunt him one day. It just hadn't occurred to him that today was it.

"Look, Tess." He felt the weight of her presence as he spoke the words, could sense her displeasure sucking the air from the room, and so his chest quickly expanded in a desperate attempt to draw in oxygen. "I… I need you to trust me. Let me handle this. Get them to call off the dogs. And then I promise I'll tell you everything."

"Why?"

"Why?" He parroted her response. "What do you mean *why*?"

"Why not tell me now? Why do I have to wait? If you can tell me everything, then why don't you just do it already?"

"Because." Yeah, he knew it was the wrong thing to say the moment the curt reply fell from his lips. However, by that time, Tessa had already jumped from the chair and pivoted on her heel before she stomped towards the door. "Because I've never told anyone… and I need to confront my demons before letting them all out of Pandora's box. You can understand that, can't you, Tess?"

She paused midstep but had yet to turn to face him. He could see the rhythmic rise and fall of her chest, the stiffness in her spine, as she stood frozen in contemplation—as though she were his judge, jury, and executioner all in this moment. After what felt like an eternity but was probably mere seconds, her shoulders dropped and she spun to face him once more.

"I suppose I can… understand. But don't make me regret it, Lucien. Don't put me in that spot again."

He wasn't entirely sure what she meant. But he also knew now was not the time to ask her to clarify. He could only assume it had something to do with her hesitance to put her trust in him. Her fear of betrayal. And if that were the case, he'd swear it on the Bible. Because there was no doubt in his mind that he would do anything to protect this woman. Even if it meant unearthing the worst skeleton of them all.

His mother.

CHAPTER 15
THE HENHOUSE

TESSA

SHE HAD MEANT to hit record, her hand gliding into her coat pocket like it had done so many times in the past before feeling along her cellular device with just enough force to tap the correct icon—the app she downloaded to ease this process and serve as a failsafe for both professional and personal matters. However, that hadn't been the case that day. In that alley. With that man.

Instead, as if guided by the petty hand of fate, her fingertips had honed in on Sterling's name. Somehow dialing his number and connecting the call. He'd heard everything, or so Tessa could only assume by the timestamps noted on the outgoing call log. As to what he thought of that exchange, she didn't know. He hadn't seemed all that surprised to see her reappearing at his office door. Though he didn't question her, she was certain that part would come later.

And she'd be ready when it did, along with her own arsenal of who, what, when, where, and whys. Until then, she would remain locked in her thoughts, mulling over what her life had become. How the game was no longer fun, the complexity no longer thrilling. She was tired. Of fighting, of arguing, of herself and her inability to do anything but fight and argue. Winning just didn't come with that same satisfaction anymore. Even writing felt stale, as though she were going through the motions, instead of feeding off the high.

She just wasn't who she saw herself becoming, and neither was she who she once was. As if, looking back, she saw a stranger just as much as she didn't recognize the person emerging from all the life choices set out in front of her. Worse yet, the girl in the mirror wasn't any more or less familiar. Like her physical form had been inhabited by some alien being, equipped enough to appear the same, but that's where the similarities ended. It was crazy talk. She knew it. She was that self-aware. And medication would be the easiest solution. But easy had never been her preferred method.

So, when given the option, Tessa had refused. She liked the way her brain worked, even on its worst days. And she feared taking something would alter the way she thought and felt and acted. While that could be good in so many ways, it was also terrifying. Because how she thought, felt, and acted was what made her… *her*. It was what made her human, and no doctor could convince her otherwise.

She knew part of it had to do with being stubborn, with refusing to accept help, even when it was for her benefit. But that same stubborn part of her was what drove her forward, refused to let her give up or give in. Especially on days like these. When everything seemed to be collapsing in around her. Because, no matter how deep her inner demons seemed to be able to drag her down and hold her under, Tessa would force her head above the water. Break the surface and fight the current.

She wasn't weak and she wasn't a quitter. Though she couldn't deny that being so damn resilient was also so fucking exhausting.

"Penny for your thoughts?"

The question seemed to jump down Tessa's infinite rabbit hole, grabbing on to her by both wrists and tugging her up and out. The grin she wore for all the world to see flashed across her face, curling back her perfectly painted lips and softening the lines in her forehead. She slid off the edge of Sterling's desk, where she had positioned herself nearly an hour ago, gliding her bare feet along the hardwood floor— having kicked her heels off and tossed them in the corner—before stomping a few inches short of her amused onlooker.

He continued to eye her curiously, as if her next move was an impossible puzzle he was trying to decipher, as she reached out to gently cup his cheek. "Oh, honey, it'll take way more than a penny," she hummed. "I hardly think you can afford me."

He narrowed his eyes, observing her features for a minute, looking for any sign of weakness. Any fracturing in her demeanor. Or so she could only assume. Before his neck craned as if on instinct, his lips lowering to just a breath away from hers. She could nearly feel his pulse racing in the air between them, her fingertips making contact with his chest, climbing upwards, and digging into his lapels for better purchase. Leverage.

She felt the sharp intake of air tensing his abdominal muscles milliseconds before she heard the barely audible sound as she watched his nostrils flare with the action. Then, as if common sense and better judgment had taken a baseball bat to the back of his skull, he cracked a smile and she shoved him aside, her face brightening with a smirk. The first real reaction throughout their entire exchange.

"What do you want, Charlie?" She laughed as she pivoted on her heel and made her way back to her spot on the desk and her view of the skyline through the expanse of windows.

He shook his head—she could sense the gesture even though she didn't turn to see it—and raked a hand through his purposely tousled hair. "You weren't going to back down, were you?"

Tessa repositioned herself on the freshly polished desk top, crossing one long leg over the other, before shifting to face him. "Never challenge me to a game of chicken, *mon chou.*"

"That is equal parts sexy and terrifying. But point taken." He shrugged. The performer had been outperformed. But he was smart enough to know when to step out of the spotlight and let someone else shine. "In all seriousness, though, are you all right?" He entered the office but seemed to think better of venturing into her personal space again, choosing to lean against the far bookcase with his arms crossed and tie now slightly askew. When she didn't answer him, he pressed on anyway. "I can feel your anxiety from here, sweetheart. You're not as good at hiding it as you think."

"Oh, I'm better than good," she taunted, because it was far easier to dance around his discomfort than admit her own.

Charles raised an eyebrow, as if he realized her game and wasn't taking the bait again. "That's going to get you in trouble one day."

"Probably. But not today." She grinned with a cocked eyebrow of her own before dropping it along with her facade. Her chest heaved on a long sigh as she finally admitted, "I honestly couldn't even begin to tell you. I guess it all just hits too close to home. They knew about my mother, Charlie." She peered up at him, finally making earnest eye contact. "I thought it was over. I tried to ignore it, you know? The realization that I put my family at risk. Brought them into my nonsense. But the truth is… the guilt has been eating me alive."

He nodded, seeming to understand that flowery words and half-hearted dismissals weren't what she needed at the moment. He crossed the distance between them, leaning on the desk to slide up beside her before wrapping an arm around her shoulder and tugging her against his chest.

Tessa needed the comfort almost as much as she hated her need for it. But she didn't allow the tears to fall. She'd regained her restraint when it came to the random displays of waterworks, just not her ability to shove all her emotions down and bury them under years of repression.

As though it were instinct, Charles tucked her head under his chin and ran a hand up and down the length of her back. And she couldn't help but think that at least it wasn't a condescending tapping of his palm. A "there, there" which really stood for: *you did this to yourself, but we can both pretend you didn't.* Regardless of how true the sentiment may have been.

They both heard the clearing of his throat before they felt his presence staring through them. "You two seem to be getting along," Sterling mumbled in greeting, the statement clearly meant to sound playful; however, his underlying annoyance was undeniable. It showed in the way his jaw ticked and his shoulders pinned back. In the way he maneuvered around the space with a purpose, his movements jerky and calculated. In how he avoided eye contact, acting as if

—despite acknowledging them with his sarcastic observation—no one else was in the room.

Ever the perpetual tormentor, Charles seemed to take note of each of these mannerisms, though he hadn't released Tessa from his embrace. And rather than tamp down his counterpart's ill mood, he chose to throw a handful of kindling on the simmering blaze. He shrugged, his eyes drawn to his target's location with that unforgiving smirk plastered across his face. "You should have seen us earlier." And he grinned through each word as they landed like grenades meant to take root in his best friend's psyche.

But they didn't just land, they exploded upon impact, as Sterling's glare shot in his heckler's direction, his head craned in an unnatural position while resembling something straight out of a horror flick. "What the fuck is that supposed to mean?"

Oh…" The zing of the paper weight carried through the air before Charles could release his two-syllable taunt. "…nothing." And the metal sphere landed across the room with a thud, bobbing in a circular motion until it found footing in a random divot embedded in the floor. Unscathed and deciding *doubling down* was far more entertaining than *backing down*, Charles tugged Tessa closer to him. "It's okay, sweetheart. I'll protect you from Luci's large, angry balls."

CHAPTER 16
THE PEARL-CLUTCHER
TWO HOURS PRIOR

STERLING

"LUCIEN." It wasn't his name itself that sent a shiver down his spine but the way she said it. The perfect pronunciation. The cadence. How a singular word could so clearly hold an underlying meaning. The disappointment. The disapproval. The disinterest that hung in the air. Like his presence alone could evoke such blatant irritation. All of it emitted from the expertly trained vocal cords of the woman in front of him.

"Mother." He could only hope his greeting conveyed as much ill will. Though he was certain it didn't. It was a talent he didn't possess. To be so cold-hearted and distant. To reject your firstborn—your only son—because he no longer fit the picture-perfect image the family sought to maintain. "I assume you know why I'm here."

"Why should I know anything when it comes to you and your comings and goings, son?" Her eyes never met his, firmly focused on the computer screen in front of her, not a hair out of place or a wrinkle in sight. She'd aged like some sort of undead creature and she was just as bloodthirsty and soul-sucking.

"Son? Really? Is that what I am to you? The last decade would say otherwise."

"Let's not start with the dramatics, boy. You chose to lock yourself away like some beast in that tower of yours. Do not seek to garner my pity for it now."

"That's rich… Pity? That's what you think I'm after, Mother? I'm glad to see nothing's changed."

This time, her gaze swept upward, the figure in front of her finally garnering her interest. Or perhaps her curiosity. "Oh, plenty has changed, like your ability to see to a proper shave."

If the debutant had a love language, it would be insults. However, Sterling was certain the four-letter word wasn't in his mother's vernacular. All the woman knew was bitterness. Incorrigibility. And degradation—giving rather than receiving it. She was an ice queen, a sea witch, and every other villainous analogy you could muster.

"Well, get on with it." She twirled her hand in an outward gesture before commanding him like one of her canines, the only beings to ever openly receive her affection. "Speak."

"Do you want me to roll over and play dead too?" he countered.

"That would be a miracle, now, wouldn't it?" she scoffed. "I'd love to see you try. Why don't you give it a go like a good boy, dear?"

This. This was why he couldn't be here. In this house. In this room. With this woman. Everything came down to him and the goddamn chair. Which, despite it being his personal burden to bear, was somehow her affliction as well. As if the accident had been intentional. His way of giving her the ultimate *fuck you*. At least that's how she seemed to view it. Like he had a choice and chose wrong. Like the only thing keeping him from walking out the door was his refusal to do so. They were the elite of society. They were strong. And they certainly weren't disabled.

"You first," he huffed in reply.

She smirked, the grotesque gesture somehow appearing more menacing than her eerie stoicism. "While I've so enjoyed this little… *disruption,* I assume you're here for more than some motherly advice."

"You know exactly why I'm here, Mother Dearest."

"I'm not a mind reader, Lucien. Spit it out or get out."

"His name. Did you have to use his name? There was no calculated, logical reason for it. You knew I'd see it. You knew I'd recognize it.

And you knew there would be no question in my mind who was behind the wire transfer. You didn't even try to cover your tracks. You wanted me to know. And you wanted me to know that you wanted me to know."

"Of course I did. You shouldn't be allowed to forget. To move on whilst he's buried in our own backyard. That name, his face, it should haunt you for the rest of your miserable existence."

"Wow… I don't even know what to say to that. You really are certifiably insane. That was two decades ago!"

"And that doesn't change the fact that you killed him!"

"I was eight! And he was a goddamn dog, Mother! A pet! I'm your son!" He hissed the words, though he knew it would be an argument with no concession. Not from either side. While his inability to "properly represent his family's legacy" had been the end of his familial relationship with the woman who bore him, Sterling was certain the beginning of the end had started nearly twenty years prior… when he had accidentally fed his mother's prized greyhound some table scraps, and the poor thing had later choked to death after a splintered chicken bone had lodged in its throat.

"You are no son of mine. My boy died in that hospital bed, or don't you remember?" Her nostrils flared with disgust as her lip curled into what could only resemble a snarl.

"How could I forget? It was the first choice I was ever allowed to make for myself."

Sterling's parents had wanted him to agree to some experimental treatment, to forgo physical therapy and undergo a series of invasive surgeries his treating physicians had strongly advised against. The risks far outweighed any conceivable reward, but it would have meant their precious heir could possibly walk again. *Possibly*, not probably. The likelihood of success was slim to none. The cost both physically and financially… *astronomical*. But the surgeons had dangled the promise of normality over his parents' heads, like an equestrian with a carrot, and the bluebloods had champed at the bit.

"But that's neither here nor there, Mother," he continued. "End it. Now. Call them, in front of me, and end this ridiculous game of yours."

"I'm not sure I know what you mean, dear." She'd already bombarded him with her usual insults, so apparently her next move was to play coy. Though the woman was about as demure as a cobra waiting to strike.

"You know very well what I mean. We've already established that I know it's you. That I know what you're trying to do. End the nonsense and leave Tess out of this." He slammed his fist down on the freshly waxed surface of her mahogany desk, and for once, the shrew actually appeared rattled.

However, it took milliseconds for her well-established mask to fall firmly into place. "That girl is no good for you. She's just after a paycheck. The family name and money."

"The family money?" Sterling threw his head back in exaggerated laughter. "You mean my money. I stopped being part of this family a long time ago. I don't owe you or them shit."

"Except for that lovely office building of yours," she was quick to bite out, the perfectly painted smirk just barely visible beneath her soured expression.

"Fine. You'll have a transfer in your account within the hour. The value of the building plus interest. Now we're even."

"We will never be even, son. I gave you life. Everything you have is because I *allow* you to have it."

Ah, yes, there were those maternal instincts again, Sterling thought to himself.

Though his spoken reply was much less sarcastic and far more corrosive. "Did you? Or did I save yours? Where would you be if I hadn't been born? If dear old Dad didn't get his male heir? Oh, that's right. *Divorced.* With a prenup and without a penny to your name. If we're discussing gratitude, then I suppose you are so very welcome." When his mother couldn't seem to muster a clever enough retort, her face puckered and her jawline squared as though she were biting on the meat of her cheeks, Sterling repeated his hissed command. "Call. Them. Off."

"I will not."

"You will." He punctuated the two words with a dip of his chin. "Or I'll contest William's claim to my inheritance."

"You wouldn't dare. You want nothing to do with the family business."

Even as his mother offered her words with conviction, Sterling could hear the uncertainty there. The doubt he'd planted in the back of her mind, to take root and bloom into dread, before the visceral reaction turned septic and all but consumed that smug facade the woman liked to present. And the moment he saw it, the crack in her demeanor, he pressed her further.

"No, I want nothing to do with *you*. But force my hand, Mother, do it. And you'll regret it. I'll play the goddamn game. I'll get every penny. Then I'll restore each and every building to its original design, starting with your home office. I'll even make it a point to work my way through all of your satellite locations. Anything with your name on it."

Her lower lip dropped just slightly. But Sterling had seen it. The breaking of her icy exterior. "I—you… Fine, I'll call them off. Now get out of my sight." She dismissed him with a wave of her hand, like she would one of her staff. But it didn't matter. He'd won.

"Gladly, as soon as you make that call."

CHAPTER 17
THE POT

THE PRESENT

TESSA

"YOU KNOW, breaking things never solves anything," Tessa clicked her tongue at the disgruntled man-child in front of her. Charles had left the pair to their own devices twenty odd minutes ago; though Sterling had yet to offer more than the occasional grunt in her direction. She didn't have the time or patience for his delicate ego today. And she'd grown tired of waiting for the sulking architect to speak up.

"Says the pot to the kettle," he muttered under his breath, swirling his second serving of Scotch in the bottom of his glass before downing the contents.

She knew he was referencing the picture frame and perhaps even his shaving mirror; however, Tessa didn't care to acknowledge the validity of his counterargument at the moment. "Lucien, are you going to tell me what happened, what's going on, or are we both wasting our time here?"

He peered up at her, his eyes finally meeting hers, and a vulnerability shown back from their depths, as if someone had pressed reset and this was their first meeting all over again. "Tess, can we just go to bed and do this in the morning? Please?"

For a moment, she hesitated. Because that honestly sounded like the best idea in the world. But she couldn't fall back on old habits. She'd made peace with their breakup. With the understanding that it was better if they just parted ways and ended their unhealthy codependence. So that moment passed as quickly as it came, and her wavering decisiveness gave way to obstinance.

Tessa crossed her arms over her chest and tapped her foot like an impatient school teacher. "No, Lucien, we can't *just go to bed*. There isn't a *we*, nor do we share a bed. Not anymore. You asked me to trust you, to wait for you to do whatever it is you had to do, and against my better judgment, I did. Now it's time for you to deliver on your word."

Sterling maneuvered around the desk and towards the office door. And Tessa sidestepped him, blocking his attempt to flee. He narrowed his eyes and glared up at her, the scent of alcohol permeating her nostrils with each word he hissed in reply. "It was my goddamn dog, Tess."

"What do you mean?" The stiffness in her shoulders laxed as confusion creased her brow.

"The name. Rem E. Steele. Remington Steele. He was the family dog. A retired greyhound. We called him Remy." He took a breath, shook his head, then paused to peer up at her again. "Can I go to bed now? It's been a real shit day, Tess. And if you aren't going to join me, just please let me pass. So I can forget about all of... this..." He gestured to the air, as if it somehow represented the entirety of the day's events. "...for a few hours."

"I'll stay." Though her reply was simple, two short words, so much more hung between them. He nodded. Almost as though he feared speaking had the potential to retract her agreement. And moved through the doorway when Tessa slid over and finally allowed him to pass. "I'll be up in a moment," she called out to his retreating back. Her voice didn't halt his movements nor elicit a response. But she was certain he'd heard her. And would be waiting.

———

She didn't know what exactly had changed her mind—okay, that was a lie. Tessa had been teetering on the edge of concession from the moment he'd asked the question. From the moment she knew he needed it more than he was asking. Regardless of her reasoning, her logic, it was the first thing to feel right since the start of this godforsaken day, month, year even.

It was the only instance where her heart was ever at war with her brain. In the presence of this man. Any other time, the two organs were in constant agreement. What felt right was in fact the right decision. The rational choice was also emotionally driven. The best option was the only option presented by her internal monologue. However, when it came to Sterling, it was as if she were somehow split in two. Each voice trying to shout over the other. One urging her forward while the other screamed at her to flee. It was why she had such a hard time knowing how to behave in his presence. Knowing which version of herself was most appropriate.

The good doctor had mentioned how she'd been losing herself to her personas. How her psyche had been fracturing and compartmentalizing under the stress. Trauma response, or so she'd been told. And it made sense, to an extent. She was cognizant of the separation. It was intentional. How she played a part and just as quickly dropped it in order to move on to the next. Though she'd yet to understand why the man acted like it was an affliction. Something he needed to treat and she needed to recover from.

Without her ability to isolate any one thought or emotion, Tessa would have fallen victim to her insecurities and self-doubts. She never would have picked herself back up and pushed past her moral dissonance, each life decision serving as a barrier to her progression, rather than a hurdle meant to be surmounted.

But none of that was of consequence at the moment. Because she didn't need to perform. Her words didn't need to be carefully chosen. Nor her actions guarded. Not tonight anyway. Because tonight, she wasn't the one falling apart. The one in dire need of being pieced back together again.

The bedroom was dark, pitch-black, but she could feel him watching her. And she could sense the weight of his burden, almost as easily as if it were her own to carry. The gentle whirling of the ceiling fan served to muffle her steps as she crossed the threshold and approached the bed. As her vision adjusted to the shadows, she could make out the even rise and fall of his chest but she knew he was awake. Despite his efforts to appear otherwise.

He hadn't showered or even bothered to change his clothing, the stench of liquor and self-pity telling her what the lack of light could not. It was as if someone had simply thrown him on the bed and left him there to rot amidst his own misery and self-loathing. She switched on the bedside lamp, only to realize her blind assumption wasn't all that far from the truth. The man appeared no better than a decaying corpse, as he stared up into the nothingness of the off-white ceiling paint. His expression lifeless and haunted.

"It was my mother," he stated, breaking the silence and answering a question she hadn't even asked. "She was having you followed. Tested. Maybe trying to pay you to disappear. Who knows? I really can't say what exactly she had in mind. Nor is it in her nature to ever tell me the truth for that matter. So I learned not to think on it too much. Not to waste my time trying to decipher the enigma that is Viola Sterling. But that's beside the point. It's been handled, Tess. Your mother is safe and you won't see those men again."

Tessa stood wordlessly, neither backing away from the bed nor making a move to join him. Of all the villains she'd imagined, who'd plagued her mind and haunted her subconscious, some stuck-up wife of a billionaire wasn't one of them. Though the woman should have made the list—perhaps it was her own innate sexism that helped keep Tessa from giving the heiress a second thought.

Then again, while she knew what it was to fear for her family, it never occurred to her that the danger could be so close to home. And she couldn't imagine what Sterling was feeling at the moment. Where his mind was going. What dark corner his sense of self was presently subjected to.

"I… I don't know what to say, Luc—"

"Don't…" Seeming to notice his harsh tone, Sterling stopped himself. And, as if swallowing his negativity, he took a deep breath and tried again. "Don't call me that. Not today. Please."

"All right." She nodded because she knew he needed it. That one concession. Especially from her. And especially now. "Do you want to talk about it?"

"Not even a little bit."

Placing one knee on the mattress, then the other, Tessa climbed on the bed beside him. Fully clothed. Until her head rested on his shoulder and his arm instinctually tugged her against him. She could feel his heavy intake of air, his chest expanding with the action as he breathed her in. And, as if her presence could somehow cure what ailed him, the tension seemed to leave his body. Though his eyes continued to bore through the ceiling's plaster.

Sterling waited several long minutes before breaking the silence for a second time. "That's not all though…" She stilled but didn't speak. "I lied to you," he admitted on a sigh.

CHAPTER 18
THE KETTLE

STERLING

"WHAT DO you mean you lied to me?" Tessa flew up from the mattress, one arm supporting her weight as she glared down at him. And the sudden chill he felt where the warmth of her body had been was like a knife to the gut—no, *worse*. A knife to the gut meant a far quicker end. This was slow torture. And the best part was that it had all been self-inflicted.

He didn't know what insane part of him decided to ruin the moment, what idiotic brain cell decided that now was a good time to open the floodgates like a dam bursting after a torrential storm; however, he found himself speaking before his common sense thought better of it. "I wanted to know what you were doing, who you were doing—"

"I already told yo—"

"I know you did, love. I know. But I couldn't accept it. I was just so sure… I couldn't get the images out of my head. I couldn't get you out of my head."

"Luc—*Sterling,* it had nothing to do with you."

"I know! I realize that now. And I'm so fucking sorry. I chose my own demons over allowing you to sort through yours."

Tessa sat upright, crossing her legs and pivoting to face him. "What did you do...?"

The weight of her eyes felt like a pile of crunched metal sitting on his chest. As if he were stuck beneath that car all over again. But he couldn't do it. He didn't know how she did. How she was able to twist the truth, bend it to her will, and carry on with her day. It ate him alive. And it had barely been a few hours.

"I asked Charles for help. To figure out where you've been going, who you've been talking to. I just needed a name. To see him. It sounds ridiculous saying it out loud. I know it wouldn't have made a difference or lessened the bullshit going on in my head. But, fuck, if it didn't feel like it would at the time."

"And?"

He could see the anxiety on her face, the growing irritation and impatience. "And he looked through your phone, at my behest." That part wasn't entirely true but it wasn't a lie either. "I know you've been seeing a doctor—*going* to a doctor," he was quick to correct himself.

"Oh..."

"Oh?" His brow furrowed as though it were drawn down subconsciously. If it wasn't for his narrowed vision, he wouldn't have even known he'd made the gesture.

"But that was today..."

"Yes..." he drew out the word. He wasn't understanding her nonchalance. It was eerie, like the calm before a storm, or the silent countdown before the bomb detonated. "You... don't seem all that... *bothered* by it." He was bracing for impact, his body stiffening, and his every nerve ending screaming at him to run—ironic, considering he barely felt most of them, and he sure as hell wasn't going anywhere.

"I mean, what the fuck!" She tapped his chest with the backside of her hand. "But, seriously, how'd he do it?"

She was enjoying this... The woman was near giddy. And while the architect was relieved she hadn't picked up the closest solid object and cracked him across the head with it, he didn't know how to respond to this reaction either.

"Your call log. He narrowed it down to the most recurring number not listed in your contacts. Then did a reverse search."

"Oh, smart." She tapped her finger on her chin, as if considering something for a moment, then quickly dropped her hand. "I didn't think of that. I disconnected my work email but it didn't occur to me to check the call log. Well, next time." Her gaze landed on him before she deadpanned, "Do you think Charlie would be interested in a little freelance work?"

"Are you serious right now?"

"Of course I am. Why?"

"I… um, I lied to you. And you don't seem… mad?"

"I don't know that I'd call it a lie as much as I'd consider it being resourceful." She shrugged.

"Of course you would…" He shook his head and dropped it back down on the pillow, his eyes returning to that unseen hole in the ceiling; though this time it was for an entirely different reason.

"Lucien, are you upset that I'm *not* upset?"

His gaze shifted to his left to glare at her through his peripherals. "I asked you not to—"

"I know." She grinned. She was fucking with him, but he'd been in the wrong, leaving him suspended between a state of annoyance over the fact she'd used his name again and gratitude for her seemingly instantaneous forgiveness. And she was enjoying every moment of his discomfort. He reached out, clutched her wrist, and yanked her forward. She landed on his chest with a thud and a squeal before breaking out into laughter.

Sterling knew it was more of a release of tension than anything else but he couldn't help but smirk at the sound. He tucked her against him, his lips pressing into her forehead as though it were second nature. And it was. It was right. It was exactly what he needed at the moment. After today. Exactly where she was supposed to be. He inhaled her scent, breathing it deep into his lungs and holding it there for as long as his respiratory system would allow him.

"You're doing okay though?" he exhaled the question.

"With…?" she hummed in response. Her body lax and her eyes closed. The telltale signs that sleep was pulling her under.

"With that doctor. He's helping you?"

"Maybe." Her lips barely parted with the singular word, as she shifted her hips to close the minute gap between them before succumbing to exhaustion.

CHAPTER 19
THE CONTROL FREAK

TESSA

"I'M GOING BACK to my apartment tonight."

"Really. Are you ready for that?"

Tessa spun on her heel and narrowed her gaze at him, her scowl an answer in itself, though she stressed her point by adding, "What kind of question is that? I wouldn't go back if I weren't."

"It's a perfectly logical question, Ms. Owens. Just last week, we discussed you staying with Ms. Gallagher for another month or so. And now, seven days later, you've decided to expedite the transition. Why the sudden change? What's brought you to this decision?"

She crossed her arms, her lips pressed into a thin line to avoid saying something she shouldn't. Because that was becoming an all-too-common occurrence. "We didn't discuss anything last week. Because there isn't a *we*. There's a you, the good doctor. And me, the dutiful patient." She watched as his eyebrow raised with the word *dutiful*. And waved her hand as if to dismiss his silent retort.

"Regardless of your choice of adjectives and misdirected anger, Ms. Owens, a change is a change. What was the catalyst?"

She was quiet for a moment, her feet drawing her back to the window as if she'd lost all autonomy and her limbs now acted on their own. Then she stared out the thin, tapered pane, the chill of glass reaching the tip of her nose and sending a shiver down her spine. "I saw him yesterday."

"You've seen him before. What was different about this time?" he prompted, and she never realized just how grating the sound of his voice had become.

She could hear it in her head at times, sometimes louder than her own, always questioning. Always urging her to think and conjecture and stop to breathe. It was irritating, constantly having someone else in your head. And suddenly her thoughts were drawn to *him* and what he'd said last night. About her being in his. How preoccupied he'd been—near obsessive—and she understood the drive. The need to know. The inability to think about anything else. It was her affliction when it came to work. And when it came to one particular man.

She knew Doc was waiting for her. He always waited. Gave her time to sort her thoughts and evaluate them; though, more often than not, she used the silence as a way to avoid him. To run the clock out as it *ticked, ticked, ticked* in the background. She would have thought he'd have caught on by now. If he had, he hadn't mentioned it. However, he didn't mention much when it came to her. Always questioning, that one. But rarely answering. Rarely giving anyone a glimpse of the cards in his hand. Which, she supposed, was a clever move on his behalf. To tilt the microscope so it only ever faced outwards.

"I don't know." Tessa shook her head.

"You don't know what?" he parroted.

"What was different. But something was."

"Something like?"

"That's an annoying habit, you know?" she threw the dig over her shoulder, refusing to actually face him this time.

"Your intentional use of deflection?" He grinned. She didn't see it but she could hear it in his voice. "You're right. It is."

And she couldn't help but smirk. Because it was true. She was deflecting. She wasn't actually irritated with the man himself. She was irritated with the fact he was redirecting her to the same thoughts she wanted to keep buried. To the issues she was more than happy to leave unresolved. Because dragging them to the surface left her uncomfortable and exposed. Like a corpse abandoned to rot amongst the elements. And she could feel her insides churning with the grotesque imagery. The bile sitting heavy in her throat.

"He needed me." She shrugged as though the admission wasn't prized from her mouth with the same force as a shiny new pair of forceps reaching in and pulling teeth.

"So the dynamic changed? That's the difference?"

"I don't know what you mean…" What she really meant to say was that she didn't want to know what he meant. She didn't want to delve that deep into her motives.

"Of course you do, Ms. Owens…"

"You can call me Tessa," she was quick to interject. Her lips curling and her fingertips tapping against her elbow.

And he dismissed her just as quickly. "I can but I won't. As we have discussed—"

"*Discussed before*… yeah, yeah." She twirled her wrist, signaling for the stubborn bastard to just get on with it.

Doc shook his head, repositioning the recording device before continuing. "As I was saying, Ms. Owens, the difference appears to lie in the change in your relationship—"

"We don't have a relationship, remember? Lucien and I ended things." Even to her own ears, the rushed clarification sounded weak.

"*You* ended things. If I recall correctly. But regardless of the specifics, how you interact with those outside your person is considered a relationship. Just as we have a doctor-patient relationship, you and Mr. Sterling maintain an interdependence. An innate dynamic, which was established during your first interaction, then morphed and reestablished with every exchange thereafter. Think of it as a balance of perceived power. Like the relationship between an irate customer and an exhausted sales clerk. Someone always feels or appears to have the upper hand. It's human nature. And who that person is—the one guiding the exchange—varies from circumstance to circumstance. That same irate customer may call in a manager, gaining the leverage. Winning, if you want to simplify the verbiage. However, take that customer and drop him in a different scenario. He leaves the store and gets pulled over for speeding. Same person. Same man. Nothing has changed except the circumstance. His relationship. And perceived lack of power."

"And who am I in this story you are painting?" she pressed. For no reason other than to indulge her curiosity. After all, it had always been just as much a blessing as it was a curse.

"You're both. Sometimes all three. The customer, the sales clerk, and the police officer. However, in a more concrete way of speaking, we don't change who we are. Suddenly shifting from being one person to the next. Instead, we shift how we respond to our outside forces and how they make us feel. When you're at your lowest, you feel like that sales clerk. That doesn't make you him. Or change your ability to overcome your obstacles. But it does change how insurmountable they feel. When you fight against a perceived wrong, you're the customer and you get that rush of adrenaline. That high of being right. Winning. Coming out on top. And then, when it wears off, and forces outside your control—or perhaps forces within it that just seem unconquerable—start to cage you in, you feel like your power is ripped away. And you're stuck. You can try to outrun the police car, you can pull over, or you can try to ignore it. Continue as if you don't see the flashing red lights behind you. But none of those responses change your reality. Just how you react to it. Lastly, when you're at that low point again—lower still because you had the power and it was taken away—you seek out another speeding car. Something to divert your attention. A wrong you can right. And once again, it works. Momentarily. Because you've taken back your power. Shifted the dynamic. The relationship."

"You like to hear yourself talk, hmm?" she postulated.

"No more than you do," the aging physician was quick to retort.

Tessa tensed her molars, tooth clenching against tooth, to hold back her sudden urge to grin. She could only assume he meant to imply the tapes she'd been confiscating after their recorded sessions; however, he made no further verbalization to indicate as much. The accusation dying on his tongue as quickly as it had arisen.

Instead, Doc leaned back into the cushion of his office chair and eyed her with the curiosity of a researcher eyeing a test subject. He watched her facial expressions, her posturing, the count of her breaths.

And she watched him watching her. The silence stretching onwards as each occupant dared the other to speak.

The audible timekeeping of the clock was beginning to irritate her. Grate on Tessa's nerves. She knew the man had a proclivity for his archaic relics but surely that sound—the continued *tick, tick, tick* of the second hand—had to get to him. Day after day. It was maddening. And so she'd concluded that the sound of her own voice was in fact a better option.

"What is it you're trying to say, Doc? Can we get to the point instead of exchanging bedtime stories?" Had her mood been better, lighter, she would have considered it a failure. Her inability to remain in the empty quietude of the room without surrendering to the innate urge to fill it.

"You, Miss Owens, are a very, very intelligent woman. One who's often not given enough credit for that asset in favor of others. I won't be so blind as to do the same. Figure it out. Explore what I've told you, apply it to yourself and your current situation with the architect, and then, when you've come to a determination, we can discuss it next week."

"Fine," she huffed the singular word, wrenching her jacket from the coatrack and shoving her fingers through the sleeves. "So grateful for all your help," she hissed. "Has anyone ever told you that you sound like a goddamn fortune cookie?"

The balding, gray-eyed, overtly unfazed man smirked. His forehead further creasing with the gesture while the glimmer in his eye gave him a near youthful appearance. At least at the moment. "Only on my good days." He then raised a hand and gestured for the door. "See you next week, Ms. Owens."

She dipped her chin in acknowledgment, grabbing the handle and pulling it inward before exiting without a reply. Her heels clicked on the dingy tile flooring all the way down the length of the hallway, her mind lost to one man's image and another's words.

CHAPTER 20
THE UPPER HAND

TESSA

SHE KNEW IT WAS A RIDDLE. Not one all that deep when she really thought about it. However, it wasn't one she wished to unravel. No matter how blatantly it waved its red flag in her face.

Because doing so meant what she feared all along. She'd been wrong. That her reasons for leaving had been far more skewed than her initial logic had promised her. That she'd hurt the one man she wanted to protect out of fear and self-preservation, rather than true insight. That she wasn't as clever as she thought herself to be. And Sterling was cannon fodder for her poor decision-making. She could see his inner turmoil, practically feel it vibrating beneath his fingertips when he reached out to embrace her. Tugging her against him, like an addict in desperate need of a fix.

And she was starting to realize she'd done that to him. All of it. She'd blown up his life just as Corey had warned her she would and then left him to cope with the aftermath. Alone. On his own. Because she insisted they weren't good for each other.

The truth was… she wasn't good for *him*. She didn't know how to fix things, only break them. And she didn't even realize that's who she'd become. Someone who created chaos, then abandoned ship when it became too difficult to navigate around the debris. She was toxic. Not him. Not them together. And yet, he chased her all the same. He wanted her. Or else he was more self-destructive than she was…

The change in circumstance—in their dynamic as Doc liked to call it—was easy enough to decipher. It was exactly as she'd mentioned. Just that simple. He needed her. He was broken. And his brokenness called to hers. Perhaps it had always been there. Tamped down in favor of protecting her. But Tessa had been far too broken herself to realize it. To see him. To recognize the pain that mirrored her own.

Then again, she knew that even if she had seen it, she would have been blind to it. Willingly so. Buried it alongside her trauma before leaving it there to rot.

But in needing her, in his state of obvious vulnerability, she felt in control again. Of her emotions, of their *relationship*, of her ability to make logic-driven choices. And being in control, feeling as though she had the upper hand, that was a comfort. Seeing as the man had watched her slowly deteriorate in such a short time. He'd watched her fall apart more than once and been there to piece her back together. And that level of dependency just wouldn't do. Not for Tessa.

It was terrifying. Allowing someone else the power—the ability—to pick you back up also presented them with the opportunity to knock you down. To push you over that ledge and watch you drown.

And that thought had her pulse racing and her palms sweating. And suddenly it hit her, how ironic it was that both fear and excitement elicited the same physical reactions.

At the moment, neither would do. She needed to focus on the task at hand. At getting her life back together and regaining some form of normalcy. Which included finishing this article, returning to her apartment, and facing Corey. Though some of those tasks were easier than others. She'd been avoiding him. Much like she had been avoiding everything. And even Tessa knew how wrong it was.

"He's on his way over," Laney interjected, as if reading the journalist's thoughts.

"Who is?"

"My brother."

"Oh, um, why?" While Tessa was eager to break the awkwardness between herself and her partner, she hadn't mentally prepared for the interaction quite yet. She hadn't choreographed the exchange, planned out the dialogue and every possible outcome.

"Because, believe it or not, the pretty boy can lift more than a beer can and you've accumulated a lot of shit in a short time." Laney scanned the moderate-sized living room before gesturing to the random piles of boxes scattered across the flooring.

Several minutes and a few knocks later, Corey was being escorted into the room. His hands tucked into his pants, his hair purposefully tousled to the side, a boyish grin curling his lips. And, for once, Tessa could see the attraction. Not feel it. But having distanced herself from the man in front of her, she suddenly saw him in a different light. He was every girl's dream. Every girl but those in present company.

"Hey, TK," he seemed to hum, the complexity of their past interactions suspended in the air between them. Tangible but unspoken. "How've you been?"

Tessa was hesitant, unsure how to carry herself in his presence after avoiding him for so long. After breaking down so completely and confessing so much more than she ever intended. But silence and evasion were no longer the answer. Nor were they really an option at the moment, as he appeared to stare through her with no escape in sight.

"I'm good. Okay. Better." The journalist flung the adjectives out with little care for their meaning as she rose from her seat on the sofa and closed the distance. Every nerve ending in her body was screaming, telling her to keep her spine straight and her head held high. But when he opened his arms, Tessa fell into his embrace as easily as if it had been moments since she'd last been there rather than weeks. Months.

Corey squeezed once before releasing her. "So I heard you have a shit-ton of boxes that need relocating. You sure about this?"

Tessa nodded, her arms folding over her chest with her hip slightly cocked. The posturing both confident and guarded. "Yeah, I need to go home. It's time."

What she didn't mention was what it was time for; though verbalizing it didn't seem necessary. Because her partner appeared to understand. It was time to face the world again. To stop hiding. And to reclaim her sanity.

It was time to remember the woman she was again. And forget the girl she used to be.

————

The door swung open to the same barely furnished space. The same white walls and lackluster decor choices. A room without personality that could belong to anyone, though it was hers. Tessa never realized just how cold her apartment felt until this moment. Until leaving the warmth of Laney's living room and Lucien's office. She thought she would be comforted by the change in atmosphere. By returning some-where, to something, that was her own. By the normalcy of it all.

However, comfort seemed to be evading her while unease took its place, the sensation crawling up her spine before settling at the base of her neck like a serpent about to strike. She didn't want to be here but she didn't want to be anywhere else either. It was a contradiction, just like everything else in her life. She didn't know why she assumed this transition would be any different. *Better.*

"Where do you want it?" Corey forced his way over the threshold, the door knob bouncing against the plaster wall as he maneuvered his way inside with far too many boxes. He was the bull in her china shop, though she had nothing worth breaking. Not anymore.

"Wherever you want to put it, handsome," she replied with an elbow to his abdomen.

"Okay, ew," Laney muttered from behind him.

And her brother was quick to agree. "Yeah, what she said."

"Sorry... sometimes it's hard to turn off." Tessa shrugged her shoulders, though she would be the first to admit that she'd made the situation far more awkward. Corey had never been the target of her false affections and shameless flirting; however, nowadays, it seemed everyone was free game. As if the journalist wore her sexuality as a coat of armor far more openly than she had in the past. Which was saying something.

Corey dropped the last box on the floor with a thud before pivoting to face her again. "What the hell is in all of these anyway?" he questioned, straightening his spine and cracking his neck to the side, the popping of his vertebrae bouncing off the walls in the hushed reticence of the room. "It didn't look like you packed this much when you left."

"Documents." She waved her hand as if to dismiss him, then caught herself. She was doing it again. Pushing him away when she was supposed to be bringing him in. He was her partner, and even after everything, after the way she treated him, he stood by her side. "Blueprints, historical records, deeds…" she clarified.

"For?" he prompted. Laney remained silent, though she watched the interaction from afar as Tessa shrunk beneath Corey's scrutiny.

"Another article… on Lucien." The irate Irishman dropped his jaw to speak but Tessa held up a hand. "It's not what you're thinking. And you are more than welcome to help. I mean… that sounded…" She dug her index fingers into her temples. Her mouth and her brain weren't communicating. Her tone was sarcastic and her posturing was defensive. She wasn't looking to initiate a fight, yet everything about her body language suggested otherwise. Tessa dropped her hands and peered up at him. "I'm sorry…" And even she knew those words sounded foreign as they reverberated off her lips. They tasted foreign too, like an overseasoned meal she couldn't quite spit out. "What I meant to say was… he requested the article—Lucien did. It's… not our typical repertoire. But I'd appreciate the help. If you're interested."

Corey grinned, the gesture both bright and genuine. "I knew you missed me—"

"Now, I didn't say—"

"Sure you didn't." He chuckled, tugging her within arm's reach before shoving her to the side and making a run for her freezer.

She shook her head, calling out to his back, "It's empty, you jackass!"

CHAPTER 21
THE TWO QUEENS

TESSA

"SO, WHAT DO YOU THINK?" She was pacing again. But no matter how hard she tried to stop her movements, it was as if her legs —her feet—pressed forward and back involuntarily. Tessa didn't know if it was nerves or the thrill of it that urged her repetitive actions; however, neither option was that far out of left field. It seemed like an eternity since she was so compelled by a lead, yet it was as if no time had passed at all. Like curiosity burned in her veins and she couldn't ignore it even if she tried.

"I think you're right. It's definitely… different." Corey appeared to chew on that last word. Though it didn't matter how uncertain he was, because the urge to press on vibrated in the journalist's bones. It breathed life into her lungs and adrenaline through her every nerve ending.

"Of course I'm right. I'm always right," she huffed, pausing midstep before turning a finger on her counterpart. "There's a story there. I'm telling you."

Corey dropped his jaw to argue with her, or perhaps to agree, but his words were severed by the buzzing of an intercom.

Tessa looked from the man in front of her to her apartment door before stalking towards the sound. She glided her fingertip across the square panel, gently depressing the button staring back at her at eye level. "Hello," she called into the receiver.

"Miss Owens?" a stuffy male voice called back.

"This is she… How can I help you?" Tessa's brow furrowed as her brain scrambled to find recognition where there was none.

"Your car is here waiting, ma'am," he replied as though it made perfect sense. It didn't.

"Thank you but I didn't order a car." She dropped her hand, prepared to step away, when the unwanted visitor halted her actions for a second time.

"No, ma'am, the car was sent by Mrs. Viola Sterling. She's requested your presence at the family estate in Glencoe."

Tessa sucked in a sharp breath before her lips curled into a cryptic smirk. She could feel Corey's eyes boring into her forehead from across the room as she leaned closer to the intercom and responded, "Right. We'll be down in a moment. Thank you."

"Yes, ma'am."

"Nope. No, no, no, no, no." Corey raised a finger in her direction, waving it back and forth as if she were a pet who'd soiled the carpet. "Don't even think about it, TK. Not happening." He pushed to his feet and crossed the room in two long strides, meeting his counterpart at the doorway where she was already slipping her arms through her coat sleeves.

"And why exactly not?"

"Tess, you can't be serious. That woman had you followed for months, threatened and attacked you—"

"Technically—"

"No! Not *technically*. She paid that man. She knew exactly the sort of people she hired and she didn't care about the ramifications. Those are the kind of snobby assholes who pay henchmen to drop your body at the bottom of the Chicago River, then grease enough palms to ensure no one goes looking."

If it were even possible, Tessa's lips seemed to upturn all the more as she adjusted her collar and fastened the four buttons on her jacket. Then she inched forward, placing a hand on each of Corey's wrists.

Peering up at him, she allowed her lashes to flutter once. Twice more. And replied with a hum, "*Mon chou,* did I ever tell you about the time I embedded myself in the New York mob?"

Corey's palm instinctively thumped against his forehead as he released an exaggerated sigh. "For fuck's sake, woman, what the hell is wrong with you?"

Choosing to ignore his question, Tessa offered him one of her own. "So, are you coming or not?"

COREY

The woman was certifiable. Though, considering the more recent events, Corey thought better of voicing that opinion. Even as they were escorted up the long driveway of the statuesque estate, lined with perfectly manicured shrubbery and the sort of landscaping that required a horde of groundskeepers to maintain. This wasn't just money; it was affluence. It was titles and trust funds. Esteem and familial recognition. Beyond anything the barely middle-class son of a factory worker could ever hope to grasp. And Corey didn't know whether to be impressed by the opulence or disgusted by the clear excess.

Though he didn't have too much time to wonder either, as they were ushered from the back of the town car and directed through the towering double doors leading into the foyer—or whatever rich people called their entryway—with its pillars, decorated vases, and shiny tile flooring. So shiny his exact image was reflected back at him any time he dared to glance downwards. His work boots tapped and echoed in the empty space, and Corey was certain his person had seen more dirt than every square inch of the residence combined.

In truth, he wasn't sure what the point was of having so much room in a house that never felt lived in. It was like visiting a museum, just as sterile and unwelcoming. Especially the piercing blue eyes that glared down at where the pair presently stood. Dull, lifeless. Unapologetic and narrowed in as if she could she see past them. Through them. If the giant portrait hanging above the entryway was this terrifying, Corey could only imagine what the corporeal version of the woman would be like. Their driver seemed to linger for a moment, before making a swift exit the same way he'd come, as though to leave the sacrificial lambs to their slaughter.

Corey turned to his counterpart, who appeared far more at ease amongst the extravagance than he'd ever be. Then again, that was Tessa. A chameleon in whatever crowd she stumbled upon. "You know, it's not too late to turn back," he muttered, the useless reminder forced through the side of his mouth.

She shook her head and grinned. She was enjoying it. His discomfort, the high of the unknown, a chance at besting someone who clearly underestimated her. Corey could see it in her eyes—that spark. That twinkle she'd been missing for months now. And he was both relieved and wary. Because, at the moment, he didn't know who was more dangerous. The woman in front of him, or the one who had yet to make herself seen. The devil he knew and sometimes feared, or the one he didn't. It was anyone's guess.

The lady of the house made them wait exactly thirty-two minutes (he'd counted) before summoning them to her parlor. A gesture meant to make them sweat; though Corey seemed to be the only one perspiring beneath the harsh lighting of the crystal chandelier. Tessa appeared unfazed, bored even, as if she'd been expecting this move all along and was none too impressed. And he could only assume that observation wasn't far from the truth. The woman lived for mind games, whereas Corey was a much simpler being. The kind of man who was content with a good beer, a great fuck, and a mediocre meal. He could hear his own stomach grumbling at the thought. He highly doubted the present company ate anything that wasn't garnished with gold flecks and served on a platter worth more than his yearly paycheck. His eyes flicked to the tray of dry biscuits laid out in front of them.

Yep, what he wouldn't give for a goddamn cheeseburger right now.

Viola Sterling made her appearance like a Hollywood starlet in a black and white film. All she was missing was the fluffy, sheer widow's robe as she floated through the doorway to greet them. "Mr. Gallagher, Ms. Owens, I see you've made yourselves comfortable. Were the refreshments not to your liking?" She gestured to the untouched platter and spotless china. She didn't really care—that much was evident—however, the question was expected of the diligent hostess. It was the polite thing to say. Proper decorum.

"Refreshments aren't exactly the reason we're here, now are they?" Tessa was quick to counter.

"Oh? Then why are you here, sweet girl?" the woman hummed as though they were an imposition, despite having imposed both her will and her driver on them, while the endearment may as well have been an insult.

"To make you feel as little and insignificant as you tried to make Lucien feel. Perhaps more so." Tessa shrugged, peering down at her nails, her lack of attention deeming the older woman a nuisance.

"Bold words. From a bold girl. But not so bold as to come alone, hm?" Viola's heels clinked across the marble flooring, the sound both irritating and ominous as she approached the wet bar to pour herself a brandy.

"Oh, he's not here for me," the journalist replied without missing a beat, before hitching a thumb in Corey's direction. "Oh, no, he's here for you, *vieille vache*, to intercept should you force me to be anything less than ladylike. Besides, I always work better with an audience."

"Audience?"

"Well, you should know. You do like watching me, don't you? Sending your little minions to observe my every move. So, here I am. Watch to your heart's content." Tessa draped her arms across the modern sofa, leaning back into the stiff cushion. Her posturing was open, confrontational. "Go on. Grab a camera. Or do you need to borrow mine?" She pushed herself forward, slamming her phone down on the coffee table, her screen clanking on the marble before she crossed her legs and resumed her position of defiance. "Now, what is it that you want, Viola?"

"Mrs. Sterling," the debutante was quick to correct. "I want what any mother would want—whatever's best for my son."

"I see. And what is it that you think is best?"

"Not you, that's for certain. So how much will it take?"

"For?"

"For you to disappear, child. Don't play coy," the aristocrat chided.

"Mmm, way more than you can afford." Tessa's lips curled into that signature smirk, the one that told Corey the punch line had yet to come.

"Try me." The woman's eyes narrowed, as if drawn to the challenge. As if feeding on it as much as it disgusted her.

"The truth." And there it was. The catch. The hidden motive.

"Excuse me?" The two words seemed to lodge in Mrs. Sterling's throat.

"Oh, you heard me. I want the truth, Viola."

"And which truth is that?"

"Lucien's paternity. Does he know about your chauffeur?"

CHAPTER 22

THE BULL'S EYE

TESSA

TESSA WATCHED the woman's throat, the tension in her jaw as she swallowed whatever lie she'd deemed insufficient, the way she flicked her eyes to the side and swirled the remnants of her brandy in her near-empty glass. Viola was hiding something. Something big. And the journalist had just begun to unravel the enormous web of deception.

"I don't know what you think you know, girl, but accusations like that could ruin a life… a career… and I don't mean mine."

The matriarch had resorted to threats. It spoke of desperation, and a lack of any real counterargument. She may as well have rolled over and presented her throat, because the only next plausible step was the woman's ultimate submission.

Tessa smirked, half because she was savoring the win and half because it was almost too easy. "I had his DNA tested, you know. Uploaded to one of those genetic sites. Your son was more than eager to provide a *sample*."

"Enough." The sound was closer to a bark than anything else. "I'll ask you this once more. What do you want?"

Tessa leaned forward, one arm still snaked along the sofa while her head and upper body lessened the distance between the two opponents. A few inches meant to demonstrate clear obstinance and an utter lack of fear. "And I'll tell you this one more time… in English… unless you have a preference? *Parlez-vous français?*" When the question was met with silence, Tessa continued. "Right, I didn't think so. English it is. I want the truth. Admit it. Tell me about his biological father and I'll walk out that door. You won't hear from me again. Nor will your son. I won't even write a story about it. I just want to hear the words. Watch them leave your lips. And that satisfaction alone is worth its weight in gold."

"I… you little—fine." Viola's jaw snapped shut like a rabid canine sinking its teeth into flesh. "Lucien's father needed an heir. And I needed to produce one. So I did what had to be done. What my dear husband couldn't. I won't feel guilty for fulfilling my obligations. That's what wives—what mothers do—whatever needs to be done. What men don't have the ingenuity to do themselves. We carry the burden and we move on."

"Is that what your son was to you? A burden?" Tessa scoffed, though she knew the answer without ever having to hear it verbalized. It was evident in the woman's eyes.

"In many ways, yes. I didn't choose motherhood. It was assigned to me. There you have it. The truth as you call it. Though I'm not sure what good it will do you now." Viola refilled her glass before chugging the contents. "No one will believe you. And that sample of yours? By tomorrow, it will be listed as a lab error and removed from whatever mediocre database you thought yourself clever enough to utilize." She pivoted on her designer heels, her eyes narrowed down at her accuser. "You think you've won, dear sweet girl, but you were never even playing my game. We're in separate leagues, you and I, and mine is on a level you have no chance of reaching—so don't strain your neck looking up."

"You're right," Tessa hummed. She could feel Corey's discomfort radiating off him like a washing machine stuck on spin cycle. His eyes boring into the side of her head as though he was attempting to see its contents. "About one thing anyway. We aren't on the same level." She slid a hand over her cellular device before flipping it over. "Though I'm afraid you've misinterpreted who is seated where."

It took several long breaths for the reality of the situation to set in, for Viola to understand what she was looking at. But Tessa could tell the moment it clicked. The moment the older woman realized she'd been recorded. Her tightly held confession cemented within a few seconds of sound waves. Something so little, so insignificant had been her undoing.

However, Viola didn't hesitate. She refused to admit defeat even in the face of it. She clicked her tongue; whether it was at herself or the adversary in front of her was unclear. "Did you really think you were leaving this house with that phone intact?" She punctuated the ambiguous question with a chuckle.

"Doesn't matter if I do. What's done is done. Did you really think I wouldn't have a back-up plan? Everything has been autosaved to a secure cloud." As if to further demonstrate her point, Tessa tossed the cellular device on the floor, standing, only to crush it with the heel of her boot before repositioning herself as though she'd never moved in the first place. "There you go. The phone is all yours. But… if you even consider trying to keep us here, that little sound bite will be sent—anonymously—to every news outlet in the midwest. Then forwarded to the east coast before my contacts in New York ensure it makes its way to the west. My remote colleague is just waiting on my word to stop that transmission from happening. Without it, he has the green light."

"You're bluffing." Viola hissed the two words between clenched teeth; though spoken with a harshness, they were missing their conviction.

"Try me." The journalist shrugged, as if each possible outcome mattered as much as the last. She didn't care. If she lived. If she died. If they all burned. Because either way she'd been the victor. She'd outsmarted the woman with the keys to the kingdom, and there was no countermove to change the trajectory of this present moment.

The sound emitting from Viola's throat was somewhere between a shriek and a battle cry. But her slumped shoulders quickly straightened in unison with her spine. She'd remembered her place, her standing, her station in life. And with each of those came the need to persevere. To adjust and bend reality to her will.

"Fine. I'll have Maurice drive you home. You're dismissed, with the assumption you'll keep your word. I'd hate to think what might happen should you break it." The lady of the house, with her mask firmly in place, waved a dismissive hand like a spider who'd grown tired of playing with the fly that had been lucky enough to escape her web.

"That won't be necessary. I've already arranged for a cab. I'm not sure I can trust Maurice to keep his wandering eyes on the road. Wouldn't want to chance another accident." Tessa grinned, enjoying how Viola visibly stiffened at the double entendre, the woman's eyes shifting as though she were trying to muster a sharper-driven quip.

"You know, you two really are an adorable couple." The matriarch gestured between her guests as she led them to the front door. "I didn't understand it before… but, yes, now I see it."

Corey's head snapped up at the implication, but Tessa didn't miss a beat in responding, "Your son and me? Yes, I know. Just took me a bit to figure it out for myself." Though she spoke the statement aloud, the last part hadn't been meant for anyone else's ears. It was directed inwardly in a moment of self-realization. As if the journalist was just now understanding the truth of her own words.

———

The cab was waiting outside when Corey and Tessa descended the stone stairs, slid into the worn leather seats, and welcomed the rush of fresh air through the lowered windows with a sense of shared freedom. It had been touch and go for a while there, and both journalists seemed to understand that.

Once the estate became no more than a blip in the rearview mirror, Corey turned to his companion, voicing the question that seemed to be dancing on his tongue since they'd escaped the confines of that stuffy room and stuffier woman. "How did you know?"

Tessa shrugged as if the events of the day had been nothing more than a normal exchange, rather than a threat against life and limb, ending in a shattered cell phone. "I didn't."

Two words. So simple and yet the man in front of her failed to comprehend them in the slightest. "What do you mean *you didn't?*"

"Exactly that. I had my suspicions after we dove into the canceled engagement and shifted through his family history. But nothing concrete."

"How? Why? I don't remember seeing anything that suggested his paternity was in question."

"It's not. It wasn't. That woman made sure of it." Tessa gestured behind them. "As you've seen, they'll do whatever it takes to maintain their squeaky-clean image. The image of the perfect family. The perfect family with perfect genes. Until that perfect blue-eyed couple produced a son lacking that particular recessive feature. Now, it could have been an abnormality—a natural fluke or mutation. But something told me it wasn't. Especially when you take into account how long it took them to conceive, prefaced by a prenup that included a clause about producing a male heir. It's funny what can be made a matter of public record if you know where to look. But that was all theory… until I took note of our driver, how his gaze seemed to linger on Viola's portrait when we were escorted inside, a gaze which included a pair of chocolate-brown eyes, as well as his age and unmistakable knowledge of the grounds. Something told me I was right. So I presented it as fact rather than conjecture. A simple roll of the dice that happened to favor the player."

"The DNA?"

"A lie." Her reply was nonchalant.

"And the recording?" he prompted.

"Another lie," she confirmed. "I did record the woman with that app I have—you know the one. But there's no cloud storage. That device was an old backup with shotty service and barely any Wi-Fi connection."

"Then why the fuck did you smash it? I don't get it… What was the point?" he huffed like a toddler who'd just learned the tooth fairy isn't real.

"To double down. Solidify the bluff. It doesn't matter what you know, just the conviction of which you say it. Besides, I was never going to use it. That's not my secret to tell, to rip away the only father he's ever known. Some things are best kept buried."

"...you're really not going to tell...?" It was a statement, even though it was presented as a question. And Tessa knew a lecture was soon to follow.

"No, I'm not. And before you try to argue otherwise, I've already thought this through. The truth doesn't always set you free, *mon chou.* Sometimes it cages you in your despair. I refuse to be the one to do that to him... again."

Corey nodded, then straightened his spine and peered up as if struck by another thought. "There's still one thing I don't understand..."

"And what's that?"

"Everything you said is verifiable. That family—that woman—is going to look for all those loose ends you mentioned: the website, the remote colleague, the cloud storage. She's not going to give up. You know that, right? What are you gonna do when she comes up empty-handed? When she comes looking for answers? Or to shut you up for good...?"

Tessa sighed, leaning back into the leather seat much like she had on the sofa at the estate. "It's exponentially more difficult to search the haystack for a needle that never existed. Because when you get to the bottom, you can never be quite sure if you missed something. So you'll start again, one wisp at a time, only to come to the same conclusion. Repeating the process over and over until you drive yourself mad. And I don't see her far from that edge to begin with." The journalist lifted a single shoulder to further solidify the sentiment.

Corey sat dumbfounded, as if he were seeing the woman in front of him in a whole new light. "I don't know if that's evil or ingenious..."

Tessa grinned, her lips curling like some villain popping up at the end of a movie. "Why can't it be both?"

CHAPTER 23
THE HOUSE OF CARDS

STERLING

IT HAD BEEN days since he'd heard from Tessa—seven to be exact. She'd answered her professional emails regarding the article but had given him little more than a curt, emotionless response. He should be grateful for that much. He knew it, but that knowledge did little to elevate the darkness that seemed to shroud his mood.

His mother had fallen off the radar. But he realized that only meant that she was plotting. Lurking in the shadows until the time was right for her to pounce, as though the woman were an antagonist in someone else's story. Since clearly she wasn't satisfied with her own.

The mindless chatter was dulling his senses, as his eyes flicked from corner to corner. Sterling didn't usually attend these sorts of events. He never had much emotionally invested in these homes. They were nothing more than a way to distract his mind. To fix something when he couldn't fix himself. But there was something different about the Victorian. It reminded him of *her*. And selling it felt wrong. Almost as though he were losing a part of her in the deal. He knew it didn't make sense. It was a piece of property. Four walls. A foundation. Several gallons of paint and plaster. Sure, some pretty stained-glass windows and more original features than he was used to salvaging. But it wasn't more than that, was it?

It was foolish of him to consider keeping it. It wasn't practical to buy a home, where he'd never venture past the first floor. And installing an elevator or chair lift wasn't an option. It would ruin what he'd worked so hard to restore. So, yes, he knew none of it was logical; however, it didn't stop him from considering it. From prolonging the inevitable for as long as he could. But the time had come and here he was.

His presence was unnecessary. He'd hired a realtor to handle the open house, Tessa's article had made certain the event was properly publicized, and his name alone (after the fiasco that was his social life for the past few months) would bring the crowds to his doorstep regardless. But each time his mind flitted back to the way she'd raced up that staircase, how her eyes begged him to salvage the interior while her mouth asked if they could *keep it*, his chest ached with something far beyond the physical.

He saw the woman's reflection in every hand-laid piece of glass tile, heard the gentle hum of her voice in each creak of the original floorboards underfoot, smelled her perfume as the wind carried the scent of the fresh-cut flowers from the table by the window into the office space he presently occupied. It was almost as if he could feel her presence within the walls, though it had been days since she inhabited them. In reality, it was the ghost of her memory that plagued the man, far more incessantly than any phantasmal apparition ever could.

The crowds had begun to line up nearly an hour ago. Some were serious buyers, others were potential investors, while most were merely curious onlookers—hoping to get a glimpse of the broken billionaire. Oddly enough, his mother would be happy to know he'd had several marriage proposals thrown his way once his lineage had been made public knowledge. Single women and their parents alike probably assuming they could lock him away in some rehab facility after garnering full access to his various bank accounts. He was a gold-digger's wet dream—nearly as enticing as an oil tycoon on his deathbed—an affluent husband they could only presume they'd never have to service.

I mean, part of him was broken so all of him must be, right? Or so he'd been told over and over again. By everyone. Everyone except her...

And so Sterling was back to where he'd started. Obsessing over a woman he was better off forgetting. A self-induced flagellation that had gone full circle. Beginning and ending with the one person who seemed to see beyond his exterior, much like he'd seen the heart of this home.

The clicking of heels through the entryway both soothed and irritated him. They reminded him of Tessa's confident stride, how she entered every room as if she didn't just own it but possessed it in a way that somehow thickened the air. But the sound also evoked the realization that each new houseguest was continuously scuffing his freshly polished floors—the higher the heel, the more exacting the damage. They may as well get it over with, pull out a penknife, and carve their initials into the floorboards. It would ultimately quicken what their clear lack of regard was already setting into motion.

Though there was something different about the present sound, about the pattern and echo of the stride. Something beyond Sterling *willing* it to be familiar. Because it was familiar. He canted his head to the side, pivoting to face the door just as someone's shadow darkened it. "Tess... what are you doing here?" He knew the way the question sounded but his mouth asked it anyway, his brain having failed to sever the transmission in order to keep his lips from moving.

She took two more steps until she'd fully breached the threshold before stopping in her tracks, her hip cocked to one side and her right hand instinctively resting against it. "Would you like me to go?" Though her tone was sarcastic, she underscored it with a grin. She was amused, while the hesitant architect prayed that it was a good thing.

Sterling paused for a breath, his disbelief getting the better of him until his smug mask slammed back into place. "If I say yes, will that make you stay?" The retort was meant to draw on her memory, remind her of what she'd confessed in the moment.

The easiest way to get me to stay is to tell me to leave.

That was what she had told him anyway. And thinking on it, he understood it to be true. The woman was the epitome of oppositional defiance, the definition of what it meant to break all the barriers and rules. She needed the challenge and fed on her ability to prove you wrong. Because her need for control meant he had to relinquish it. He had to admit that there was absolutely nothing he could do to make her stay.

"It just might…" She smirked, and he knew she remembered—more so, she liked that he had too. That he took her words and tossed them back at her with the ease of a worthy opponent.

The voices were growing louder in the distance, the crowds filtering in and out from room to room, partaking in the hors d'oeuvres and cheap champagne. It wouldn't be long before their exchange was interrupted. The thought crossed his mind as he eyed the closed door from across the intimate space. But before he could formulate a proper thought, anything to prolong the moment, Tessa drew a piece of white cardstock from her back pocket. Sterling recognized the font choice and script at a glance.

It was a personalized invitation to the day's event, though he hadn't been the one to send it. He'd thought about it. More than once. But thinking about it only served to solidify his conclusion: she wanted to be left alone. Otherwise, she wouldn't be. That was what all the unanswered texts, phone calls, and emails seemed to tell him anyway.

She tapped the cardstock against her jawline, one arm crossed over and just below her chest while the other rested vertically against it. "You know most guys send flowers," she seemed to hum.

"Most guys don't make it past your front door," Sterling was quick to remind her. He could only assume the invitation had been Charlie's doing, though his best friend's constant interference appeared to be working in his favor. *For once.*

"Touché," she *tsked* her tongue, as if tasting the word in agreement before crossing the room to seat herself on the professionally staged desk top. Sterling understood the importance of the staging process; however, as his eyes bounced from object to object purposely situated across the shiny ebony finish, he couldn't help but focus on the fact that none of the decor made for a functional workspace. It was an odd thought to have, considering the circumstances, yet his brain seemed to need the minuscule distraction.

He watched as Tessa scooted back so that her legs draped over the edge at the perfect angle to draw his eyes up the length of her jean-clad thighs, to the curve of her hourglass hips, accentuated by the sheer material of her blush-pink blouse. Her posture was somehow equal parts seductive and professional as she straightened her spine and consequently enhanced the protrusion of her chest. Even the sunlight seemed to favor her as it flitted through the bay window to their left to illuminate the sharp lines of her profile, projecting her mirror image on the wall beside them.

As if the world could handle two of her. Certainly he couldn't, or so he mused to himself.

It was obvious, the way he watched her. He knew it. He knew she could feel the weight of his gaze as it skimmed across the exposed flesh of her collarbone, daring to sink lower with each rise and fall of her chest. And he also knew she enjoyed it. Not from most men but from him. It was a thought that jolted his system, yet felt true all the same. Despite his insecurities, despite his self-deemed inadequacies, she wanted him. She chose him. Right here and right now. And it was a startling realization, though it had never been spoken aloud.

"What are you really doing here, Tess?" he breathed the question, inhaling the subtle scent of her perfume as he did so.

"You invited me, remember?"

"And called you, and emailed you—fuck, I would have sent a carrier pigeon or hired a skywriter if I thought it'd make a differ-ence…" He shook his head. "So why now? Why today?"

She seemed to ponder the question for a moment, sucking her plump bottom lip between her teeth to chew on the supple meat before meeting his gaze again. Something passed across her features, some-thing he didn't recognize. Something dark. Though it lasted but a moment, then she quickly tucked it away as if it never existed. "I saw your mother."

Prior to this exact point in time, Sterling would have argued that four simple words couldn't possibly have the power to stop his heart midbeat. Yet, here he sat, choking on air. The organ in his chest, which had been pounding in rhythm with his quickened breaths mere seconds ago, eerily silent and immobile.

CHAPTER 24
THE BEST MEDICINE
THREE DAYS PRIOR

DOC

HE WASN'T INTO LABELS. Patients, people, were more than their diagnoses. What applied to some was out of the realm of comfort for others. However—and this thought gave him pause—should he be so inclined to list *hers*, he'd need a new sheet of paper.

PTSD with dissociative tendencies, ODD stemming from trauma response, and disorganized attachment disorder… were just a few that came to mind.

The woman was both brilliant and baffling. Someone who was so brutally unaware of her self-sabotage, her intelligence so overshadowed by her denial that her ability to problem solve regressed to the point of being nonexistent. At least when it came to anything of meaning and substance—such as promoting, establishing, and maintaining healthy relationships.

She was fascinating, which was likely the only reason he kept indulging her sessions. Because it sure as hell didn't benefit his sanity. She aged him each time she walked through his office door, took years off his life with the psychological warfare she used in place of physical armor. Even now, as she stomped her heeled boots back and forth across the vinyl flooring, he could feel his will to live seeping from his pores, nearly pinpoint the brain aneurysm ready to burst beneath his skull. Yet he schooled his features, relaxed his posture, and remained outwardly unaffected. She fed off her opponent's reactions, first consumed then regurgitated whatever response was most likely to achieve her desired outcome. Stoicism was maddening to her—it fueled her insecurities, eventually provoking an outburst. And only when she lost control did she offer him something real.

She pivoted midstep, as if sensing his gaze on her, and crossed her arms over her chest. Her hair was slightly wild today, rather than pulled up and tight, and matched the sudden gleam in her eyes. He watched on as she rushed air through her nostrils, into her lungs, and back out again. She was either on the brink of opening up or shutting down; both options were just as likely.

He clicked his pen in hand, the sound rhythmic, soothing, and keeping in time with the ticking of the clock. You didn't need a pendulum to lull someone into a state of complacency. A simple, repetitive beat would do the trick. The body instinctively sought to keep pace, to inhale and exhale, increasing blood flow to the brain while releasing a low dose of serotonin to relax the muscles and allow the mind a semblance of plasticity.

She hadn't caught on to his methods as of yet. But he knew it was a matter of time before he'd have to adjust and refocus his efforts. That, or finally succumb to the strain she was surely exacting on his aging heart. Her blinking slowed, her eyelids comfortably hooded, as she fell into the chair in front of him with a sigh.

"*Mon dieu*, I love the idiot," she huffed.

As though that wasn't obvious, he couldn't help but think.

Though the good doctor was smart enough to keep that opinion to himself. He had to choose his wording carefully, like the next move in a game of chess. The usual *how does that make you feel* or *what do you think that means* did little more than irritate the girl before sending her stomping through the door. That being said, verbalizing what he really wanted to say—something along the lines of *duh*—would likely earn the man a knee to the groin. The odds certainly weren't in the physician's favor.

"Well, are you going to say something or simply stare at me for the entirety of the hour?" she huffed, her posture tensing, and he continued the clicking until she settled into the seat for a second time.

"What is there to say?" He shrugged. "It's not for me to tell you how you feel, Miss Owens."

"Since when?" She narrowed her eyes as she tossed the words at him. "That never seemed to be an issue before."

He knew what she was doing. Deflecting was a favored weapon in her arsenal, anger the fuel that spurred her onward. "Let's agree to disagree and remain on topic, shall we?" When she didn't immediately argue, he pressed on. "What's driven you to this conclusion?"

"His mother."

That was not the answer the physician was expecting, but it did garner his interest. "His mother told you that you love him?"

"No—*con comme une valise sans poignée*—she threatened me to stay away. Assumed I wasn't good enough." The woman waved her hand as if to dismiss the ridiculous thought.

His French was rusty but he was near certain his patient just called him a *suitcase*. He dismissed the odd insult, choosing to focus on the matter at hand. "Please humor me and explain your logic..." he prompted, because honestly he was grasping for a connection. "Have you considered that perhaps this is an act of defiance on your part? Like telling a child they can't have something and suddenly they want it more?" He knew she wouldn't take the accusation kindly, but it needed to be said. Especially considering her pattern of behaviors.

He expected resistance, though she remained relaxed, her chest rising with a single inhalation as her eyes flicked to one side. "Actually, I have. I'm not as oblivious as you assume, as you annotate in your notes." The old man quirked a brow but she continued without acknowledgment. "It's why I waited a few days, let everything sink in, before I scheduled this appointment. To avoid being rash, impulsive. To avoid hurting him again."

Doc wanted to comment, to compliment his patient on her process and self-reflection, but he knew better than to interrupt her. She didn't need the praise, nor did she want it. So he remained silent, impassive in the face of unexpected pragmatism.

"I wanted to protect him. From her and myself. I went in without a failsafe, without a concrete escape plan. It was terrifying and I was heated—I admit. And there was nothing unusual in those aspects. I'm aware I enjoy the thrill. That being said, there was no ulterior motive in the back of my mind, nothing for me to hold on to, on the off chance an opportunity presented itself. I could have made it worth my while. The story I could have told…" She sighed as if she were picturing it. "Bigger than anything I've seen before. And I instantly didn't want it. It didn't matter. Because he was hurting and she was the cause."

"So you put his needs above your own. That's part of being human, Miss Owens. Why do you appear disgusted with yourself? Do you regret your decision?"

Her eyes traveled from the far wall, back to the man in front of her, her lash line weighed down by the moisture of unshed tears. "Oh, I regret plenty. I'm just not sure that it matters. That it's fixable."

CHAPTER 25
THE STONE WALL
THE PRESENT

STERLING

"I SAW YOUR MOTHER."

Those four words clung to the dust particles between them with the viscosity of cement. Their meaning causing Sterling to choke on air with each new draw of breath he was attempting to force into his lungs. The walls were creeping forward, breaking free from their structural framing to gradually encroach on his personal space, as if the inanimate materials somehow had minds of their own. The architect could feel himself sinking, though he hadn't moved the slightest muscle, his deadened limbs tingling with a sharpness that ghosted up his spine before making a nest of agony at the base of his skull.

It wasn't the sort of reaction any son should have for his mother; however, that did little to alter his reality. The woman was capable of anything, had criminals at her disposal, and combined with her lack of moral grounding, she was both lethal and unpredictable. Sterling had no qualms when it came to challenging the matriarch, as long as his was the only well-being at risk. As long as he had nothing more to lose. But Tessa added a hitch to that foundation, and everything could come tumbling down with the flick of a manicured wrist.

"What did she do?" The question left his mouth on a heavy exhale.

"Told me to name my price."

"For…?"

"For my swift disappearance, likely my silence, perhaps to further my career." She shrugged, as if the specifics didn't matter.

"And what did you say, Tess?"

She smirked, her lips curling round much like they had during their first meeting. "I'm here, aren't I? What do you think I said, Lucien?"

"I haven't the fucking slightest. You haven't spoken to me in days, avoided me for months." He threw his hands in the air before dropping a palm on his head and raking it down his face. His eyes burned, and the whites were probably bloodshot by this point—the red veining more prominent than a good slab of Carrara marble. What he needed was a goddamn drink, something to still the trembling in his fingertips. "Please… just stop… just tell me why you're here and what you want. I'm exhausted, Tess, fucking suffocating in my own skin. Whatever it is you have to say, I'm begging you to just say it."

"I, um, I'm…" She paused, her gaze drifting to the floorboards and quickly flicking upward to pin him in place. "…sorry…" She pushed herself up from her makeshift seat on the desk, in an attempt to beeline it to the doorway. Sterling reached a hand out to grab her wrist, tugging her backwards before she could take a full step.

He'd seen it in her eyes. In how her lips parted, then changed direction. How her pupils dilated and refocused. She was lying… about something. And *sorry* certainly wasn't what she was about to say. "Tell me," he prompted. Nothing more needed to be said. He knew she understood his meaning. Her facade had dropped momentarily and he'd read her like a front-page headline. Worse yet, neither had meant to lower their guards. And despite the best of intentions, both were frozen in place. Their chest cavities flayed open and exposed for each to view.

Tessa dropped her gaze to where his warm palm encircled her wrist, his fingers meeting at her pulse point. He could feel the increased rhythm of her heartbeat thrumming beneath his thumb, as if trying to break free from its confines. She reached a hand forward, her curled knuckle pressing into the underside of his sharp stubbled jawline and tipping it upwards, until his eyes aligned with hers. He sat stock-still as he zeroed in on the image reflected in her dilated pupils. He could only imagine how she saw him now, how weak she likely regarded him to be. He was damn near thirty years old, his social life was in shambles, he was stuck in this goddamn chair for the foreseeable future, and Mommy Dearest was still running the show.

Every ounce of confidence that had been brewing in his veins tempered at the realization he would never escape his namesake, which meant neither would she, should she ever choose to be with him. Though this knowledge did little to loosen his grip. He was anchored by indecision, unable to keep her, yet unwilling to let her go either.

"Tell me," he repeated the order on a hushed breath, hanging on the unspoken answer as if he knew it would somehow be the catalyst for everything to follow. She tugged away, and he gripped her harder —his hold bruising, unrelenting, and unapologetic.

Enough running.

He didn't speak the words aloud, but the understanding was nearly as tangible as the forced air now parting her lips.

"Lucien…" His name was pressed out on a hiss.

"Tess," he countered. "All you have to do is tell me what you were going to say. It really is that simple. I don't know why you're making it so difficult for yourself."

Her creased brows softened, as though she didn't know the answer either. As though the task felt impossible and she herself couldn't understand the reasoning. She leaned forward, her fingers closing around his lapels while his hand slipped down her forearm, loose enough to graze her flesh but tight enough to keep her from fleeing. Her lips brushed against the shell of his ear, her tongue flicking out to taste him as he inhaled the fragrant air now thickened by her presence. He could feel the swell of her chest as she sucked in a breath, the vibration of her vocal cords as they prepared to speak, and the fluttering of her lashes as the fine hairs brushed his cheek. And just as she swallowed, the muscles in her throat tensing, magnifying, and enriching the sound of her melodic voice—the first notes of sound reaching his eardrums—the impatient rattling of the doorknob breached the tension of the moment, plowing through Tessa's resolve and unwittingly releasing Sterling's grip.

The daydream was shattered and she crossed the threshold before he was even fully cognizant of her sudden absence.

TESSA

"Yeah, no, nuh-uh, not happening." Charles positioned himself in front of the large double doors, his arms crossed, his foot tapping, and his broad shoulders effectively blocking the journalist's closest point of escape. "You get your pretty little ass back in there and play nice," he huffed, his chin jutting towards the room she'd just fled.

She could run, find another exit, and make it to her car long before he could catch her. But that felt too much like a blow to her dignity, especially with the growing crowd. She would walk out of here with her spine straight and her head held high, not like some back-alley whore with something to hide. That being said, she wasn't about to make it easy for the stubborn prick currently forcing her hand— because nothing about this woman was easy. Something Charles Fox had yet to learn, though she was certain he would.

"What do you expect me to do, Charlie?" She mirrored his posturing. "Go in there and say what, exactly?" She could feel eyes shifting her way, the occasional onlooker hooked on a taste of gossip while hoping for a bigger bite. Fuck it, she was used to the stares. If they wanted a show, she'd give them an encore.

"For starters? How about something along the lines of *your friend may be better looking with a bigger cock*—it is by the way, much bigger actually." He paused, an index finger pressed to his chin as if he were envisioning his grandiose claim before clearing his throat and continuing, his voice low enough so that only she could hear him now. "I want to make sure that part makes print." He grinned, his head dipping towards the throng of reporters hanging on his every word. Then his face softened, a hand reaching out to cup her cheek, the gesture almost intimate. "Tess, just go the fuck in there and be honest. For once, tell the man how the fuck you feel. And if it's really so minute that you can turn your back and walk away, then do it. Cut the poor bastard off… just make sure it's permanent this time. He's a good man, he loves you, and he deserves that much."

She sucked in a lungful of air but had somehow forgotten how to release it, her bodily functions seemingly suspended. The son of a bitch was right. About everything. About everything other than his inflated ego, or so she could only assume. Though it did give her momentary pause to wonder about the validity of his claim—not enough pause to drive her to investigate. That mystery would remain unsolved. While another question hung in the air…

How *did* she feel?

Everything had seemed so clear at his mother's house, amidst the tumultuous few days between this present moment and her session with Doc, and even during the drive over. However, it was as if that confidence had seeped from her pores, pooling at her feet and leaving her speechless the second she had hoped to tap into it. As if she were being pummeled by insecurities and biting off her own tongue was a more appetizing outcome than being forced to give voice to her emotions. As if *can't* and *won't* were synonymous and she'd yet to determine the meaning of either.

And so Tessa was left wondering if she didn't want to be with him, or if she simply didn't know how…

————

The darkness was a part of her. It always had been. Maybe not always…

That was a little dramatic and drama was Charlie's department, not hers. But since Tessa was old enough to grasp and understand the cruel nature of mankind, the shadows seemed to follow her wherever she went, saturating her world in shades of gray. Tamping down the slightest flicker of light. Because survival meant expecting the worst from people. It meant being prepared for disappointment and only trusting in yourself and your own capabilities. Which in turn meant being alone.

And that's where she found herself, at the threshold of the door, heels in hand and feet bare, as she watched the man she loved fall apart by her own doing. All because she didn't know how to *not* be alone. Because *being with him* seemed as unbearable as *not being with him*. Because difficult was her default setting and giving in felt like giving up. Like lying down and accepting defeat. Instead of fighting. But fighting was so incredibly exhausting. And she finally understood that there wasn't anything to win.

He hadn't sensed her presence yet, so lost to his own thoughts—perhaps misery—as he stared out the bay window, a rogue stream of sunlight illuminating his aristocratic features. He was eye-catching if nothing else. Though he was also so much more. And that was likely what terrified her. What gave her pause for a second time, as she considered pivoting on her heel and walking out. However, she could feel Charlie's eyes boring holes into the back of her head and thought better of making another escape attempt. The choice was simple: in here with Lucien or out there with the vultures. And as much as Tessa enjoyed journalism, she hated making the news.

She could feel it, the moment he *felt* her, as his head finally snapped in her direction, his eyes shrouded by grief and his jaw set with forced indifference. He pretended not to care, to remain unaffected, but it was as much a mask as the one Tessa donned regularly. She raised a hand to keep him from speaking—she had noted the flair of his nostrils that indicated he was a breath away from breaking the silence—and spun to close and lock the door. There were far too many prying eyes, and the man's privacy had been invaded more than enough, thanks to her.

But she didn't move closer, fearing she would revert to more carnal instincts given the choice between emotional and physical intimacy. One always came far more naturally.

"Lucien, you asked me why I was here and what I was going to say…" She lifted a finger, anticipating his protest before he could verbalize it, and continued. "And even now, I'm at a loss for words. *Comment dire au soleil qu'il est trop brillant? Comment dire à une fleur qu'elle est trop parfumée?* It's impossible. And simply saying how I feel… it just seems to fall short."

"Bullshit," he hissed between clenched teeth.

"Wha—"

"Tess, that's bullshit and you know it. Pretty words aren't the issue, nor is the implied inadequacy of your ability to verbalize them. You're just fucking terrified. And too goddamn stubborn to admit it. Ignoring your emotions doesn't make you strong and me weak. It doesn't make you fucking better or more intelligent than I am. It just makes you a fucking coward."

The pointed insult landed with the force of a direct blow, sending Tessa back a step as if the impact had been corporeal rather than just cleverly articulated. She was equal parts impressed and incensed. Both hurt and heated. Sickened and thoroughly seduced.

"Coward? *Tu penses que je suis un lâche?*" she parroted the rhetorical question. "Fuck you, I'm not a coward. *Je t'aime, espèce d'idiot.* Happy?"

"I love you too, Tess. But you already knew that. Because I've told you more than once." As if noticing the slight tilt of her head and the curious eyebrow, he added with a grin, "Ah, my apologies. It must have slipped my mind, love. Did I forget to mention I've been working on my French?"

CHAPTER 26
THE CAKE WALK

TESSA

"MARRY ME…" he asked for the third time in as many weeks, the words breathless and offered with a labored intake of air. And she shook her head for the third time *in as many weeks*. Because the man was out of his mind if he thought a little post-coital bliss would lull her into an endless barrage of white dresses and an onslaught of cake tastings. Though it could be argued that that last bit was rather tempting at the moment.

Tessa rolled out of bed with that thought in mind, driven by her need to indulge in something sweet and definitely nothing resembling a wedding gown.

"Where are you going?" Sterling reached out to tug her back onto the mattress, but the prior exertion had his hand missing her waist and swiping through air instead.

"To the kitchen." She shrugged as though the answer were obvious. It should have been. It had become routine. She threw on his button-down dress shirt, leaving it undone, as she padded through the hallway and took the freight elevator down to the second floor. Normally she didn't mind using the stairs, but she was more than willing to admit that her thighs were aching, her muscles pulsating, her libido well-satisfied, and her bodily fluids in desperate need of repletion. The man was certainly not lacking in stamina…

Her eyes scanned the digital clock glaring back at her from the oven's stainless-steel control panel, the time flashing in front of her like some ominous Easter egg in a poorly rated horror flick.

Nothing good ever happened after midnight.

It was superstitious, she knew. Especially for someone so logical, but she couldn't stop the feeling of dread that seemed to be eating away at her subconscious. Telling her she shouldn't be here. Not now.

And as if materializing from the shadows, the glowing red numerals morphed into a pair of glowing red eyes. Eyes that could see through her, past her, and somehow froze her limbs in place. The ground shifted like quicksand, reaching up, enclosing around her ankles, and tugging her downward until the tiny granules were sucked into her throat, accumulating in her lungs and replacing the oxygen. She was choking, her lips sputtering in an effort to rid her body of the foreign objects slowly suffocating her. But it was as if the harder she fought, the more constrictive her airway.

She couldn't breathe. She needed to breathe.

Tessa clutched at her throat, her jaw, clawing until her fingernails broke flesh, the tips warm and wet as they broached her trachea and tore at her vocal cords. But the screaming didn't stop. She could hear it, even as she pried ligament from bone, sand cascading over her neckline and sticking to the perspiration coating her chest. The sound was god-awful. The kind of shrieking that perforated eardrums and popped blood vessels.

It wasn't until she felt a temperate palm massaging her shoulder that her lashes fluttered open and refocused on her surroundings. Her hands shot to her throat and collarbone, her fingertips taking inventory of each plane and divot of flesh in search of the slightest abnormality, though quickly coming up empty.

"It happened again, didn't it, Tess?" Sterling pushed himself upright, pressing his lips to the back of her head while tugging her into his embrace. "What'd you see this time, love? You wanna talk about it?" he prompted when she didn't answer.

She didn't want to talk about it. She didn't even want to think about it. She'd yet to determine how much had been real, and how much was her mind continuing its unyielding torture of her subconscious. Ignoring the bombardment of questions, she focused on her breathing, counting to five in her head and back down again, like Doc had instructed her. Sterling ran a hand along her spine, holding his tongue as Tessa took in her surroundings.

She was in his bedroom. His home. She glanced at the clock. A quarter to midnight. So she hadn't made it to the kitchen… Had she even left the bed? She peered down at her state of undress. It didn't seem likely. Though the sex, that most certainly had been real. Her body still ached from the exertion, her veins pumped with the surge of oxytocin, and her heart thumped with that satisfaction she only ever felt post-bliss. Her flesh buzzed with the need to sink back into him. On him. Anything to distract her thoughts. To help her forget the terror plaguing her mind.

Tessa pushed Sterling back against the headboard, his skull landing with a thud as she shifted her body to straddle him. His mouth parted in protest, to stop her, to likely interrogate her further, and she bit down, capturing his bottom lip between her teeth and tugging. Almost to the point of drawing blood. He hissed out a groan, half-pained, half-pleasured by her animalistic need to taste him.

"Tess," he tried again. "We should probably talk…" His lackluster plea died off the moment she slipped beneath the sheets and seized him in her mouth. Though he seemed to completely forget it altogether when she hollowed out her cheeks and pulled back, gliding her tongue along the length of him in one fluid motion. "Fuck," he hissed between shallow breaths, his calloused hands splayed across her head and delving into her hair as he attempted to draw her upwards.

But she needed the control. She needed the distraction. To ground herself in the physical and disregard the mental. She needed to feel him, instead of feeling herself. Instead of feeling *like* herself. Instead of feeling anything…

Tessa embedded her nails in his thighs, keeping him at her mercy as she ran her tongue along the underside of his shaft, the nimble appendage paying careful attention to the large vein pulsing beneath his flesh. She knew how to play him like an instrument, which nerve endings to manipulate, where to hyperfocus her attention, how to elicit those groans that sent goose bumps rising along her skin. Her body so in tune with his that the satisfaction was nearly mutual. She relaxed her jaw muscles, taking him back into the depths of her throat, and swallowed, regulating her breathing while disabling her gag reflex.

He ground out a string of expletives, his eyes screwed tight and his hands grasping at the bedsheets. She watched him from where she perched her elbows between his legs, resisting the urge to drop a hand and bring herself to completion. The ability to dominate his senses was intoxicating, to watch him come undone addictive. And while she knew there were issues with that fact in of itself, she didn't care to delve into the underlying meaning. No, she preferred the rush of endorphins, the heady sensation of bringing such a strong-willed man to his figurative knees.

His thighs trembled, likely ached from overuse, and she could feel his pulse point throbbing between her lips as she drew them back at a leisurely pace before quickly intensifying her efforts. Sterling hissed her name in both reverence and damnation, worshiping her chronic attention while cursing her well-practiced form of slow torture as she nudged him towards the edge of euphoria before tugging him back again with a sudden change in rhythm. She knew exactly what she was doing and she enjoyed it. More so, she knew he knew it as well.

He wanted it to end as much as he hoped it would continue. She saw it in the conflicting way he both pulled her down while also attempting to yank her off. In how he soothed her hair one moment and tugged at the strands another. How his breath hitched, only to still. She didn't feel the ache in her jaw, nor the saliva trailing down her chin and along her neckline. It was inconsequential when her sole focus was on bending this man to her will. To only release him from her spell when she deemed it appropriate. If she deemed it so. To make him beg for it, need it, in a way men like him didn't need anything or anyone.

That thought gave her momentary pause, though not in action only concentration, as she realized how mad that accusation was. He wasn't *all men*. He wasn't anyone who'd ever hurt her. And there was no one *like him*. That had always been the problem. How different he was from everyone else. How he considered her his equal. His better.

She grazed her tongue along the very tip of his length, savoring the salty aftertaste as her mouth sank down to the base, her nose flush against his pubic bone. She inhaled the natural smell of him, enhanced by the lightly scented soap he used in the shower—something so woodsy and masculine—and rolled her throat muscles. The viselike, pulsing sensation shoved him over that final ledge, and his hips bucked in time with her well-versed withdrawal. Until he was left gasping between hollow bouts of laughter. Like a condemned man spared the noose seconds before that final drop. Like a pedestrian tugged back the moment a speeding freight train crossed the tracks. A jumper whose parachute didn't open until his feet brushed the ground. He saw his end and chuckled in the face of it. Realizing he'd been both sentenced to an agonizing death, and just as suddenly given reprieve.

Tessa crawled up the length of Sterling's torso before carefully positioning herself at his side, her spine pressed against his rib cage as she stared out into the shadows, her eyes focused on the darkness beyond the wall of windows. After a moment of silence filled only with the sound of his evened breaths and her gentle respirations, Sterling used the leverage of his extended arm to pivot her to face him. Her head tucked against his pectoral muscle as if she belonged there. And he sighed into her hair, drawing her in with each new intake of air.

"We need to tell him, you know," he shattered the white noise of the fan with the ominous declaration. And the journalist promptly ignored the comment, looking to straddle him a second time. "Tess, I couldn't… even if I wanted to."

"Are you implying you don't want to?" she was quick to counter; though she was certain he could hear her grin if not see it in the obscurity of the shadow-cast room.

"You're well aware that that's not what I mean." He pressed his lips to the top of her head before continuing. "And I know what you're doing."

"And yet you didn't stop me," she hummed the retort, as if content with the knowledge. Because she was. She relished his submission nearly as much as his fight; and she believed he likely felt the same when the roles were reversed.

"Because there *is* no stopping you, love. Not when you have your mind set on something. The sooner I realized that, the better it's been for my sanity."

Tessa could feel the curl of his smirk against her hair, and she couldn't help but mirror the expression. She tipped her chin up to kiss him, the gesture quickly transitioning from pliable and soft to fevered and demanding, as her newly polished nails skimmed a path along the surface of his chest before treading downwards. Sterling caught her wrist mid-descent, clutching it against his chest as he dominated her mouth with his, effectively decelerating her frenzied distraction.

He wanted her. She knew it. She could feel it. No matter how vocal his protests. But she also knew that the son of a bitch was nearly as stubborn as she was on a good day. And more so on a bad one. Like his balls somehow steeled whenever her well-being was in question. She couldn't fault him for it. But she didn't have to like it either.

She only hoped he couldn't make out the details of her pout, as her bottom lip jutted slightly outward with her displeasure. She was far too old to be making expressions reminiscent of her prepubescent years. And far too proud to outwardly admit defeat even as the words left her mouth.

"Fine. I'll call him in the morning. But he's just going to insist you come with me."

"And...?"

"*And* that's just... well," she struggled to vocalize all the insecurities playing out in her mind. "I don't know... very intimate, Lucien." She bounced with the sudden jarring movement of his chest as he chuckled in response. "It's not funny!"

"No, it's not. Because it's goddamn hysterical, Tess." When she didn't seem to grasp his meaning, he clarified, "That's intimate? But this isn't?" She watched as he gestured between them. "I think your vocabulary is a little skewed, love."

"Don't you dare insult my vocabulary," she chided, her eyes narrowed in his direction though she was certain he couldn't see them. "Sex isn't intimate, Lucien. It happens between strangers on a daily basis. The dictionary definition of intimacy is sharing something of a personal or private nature. Exchanging it willingly, without coercion. And sexual acts?" she scoffed. "They can be stolen, forced. Nothing about intercourse is intimate, Lucien. But my thoughts, my emotions, those are mine. And no one can take them from me. Not without my consent."

Her meaning thickened the air, weighed it down with the burden of her truth, congealed it till her lungs burned with each sharp intake of air. Like glass embedding itself in the supple meat of her bronchi. While his lack of a counter argument only served to solidify Tessa's resolve in her belief that intruding on her innermost thoughts was far more invasive than indulging in her body.

CHAPTER 27

THE ART OF DISTRACTION

DOC

"HE KEEPS ASKING me to marry him," Tessa huffed the accusation within seconds of entering the physician's office, her rear barely making contact with the chair's cushion before she was spewing a variety of expletives.

"Right, well…" the old man began and was cut off just as quickly.

"Clearly he needs your help more than I do—*putain de fou*." She threw her hands in the air, as if to further emphasize her point. *He was crazy,* or so she seemed to indict, assuming his quick translation was accurate.

Doc dropped his eyes to the supposed madman in question, raising an eyebrow as if to silently interrogate the architect before attempting to speak again. "So… this unscheduled appointment is meant to be what…? What is the goal here, Miss Owens?"

She straightened her spine, transitioning from the guise of a pouting teenager into that of a woman well beyond her years and in control of her somewhat turbulent emotions. It was like watching a scene locked in a view-master, and with each click, his patient donned another mask. A different persona. Her worlds were once again colliding and she didn't know who she was meant to be in the moment. It would be fascinating if it weren't so clinically damaging to her psyche.

He shook his head, returning to the task at hand before his naturally inquisitive mind sent him spiraling. "Miss Owens?" he prompted for a second time, having realized she'd yet to answer him.

She released an exaggerated exhale as if stuck between the two emotional age brackets. "Fix him. Make him stop."

"So that's why you're here…" he broached the topic carefully, like a man looking to tame an alligator without getting bit. "To discuss marriage—the possibility *or lack thereof…*"

"Tess, that's not at all why we're here and you know it." Her would-be suitor waited until this moment to finally speak up, as though he knew better than to confront her mid-tantrum.

Good man, the physician chuckled to himself while refraining from speaking the compliment aloud.

"Then please enlighten us, Mr. Sterling, so that we may move forward with the session." When his hand shifted to idle above the vintage RECORD button, the therapist couldn't help but notice how flagrantly the disgruntled billionaire eyed him with suspicion.

Ah, yes, this was the boy's first joint session and it wasn't surprising that the wayward patient had kept that little secret to herself.

She hadn't mentioned that all of their interactions had been made permanent in the form of a stack of cassette tapes. That her most intimate thoughts could very well be accessed by an individual with both the means and the knowledge. He could see Lucien's wheels turning— his curiosity getting the better of him—though the aging man couldn't blame the boy. If it were his lady, he'd want to know too. Despite the morality of the situation, the lovesick kid was still human.

That being said, it was far too late for that form of underhandedness, considering each recording "magically" disappeared within hours of being stored in Doc's filing cabinet. Magic that he was certain came in the form of someone in their midst.

Lucien cleared his throat, the irritated abrasive sound also the first to be captured by the audio device.

"As this is your first joint session with Miss Owens, I must inform you that you're being recorded for the duration of your time here. So, please continue. We were discussing the reason for your attendance today, Mr. Sterling…"

"Um… right." He glanced at Tessa before looking forward again. "The… a… the nightmares are back. Or… I suppose they're more like daydreams sometimes." The man was clearly struggling to find the right words, partially because he didn't understand what was happening and partially because the woman beside him was glaring daggers through the side of his head. "I'll find her staring out at nothing. She doesn't respond to my questions, almost like she can't hear me, and if I'm too quick to reach out, she'll collapse in on herself—scream. Practically clawing at her limbs until she breaks skin." He paused, gesturing at the blaring marks on Tessa's throat while she scrambled to raise the collar of her blouse. "Last night it was as if she was choking on air. And she struggled to breathe."

The physician hummed for a moment, flicking his eyes to the ceiling in thought. *Trauma-induced hallucinations*, he surmised, though aloud he said, "Similar to the incident that first led you here, Miss Owens." She hadn't experienced a repeat since then, leading him to question, "Were there any identifiable triggers? Anything that seems to correspond with the hours, minutes, seconds prior to the event?"

Tessa grinned while her counterpart appeared to sink lower into his seat, his brow creasing and his neckline flushing. Clearly uncomfortable with the topic at hand. "Sex…" she stated simply with a shrug of her shoulders, likely feeding off her lover's unease. It was another form of control—one the aging therapist had come to recognize. She enjoyed watching men squirm, this man in particular, and pushed boundaries as far as anyone would let them bend. Then she'd snap them farther.

"Which makes sense, considering your history…" When Lucien didn't immediately react to the implication, Doc realized Tessa must have confided in him. That in itself was progress. "But why now? Though we've not discussed it in detail…" *For the record.* "I can only assume these… *exchanges* weren't the first you've shared. So I must ask you again, Miss Owens, what could be the potential catalyst for your regression?"

"You tell me, Doc," she was quick to counter, without giving his request for self-reflection the required thought.

"Right, well, let's revisit that question before the end of the session. In the interim, I want you to consider this one: when was the last time you were in a romantic relationship?" He knew the answer. He and his reluctant patient both did. And with the current company in mind, he knew the insinuation wouldn't be received well. Likely from either party. "Miss Owens, I think it's time we discussed your brief courtship with Marco Agostino." Again.

———

"And did you have feelings for him? At any point during the assignment?"

"No, of course not." She spun on her heel as if the very idea propelled her forward. "Do you think I make it a habit of crossing professional boundaries? He had something I wanted, and I got it. End of story."

"I see…"

"Are you insinuating I deserved this?"

"Miss Owens, no one deserves what you endured. That's not at all what I'm suggesting." Doc sighed. The physician was as exhausted with fighting with her as she was with putting up a fight against him. "There's a pattern in the sort of relationships you maintain and the only way to break it, to alter it, is to first acknowledge its existence. And it all begins there. In New York. With that assignment."

"It wasn't a relationship. It was a stor—"

"For one of you, maybe. If we're reverting to your definition of relationships. That being said, it's hard to fake emotions without a point of reference. Meaning some part of you, some part of your psyche is still connected to that man. As well as your former partner. And everything you perceived you lost to each of them."

———

"Or should we start with Sebastian today?" Doc prompted when his patient didn't immediately react, allowing her to pick her poison for the remaining forty-odd minutes she had left in today's session.

CHAPTER 28
THE KINK IN HER ARMOR

TESSA

THE MAN WAS INSANE—NO, both of them were insane—to insinuate *he* had anything to do with her present… resistance. They wanted to place her in a clinical box, to find a connection where there was none and explain away what was blatantly simple. What was obvious. She wasn't the problem. They were. Them and their inability to see past their noses or the dicks between their legs. It was a mistake to bring Lucien there. To believe he'd see sense, when clearly the guy was delusional.

Who did he think she was? And why did he always seek to ruin a good thing? They were comfortable. Enjoying their time together without the pressure of labels, without the lies and insecurities. But he had to fucking ruin it. To push for more when she'd given all of herself that there was to give. That she could. There wasn't *more*.

And instead of taking her side and making Lucien see reason, Doc had turned the tables on her. Tag-teaming the journalist in a match of wits while giving her opponent an unfair advantage.

She should have stormed out of the office. But she was trying to be better. To face things head-on, rather than attempting to maneuver her way around or over them. It was progress or so she'd been told.

Because at the moment it felt like anything but. It felt like insects were crawling under her skin and prickling the flesh. As though she couldn't scratch hard enough to rid her nerve endings of the sensation.

She glanced down to find the undersides of her arms red and raw, the four parallel lines proving they had been of her own doing. Each step towards normality seemed to be accompanied by several more teetering on the edge of chaos. As if Tessa couldn't escape it any more than she could escape the confines of her skin.

"That's not how it was supposed to go," she hissed the words in Lucien's direction, her anger directed outward, though it was her subconscious that should have been the target.

"No, that's not how *you* wanted it to go, love," he corrected, and the hint of condescension—whether real or imagined—was enough to tip the scales of irritation to full-scale rage.

Tessa pivoted on her heel, an accusatory finger shooting towards his face as her glare landed on the object of her present contempt. "Don't. Don't you fucking dare talk to me like that."

"Like what?" he asked her with a grin because, for whatever reason, this man enjoyed spinning her up, almost as much as she enjoyed watching him squirm.

"Like you're my doctor. Like you know so much better. One of those is more than enough." She crossed her arms over her chest, though it was getting more difficult to maintain the same level of irritation when he looked at her like that. She could feel it dissipating, transitioning from a boil to a low simmering, no matter how much she attempted to turn up the heat.

"But, Tess…" He swung his arms out, wrapping them around her waist and tugging her forward. "I do know better."

His lips tipped up at one side moments before he forced her to lose her leverage as her arms shot out to brace themselves, and he grabbed her chin to draw her mouth to his. She melted into him, her brain fighting against her compliance at the same time her body waved a white flag in surrender. Sterling trailed his lips across the soft edges of her perfect jawline as Tessa battled between collapsing into his lap and standing upright.

His teeth made contact with her earlobe, sank down and tugged, before he breathed out the word, "See?"

She could feel his grin, his self-assurance as he purposely raised the skin along her neckline, the sensation traveling across each arm and ultimately curling her toes, and it both agitated and aroused her in equal measure. Which was honestly nothing new. If she wasn't pissed at the man, she was fucking him. And if she wasn't fucking him, she was looking for a way to frustrate him. Sometimes a combination of two, and more times than she would like to admit, sometimes all three at once. Anything else would likely lose her attention. She needed to provoke just as much as she needed to be provoked. Boredom nearly as deadly as her fear of complacency.

Tessa took a deep breath, drawing oxygen into her lungs and holding it there for a moment before releasing it on a sigh. The fresh air reset her neurons and awakened some semblance of her common sense. She dropped her lips to capture his in an animalistic kiss, both unbridled and wholly intentional as she straddled his lap, a knee pinning each of his thighs in place. Then she leaned forward and whispered against his mouth. "The only thing I see, *mon nounours.*" She nipped his bottom lip and grazed a hand across his zipper. "Is how easily distracted you are."

She shot up from his chair, shuffling away a few steps in order to force distance between them. However, Sterling's right arm launched forward as his hand clamped against her wrist to yank her back in place.

"You and me both, love." He raised an eyebrow in challenge, and she didn't know if she wanted to scream or laugh.

Charles broke the tension with a clearing of his throat, knocking on the open door before sidling inside the occupied space without being invited. "I've exceeded my daily allowance of porn for the evening, so if you two could just *not,* it would be greatly appreciated." He shivered as if trying to clear the images from his head.

Tessa leaned against Sterling's chest, kicking one leg over an armrest as she replied, "Don't be coy, Charlie. We both know you enjoy a little voyeurism now and again." She winked, and he immediately paled, his gaze shifting towards the audible growl sounding from the man at Tessa's back.

"And how exactly did this come up in conversation?" Sterling asked the question to the room, but it was clearly directed at one of them in particular. The same one currently reaching out to adjust his suddenly constrictive shirt collar.

"Well, I—"

"It didn't," Tessa was quick to interject. "I can just tell… People wear their kinks a lot closer to the surface than they think." She paused as if considering her words before elaborating further. "Charlie likes to eavesdrop; he gets a thrill from hearing and seeing things he shouldn't. So it's only natural for that to carry into the bedroom." She could feel the tension lift from his shoulders as Sterling sighed into her hair.

"And what's my kink then, love? What's my tell?"

The journalist hummed as though she actually had to think about it. She didn't. And pressed a finger to her chin. "You, Lucien, seek control in every aspect of your life, in your relationships, to compensate…" She pivoted towards his arched brow and held up a hand, signaling for him to let her finish. "To *compensate* for your perceived lack of control in your youth. *However*, managing all those puppet strings is daunting, exhausting, so in the bedroom, you want to unwind. Relax. Toss the reins aside and let someone else ride that horse." Her hand dropped with the obvious innuendo, her fingertips trailing down his chest to his belt buckle.

Sterling grasped her wrist for a second time, stopping her progression as he feigned a cough and shook out his shoulders. "I think you've been spending a little too much time with that shrink of yours," he countered.

STERLING

"Why don't we just stay in tonight? I can have Gus make whatever you want? Or we can order in. Something greasy and artery clogging?"

"As tempting as that sounds, I'm gonna have to pass. I've been *staying in* for months now. And honestly, the walls are closing in on me. The solitude is stifling." Tessa shivered, visibly chilled by the thought.

"Solitude would suggest you're alone, love." Sterling tugged her closer to his side, pressing a kiss to her temple as he stared out and into nothing. Tessa was a lot like Charles in some ways, though it pained the architect to admit it. She needed to be out in the world. To take the stage and captivate her audience. Just one set of eyes on her would never be enough. As much as he wished it were, he also wouldn't change a thing.

She was the starlet to his stagehand, and he was captivated by the image of her in the spotlight. So sharing it—the attention, the onlookers, the fame, and infamy—was never the issue. No, it wasn't the fact that all eyes turned to her, no matter the company they were in. It was how they judged *them*—the couple, the odd pairing—that kept the man from wanting to venture past his doorstep. And it wasn't even their opinion that bothered him. It was his own fear that they were right. That he and Tessa didn't belong together. That he was kidding himself to think otherwise. That she pitied him. He was a charity fuck. And it wouldn't be long before she realized it herself. If she hadn't already.

But the woman wasn't a pretty pet meant to be kept in a cage. Nor did he have the ability to do so. He'd seen his kitten's claws, and they were far sharper than she let on.

"That's not what I meant and you know it." He could hear the irritation in her voice. "I want to go out. To people watch. I need to. I need to remember what it's like before I lose my touch."

"Oh, you certainly haven't lost your touch, love." Sterling grinned and Tessa flung a hand out to tap him across the chest.

"Also not what I meant." She rolled her eyes. "I have to get back to work. Or everything I've done is as good as forgotten. I'll be replaced, *literally*, like yesterday's news. And going out. Tonight. Is the first step in getting back out into the real world. Into remembering why I love what I do." She scratched at her skin as though her memories could somehow crawl up her arms before settling in the pit of her stomach. "I need a puzzle to solve, Lucien, or I may as well be brain dead."

"I know you do, Tess. I know you do." He sighed against the top of her head, his heart thrumming in an uneven beat in time with his forced breaths. He didn't want to let her go. But he couldn't make her stay either. And that realization was worse than death itself.

CHAPTER 29
THE STICK IN THE MUD

STERLING

THE CANDLELIGHT ILLUMINATED her features in a way that was both haunting and ethereal, the shadows dancing across her skin as if to tempt him into believing he saw more (or less) than what was there, as Tessa sat opposite him with a menu in hand. It had been years since he'd stepped foot in a restaurant, longer still if he were to be literal. The last time being the night of the accident.

It sounded ridiculous, even as he thought it. Of course, a woman, a girlfriend, *a wife* would want to be taken out, fed, and spoiled. It wasn't as though he could avoid the public eye forever. Then again, he never saw himself entertaining his present company. Or any company for that matter. He had accepted his fate, his state of perpetual confinement, and the unlikelihood of ever having more.

A family, a partner in life, kids…

It was the latter of the three that weighed heavily on his mind. The one thing money couldn't buy, not in any true sense. The one thing, if she asked for it, wanted it, he could never give her. But someone else could…

As if sensing his racing thoughts, Tessa reached forward and grabbed his hand, squeezing once before returning her attention to the selections in front of her.

"Tess, I…"

"What do you think about the—"

They each spoke at the same time. And Sterling could feel the weight of everyone's eyes on him. Questioning, judging, wondering whether the gorgeous woman in front of him was a relative or caregiver. Whether she was using or pitying him. He glanced to the side, and he could hear their thoughts, more so when he realized they weren't all that different from his own…

Why was she here? With him? And for how long? Was it right? For him to ask that of her…? To have pursued her so fervently that she could no longer bear the thought of saying no. He should have known better. Known that Tessa was far too obstinate to do anything other than exactly what she wanted to do. However, that sort of logic evaded him when he was spiraling. And common sense was just out of reach for the man bound to far more than just a chair. It was his insecurities that disabled him. Held him down and kept him from progressing.

"I—Tess, I can't do this." He was sweating, his skin itching, and his heart beating out of his chest in a way that suggested it would soon break free. As quickly as he'd been overcome by a sudden state of immobility, freezing to his spot when all he wanted to do was run, his limbs gave way to movement. And he pivoted from the dining table, brushed and knocked over a nearby chair, and fled through the front door and into the early evening air.

The sounds of the city nightlife and the veritable chill of the breeze did little to ease the rising panic or even shock it from his system as Sterling pushed through the crowded streets and rounded the familiar corner he knew would lead him to a vacant plot of grass. The ground was soft. Softer than he'd normally think to venture across. However, the architect wasn't thinking. He was acting. Driven by instinct rather than logic, as his inherent need to escape had his heart beating faster, his blood pumping more readily, and sweat beading across his forehead. And suddenly he knew what it felt like to be *her*. To feel as though there was no other option but to flee, for it to seem as though you could suffocate in open air.

The treads were losing traction, his movements slowing as his muscles waned against the force required to press him forward. He sensed himself slipping long before his palms met the mud, and his lower limbs twisted and bent in a way that would be painfully unnatural if he could feel anything at all.

And he was back there. Grasping at blades of grass while trying to pull himself along the shifting terrain. He could hear the glass shattering, the sound of the metal crunching, the white noise, and distant screams. He peered over his shoulder, and the upturned chair morphed into an overturned car as if the two were one and the same, and Sterling realized his past wasn't all that different from his present. He was helpless in either instance.

Then he saw her, in front of him, instead of staring back at him through that reflection in the glass—the one that haunted his dreams. She was beside him, instead of calling out to him from the wreckage. And she was real, instead of a phantasmal apparition conjured by his psyche. Tessa dropped to her knees and forced him upright and into a sitting position as each of them sucked in labored breaths, their backs leaning against the closest solid surface. A park bench or some sort of monument. Sterling didn't care to look to determine which.

The silence blanketed them, several moments passing with each lost to their own thoughts, their separate yet well-acquainted demons taking the reins once more. Tessa was the first to break, to grip reality and tug it back in place, as she reached out and took Sterling's hand.

"Come on, let's go home." She didn't question him, didn't push him to explain himself or his outburst. Because she knew. She knew what it was like to feel her world crashing down on her. And she knew that quiet acceptance was invaluable. But it didn't matter what she knew, how readily she accepted him, because he didn't accept himself. And he wouldn't accept this life for her.

"Is this what you want?" he hissed the question, near breathlessly, his chest heaving with the effort.

"What do you mean?"

"This!" Sterling gestured to his legs, as though they were all the explanation in the world. "To be a caregiver for the rest of your life? To watch me deteriorate by the day. To carry my burdens as if they are your own. To watch everyone else thrive while you're held back by two hundred pounds of dead weight." And the words formed on his lips before he could stop them, and they continued despite how sour they tasted. "You want to end up like your parents? Like your father?" And he immediately shut his mouth, opening it several times before attempting to form a coherent sentence. "I ... Tess... that's... that's not what I meant... I didn't mean... I'm sorry... I shouldn't have said that."

"No. That's exactly what you meant." Both knew it was true. "But it's okay. I'm not upset with you. Because I just realized something. You're exactly right. That's exactly what it would be like. Like my parents. Like my father. And now that you say it, I understand. I get it. And the funny thing is... it, *that*, is EXACTLY what I want. What I've always wanted. To end up just like them. Have exactly what they have. To have someone who, even at their very worst, is so much better than anyone else's best." She huffed a sigh. "Is it easy for them? No, of course not. But my father is happy every single day that he wakes up next to my mother. Even when he can barely understand a word she says. It doesn't matter. He doesn't need to understand. Because he knows. And if you're telling me that we are, that we *could be* anything like them, that that's what being with you would mean, then I have never been more certain of anything in my life. Because the only thing worse than losing you right now would be never having had you to begin with. Don't you get it, *mon nounours*? I love you..."

"I... I don't even know if I could ever give you children. That's what life would be like with me. Solitary. Our families, our heritage, our names—they would die with us."

"And? Could you imagine children with our combined intelligence and good looks? The world wouldn't be able to handle them anyway." Tessa grinned, and Sterling knew she believed it. The last part at least.

"I know what you're doing. You're deflecting. I know you want to be a mother someday. Even if you deny it now, you'll look back and you'll regret it, Tess. You'll resent me for taking that away from you."

"When have I *ever* said I wanted children, Lucien? Ever? But I'll humor you, because I know where your mind is at, and that place is dark. It doesn't see reason. So let's say... sure, someday, maybe I want children—I don't—but let's play Devil's advocate and say I do. What's your point? What does it matter if it's not easy? Since when do you back down from a challenge? And better yet, since when do I?"

He flicked his eyes to the side and up, finally meeting her gaze, unsure of what he'd see staring back at him. "You can't mean that, Tess. I've been kidding myself, thinking it'd be enough. That I could give you enough. That I could be enough. But I can't even take you out to fucking dinner. I can't do all the shit you deserve to do. All the things a man should do for the woman he loves." The last part lodged in his throat, the truth he felt behind the admission choking him where he sat.

Sterling reached out a hand, dirt and grime embedded beneath his fingernails as he tipped her chin upward and drew her near. The gesture was gentle, unrushed, her mouth pliable as he sought to convey what words could not. He loved her. Adored her. Obsessed over her. But none of that mattered. None of it meant he deserved her. She responded to his silent plea with one of her own. Though it was far less subtle.

Tessa pulled away, placing both of her hands on his chest and shoving him backwards. The force jarring but not violent. "You're an idiot." She spoke as though it were fact rather than her present opinion, crossing her arms over her chest in blatant challenge as if daring him to tell her otherwise. "You can do whatever it is you set your mind to do. *I know.* I've seen it firsthand. You just don't want to. It's easier to sulk in your own misery and blame it on fate than admit it has more to do with your lack of trying."

His jaw dropped in an attempt to respond. But she cut him off.

"No. No more bullshit. No more feeling sorry for yourself or wishing circumstances were different. You fail to realize that if they were, I wouldn't be here. And you'd be married. Not just married but married to someone else. To someone who isn't me. And before you get any ideas in that thick skull of yours, I'm not saying I want it to be me. That I ever want to be shoved into a white dress and paraded down a church aisle like a cow at auction. *However,* I don't much like the idea of you choosing different livestock either. In fact, if I'm not in the picture, I suggest you just go vegan. No point in trying to compare."

He knew she was humoring him, attempting to lighten the mood much like he would if the roles were reversed. And he couldn't stop the corner of his mouth from curling, even if he'd wanted to. "I love you, Tess."

"I know you do. Now if only you'd stop being so goddamn stubborn, we could grab our takeout, change out of these clothes, curl up on the couch at home, and finally eat."

Home. He quirked a brow but didn't press her on the matter. It was her home, whether she realized it or not. Whether *he* did. She belonged there. And it was then that it hit him…

"Wait, you stayed back to order takeout?"

She shrugged. "What do you think took me so long? I was starving, Lucien. Your temper tantrum could wait."

"It wasn't a—"

"Oh, but it was."

CHAPTER 30
THE DEVIL IN THE DETAILS

TESSA

"I KNOW you're lying to me." She'd known it for weeks. She could feel it in her bones, like a vibration that traveled from the base of her spine and up her neck. Where it sat and snaked around her throat. Choking her. Whispering in her ear. And taunting her. Telling her everything she knew had been a facade. And this man wasn't who she thought he was.

He hadn't been the same since that day in the park. He was pretending, though he hid it well. Tessa saw the minute differences. Saw the way he observed her whenever she entered a room, as if he were trying to read her. *Did she know? Had she figured it out?* She knew that look all too well. She saw it with each of the whispered phone calls when he thought she was preoccupied. In how his mind seemed to be somewhere else. Plotting. Scheming. Perhaps his mother had gotten to him. That woman wasn't one to roll over easily. Even if she'd been left to her own devices, there was only so long a dog could chase its tail before it grew bored and began digging for more skeletons. And if there was something that Tessa didn't want dug up, it was all those bones buried in the deep closets of her past.

"Tess, love, I'm not lying to you. I don't lie to you." Sterling tugged her forward, his brow knitting in that way it did whenever he hoped to express sincerity. However, wanting to express it and actually expressing it were two different matters. Something Tessa knew all too well.

She snagged her wrist away and pivoted out of reach. Her boots thundering along on the hardwood flooring—she'd foregone the heels. "You didn't used to, but you are now. I'm many things, Lucien, but a fool isn't one of them. Something is off. You haven't been the same. You don't look at me the same. You've barely touched me in weeks." She hissed the last part. Because it stung.

It shouldn't. She knew how irrelevant physical aspects of human interactions were. They didn't mean anything. Sex was sex. It didn't equate emotion. They'd had this conversation more than once. However, the change startled her. It tossed her into a state of emotional upheaval. As much as the woman thrived in chaos, she was comforted by predictability, by structure, and consistency. And nothing about Sterling was predictable at the moment.

He'd been spending an inordinate amount of time in physical therapy, coming to bed late in the night exhausted and too sore to do more than toss back a few pain relievers and pass out. His drinking had all but subsided; though his new drug of choice was manual exertion and it wasn't the type that Tessa was happy to indulge in. Without it, without the euphoric distraction, her mind was left to wonder, to calculate, and draw conclusions. And she didn't like where those thoughts were sending her.

There was someone else. Something else occupying his time.

Lucien shifted around the desk to meet her on the other side. She didn't stop pacing, even as she felt his presence looming at her back. "You know why that is, love." And he proceeded to remind her. "Joe has me on a new regimen. I'm exhausted, Tess. The cocktail of medications they've thrown my way barely takes the edge off, and I'm trying to stay away from medicating myself… other ways. For you, Tess. Not to spite you. Look at me."

When she shook her head and refused to face him, he grabbed her waist and spun her in his direction, tipping her jaw downward and forcing her eyes to meet his.

"This is for me too. I need to be the man you deserve. Then maybe you'll finally agree to marry me." She dropped her bottom lip in protest, and he pushed it upward and closed again. "I'm not asking you. I've learned my lesson. You're not ready for that. You've made it loud and clear. But I'm hoping one day you will be. And I need to make sure I'm up for that challenge. That I can live up to my own expectations—if not yours."

She nodded because what else could she say to that? To all the pretty, perfectly punctuated words? They sounded nice. They made her heart rate quicken at the possibilities. But she wouldn't let herself believe them. She couldn't. It felt impossible. Foolish. To blindly trust them.

———

She didn't trust anyone. Not even herself anymore. Tessa's emotions had clouded her judgment since that wedding. Since the moment she allowed Sterling to have the upper hand and swipe her SD card. That's when her sanity first started slipping. Despite how much Doc argued otherwise. Though if truth be told, the man didn't argue. He strongly *implied*. To the point he hoped the idea seemed like yours all along. Emotional or not, however, Tessa wasn't about to concede to the old man. Or any man for that matter. She wasn't about to have her power stripped away. Be made to feel like anything was out of her realm of control.

And that's what trust meant. It meant relinquishing control. It meant tossing caution to the wind, and your counter plans to the side. To remove your back from the wall like a target waiting to be stabbed on a whim. And Tessa had had enough unwanted penetration to last her a lifetime.

Her nail beds were bleeding from where she had torn the flesh away with her teeth, the meat around her fingertips tender and her cuticles nonexistent. Whereas solving riddles had once stimulated her nerve endings, in the case of one man—this man—they served to disarm her. Render her both numb and aching. His words conflicted his every action, speaking of affection while offering none. And she'd never felt as cold as she did alone in his room. In his bed. Beneath his sheets. The hint of his cologne surrounding her, as if only to further mock her solitude.

It would be easy enough to say *fuck it*. To admit her discontent and leave it. Easy enough for anyone who wasn't her and with any man who wasn't him. Because as it stood, it felt like equal parts necessary and impossible. Like her only chance of recourse was also the one thing she could never force herself to do. Because breathing felt like a hardship without him. It was goddamn pathetic. She knew it even as she thought it. But it did little to alter her reality. To change what she knew wholeheartedly to be true.

She was fucked. Just as much as she currently *wasn't*.

She could do the job herself. But the satisfaction wasn't the same. Like popping a piece of chewing gum when all you really wanted was to bite into a nice juicy morsel of steak. And she had neither the will nor the energy to try.

She could hear the familiar sounds of his approach from down the hall. He would either lower himself onto the mattress and pass out within seconds of his head hitting the pillow, or twist and turn all night, plagued by the agony of the muscles he could feel while grieving those he couldn't. It had been the same routine over the last few weeks. No deviations. No change in procedure. As if the man had his mind set on one thing. And it sure as hell wasn't Tessa.

Unless she refused to accept defeat. Unless she forced his hand and called his bluff.

Tessa curled onto her side, an arm tucked up and under her pillow as she feigned her own exhaustion. She felt it. The moment the mattress dipped and he carefully shifted himself beside her, so as not to disturb her. And he attempted to mask his shock, when she pivoted to face then mount him, pinning his arms above his head while using his surprise as leverage.

She captured his mouth in hers, her teeth sinking into his lower lip and tugging it forward. He groaned but not in the usual way, not in the way that would spur her onward. No, the sound was pained. She released her grip and sat upright, still straddling his waist but bearing her own weight on her thighs.

"Lucien…?" It was a question, though she wasn't even sure what she was asking.

And he responded in like. "Tess…" He gritted out her name between clenched teeth, the singular word nearly hissed.

She could read each line of agony etched in his face, the veins of his neck popping and straining beneath his skin. His hands gripping the taut meat of her calves, his manicured nails creating crescent shapes in her malleable flesh, as his tendons expanded and clenched, loosened and tightened with each fresh new wave of pain.

And she felt small in this moment. Like a minuscule version of herself. Compared to the woman who was known to command the room. As if confidence had seeped from her pores and evaporated into the air. She didn't dare speak, for fear her voice would reveal her every insecurity in a huff of breath. However, she couldn't shift herself into action either, frozen in place like a statue waiting for its creator to return and finish carving.

"I need you to move, love," he added the endearment at the end, as though hoping to soften the intensity of his sharpened words. And as much as she had been wanting to hear that exact phrasing, this was far different context.

Like a sullen child, Tessa slid one leg back in place, then the other. Returning to her side of the bed with only the sound of her own heart-beat vibrating in her eardrums before the most sour-tasting words fell from her lips like a confession. "I'm sorry." She didn't know what else to say.

"I know you are, Tess. And so am I." He paused, allowing his respirations to even out before continuing. "This was never what I wanted for you. It's selfish of me to keep you here. But I can't let you go either. I want to… nearly as much as I don't. And for the life of me, I don't know which devil on my shoulder is whispering the lesser evil."

"You can't make me leave any more than you can make me stay, *roi des cons*. When are you going to learn, Lucien?"

"As soon as you do, *ma reine*." She quirked a brow in response, and he chuckled despite his obvious agony. "Not so fun when I understand your insults, eh?" He grinned at her pursed lips, and she couldn't maintain her feigned irritation.

"Why did you do it anyway?" she questioned after several moments of silence, each staring up at the ceiling and lost to their own thoughts.

"What's that, love?"

"Learn French. You never told me why."

The movement was minute, the slightest shrug of his shoulder as if he were still afraid to induce another jolt of pain. "I wanted to be able to talk to your mother one day. She seems like a remarkable woman."

"She was," Tessa breathed the words, and Sterling quickly corrected her.

"Still is, love." Then he reached out to tug her against his side, pressing a kiss to her head in silent understanding.

CHAPTER 31
THE MAD HATTER

TESSA

SHE WAS SPIRALING. She knew it, even as she fell deeper and deeper into that rabbit hole. The one she'd barely climbed out of in the months prior. But she couldn't stop her descent. Any more than she could stop breathing and press forward. Her lifeline was her work and even that tasted bland more recently. She missed the thrill of the hunt. The city life. She missed New York and the brief time she'd spent there. Not enough to leave everything and everyone behind. But enough to consider it. As selfish as those thoughts were, they were also her own.

She didn't have to share them with anyone. And so Tessa swallowed her shame and kept it close to her heart. She was aware of the contributing factor. The insecurities she carried with her as elegantly as her confidence. She'd admitted how she felt to Lucien. She'd laid herself bare in a way that was far more vulnerable than being naked. And then he'd changed. Tugged the security of her walls from beneath her feet and left her guessing as to what was the catalyst. To assume. To take his word as anything more than empty promises. And she understood this had far more to do with herself than the man in question; however, that didn't mitigate her unease. If anything, the self-awareness heightened it. Made her feel helpless to alter her circumstance. Helpless to feel anything but helpless.

Her appetite had waned and if she wasn't sleeping, she was staring out into space, her mind either lost or hyperfocused on a puzzle that was never meant to be solved. And she hated it. She hated herself and who she'd become. And more so, she hated how it could all be traced back to a man. She'd become *that girl*. The one who allowed her emotions, her mood, to be poked, prodded, her strings loosened and tugged by a man. It was toxic…

Then again, so was she. Her mind was her own worst enemy and it was the true villain in all this. The chemicals, neurons, synapses, the microscopic pathways that lit up her gray matter like a metro station and misfired when it was supposed to be speeding down the track towards sanity.

Love didn't look good on her. It was a shade or two too pale for Tessa's complexion. Her cheeks slightly more sunken and her pallor lacking that rosy color. And the journalist suddenly understood the term *lovesick*. Because it was the very definition of everything that ailed her. And fuck if she knew what to do about it. She couldn't give him up any more than she could stand to keep feeling this way. She'd sooner grab a violin and go down with the captain than jump ship and attempt to paddle alone. And that realization gave her pause.

She'd never been afraid of fighting for what she wanted before. So why now? If she'd been the one to hand over the metaphorical leash around her neck, she could be the same one to take it back. She was no one's pet, and she wasn't about to sit here and overpluck her feathers till she'd unwittingly left herself unable to fly. She wasn't about to impose her own gilded cage.

Tessa pushed to her feet, allowing the bedsheets to flutter to the floor, and stalked towards the adjoining bathroom. Because the first step after getting knocked down—even when your opponent was yourself—was to get up. Her bare feet padded across the threshold, her steps quickened by the cold tile floors until she reached the marble sink top. She gripped the vanity edges and glared at the woman she saw staring back at her in the mirror. A self-imposed challenge to pull herself together again. To take all those jagged shards and force them back in place. Even if the resulting image was slightly askew.

Determination settling in, Tessa stormed towards the shower stall, placed the jets on the highest and hottest setting, and allowed the water to pelt her quickly reddening skin, sending her reservations spiraling down the drain. Where they belonged. The change in temperature appeared to shock her system into compliance, the sharp sting of rapidly propelled water meeting flesh seeming to engage a cerebral reset button. She twisted the handle back in place and stepped out onto the soft floor mat, the woman who presently exited the stall a different version than the one who had entered it. It may have been a mask, a newly adorned defense mechanism, but if it meant Tessa could feel some semblance of normalcy, she'd gladly wear it.

She slid into a pair of dark-wash skinny jeans, a white top, and her favorite worn-in brown leather jacket before painting on her brightest-red lipstick and shoving her feet into a pair of matching ankle boots. Her hair was pulled high, neat and tight, with her long naturally dried locks cascading down her back. The weight straightened her spine, drew her head up, and tipped her chin into a state of forced posturing. Projecting confidence, whether or not she felt it in the moment. She tugged her thin yellow belt in place, centered the buckle, and allowed her chest to rise and fall in a pattern of slow but heavy breaths.

She repeated the breathing technique Doc had taught her several more times. Then she steeled her resolve and marched towards the downstairs gym and the object of both her obsession and *contention*.

Tessa was certain he could hear her coming long before she plowed through the double doors. A woman on a mission. Her steps loud and determined as she stomped her way down the hallway. However, that didn't stop the look of shock from knitting his brows the moment their eyes met. Nor hers, as she took in the scene in front of her.

"Tess, love, this isn't what it looks like," Sterling was quick to assure her. Though his less-than-appropriate and more-than-compromising position suggested otherwise. His hand settling on the thigh of the man in front of him, his face dipped at a salacious angle, and his chair suspiciously absent while his knees dug into the floor mat.

"Don't lie to the poor girl, Luci. I bet she'd be into a threesome. Wouldn't you, sweetheart?" Charlie's lips quirked at one side, seconds before they dropped, as a pair of knuckles collided with his jaw and tipped him backwards and off his perch atop the stationary workout bench.

CHAPTER 32
THE DAMAGED GOODS

CHARLES EDISON FOX had been in love with his best friend from the time he was old enough to know what it meant to be different. To be wrong. To have the sort of feelings his aristocratic parents insisted were unbecoming of someone of his breeding and stature. Because to be wealthy and attracted to men was just too far out of the realm of possibility. In their circle anyway.

So their outgoing, slightly overdramatic offspring learned what it was to play a part long before he understood what it meant to have the world as his stage. But their denial didn't squash his spirit like it might have with others in his place. Because the first person to accept him as he was and for who he was, was also the same person who remained just out of reach—dangling happiness in front of him without any chance of ever grasping it. So what did it matter if he never fully verbalized his needs to the outside world when they'd go forever unmet?

And that was okay. It wasn't great. But it was something. And something with Luci was better than nothing without him, while being fluid in his sexuality also meant never having to explain his lack of a permanent partner to his longtime confidant.

Charlie fucked women. At times, he even enjoyed it. The sensation anyway. But it was never their lips he imagined around his cock. Nor their hands clutching his balls. No, it was always one man. One person who satisfied his deepest desires. And he had almost lost him that day.

————

He looked much smaller in the hospital bed than Charles remembered. Weaker. Paler too. And nothing like the man he remembered. He always knew he would lose him one day, but the perpetual comedian had assumed it would be to a wife and kids. Not to… this. Not like *this. It was far more tragic than unrequited love. Because it was wasted potential.*

At first, he'd blamed Madelyn. That woman. Her family and their combined influence. But as the shock subsided, Charles knew it had been Lucien's destiny. The greater the man, the greater the fall. And his friend had been on the road to destruction long before the blonde with the high cheekbones had entered the picture. Charles had never seen one person so effortlessly fall into the role they were given at birth while simultaneously fighting it at every turn.

He took in Lucien's sharp jawline, set in determination despite his lack of consciousness. His hair had grown longer without anyone to trim it, while the smattering of healed-over abrasions along his face and arms gave him a more formidable appearance, discounting the loss of muscle mass.

The prognosis wasn't good. If he woke up, the physicians were convinced his friend would never walk again. And the damage to his brain function had yet to be determined. Though, regardless of the outcome, Charles was resolute to stay by his side. Because that's what love meant. It was unconditional. In sickness and in health. And it sure as fuck wasn't whatever Luci shared with his conveniently absent fiancée. Her parents had an image to maintain after all. And none of them could be bothered to step foot in the sterile hospital setting or wait at the bedside of a man who may not even recognize them. Lucien became as disposable to them as last year's spring line of Armani. No longer as shiny or desirable. Because these people didn't know what it meant to cherish something. To wear it until it felt like a second skin. To find comfort in the familiar. And so they all sought the thrill of the new.

But not him. Not Charles. He didn't need an expansive wardrobe, when his perfect fit was right in front of him.

Visiting hours were coming to a close and it was only a matter of time before the head nurse would shoo him out again. So Charles squeezed Luci's hand once more, leaning down to place a kiss to the prone man's forehead, when the reciprocated gesture froze him stock-still. His eyes dropped to where their palms remained joined before flicking up again. Lucien's eyes were fluttering open, though obviously unseeing as he spoke. "You're here."

The words were stuck in Charles's throat even as he thought to confirm his friend's observation. But before he could force them free, Lucien continued.

"Maddie?"

And the rejected lover's heart sank to the pit of his stomach, where Charles sought to harden, then bury it. "No, it's me, Luci. But I'll call her. She… she went back to the estate. To get some rest. But she's waiting for you, mate." The lies slipped off his tongue because that's what he'd been bred to do. Besides, the truth was known to do more damage than good. Especially in this instance. And Charles didn't have the heart to shatter the man all over again.

The weight of a closed fist making contact with his chin knocked Charles back into his present reality. Though it wasn't all that different from his past. He was still by that same man's side. Still dedicated to helping Luci, even if it meant sacrificing his personal happiness. And he was still watching him from the sidelines. Always present though rarely participating. And that's why, when the opportunity presented itself, Charles couldn't help but toss the idea out there…

Though clearly it hadn't been well received.

CHAPTER 33

THE BIRDS AND THE BEES
SEVERAL WEEKS PRIOR

STERLING

"YOU DO REALIZE you're insane, right? That your common sense is clearly lacking." Charles shook his head, more flustered than his counterpart had seen him in ages.

"You wanted me to have a life. This is me having a life. I don't see the issue." Sterling shrugged, pivoting his chair to round the desk and position himself behind it.

"Yes, we're all very happy that you're once again getting laid—kudos, mate, you're glowing. But *this*…? This goes beyond having a good time and getting your rocks off. This is permanent. Forever."

"I hope so," Sterling added with a grin. It didn't matter what Charles said. Sterling knew what he wanted. That was the thing about the stubborn architect: regardless of the obstacle, when his mind was set to something, he found a way to get it done. "I'm going to marry her."

"And does she know this?" Charles countered. "Because I saw how well that impromptu proposal was received the first time—God, Luci, please tell me that was the first time…"

Sterling flicked his gaze up from his computer screen. "It was."

"Thank fuck, because that was painful." Charles threw himself down on the leather chair with a dramatic huff.

"But there've been several since," the architect quickly added with a knowing smirk.

"What the fuck… like I said, bloody insane. Didn't your mother ever teach you that no means no?"

"You've met my mother. She doesn't know the meaning of the word, Chuck."

"Right, my mistake. I forgot you all belong in the looney bin—myself included—for indulging in this ridiculous conversation."

Silence fell between them for a few moments, one man lost to his incredulous grumblings while the other one designed a plan of action. Until Sterling broke it with a click of his tongue. "I think I've been going about this all wrong."

"You think? Finally! I guess there's a brain cell left in that head of yours after all. I was honestly beginning to have my doubts…"

Ignoring the superfluous commentary, Sterling continued. "Her shrink had a point—"

"Whoa, back up. Now you're talking to her shrink?" Charles dropped his feet to the floor with a thud, having propped them up on the desk, and gripped the arms of the chair. As if grasping for purchase while simultaneously trying to grasp the severity of his friend's descent into madness.

Sterling waved a dismissive hand. "She knows. She was there. But that's beside the point." He paused, mulling over his next words before deeming them appropriate. "I need to speak to her father."

"Yeah, no, I take back the comment about brain cells. If you really think asking Papa Bear for her hand in marriage is the way to go with this thing, you obviously don't know the girl at all."

"That's not what I meant, idiot. If I tried asking for her hand, she'd sooner cut it off than allow someone else to give it to me."

Charles pointed a finger at the man behind the desk before lifting it to his own face and tapping his nose, in a gesture meant to emphasize his agreement.

"I think I should just go there and speak with him." Sterling nodded as if cementing the idea in his head. Verifying that it was the most promising course. "Get an idea as to what I'm doing wrong."

"Everything," Charles seemed to mouth, though Sterling continued to ignore the chronic jester, his thoughts bouncing from one idea to the next.

"Can you keep her occupied?" The architect landed his gaze on the man in front of him, his fingertips tapping along the surface of the desk as he asked the question.

"Her who?"

"Don't play dumb. Tessa. Can you distract her for a few hours? I'll call for a driver and return before dinner." He was rounding the desk and making his way to the door without waiting for a reply.

"You're joking, right? You don't even know if the man's there. You're just going to knock on his front door and make yourself at home?"

"It wouldn't be the first time," Sterling reminded him with a shrug. "She ran to her office but she'll be back by three. A few hours. That's all I'm asking for."

"She's going to know something's up. She can smell it when I'm lying."

"Then take a shower," he countered before adding more seriously, "or just don't lie. Give her just enough info and steer the conversation elsewhere. Say I'm out running an errand and leave it at that."

"For fuck's sake, she really is rubbing off on you, mate."

Sterling grinned. "In all the best ways."

———

The second drive to the Owens' residence was much like the first. Filled with self-doubt, uncertainty, all while Sterling questioned if he really was losing his mind. However, those emotions—the negative thoughts—were tamped down by his need for this to be right. By his unwavering resolve that there was no one else. She was it. It was a life with Tessa by his side or a life of solitude. There was no between.

He felt it in his bones, like he'd felt nothing else. She was his obsession, his salvation, his future if he ever had one. And being without her was like breathing without air. Like going through the motions with your head underwater. Nothing felt the same, smelled the same, tasted the same. And waking up to her each morning was far more brilliant than any sunrise, more invigorating than a hot shower.

Their relationship wasn't perfect. Fuck, the woman herself wasn't perfect. And of course, neither was he. But that was what made it so… perfect. The fact that her flaws made her who she was and complimented his own as if they were two pieces of the same fucked-up puzzle. As if who he was before her was as inconsequential as who he'd be without her. Failure wasn't an option, a possibility. He just couldn't imagine it. Give it voice, for fear the concept would somehow take root in a reality where it didn't belong.

So Sterling refused to believe anything otherwise. Refused to accept she may not want the life he envisioned for them, because the thought had his hand wavering as it loomed over the solid wood paneling of Jack Owen's front door.

Much like their prior interaction, the retired military sergeant seemed to sense Sterling's presence before the knock could register. The man didn't speak as he swung an arm out, beckoning his uninvited guest inside.

"You don't seem surprised to see me…" The architect was the first to break the silence several minutes later, his voice guarded as his fingers tapped along his sleek armrest.

"Hope for the best, prepare for the worst… as the proverb says."

"And which is this?" Sterling couldn't help his inquisitive nature. His need to probe the wound to see how deep it went.

"You tell me, boy. You're the one who appeared on my doorstep." While his words were clipped, harsh, Jack's mannerisms were contradictory as he supplied his visitor with a cup of tea and a platter of baked goods. As though he were the male version of a disgruntled 1950s housewife—all that was missing was the floral apron.

"Straight to the point, aye?" Sterling tugged at his collar, his counterpart's presence suddenly stifling and overbearing.

"No time for bullshit." Jack dropped the spoon in his mug with a clatter as if to emphasize his point.

"I want to marry your daughter." It didn't get much more straight-forward than that.

"And what do you expect me to do about it? Offer you some goats and chickens and call it a day? That girl isn't my property to be given away. Nor is she yours to be taken." The sentiment was delivered with a pair of narrowed eyes and that spoon lifted up and aimed in Sterling's direction. Though the inanimate object felt more like a set of crosshairs zooming in on their target.

"Damn fucking right she's not." A fist meeting the table top caused the ceramic glasses to shift. Jack raised a brow in response, seemingly unfazed by the speaker's outburst. And Sterling cleared his throat. "I apologize for the language. What I meant to say is I'm aware Tess isn't some sort of object to be passed from hand to hand, or offered in some backroom exchange. That's not why I'm here."

"Then I'll ask you again. Why are you here, Lucien?"

"As I've stated, I want to marry your daughter. Though, she… is less than thrilled about the idea." When Jack dropped his jaw to verbalize his protest, Sterling was quick to interject. "I'm not asking you to change her mind, or twist her arm. I guess, what I'm asking for is… *advice*. How to show her it doesn't need to be like anything she's experienced in the past, that it can be like what you and Mrs. Owens have. That she doesn't need to change for me. I want to make her happy, Jack. Support her. Watch her take on the world, not deliver it at her feet." He was rambling. He knew it, but he couldn't stop the influx of words from tumbling out of his mouth. "I'm doing something wrong. I know I am. Something I need to fix. I'm just not sure what it is."

Jack seemed unconvinced, his face devoid of emotion but his eyes focused, as though he could sear beneath layers of flesh, blood, and muscle and through to the truth. As though he could dig it out and serve it up to the man behind all the pretty words and lack of action. "And what exactly is it that you've been doing with my daughter?"

"Excuse me?"

"You heard me, boy. Never was one to repeat myself." The retired sergeant leaned back into his seat, one arm resting over the top rail of the chair next to him.

"I... I'm confused by the context..." Sterling began, his expression much like a deer in headlights. I mean, how did one discuss their sexual relationship with the daughter of someone like Jack Owens? The answer was simple: *one didn't*. Not if he didn't want to end up with a butter knife to the jugular. The would-be groom eyed the object in question as its wielder twirled its edge around the tabletop. As if her father shared the same thought.

"You said you've been doing something wrong, so what have you been doing?"

Sterling's shoulders laxed with the question, his breathing noticeably more even and his pallor several shades brighter. "Right. I'm— well, I'm honestly not sure. Or else I wouldn't be here, sir."

"Jack," he corrected. "Or Mr. Owens if you'd prefer. Especially if it's your goal to be part of this family." Sterling nodded and the aging man continued. "So where is it?" Seeming to note his counterpart's confusion, Jack clarified, "The ring. The one you plan on using to propose to my bumble bee—don't tell me..." He dropped the utensil and slammed an open palm on the table in front of him, the sound deadened by the decorative cloth covering it. "Didn't your old man teach ya anything?"

"My *old man* didn't care about teaching me much past learning to count the zeros in our bank accounts. Marriages were business agreements. There was nothing hanging in the balance, other than the failure to produce a viable heir." Sterling gestured to his lap to further emphasize his point. "Once that outcome was put into question, I became disposable."

The architect didn't know why he was willingly jumping down the familial rabbit hole, but the man had hit a nerve. And if he respected honesty, this was as transparent as it got: *Sterling was rich. He was disinherited. And he was desperate.* But that desperation stemmed from needing a certain woman in his life and had little to do with anything else. If he was just looking for a pretty girl to stand at his side, or compensate for his inability to do so on his own, he was more than capable of finding someone willing. Someone to play the game until he was too old to move the pieces, or too weak to try.

"If you're looking for sympathy—"

"I'd look between shit and syphilis in the dictionary."

This had the older of the two men grinning, likely reminding him of his greatest accomplishments: his daughter and his time in the military. "My girl teach you that one?"

"No, an old roommate of mine. But I think you'd like him. He loved to give me shit too. Made his day by trying to get under my skin. Pretty sure he earned some kind of medal for it by the end."

"Sounds like a good man," Jack added with a nod of his head.

"He was. But he's dead now. So looks like I'm stuck with you."

"Right," he drew out the word, as if tasting it for a minute before waving his hand in a *follow me* gesture. "If you got your heart set on my girl, best you start with a ring, eh?"

———

Sterling stared at the box in his hand, almost afraid to open it for fear of what new horror may lie inside. Popping back the aging hinge, he was met by an oddly tinged gem with an obvious vintage setting. It was ostentatious, yet somehow understated. He flicked his eyes up to the man opposite him, as though to ask for further explanation.

"It was her mother's. Sandstone from the beach where we met, set in my mother's wedding band. One of a kind, like my daughter." Jack looked off in the distance, seemingly lost in thought or memory, before his head snapped back again. "We actually gave that to her—to Tessa —on her sixteenth birthday. She wore it every day, until she didn't. She was busy writing at the time, so we figured it was just too bulky for her keyboard. Then, a few years back, I received an unmarked envelope. The only thing inside was that ring, in that box. The sheen suggested it had been freshly polished." Jack leaned into the support of the wingback chair, his ankle crossing over the opposite knee with a hand tapping against his thigh. "So I tucked it away. And waited for her to tell us. To mention having lost it. When she didn't, I figured I'd let her sweat it out. But she never brought it up, and I never questioned her. Guess now's as good a time as any to get it back where it belongs."

"It's yellow," Sterling commented, as he had so many times before. "Her favorite color."

Jack lifted a brow in question. "You need more help than I thought. Yellow isn't her favorite color. It's red. Always has been. She would have painted her room to match the rose garden out back had her mother not forbad it. Em thought it too harsh a choice for a bedroom."

Sterling furrowed his brows. Yet another curiosity in the list of quirks that made up this woman. "Are you sure? She gravitates to it. She's always wearing it in some form or another. It can't be a coincidence…"

"I did notice that. Though it became more obvious after she misplaced *that*." Jack extended a finger towards the jewelry box. "But it's not because she likes the color. It was something we started when she was little. Used to tie a yellow ribbon in her hair. Told her it was to remind her that like a bee—my little killer, my bumblebee—it wasn't her size that mattered but the bite of her sting. When she was too old for ribbons, we moved to yellow shoelaces. So on and so forth. She just kinda kept the tradition going, so it seems. Replacing the shoelaces with that ring, then the occasional odds and ends. To remind herself never to give up. That small doesn't mean weak; that being a girl doesn't mean *less than*."

Sterling nodded, and comfortable silence fell between them. Though perhaps comfortable wasn't the right word. Maybe contemplative was more accurate. As both men seemed to consider the potential of their intertwined futures and what that actually meant.

Despite the early evening hour, the study was cloaked in darkness. The shade on the singular window drawn down and the distant lamp across the room the only other form of illumination. Sterling was the first to speak again, the crackling fireplace adding a hint of foreboding as the shadows danced across the walls. "You trust me to take care of your daughter?" he asked the question that had been haunting his subconscious since the first moment he laid eyes on the woman, even if it took him much longer to admit it. "Like *this*?"

Jack leaned back into his seat, something he had done several times throughout the course of their verbal exchange. The architect took note of his counterpart's mannerisms in everything he did and said. Despite his stoic demeanor, Tessa's father had his tells. And this was one of them. He sank into his chair whenever he was considering his words, choosing them carefully while garnering a panoramic view of whomever sat opposite him.

Several moments stretched between them before he replied. "Son, there isn't a man on this earth I trust to take care of my daughter, which is exactly why I raised that girl to take care of herself."

CHAPTER 34
THE END GAME
THE PRESENT

TESSA

TESSA STOOD BACK, watching the scene unfold as if she'd been sat in front of a giant screen while someone else operated the projector. He'd said it wasn't what it looked like, but she couldn't quite grasp what *that* was. As if her brain had shut itself off, pressing pause on her ability to conceptualize and conjecture.

She hadn't even flinched when Sterling's fist launched forward and landed across Charlie's face. Nor had she yet to understand why. Likely it had been whatever the latter had said; however, the words had been indecipherable to her ears—the sounds audible yet unrecognizable. Foreign. Though she did grasp the meaning of the string of expletives that followed.

She canted her head to the side, whether instinctually or coincidentally was unclear; nonetheless, the sensation of her hair brushing from one side of her neck to the other jarred her thin hold on reality and sent her plummeting back into the moment. Into the present.

"Then what is it, Lucien?" Her voice spoke the words, though it had yet to feel like her own. As though some other part of her consciousness had taken over and verbalized the question for her. She felt her lips move, but couldn't remember telling them to do so. She crossed her arms over her chest, the posturing meant to appear intimidating. Though, in truth, it was more out of self-soothing than anything else.

Charlie had been stunned silent. He'd yet to move, a palm pressed firmly to his cheek, a frown dipping the one visible side, and his glare focused on the man still kneeling in front of him. Like a child plotting revenge after having been rightfully chastised.

Sterling dropped his head and sighed, one hand gesturing to another figure in the corner—one Tessa had yet to spot amidst all the chaos. Joe stepped forward, his expression that of a man looking for the quickest escape while realizing it wasn't likely. *Or possible.* Before he squatted beside the bench, slipped an arm around his employer's shoulder, and assisted in pivoting Sterling towards the door. Towards the one female amongst them. As if the dance had been rehearsed, Charlie pushed to his feet, though far more reluctantly, and gripped his friend on his unsupported side.

And an awkward silence blanketed the room as Sterling hissed a labored breath, agony etched into each of the taut muscles of his face, his pinched brows, and set jawline. She could nearly hear the grinding as his back molars scraped away at the first layer of enamel. When his cinched lashes fluttered open again, he seemed to stare right through the journalist. As though he were willing her to see him as perfectly as he saw her. The two men flanking his sides each dropped to their haunches and worked in unison to adjust Sterling's posturing. Until the figure between them had been repositioned with one foot flat in front of him, the other tucked behind him and parallel with the ground.

The architect shoved Charlie to the side, using his free hand to reach into his pocket to withdraw the velvet box that must have been weighing almost as heavily as his conscience over the past few weeks —if the look darkening his features was anything to go by. And the oxygen was sucked from Tess's lungs, the air from the room, when he clicked the box open and began to speak.

"This wasn't how I imagined doing this, Tess." His eyes flicked down and back up, locking hers in place. "But nothing about you, about us, or our time together has been anything close to what I'd imagined. You are everything I'm not, love. A lot I can't even begin to understand, and above all else, the one thing I can't do without. You drive me nuts."

His lips curled into a grin in time with hers. Because they both knew it to be true.

"Yet, somehow, you're also the only person who's been able to keep me sane. Grounded. Coaxing me forward with a force greater than the combined weight of the self-imposed burdens from the life I thought I lost. But that wasn't living, Tess. I didn't know what it was to live before I met you. I knew how to follow rules. Not break them. I knew how to fit an image. Not create my own. And I knew how to stand up. Not stand out. Because that's what you do, love. You outshine everyone in the room. You draw them in and hold them there. For how ever long it is you want to keep them. So, I guess, what I'm trying to say. To ask you. Again. Is if you'll let me keep you too? If you'll allow me to hold you not just tonight but every night? If you'll marry me, Tess."

He took a breath, as if recognizing her hesitance and preparing himself for the worst.

"And not because I need you to be my wife. Or because I'm looking to own you. But because I want to be your husband. I want to be the one person who gets to see that softer side of you. The side you protect for fear of what will happen to it if you don't. I know it's exhausting. I know what it's like to want to hide that part of yourself from the rest of the world. So let me do it for you. Let me fight your demons as wholeheartedly as you've helped me fight mine. And I promise to never make you regret it. I swear, love, say it. Say yes and I'll spend whatever time I have left on this earth feeding that fire inside you, the same fire that had you bursting through those doors and ruining weeks of careful planning. I will do everything in my power to heighten that chaotic flame. Not extinguish it."

"I-I don't know what to say, Lucien," she stuttered.

"I told you what to say, Tess." Then he grinned, as if an idea had suddenly sparked in the back of his mind. "And if all of that wasn't enough to convince you, I have no qualms in telling you that my mother's forbidden it. Said she'd show up and cause a scene if I even *thought* about making a fool of her by marrying you."

"She did not! She wouldn't!" Tessa gasped, though it wasn't all that shocking of a revelation.

"Only one way to find out, love," he reminded her.

"Okay."

"Okay?" he parroted, and she smirked.

"Yes, Lucien. I think I'd like to keep you too." She paused before adding, "But I need to know something first."

He swallowed, the sound nearly as obvious as the motion of his Adam's apple bobbing in his throat. "And what's that?"

"How… where did you find my mother's ring? How?" Her eyes hadn't left the gem since the moment it appeared in front of her. At first, she was convinced it was a replica. But the longer she stared, the more certain she'd become that they were one and the same.

Lucien cocked an eyebrow before tossing out the exact words she'd used on him all those months ago, back when she assumed he was nothing more than a mark and far less than an obsession. "You have your tricks, Tess, and I have mine."

CHAPTER 35
THE PURSE STRINGS
SIX MONTHS LATER

TESSA

THE MAN WAS A CONTROL FREAK. And that meant something coming from her. Tessa knew what it felt like to need it. To need to control all the strings, each loose end, and wayward thread. However, this was beyond even her need for complete autonomy. Lucien had become the male version of every event coordinator and stylist's worst nightmare. He had an eye for detail and demanded perfection, despite his proclivity for a woman who was anything but. That being said, the quirk was almost endearing when it wasn't so god-awful and irritating.

Even as the thought flitted through Tessa's mind, she couldn't help but grin. He'd never been invested in his and Madelyn's wedding—she'd heard all the stories. Charles was a talker and more than that, the man was a gossip. So she knew Lucien's... *intensity* was as much a display of his affections as everything he'd shown her physically over the last few months. No matter how much he fought it, spending was in his blood. He couldn't deny it any more than he could deny his spotty lineage. A fact that had been weighing heavily on Tessa's heart, regardless of how deep she tried to bury it.

It was a moral dilemma she found herself facing more and more in her line of work. When was a lie better than the truth? And not just better for her and her motives. No, this question was far less self-serving. When was it better for those around her? Those left in the blast radius and forced to endure the aftermath.

Something deep in her gut turned and soured each time she looked at the man and bit her tongue. Each time she forced a smile and offered a polite nod, though she hadn't heard a word he'd spoken.

Much like the present moment. Lucien had been flipping through venue options, scanning the architecture with the wide eyes of a child anticipating Christmas morning, while gesturing to various authentic features. And Tessa hadn't heard a word of it, so lost to her own thoughts that even she realized how selfish she was being.

"Lucien, I can't do this…"

"That's fine, love." He grinned, placing a kiss to her forehead before closing his laptop, depositing the device on his nightstand, and shifting her closer. "It wasn't my favorite anyway. I was thinking maybe we should look at something outside the area, even consider the east coast… New York perhaps?"

She wasn't sure if he was joking or not; though the hand she landed across his chest told him she didn't think it was funny either way. "That's a hard pass. And not what I meant." The journalist drew in a sharp breath, her pulse increasing with her looming anxiety. "There's something I need to tell you. And I'm not certain if my reasoning is for me or not. If it's to ease my own conscience or to actually keep my promise to be more honest with you."

"More?" Lucien raised an eyebrow. She wasn't looking at him, her head tucked under his chin, but she knew the man well enough to feel the telling muscle movements that came with the gesture.

"Sometimes it's best to take what you can get, *mon nounours*."

"Right. Go on, then. What aren't you telling me? Is there a husband out there I need to pay off? A few judges' hands I need to grease? Say the word, love, and it's done. Because you aren't getting out of this now." He was smirking. She could tell that too.

"While I appreciate your attempt at humor, this isn't actually about me." Tessa pushed up on her elbow, a hand resting on his chest as she searched his eyes. Whatever she was looking for—anger, irritation, rejection—none of it was there, staring back at her.

She lowered her mouth to his, overcome by the weight of the emotions this man seemed to elicit from her without even speaking a word. And he reciprocated, his tongue welcoming hers as though she were more essential to his survival than the air he breathed. She could feel it in the way his hands gripped each side of her face. Not forcefully. Not pain-inducing. But with the sort of firmness and resolve that told her he wouldn't let her go either. That he owned her as much as any one person could own another. And he also didn't. Because it was impossible to clutch a butterfly without the fear of tearing its wings.

"Tess," he groaned when her hand dipped beneath his waistband, before adding, "As much as I'm the first to admit that the art of your distraction is refining each day, let's agree to stay on the topic at hand—not the topic in your hand." His lips curled with the lazy word play, and Tessa laughed at his efforts.

"I—well…" She chewed her bottom lip and huffed a breath. "I don't think your mother has been entirely honest with you." His face twisted into an expression of mock skepticism, and she quickly gestured for him to listen, a finger landing on his pursed lips in an effort to keep his impending smart-ass remark at bay. "Let me finish. Or I'll stop talking altogether." She waited for his silent agreement before continuing. "I don't think your mother has been honest with you about your… paternity. Now, before you—"

"I know."

"You know…?"

"Of course I know. It was one of the reasons she was so cold after the accident. She feared it was a matter of time before the odd blood sample or lab result got into the wrong hands. It's why she convinced my father to disown me, in favor of my cousin. It was easier that way. Less messy. And I honestly didn't want it at the time. Or *ever*, I came to realize. So I had no motive to fight it. Or her. My mother thought she won, when in actuality, the game had been rained out. And she was the only player to arrive at the field."

It made sense. It made too much sense for it all to remain so neatly swept under the rug; and Tessa didn't understand how she hadn't connected the pieces sooner. Viola Sterling wasn't some evil super villain. Though she wasn't a saint either. It was much simpler than that. She was a selfish, desperate woman, grasping at whatever lifeline was within her reach. Even if it meant prying away someone else's grip. It was survival of the fittest, and the heiress refused to starve. She would sacrifice one or all of her pups if it meant she'd eat tomorrow.

"And your birth father… he's…? Does he know?"

"Who do you think gifted me my first set of drafting pens?" Lucien paused as if lost to the memory. "*That one* nearly got the man fired."

The buzzing of the ventilation system hummed to life and accompanied the silence that fell between them, as Tessa lowered herself back down to the comfort of Lucien's embrace and hummed her appreciation. "New York is off the table, but what about Virginia? I heard the Kennedys like to frequent the area." And once again she could feel Lucien's grin as he reached for his laptop and opened it in front of them, his fingertips frantic in their efforts to keep up with his new flurry of ideas.

CHAPTER 36
THE PUPPET MASTER

MADELYN

IF EVERY STORY HAD A VILLAIN, and every villain had a story, where exactly did Madelyn DeLacy fall? She certainly wasn't the protagonist. Nor a minor subplot. No, she was too complex to sit pretty as a forgettable side character. The girl was the fire beneath the refinery. If anything, the ex-lover, turned confident, turned match-maker was the narrative's puppet master. The incident inciter, the one who set the entire plot into action. From meet-cute to forced proximity, and finally to the resolution. So that everyone had earned their happily ever after.

Everyone except her.

She thought she had it. But that was a lifetime ago. When she was a different person altogether, and evidently so was he. Madelyn was resolute in this knowledge. That fairy tales just weren't meant for girls like her. She was the rule, prim and proper. Not the exception, currently draped in champagne lace and marrying the man who was meant to stand beside *her* all those years ago. The same man, though no longer standing, who also appeared more engaged and love-stricken than he'd ever been picking out napkin colors and table settings with the woman who would never be his wife.

But green didn't fare well with Madelyn's complexion, and if truth be told, she wasn't jealous of Tessa. No, she was envious of what the two shared. Of the push and pull, the fight, the obstacles each threw in the other's way before finally meeting at the altar. She didn't know what it was like to "feel" anything anymore. Not beyond obligation. You see, arranged marriages weren't as romantic as all the storybooks made them seem, though that was a thought for another day. Today was about Luci and his bride, and how far they had both come.

Yes, self-pity was not appropriate decorum for a lady of her upbringing, not outwardly anyway. So Maddy shoved it down to the pit of her stomach, where she could only hope it would fester and turn cancerous before ending her miserable existence.

She should be enjoying her handiwork, the culmination of her actions. The same actions she didn't even realize would rise as they had. The debutant didn't know what she was thinking when she sent those invitations—*anonymously*—to every news outlet within driving distance. Nor did she really consider what it would mean for her when she slipped the hired security team a generous bribe while ordering them to look the other way, should members of the media sneak in to get a glimpse of "the wedding of the year." Surely, it was nothing outside of what the men were used to. Bluebloods loved to pretend they wanted their privacy while doing everything they could to ensure they never obtained it. Because privacy meant no one saw what they had and what was the point of having it, if you couldn't flaunt it?

That crisp dove-white envelope with monogrammed gold lettering had landed on the desk of the executive editor at The Maverick Magazine, before flitting through the less-than-perfectly manicured fingers of none other than The Knockout Columnist herself, the snake who slinked in and out of exclusive events like a ghost haunting the halls. No one expected the persona non grata, the broadcaster of the elite's secrets, to be a woman.

Though it was fitting, now that Maddy thought about it.

And so what if she had been the one to whisper in her former mother-in-law's ear, warning the volatile matriarch about the girl she'd seen flirting with her ex-fiancé in the background of several of her wedding photos? Madelyn knew Viola would do all the work for her, while insisting the idea had always been her own. Mrs. Sterling was short-sighted when it came to her plotting, driven by anger rather than cunning, though insistent she was well versed in the latter.

Then, after Lucien had confessed his feelings for the woman, or rather ranted about how much she irritated him (the two were mutually inclusive when it came to her onetime lover), Madelyn couldn't help herself. She needed to see them together, to see if it really was different. If *he* was different. And so, she did what every socialite did when there was an obstacle in front of her, she threw money at the problem. It had been easy enough—Sterling was nothing if not predictable—and it took her two guesses to hack into his email account, type the inquiry, transfer the funds, and press send. She didn't bother deleting it from his outbox; it wasn't necessary. She knew he would be drinking himself into oblivion and likely wouldn't remember what he'd done the night before.

So, yes, Maddy had tugged those puppet strings, manipulated the chess board, positioned the king and queen in line with each other. Forcing the two to face off or forfeit the game. Something she was near certain neither would do. And she'd guessed right. Instead of admitting defeat, the soon-to-be bride and groom fought harder. Better yet, the pawns hadn't even realized Madelyn had been the one at the helm. A secret she would likely take to the grave. Along with all the carefully orchestrated tactics that had yet to come to fruition. Because, for once, it was really and truly hers. Something she owned. That little bit of knowledge.

And the sick joy it brought her not to share it.

EPILOGUE
THE FIRST DANCE

THE GUEST

THE CRISP, off-white envelope with embossed lettering was tucked inside his jacket pocket, the weight of the contents far heavier than the cardstock itself.

It wasn't wedding crashing. Not when you received an invitation from your ex, regardless of her motives. His eyes scanned his surroundings, faces both familiar and unfamiliar in equal waves while he sat the stranger amongst them.

This was it, right?

The thought popped into his head as he cataloged the banality of it all. This was what every woman wanted, what every decent man should give her.

The flowers, the white dress, the three-tiered cake, the partygoers whispering their compliments and criticisms in the foreground like judgmental gods in the presence of mortals.

Yes, this was where the story ended, where the chapter concluded, and the characters lived happily ever after. Or whatever it was they said at the culmination of every fairy tale, as the pages whittled down and the book closed.

There was no last-minute plot twist. No "ah-hah" moment. No

sudden turn of events that could unexpectedly alter the finality of these words. Because, as if circumstance begot reason, he understood there was no undoing what had been done. What had veered the story. His story. And her story too. So off course.

He wasn't blind to the truth. He knew what their vows signified. Those promises uttered in a breathy whisper as he watched her make them without a hint of duress. Without regret. But mostly, he knew now what he should have known back then. At the beginning. It was inevitable. Because this supposed storybook ending was just that. An ending. With none of the revelry.

After all, he'd come to accept the cold embrace of his latest mistress —fate—and the ill-tempered hand she'd dealt him.

Cross the T.

Loop the E.

The End...

———

But then again, that was the irony of his presence. Here. Today. That the conclusion of one narrative was merely the start of another.

Staring up at the feminine silhouette, who was now nothing more than an apparition from his past... A reminder of a life that no longer seemed like it was ever his own. A souvenir representing his younger self, a different self altogether. And the catalyst for the series of events which led him to this present moment.

Yes, as he watched the figure who was so much more than a bride, it was evident how a man could be utterly oblivious to the delicate changes time inflicts on a woman on a daily basis. How a romanticized memory could replace what someone else saw as their reality. Especially when it stared back at them in the mirror.

It wasn't for lack of consideration—though most women would argue otherwise—but rather, he suddenly realized he would never envision her any other way than how she appeared at this moment, on this day. The image of her, with him, replacing the recollection so ingrained in his mind of their time together.

In this instance, though cognizant of the fact that he was just another face in the crowd, words were meaningless and his were utterly lacking. Because, despite everything—and this seemed to irrationally plague him the most—she was not his. Not how he had once considered her... even if only in a memory. She would never be... Not ever again. And not in the way he'd once wanted.

He forced a smile, or the closest thing he could muster, something more like a grimace.

No, that wouldn't do, he chastised himself.

A smile would be foreign on his face as of late... a clear sign that things were not as "well" as he affronted. So, instead, he figured it would be better to neither smile nor frown.

He would remain a steadfast figure of stoicism; indifference would act as a mask for the mix of emotions he shoved down to his innermost viscera and was resolute to ignore until they finally consumed and destroyed him from the inside out.

But enough of that self-pity. Enough of the guilt he carried with him until now. Until he saw for himself.

This was not a day to agonize over what "was." This was a day for closure. This was the day that clearly defined "what had never been."

He should be thankful that they could both finally move forward, and he was thankful. For her, anyway. She deserved this life, the normalcy of it, the kind of life he would have never been able to give her. Or anyone else. Because he wasn't normal. And nothing about his life was either.

Marco shifted towards the back of the crowd, slipping past skeptics and celebrants alike, his eyes glued to the exit. She'd been watching him as he watched Tessa. The blonde in the front row, her eyes flitting towards him throughout the course of the ceremony. The mafia Don's baby brother was used to the stares—for one reason or another— however, he wasn't used to them so far outside the city. His city. Or rather, his family's city. Because it would never really be his. That just wasn't in the cards for Mario Agostino's youngest son, the spare to his elder brother's heir.

And while she hadn't been scrutinizing him with anything resembling recognition, it hadn't been his obvious good looks that had caught her attention either. Her gaze had been curious, her appreciation deeper than Marco's boyish exterior. The woman had been observing him like an oddity, as though she wondered what his next move would be.

He didn't really have a plan, a reason for his attendance, other than to prove the rumors were true. And that he hadn't been crazy when he'd sworn he'd seen a dead girl drive past him on the busy streets of New York, no matter what his brother's lapdog of an enforcer tried to tell him.

Tessa's blood wasn't on his hands. And that knowledge alone had put many of his demons to bed. He'd never loved the girl. He wasn't capable of it back then. In fact, he barely knew her. Scratch that: he didn't know her at all, just a role she played. A version of herself she wore, a temptress urging him to slip a hand beneath her skirt so that she could *slip* into his bed. He couldn't fault her for it. For using him. Not really. Not when that's what he had been doing all along. To everyone. Treating them like toys, discarding them as soon as he grew bored and something shinier came along.

Something like the blonde currently blocking the door with a hand pressed to her hip and a scowl knitting her brows. Shiny was definitely the right word for her, though not in the initial sense. She shined with a certain indignation, like that of a woman who'd been crossed one too many times and would make sure as hell she wasn't crossed again. His lips tipped up at one corner. He liked that sort of woman. They were fiery in bed, taking as much as they offered, if not more.

"Who are you?" The question was hissed his way as her eyes flicked to the left, then the right. Though it was obvious no one was paying either of them any mind.

The other side of Marco's mouth curled to match its counterpart in a wide grin. "Just a ghost." He lifted a shoulder in a half shrug as he buttoned his suit jacket and brushed past her. He had made it down the walkway and towards the parking lot before his steps faltered as her ominous reply was launched at his back.

"I didn't know ghosts accepted wedding invitations. Make sure to have your parking validated, Mr. Agostino."

BONUS CHAPTER

THE EYES OF THE BEHOLDER

DOC

"WHY DO you keep recording the sessions when you know she's just going to steal the tapes?"

The older gentleman smiled, and though his back was turned to his associate, he was certain the rise and fall of his shoulders conveyed the truth without the verbal confession accompanying it. "The tapes were never for me. They aren't about me. They're about her. About Miss Owens taking her control back. About writing her own narrative." Seeing that the younger woman still didn't grasp his meaning, he continued. "The tapes themselves have always been inconsequential. It's the symbolism behind them, what they represent, that's truly therapeutic. They're a tool, a representation of what she lost, and a way for her to find it again. A way for her to choose who is worthy of her trust and her secrets. Even if the only person she offers them to is herself."

Conveying her understanding in the form of a nod, the nurse practitioner crossed her arms over her chest. "I'd hate to be you if she ever finds out you are allowing her to take them."

"Who said anything about *allowing* her?" With a knowing smirk, the psychiatrist placed the labeled cassette tape into the metal cabinet, before turning the locking mechanism into place, punching in his security code, and proceeding to secure his office door.

As the pair traversed the hall of the empty medical facility, a voice impeded their nightly routine. "Hey, Doc, Laney sent me. She said you'd know what that means." The girl punctuated the ominous statement with the popping of her bubble gum.

The physician knew exactly what that meant, though he was none too happy about the matter. Because it meant another headcase, for lack of a better, more medically appropriate term. But this late in the evening, he didn't have much patience left. Nor time to rack his brain for any number of possible diagnoses he was sure this young woman possessed.

He shook his head and reminded himself of his Hippocratic oath, before shooting his colleague an apologetic grin and leading his uninvited guest into an examination room. Once the woman had settled into a chair, he passed her a clipboard and a bundle of his usual forms. She glanced down once, raised her eyes to meet his, then tossed the paperwork aside.

"Yeah, I'm not really the formal type," she huffed.

He could tell this was going to be a long night. As it tended to be with all of Delaney Gallagher's *referrals*. "Right, well, I at least need a name for the file." He pressed the girl further. After all, it wasn't the billability of the session which concerned him, but rather the status of his medical license.

"Dani. That should be enough for your *file*," she spat, though her anger seemed to belie a deeper vulnerability. He nodded in response while gesturing for her to continue. "So, Doc, tell me... how familiar are ya with lost time?"

COMING SOON
HALF COCKED

(A standalone, full-length novel in the Truth and Lies Duet world)

BLURB:

Good guys finished last, but smart women finished on top.

It made for a quick climax and an even quicker escape.

Especially when you left 'em zip tied to the headboard with a wink and a wave of the middle finger.

Mine wasn't a love story. It was a cautionary tale. A how-to of what not to do, if ever caught in a similar predicament.

How not to fall for the bad boy, who promised you the world and left you with a bullet in your skull instead.

How not to fall harder for the good guy, the right guy, who decided to appear at exactly the wrong time. Every time.

And how not to use sex and adrenaline to cope with both.

Yup, my life wasn't just complicated. It was fucked. And so was the pretty boy with the green eyes and the greener complexion.

The same one with a limp in his step and a slightly tender set of balls because he was dumb enough to stand between me and my next paycheck.

But, for some reason, the poor bastard still thought I was girlfriend material.

One of us was about to learn a hard lesson, and I sure as fuck hoped it wasn't me...

Check out an excerpt of **Half Cocked** on the next page.

HALF COCKED

PROLOGUE

DANI

THE DARK, sanguine liquid stuck to my fingers like honey, the translucent film popping when I first pinched, then pried my thumb from my middle digit.

Blood.

At this point, I didn't know if it was mine or not. And, at this point, it didn't matter. Then again, when did it ever? Certainly not the first time I felt the rhythmic bolt action of a 357 Magnum beneath my grip. Nor the last time I inhaled the biting sulfuric smell of a crisp copper jacket whirling through a clean barrel. Nor any of the times between.

So, no, pain… death… none of it bothered me. However, uncertainty did. The not knowing was a real kick to the proverbial balls. You see, morals (much like my sexuality) were fluid—they could twist, bend, and come undone with just the right amount of coaxing. And, currently, I didn't have any. Morals, that was.

But I've digressed…

"Bitch, you shot me!" *Well, that answers that. Not my blood.*

"Please, it barely grazed you." *Because if I shot you, you'd be dead.*

Shoot to kill, Dani. Always shoot to kill. There's a lot less chatter that way.

I reprimanded myself internally.

"Hey! Headcase!" The man-child with barely enough stubble to deem it a five o'clock shadow was squawking in my ear again. "Are you going to untie me or what?!" The fresh streak along his cheekbone was beginning to coagulate.

I wonder how much time has passed. My best guess with this information would be two to eight minutes. Two to eight minutes of lost time.

The blackouts (if you could even call them that) were getting more frequent. Not that it really had much effect on my operation. My body would switch to autopilot, muscle movement, and instinct. It was my brain that remained a little foggy—*I should probably get that checked out.*

Yeah, right…

"Hey! Bitch!" He was spitting now. Good looks (if you could call them that) didn't make up for bad manners. *Someone should really teach the fucker as much.*

The sound of his nasal cavity caving in beneath the force of my ruptured knuckles was worth the throb now radiating up my arm.

Guess I was that someone.

HALF COCKED
CHAPTER 1

DANI

"SORRY, NO DICE, DOLLFACE." He punctuated the unwanted pet name with a wink. "Better luck next time."

"I don't need luck, *dickwad*." Perhaps I needed to work on my own vocabulary. "My name is on that list of yours. So, go on, tuck your cock between your legs, and let a lady through."

"Lady?" I didn't appreciate the way the venomous word came out of his mouth more like a question. I could be a lady if I wanted to be. I glanced down at my leather riding pants and matching vest. All right, not a lady. But that was beside the point.

"Yeah, lady." I crossed my arms and stuck to my guns, knowing that the stance would accentuate my chest in doing so.

"Okay, then, *ma'am*," he mocked. "This name most certainly is on the list." He paused, tapping my ID card. "But it's not yours." My posture sank and he raised a brow. "Should probably look into getting a better fake. I know a guy… if you are so inclined."

"Really?" I shouldn't have sounded so eager. But a good counterfeiter was hard to find.

"Fuck no!" He laughed. A genuine, real laughter that softened the creases along his eyes. "But you dropped that scowl for a second, didn't ya?"

Son of a…

I stared up at him through the fan of my black lashes, allowing the strain to prick my eyes. The tears fell without thought. "You don't understand… he's in there… and if I don't bring him home… I need him home. He's… my brother's… the only one who can talk Papa down when he's been drinking…"

His features softened at my confession, his posture relaxed. "I… are you being serious?"

"Fuck no!" was my response as my already damaged fist made contact with his glass jaw.

———

It was cliché but the big ones always did fall the hardest—the force of gravity and all that.

As was human nature, onlookers gasped and cooed but not one of them stepped forward to intervene when the glorified door guard toppled to the ground. I smiled. It was always the same. That was the one constant you could count on. Cowardice.

The combination of strobing lights and overused bass, along with the noxious odor of perspiration, was the thing of my nightmares. And far worse than any bogeyman I could conjure up.

At most, I had a few minutes to lock eyes on my target before: one, the bouncer came to or two, the son of a bitch manning the security cameras called out "man down." Either option was an inconvenience I just didn't have the patience for tonight.

My head was still pounding from the altercation this morning—I really should have passed this case off. But my work was like a drug and I needed a quick fix. A distraction. Liquor and faceless sex just weren't doing the trick nowadays. *Shocking, I know.*

Glancing down at my watch, I hissed. *Better make this quick. In and out like a short dick on prom night.*

I recited the profile for one John Porter. If ever there was an alias…

Thirty-four-year-old male: shaved head, generic tribal tattoos (bilateral arms) and an eyebrow piercing (left). Call sign: Douche with a side of mommy issues.

Okay, I may have made up that last part but it was fitting nonetheless.

————

Ticktock, Dani Girl, you ain't getting any younger.

"Here, kitty, kitty." This I purred outwardly among the waves of body odor and pheromones. "Bingo!" It was like the mugshot had jumped off the folded piece of paper and materialized with an arm slung along the bar top—six empty beer bottles acting as witness to his overly inflated ego and misplaced machismo. "Long time no see, lover boy," I hummed, dropping the instinctual edge that tended to pleat my voice.

"Aren't you a little sweet thing?" His grin curled like something out of a horror flick, his eyebrows so narrow they looked drawn on, unnatural. I cocked my head at his choice of adjectives.

"Oh, Johnny, Johnny, Johnny," I continued, sidling up next to him on the empty barstool. I skimmed my lips along the arch of his ear, trying not to choke on the punch of stale cigarettes and cheap liquor that assaulted my nostrils. "Five minutes. Meet me out back." It wasn't a request and the sick bastard liked it.

He didn't question the name drop. Nor did he argue its accuracy. That was all the confirmation I needed. The male species really had no chance of survival if the sons of bitches didn't start thinking with the larger of their two heads.

I beelined for the neon EXIT sign. *Do not look back. Do not stand out.* I needed to remain just another silhouette in the swarm of buzzing partygoers. As my cheeks were clouted by the crisp night air, I shuffled a step, flicking my gaze downward at the pointer finger and thumb currently clasping my wrist.

Well, ain't that a bitch? Looks like his momma blessed him with chiseled features AND a quick recovery time. Some guys get all the luck!

"Miss me already?" I always did like to push my limits. There was just something about poking the metaphorical bear that always got my panties in a twist.

"Not so fast, dollface…" This time the endearment was a little less, well, *endearing* as he yanked me backwards and against the bite of the cold brick wall.

"When you say doll, what are we talking about here? 'Cuz you know there's a difference between Precious Moments and the Bride of Chucky." I tapped my chin with my free hand while puckering my lips and biting the inside of my cheek.

"More like fucking Annabelle." It was a hiss, his analogy, one meant to straighten my spine but resulting in a raise of my eyebrow instead.

"The cinematic version or the good old-fashioned Raggedy Anne Doll?" I countered.

"Enough with the games already."

"Games? Sorry, but you're not exactly my type when it comes to playing." I smirked. "No, this isn't a game, *Romeo*. I'm just trying to determine exactly how condescending you're being. But it seems your ego is just as fragile as your jaw."

"Awfully proud of that cheap shot, aren't ya?"

"Nothing about me's cheap." I winked, mimicking his patronizing gesture from earlier and wasting more time than I had to spare.

Something about this fucker left me sidetracked, veering off a course that should have been locked on cruise control.

"What the fuck!" Johnny Boy's expletives were exactly the slap to the face I needed to jerk the steering wheel back on the road.

Imparting a good old-fashioned knee between the legs, I dislodged my wrist from the bouncer's collapsing frame before returning my attention to my target. But the dilation of Johnny's eyes offered what his lips reiterated.

"Oh, fuck no." He threw his hand up in a dismissive wave before pivoting towards the asylum of the open club door. "Not sure what the fuck you are into, but that ain't my thing." He clarified, with a shuffle in his step that told me he was clamping his thighs together—as if attempting to safeguard his family jewels even from afar.

"*Fuck!*" I echoed Johnny's sentiment. "Do you even know how much money you've just cost me?" I crossed my arms and glared at the figure currently hunched over a trash can, his hand in the air wordlessly suggesting that I "hold that thought." Or so I assumed. He slammed his palm down on the metal lid, brandishing a slew of vocabulary colorful enough to make a sailor blush, before sucking in a breath.

"What are you? Some kind of hooker or something?" He choked out the insult as tears burned his lash line.

"Do I look like some kind of hooker?" His hesitancy as his eyes raked along my silhouette led me to add, "It's like you want another kick to the balls… Is that *your* thing?"

FINAL NOTES BY THE AUTHOR:

This is it. There's no more to tell. Though some of you may have noticed that several questions have been left unanswered. Please note that this was intentional. This was meant to be Sterling and Tessa's story only. Other players will have their own narratives down the line, which will resolve some side plots; however, none of it is pertinent to the story the author wanted to tell here.

If you are interested in Tessa's time spent undercover, what happened to Bash, who sent the ring to Jack, and so on… keep your eyes open for future titles by Sybil Knight and Dahlia Reign, where these subplots hold more significance to another character's tale. As it stands, stories are planned for Corey, Madelyn, the mysterious Russian from the warehouse, Marco, and Laney.

The author appreciates the time you took to read this duet and looks forward to hearing your thoughts.

**Other titles in the same world by
Dahlia Reign:**

Contracted to the Devil
Clever as the Devil
Beautiful Deception

And Twice as Twisted
Bittersweet Revenge
Original Sin
Infinite Sorrows
Endless Deceit

ACKNOWLEDGMENTS

Thanks to everyone who has been a continuous part of this three-year-long process. A special thanks to my dads for *not* giving me daddy issues. To Dahlia Reign, for too much to name. To Kat Pagan, for putting up with my shit. To Frankie Page, for formatting my paper-back. To my beta and ARC readers. To the members of my reader group. To the authors who agreed to be part of my release. And everyone who's supported me on my socials.

ALSO BY SYBIL KNIGHT

The Sweeter the Lies

Sins of Our Fathers

Half Cocked

Skin

More titles to come…

ABOUT THE AUTHOR

Sybil is a career-driven Philadelphian native. A crime show enthusiast by day, and a BDSM club hopper by night. When she isn't working or writing, she is talking about working or writing. She is a single mom to her beta fish (Fish) and way too many dead houseplants.

Her stories range from gray to black, with darker themes throughout. She prefers heroines with a kick-ass mentality and the heroes who know how to rein them in. The mental and medical aspects of her books are well-researched, though they are given a humanistic approach and diagnoses aren't the focal points. She believes her characters don't need to wear labels in order to get their messages across.

Her books are mostly standalones, though her characters may interact and intersect worlds. Additionally, she works closely with and writes alongside author Dahlia Reign and some characters will appear in cameos in each of their publications.

———

Sybil welcomes emails from readers if there are concerns or questions regarding any of her publications.

Email: authorsybilknight@gmail.com